18 WHEELS OF HORROR

18 WHEELS OF HORROR

A Trailer full of Trucking Terrors

Loaded, Driven, and

EDITED BY ERIC MILLER

Big Time Books™
Los Angeles, California
www.BigTimeBooks.com

18 WHEELS OF HORROR
A Trailer Full Of Trucking Terrors

Anthology, Cover, Title, Front and Back Material all copyright © 2015
Eric Miller dba Big Time Books™

Interior and E-Book layout by Steven W. Booth,
www.GeniusBookServices.com

If you like this book, we want to know.
Email us at: Contact@BigTimeBooks.com

Dedicated to

*John DeTroia, Chris Mendoza,
Charles Moore, and other
absent driver friends*

*See you again someday at the
truck stop in the sky...*

CONTENTS

ACKNOWLEDGMENTS

Welcome to *18 Wheels of Horror,* an anthology of trucking horror stories born out of my love for dark fiction, trucking stories, and the open road. In spite of there being millions of truckers plying the highways around the world, there's not a lot of dedicated trucking fiction, so I wanted to add some great stories to the existing body of work and hopefully inspire more. I think the writers and I did a damn fine job, and we hope you agree.

If you're not a trucker, don't worry; you can still enjoy these stories. Anyone who likes good genre fiction will find many a good read in these pages, and might also learn something about the trucking world.

As with any book, a lot of thanks are in order, the unsung heroes that make it all possible. So in no particular order I'd like to thank:

Everyone who has supported Big Time Books over the last few years. The fans, the writers, the reviewers all made it clear they liked what we were doing and wanted more.

The Horror Writers Association. I am still amazed at all the talented, professional, and friendly people that I have come to know since joining. Proud to be a member and help the organization—and the horror genre—grow.

Paul Carlson. His trucking fiction list at www.cuebon.com introduced me to lots of new trucking stories and books I wasn't aware of, as well as his own fiction. Paul is a rare breed, a driver and a writer. Wish there were more.

Elie Littauer. Driver, Beta Reader, and much more.

Steven W. Booth and Leya Booth at Genius Book Services. Their formatting, design, and proofreading skills help turn words into a real book. Magic.

John Palisano, Shane Bitterling, Patrick Shiffrar, and the rest of the Big Time Books Irregulars. For all the behind the scenes support.

Keven Carter. For the kick-ass cover art and title design.

Red Sovine, C.W. McCall, Jerry Reed, and all the other singers and writers of trucking songs over the years. You inspired generations to hit the road and showed that there were real people behind the wheel.

Jack Burton. The greatest (fictional) driver of all time. Still out there somewhere, driving the Pork Chop Express through hell and high water, keeping the world safe from evil.

Richard Matheson. He wrote a lot of amazing things, but "Duel" was the grandaddy of all trucking horror stories and this book wouldn't exist without it.

Truck Drivers everywhere. You literally move the world. From big rigs to box trucks to delivery vans, without you everything would stop. It's a lonely, hard job, so I hope this book gives you a break from the road and gives you some entertainment.

And special thanks to every one of you that blasted the horn without fail when a kid gave you the sign.

One final note to the truckers: The writers that made this book happen are terrific storytellers, but most are not drivers. And though I have a CDL and have been a professional driver for many years, a few things might have gotten past me, or I let them go for sake of the story. So I hope you will overlook any "mistakes" and enjoy the tales anyway.

Eric Miller
Los Angeles, California
July, 2015

FOREWORD

Civilization rolls on eighteen wheels. Truckers are out there, day and night on roadways all over, bringing darned near every item your family might want or need.

Truckers are a welcoming bunch. It doesn't matter if you're a tattooed ex-con or a burned-out neurosurgeon, if you can pass the requisite tests you'll soon find yourself behind the wheel of a big rig.

Every trucker has some gripping tales to tell, about a whole range of unusual experiences. Even so, such literature has always been rare, whether written by truckers or about them. Several dozen Romance novels center upon truckers, along with a similar number of Science Fiction stories. As for trucking Mystery tales, there are, to the best of my knowledge, only two in print: one novel and one short story.

Ah, and then there's Horror. Truckers are often far from home, in unfamiliar places, working alongside complete strangers. The possibilities for trouble are endless.

Here in your hands is a great new anthology, with eighteen hair-raising stories from talented authors. Read and enjoy, then say a prayer for those intrepid truckers, who are speeding past you in the evening gloom.

Paul Carlson
Driver and Writer
www.cuebon.com

LET'S ROLL...

With over sixty books to his credit, including the trucking hor-
ror classic Lot Lizards, *the* Bram Stoker Award-*nominated* Live
Girls, *and* The Loveliest Dead, *Ray Garton is indeed a* Grand
Master of Horror, *the award given to him at the 2006 World*
Horror Convention. *He has also written thrillers such as* Sex
and Violence in Hollywood *and* Murder Was My Alibi, *movie*
and TV novelizations for shows like Buffy the Vampire Slayer
and A Nightmare on Elm Street, *several short story collections,*
and a series of young adult novels under the pseudonym Jo-
seph Locke. He and his wife live in Northern California.

A DARK ROAD

Ray Garton

SPENCE HAD ALWAYS FOUND that passing through the long
stretches of nothingness in Nevada was much easier to handle
at night. His schedules did not always permit him that luxury, of course, but that, whenever possible, was his preference.
During the day, the desert was nothing but empty space stretching in every direction, interrupted only by some hills and the
occasional rocky butte, all beneath a sky that went on forever.
He'd never liked driving his rig through Nevada during the day
for that reason. The night concealed all that emptiness under a
blanket of darkness. Now, it hardly seemed to matter because
his whole life had become one long drive through an empty desert.

He saw no other lights on the road ahead or behind him and
hadn't passed another vehicle in at least twenty minutes, maybe
longer. He turned on the radio and made his way up and down
the AM dial twice. On such a clear night in the desert, he picked
up radio stations from all over the country, but there was nothing to choose from but a call-in show about the paranormal that
was simultaneously carried on most stations at that hour, hell-

fire-and-damnation religion, and sports. He left it on a sports station for a while to banish the deadly silence, but he couldn't take it for long. It was a call-in show. Lots of yelling.

Spence often wondered why men always sounded so stupid when they talked about sports. Judging by their comments and the way they talked, the men who called the show probably should never be allowed to operate heavy machinery or work with the general public in any way. He was sure they were, for the most part, fully functional and responsible adults, but they didn't sound like it on that radio show. Was it the sports jargon? Was it the hyperbolic passion they showed for something so inconsequential? Was it their encyclopedic knowledge of a particular sport or player? He wasn't sure. But he couldn't take it for very long. Spence enjoyed a good game as much as the next guy, but he had other interests.

He tuned to another station and listened for a while as a woman described what it had been like to be impregnated by the aliens who'd abducted her. None of the callers expressed a hint of skepticism because on this radio show, everything was real—ghosts, aliens, Bigfoot, government conspiracies to poison and/or enslave the human race, and even the "natural" miracle cures and freeze-dried food to eat after the collapse of civilization that were offered during the commercial breaks.

Who needed *that* shit? He turned off the radio.

He had plenty of music and audiobooks to choose from, but he wasn't in the mood for either. He was in the mood for conversation, the interaction of voices. Yelling was fine, but only if people were yelling about something interesting. He was too tired for music, too tired to be read to, and he'd been left alone with his own thoughts too long. He needed some voices from out there to drown out the voices in his head. Voices he would never hear again but could not stop remembering. Among them was his own voice speaking those last bitter words exchanged with his wife Nan and teenage daughter Jillian. The last words he'd spoken to them before they were killed.

Sometimes—like right now, in all that lonely darkness—all he could hear were Nan's and Jillian's screams for help deep inside his head.

He did something he did not do often: He turned on his CB radio.

It was handy for truckers. It allowed them to communicate with other truckers, avoid cops, check the conditions ahead. Like anything else, though, it was, for the most part, a gathering of loud idiots who talked and talked and said absolutely nothing. Spence normally didn't turn it on unless he had a good reason because his tolerance for most of what passed for dialogue on CB radio, like his tolerance for sports talk and alien abductions, was limited.

Spence talked on the radio even less than he listened to it. He had never been able to use CB jargon without feeling self-conscious, as if he were doing a Burt Reynolds impression in front of an audience of strangers. He'd been driving so long that he knew the jargon well, and he wincingly used it—he had to or nobody would talk to him—but, as he liked to say, he didn't inhale.

He moved through the channels slowly but heard little activity. A few staticky voices faded in and out, distant and ghostly, but nothing close.

"...the chicken choker on the backstroke and I got me a fierce case of beaver fever 'cause I been gone for..."

"...lookin' for Pattycakes, you got your ears on? Pattycakes, come in, this is..."

"...heard they's a beer bust over at the creek..."

He let the radio scan the channels for a while. Voices rose from the static now and then before sinking away again. It wasn't what he was hoping for, but it would do for now.

The yellow shafts painted down the center of the road raced toward him like missiles in the glow of his Freightliner's headlights. The darkness hugged that glow, surrounded him, moved down the interstate with him, waiting for an opportunity to rush in and join him, maybe take the wheel from his hands.

"...got three kids already, what the hell's he want with..."

He and Nan were going to have three kids. That had been the plan, anyway. But Jillian's birth had been complicated by a severe case of endometritis. Damage to Nan's fallopian tubes prevented any future children.

They had been perfectly happy with one, an angelic baby and a well-behaved child. But in the two years before she'd been killed, Spence had noticed that Jillian was becoming somewhat morose. The change was not abrupt but gradual enough to sneak up on him. He and Nan had discussed it in some of their last conversations but had been unable to decide how to address the problem. Now it was no longer a problem.

But Spence thought about it as if it were still a problem. He fantasized about how they might have handled it had things turned out differently, how they would have brought it up with Jillian and tried to find out what was really going on in her life. They did not like the idea of snooping on her and tried to give Jillian her privacy as she got older. But sometimes it was difficult not to take advantage of some of the many snooping options available to modern parents. They kept it to a minimum, but they made sure she wasn't spending her limited time online visiting any dangerous places or having private conversations with strangers, and a couple of times they'd used GPS to make sure she was where she claimed to be.

Earlier that night, Spence had been torn from a deep sleep and sat up in his sleeper dripping with sweat and filled with a strangling fear that Nan and Jillian were in danger and needed his help. He'd started to get dressed before realizing he was dreaming. Before remembering that the danger was over and they were already gone. He couldn't get back to sleep because, after remembering they were gone, he started remembering how they were killed. He'd gotten up and hit the road.

"How many truckers we got out there in the desert, come back?"

The voice boomed out of the radio so suddenly and loudly that Spence jumped at the wheel. He reached over and turned down the volume a bit. The man sounded like he was shouting from the passenger seat.

Spence listened but there was no response at first. The silence went on so long that he frowned at the radio. He knew he wasn't the only trucker on this road because he'd seen others. Not in a while, but they were out there.

"C'mon, truckers," the voice said. "I know you're there. Traveling the highways like blood flowing through veins and arteries. That's what you are, you know, you're the blood in America's veins, you truckers. Somebody's gotta have their ears on out there *somewhere*. Come on back!"

Spence waited and listened. Another long silence followed. Nothing.

The man lowered his voice the next time he spoke and sounded more relaxed. "I know most of you are alone out there with nothing but voices to keep you company. You've left your families at home, maybe haven't seen 'em for quite a while. You long-haul truckers know what I'm talkin' 'bout, right? You don't see the family for weeks sometimes. All alone out there on the road. You can't wait to get home and see them. Or maybe...maybe..."

There was another silence, but he did not release the call button.

"...maybe you got no family to go home to. That'd be worse, I think. Missing them is one thing, but if they don't exist...well, that would be sad."

The man lifted his thumb from the call button with a faint click of disconnection. Spence realized the man had not identified himself, which was virtually unheard of on the CB radio. But Spence already had an image in his head. The man sounded like the actor Sam Shepherd, but without the drawl. Any drawling this guy did was simply lazy speech.

He listened for a response, for Sam Shepherd to continue. It took a while, but he finally keyed his microphone again.

"I guess the only thing worse than having no family to go home to would be having a family and then losing 'em. Then you *used* to have a family to go home to, but...not anymore. Yeah, I think that'd be worse than just about anything."

Spence realized the muscles in his back and shoulders were tense and he was starting to feel fidgety. He knew it was irrational, but he had the sickening feeling that the man was talking to him. That was impossible, of course.

He continued, his voice still coming through with perfect clarity: "Now, I've known some truckers who take the wife with 'em. Maybe the kids, too, I dunno. That way you don't have to go home to the family, they're right there with you. All safe and sound where nobody can hurt 'em."

Spence's insides began to slowly twist themselves into a knot as his eyes moved back and forth between the road and the radio. His stomach felt queasy. There were other voices on the radio, but none as strong as that one.

"Yeah, that'd be the best thing to do, I think. Take 'em with you. No reason not to."

Spence's head jerked toward the green numbers. He did not reach for the mic, but he spoke to the radio. "No reason not—ever heard of something called regulations, assmunch?"

"Yeah, that'd be the safest thing to do. 'Specially these days. There's a lotta sick, twisted people in the world. And these days, most police departments can't afford to do a thing about it. They're just runnin' around and fittin' in, but they're not like everybody else. They enjoy doin' bad things. Usually to good people. It's an ugly world, and it's just gettin' uglier when a man's family isn't safe in their own home."

It had been the kind of crime scene that perpetuated a belief in evil. The supernatural kind of evil. It was horrible. Torture, stabbing, dismemberment, sexual assault before and after death. Blood everywhere. The kind of crime scene that practically replayed the screams for anyone who saw it. It was enough to make anybody wonder about the possibility of a non-human evil force.

Spence had given the idea a lot of thought, but had rejected it years ago. He was a history buff and an avid reader—he listened to a lot of audiobooks on the road—and he had not, as yet, encountered anything in human history that even vaguely suggested the necessity for a supernatural force of evil. Humankind had, from the beginning, proven itself quite capable of evil without any assistance whatsoever. Whenever someone asked him if he believed in the devil, he always said, "No, I think it's pretty obvious we're self-taught."

The unidentified voice on the radio had sounded like a regular guy at first. But after those remarks, his voice took on a sinister quality. Spence didn't think it would register with anyone else. It was only from his point of view, he was sure. Because it would be insane to think Sam Shepherd was speaking directly to him. That would be delusional.

"You're awful quiet tonight," Sam said. "Isn't there anybody out there who knows what I'm talkin' 'bout?"

Spence wanted a cigarette. He ran the tip of his tongue over his lips, looking for that Marlboro filter. He'd stopped eight years ago and hadn't craved one in half that time. This sudden craving was more of a need. But he knew how hard they were to quit and how easy it was to start them up again. Just one cigarette, that was all it would take. Because one cigarette always came with nineteen others and what nicotine addict, no matter how long it had been since the last puff, could let them just *sit* there?

It wasn't a problem, though, because he had no cigarettes in the truck and it was a long way to the next gas station or convenience store.

"Or are you one of them truckers who can't wait to put his family behind him?" Sam said. "Gettin' away from 'em as fast as possible so you can hit the truck stops and roll around with the lot lizards? If so, shame on you. That's a good way to get a disease that'll make your junk fall off. Or get your throat slit by one of them creatures. And shame on you for doin' that to your family. Leadin' 'em on like that. They'd be better off without you if that's how you feel, ya snake."

The glow of headlights crept around a hill that the road hugged, and a moment later, the lights themselves appeared like eyes in the night. A Volkswagen Beetle zipped by, resembling its namesake from Spence's vantage point.

"Boy, I guess nothin's gonna rouse you tonight, huh? It's just dead out there, isn't it? And sad, real sad. Like a graveyard fulla dead whores."

The darkness sped by as he waited for Sam Shepherd to continue and drown out the voices that sounded like ghosts gibbering in the night. He listened for the faint sound of that microphone being keyed.

It didn't come.

"...smokey's not too busy tonight, but about an hour ago, I saw..."

A bobcat darted across the road at the very edge of his high beams. It almost looked like a shadow except for the brief glint of its eyes as it tossed a glance Spence's way.

Spence eyed the CB microphone on its hook, considered reaching for it, but didn't.

"...Sweet Tart, lookin' for the Sweet Tart, are you out there, baby, or am I gonna have to..."

Farther down the road, a pale barn owl swooped out of the darkness and into the glow of his headlights for an instant, then banked away from Spence's oncoming truck and shot upward, back into the night.

With only darkness outside the truck, there was nothing to see beyond the reach of the headlights.

He kept glancing at the radio. Waiting for that voice.

The radio fell silent. No voices at all.

His right hand struck like a snake, snatched the microphone from its hook and keyed it as he brought it to his mouth.

"I'm a trucker," Spence said. He lifted his thumb.

"*There* you are," Sam Shepherd said with a soft laugh. "I was wonderin' how long it would take. I knew you were out there."

"What's your handle?" Spence said.

No response.

Spence said, "You got the Sidewinder here."

"You headin' back home, Sidewinder? Headin' home to—" he chuckled, "—the family?"

A deep chill moved through Spence and raised gooseflesh on his back and neck. He lifted the mic again, but said nothing because he did not trust his voice. A glut of emotions were lodged in his throat.

That chuckle had been made of ice and Sam Shepherd's words sounded like they were spoken through a smile. But it wasn't a pleasant smile, Spence knew that. Whoever this man was, he knew exactly who he was talking to and he was having some sick fun.

He keyed the mic and opened his mouth to speak but couldn't because what he was thinking was—

His thumb snapped away from the button as if it were hot.

"Crazy," he muttered. "It's crazy."

Since the murders, he'd been afraid of losing his mind because, after losing both of them at once, it felt like a real possibility. He kept reminding himself of all the times he'd read and heard that if you wondered if you were crazy, you couldn't be, or you wouldn't be wondering.

"Who am I talking to?" Spence said.

"Think of me as a friend of the family, Sidewinder."

He worried that he might vomit and considered pulling his truck over and parking for a bit until he pulled himself together. But he didn't.

"You son of a bitch," he said to the road. He lifted the mic and said, "You sound pretty close. *Friend.* You're real loud and real clear. What's your 20?"

"Oh, I'm...around. You're on the move, though, right?"

Spence decided it would be good to keep him engaged in small talk for a while. Maybe he could learn a few things about him unobtrusively, without questioning him directly. "Yeah, I'm on the road with a load of appliances."

"Yep. You truckers are the blood in America's veins, keepin' the country alive. Movin' the products we need back and forth to the places where we need 'em. While your loyal family waits for you at home. Ain't that right, Sidewinder?"

Had he put the slightest emphasis on "loyal family"? Had he dragged those two words out just a bit?

For an unpleasant moment, Spence thought the rig was making a deep, ugly grinding sound and was relieved that it was only his teeth. He clenched the microphone so tightly that the plastic crackled.

With teeth still clenched, Spence said, "You keep bringing up my family. What do you know about my family?"

"Breaker 19, breaker 19."

"Go ahead, breaker," Spence said, and when he heard the angry snap in his voice, he took a deep breath. His hands were shaking.

The man sounded a little slurry. "You got Grandpa Moses, here, and I got my grandkid with me. So if you don't mind watching the language—"

The deep breath didn't help. "What the fuck is your grandkid doing up this late on a school night?"

After a moment: "I don't see's how that's any of your goddamned bidness!"

Sam Shepherd spoke up, wiping out all other sounds on the radio: "There goes the neighborhood. Look, Sidewinder, you wanna keep jawin', switch up."

Still holding the mic, he reached out his right hand to change the channel, but he waited.

"You still there, you crazy bastard?" Grandpa Moses said. "These are all *public* channels, you goddamned freak, so you never know who's listening!"

A memory bobbed to the surface from the depths of hours he'd spent as a child watching TV. He brought the mic back to his mouth and said, "This has been a production of the Children's Broadcasting Network."

As he switched to channel 20, something caught his attention. It was a glimmer of light somewhere up ahead and to the right.

"Come on, Sidewinder."

He heard that grinding sound again.

Spence said, "Who are you? What's your handle?"

"Those are two different questions, Sidewinder. Which one do you want me to answer first?"

"What do I *call* you?"

"You can call me whatever you want."

"Oh, I have been, believe me. But you saw how that kind of language goes over on the radio."

His eyes kept searching the darkness on the right side of the highway.

"Ha! Nice to see you haven't lost your sense of humor, Sidewinder. You know...you seem to think you know me. Am I right about that, come back?"

"No. No, I think *you* know *me*."

"Ah. Well, that's a different thing, then. But, Sidewinder, you're just a voice on the radio. How would I know you?"

Spence's throat burned, his nose began to run, and the lights on his console bled together for a moment.

"You tell me," he said.

Silence for a while, then: "I guess the only way to find out if either one of us knows the other would be to meet in person. Don'tcha think, Sidey? Winder, old boy?"

"Sure. Give me directions and I'll just zip my little 18-wheeler straight to your door. Very funny."

"Hey, I'm just up the road from you. You're headin' straight for me. There's a turnout up ahead. Take it and park."

"Are you serious?"

"Course I'm serious. You can't miss it."

A sign oozed out of the darkness. TURN-OUT 1 MI.

He *was* serious. But how had he known exactly where Spence's truck was at that particular moment? How could that be possible?

"Drones," he muttered. Drones were for sale to the public now. Anybody could buy one. Maybe he was being tracked from above.

Spence was convinced that Sam Shepherd—whoever he was—knew something about what had happened to Nan and

Jillian. Maybe he was the killer. And he was waiting for Spence up ahead. All he had to do was pull the truck over and park.

He decided to do it. He had a .45 tucked under the mattress in his sleeper. He would have to be crazy not to take it with him. But somehow, that gave him little comfort.

He trembled all over. He was as scared as a little boy all alone in the dark.

ᆼᅩ

Once the engine stopped, Spence heard nothing. He looked around and saw a couple of picnic tables and a sign with some information about the area. After he killed the lights, he couldn't even see that much. It wasn't a rest stop and there were no facilities. Just a place for people to pull over and stretch their legs.

"Sidewinder!" the voice boomed from the radio. "Come back, Sidewinder."

"Yeah, I'm here. I'm parked and waiting."

"Take a look to your right. Out at the desert."

He turned his head slowly, more than a little afraid of what he might see. A small part of Spence's mind expected to find the guy in the passenger seat, grinning in the dark.

A small cluster of lights glowed some distance from the roadside turnout. He suspected that cluster was the light he'd seen while driving shortly before deciding to stop.

"See that light, Sidewinder? That's me. Come on out to the camp trailer and pull up a chair. I am 10-7."

"How the hell did you know I was driving through here right now?" Spence said.

Sam Shepherd did not respond.

"Were you sitting out there *waiting* for me?"

Nothing.

"*Answer* me, goddammit!"

But Spence knew he wasn't going to answer. He'd signed off, and now he was waiting for Spence to show up.

He got his .45 from under the mattress and, two minutes later, his shoes were crunching over the ground and he was walking through the chilly night. In his jacket pocket, his right hand touched cold metal. His left hand held a small, bright flashlight and he swept the beam over the ground ahead. He avoided rocks and holes while keeping half his attention on the lights out there, lights that cast pools around a long camp trailer attached to a big, white Dodge Ram. There were three sources of light: The light over the door, the bright light coming from the windows, and a light mounted on the roof of the camp trailer near the front.

He heard a small sound that grew steadily louder as he got closer to the trailer. Someone was playing music inside. As he got a little closer, he recognized Barry Manilow's voice. An obscure song from the 1970s, "Starting Again." He remembered that only because Nan had been a lifelong Manilow fan and had all of his albums.

His crunching footsteps stopped abruptly and Spence thought, *Am I dreaming?*

Something small skittered over the ground inches from his feet. An owl hooted somewhere. He wasn't dreaming.

There were pale curtains over the windows, but vague shadows shifted around inside. The old song played. Creatures moved in the night.

This was a crazy, stupid thing to—

Spence would later swear that, at that moment, he was struck on the back of the head with something heavy and hard, and the night disappeared.

❧

He regained consciousness thinking, *Which album is that?* while Barry Manilow sang "Losing Touch."

As he became more aware of his environment, he wondered why he couldn't feel the hard, rocky ground on which he'd fallen. He seemed to be lying on a flat, cushiony surface. Then his right arm slipped off that surface and dropped a foot or so to a harder one. He was holding something in his hand. Clutching it. He tried to loosen his grip but could not. The muscles of his hand felt frozen in place.

Spence opened his eyes and sat up. Looked around.

He was on a couch in a surprisingly spacious, well-appointed camp trailer. It was the camp trailer, of course, that he had been approaching...how long ago?

There were other people in the trailer with him—a man and woman in their thirties, two kids—but they were all dead and sprawled in black pools of their own blood, their faces, throats, limbs, and bodies crisscrossed with slashes and slotted with stab wounds.

"What?" Spence said, his voice a hoarse croak as his head turned in short jerks and his eyes got bigger with each movement.

Am I dreaming?

He smelled the blood. He wasn't dreaming.

"Hello?" he said, standing. "Who's here?" He turned his head to the right and leaned forward to look down the narrow, dark hall.

There were no other sounds in the trailer besides Barry's singing and Spence's thudding heart.

He realized he was panting as panic burned his nostrils like a toxic gas. He saw the CB radio on the sideboard in the small dining area. It was on and had two orange numbers on its face: 20. The channel Spence had been on...when was it? How long ago?

He was not going to talk to him on the radio. Not this time. He shouted, "Where are you, you son of a bitch?"

Tears blurred his vision and made all that blood look soft and pretty.

"Where the fuck are you?"

Sam Shepherd did not answer. No one did.

He experienced the next few minutes in a series of jarring cuts.

Screaming because he couldn't help himself, just screaming and screaming when he saw the bloody knife he was gripping in his right hand, a big one, the kind that brought the word "butcher" to mind, the kind that—

Babbling incoherently as he tried to get out of the trailer, but he slipped and fell in all that blood and hit his elbow on the corner of the counter, his head on the floor, tripping on a limp, staring girl of about eight and—

Running through the night, crying, laughing, shouting at himself, looking for the truck, where was the goddamned—

Making that engine wake up with a rumble that chewed over his sobbing and whimpering, fastening his seatbelt and feeling the stickiness of the drying blood on his hands—

Watching those blurred yellow missiles being fired silently at him, so blurred they almost looked like a single line as he cut through the night fast.

Something, a small animal of some kind, dashed into the road and died under his tires.

The chatter on the CB was nothing but babble through the screams inside his head. Unfamiliar screams from strangers pleading for their lives. At the Copa. Copacabana.

"Breaker twenny, breaker two-zero, lookin' for the Sidewinder, come back."

Rage moved through Spence's body like an electrical current and he gripped the wheel so hard that he was sure it would come off the steering column in his fists. But he did not respond. He could not remember turning the radio on when he'd gotten in the truck. But he didn't remember turning it off when he'd gotten out earlier, either. He loosened his right hand from the wheel and reached over to turn off the CB, but—

"Come on, Sidewinder, I know you're out there. Did you have a good time with the DiLucas? They're vacationing from Seattle."

A miserable sound filled the truck, a shrill whimpering. When Spence realized it was coming from him, he stopped and grabbed the microphone.

"What the fuck did you do, you prick? You sick, sadistic *prick!*"

"What did *I* do?"

"You set me up!"

"Oh, Sidey, Sidey. Winder, old buddy, you really shouldn't drive while you're sleepin'."

"Stop it! I'm not your fucking *buddy!*" His saliva spattered on the microphone. "You set me up, you killed that family and you fucking set me up!"

He waited. The yellow missiles came. The road continued to unroll ahead of him.

No response from Sam Shepherd.

"Talk to me, you fucker!"

He did not talk. Others did, but they were nothing more than babble to Spence.

"...to me like somebody's had too much meth, if you wanna know the..."

Watching the road while his concentration was focused on hearing Sam Shepherd's voice, Spence seemed to exist in a narrow tunnel.

"...and get off the damned radio, you drunken..."

But that voice didn't come.

"...the hell is wrong with that guy, who the hell's he talking to, anyway, 'cause I don't hear..."

The steady thrum of the road beneath the wheels calmed him and he took comfort in the sound of the smooth-running engine.

"...talking to *himself*, the nutjob!"

Spence did not hear the voices or the laughter. He turned off the CB and decided to listen to some music.

And the missiles kept coming.

Brad C. Hodson is the son of a trucker who grew up on Smokey and the Bandit *and reruns of* BJ and the Bear. *He's also a screenwriter and novelist in Los Angeles and his first novel,* Darling, *is currently being adapted into a movie. For information on him or where to find more of his short fiction, please check out* www.brad-hodson.com.

RISING FAWN

Brad C. Hodson

HE HAD BEEN AWAKE for thirty-six hours when he came down the hill outside of Chattanooga and first had the thought that he needed to see Lucille. He'd been going non-stop since leaving Baltimore, downing Yellow Jackets with sugar-free Red Bull every few hours just to keep his hands on the wheel. Trying to fight it anymore was useless. He could only give in and find Lucille.

It had been a rough six months. Sleep eluded him even when home between runs. He found himself more often than not in front of the television at three in the morning, eyes tired, ass numb, switching channels so rapidly that the random voices and sound effects and bits of music created an odd rhythm. It was like a tribal chant issued from his idiot box. It would lull him to sleep for an hour or two but then he would see *her* face and bolt awake to an infomercial for weight loss aids or fabric cleaner. Those ads pretended to be talk show segments so well that it often took him several minutes to realize what he was watching.

The Peterbilt eased off of the hill and passed the small lake he had always thought of as the edge of civilization. It wasn't so bad these days. When he had first started driving, there was only one exit with a small gas station for the next two hundred fifty miles. Well, one exit worth a damn. There were several others, of course, each charting its own path into those ancient hills that ran from Tennessee through Georgia and into Alabama, but they were dark and lonely things that someone driving a truck this size had no reason to head down. For him there had only been the interstate to keep him company in those days before cell phones and satellite radio. In the last ten years more and more restaurants and gas stations had appeared along this stretch. Each came suddenly with no visible construction as though they had grown in the fertile soil, their seeds carried by thunderstorm winds rolling down through the Cumberland Gap or up from the Gulf Coast.

This time of night, the lake was little more than a dark hole, a pitch black abyss that beckoned him to turn his wheel hard to the right, crash through the guard rail, and tumble down into angry oblivion. It would be so easy, he knew.

He kept driving.

Even with the sporadic developments appearing down this stretch of interstate, he still had a long patch of nothing ahead of him. The rumble of his engine and the sound of his windshield wipers worked at him. He wanted sleep so bad that he thought if he pulled over onto the side of the road right now he might actually be able to get it. But he had to be in Birmingham in four hours to drop off a load of printer ink. He'd have time for a long nap while they emptied his trailer and reloaded it with plumbing fixtures and then he would be on the road again, this time to...

He couldn't remember.

He took a deep breath and scratched his scalp and said the names of a few cities aloud, places like Tampa and Austin and Kansas City, but none of them sounded right. Damn, was he tired.

Rolling the window down to let the cold November wind pelt his face, he woke a little. Wherever he headed next didn't matter. He'd examine the manifest when the plumbing supplies were loaded and then he would be fine. All he needed to know was what direction he was going. One destination at a time, his father always said.

Had the old man said that? It sounded right, but Randy couldn't be certain.

The Yellow Jackets were gone and the Red Bull had been reduced to a few empty cans knocking against one another on the passenger side floorboard. What he needed was to see Lucille.

Grabbing the CB handset, he squawked a quick greeting and asked if anyone had seen her.

His radio crackled. "Flying Dutchman, this is Tricky Dick. You're breaking up. Come back."

Tricky Dick was receiving poorly and wanted him to repeat the message. He held the button down and spoke a little louder. "Tricky Dick, this is Flying Dutchman. I'm calling out to see if anyone knows where I can find Lucille."

"10-4. I know a Truck Stop Tommy or two might know where she is. What's your 20?"

"I'm on I-24 West heading to the I-59 split down to Birmingham."

"Rising Fawn."

"Come back?"

"The Rising Fawn exit. There's a big ass truck stop there, rain lockers, Subway sandwiches, the whole shebang."

"You seen Lucille there?"

"Saw her there earlier tonight, as a matter of fact. Her pearly white smile is the only thing keeping me going right now."

"10-4, Tricky Dick."

"And Flying Dutchman? You back off the hammer coming down south from that exit. Sometimes there's a picture taker inviting folks to feed the bear a little further down the road. Don't wanna end up with a driving award around these parts, I guarantee you that."

"Much obliged." Randy wasn't much of a speed demon as it was, but he appreciated Tricky Dick's warning. He did not want to get a ticket, especially right after seeing Lucille. That could be ten to twenty these days.

The last time he had seen Lucille had been *that* night. He had gone cold turkey after that and was surprised that he had made it this long. Yet every run he went on over the past six months, he had almost gotten on the horn and asked about her. He wasn't disappointed so much that he was giving in tonight as he was relieved. He'd known the day would come, after all. How could he have not? The constant fight had been exhausting.

Just because he knew where she was didn't mean he had to act on it, he reminded himself. He could keep driving through the cold rain and push toward month seven.

His headlights illuminated a sign ahead. "Rising Fawn," it said.

He flipped on his blinker.

Turning off the interstate, he rose up the hill to a small road. To the east was darkness, a cold black that devoured the pavement. To the west was a near deserted BP, a minivan at one of the pumps and an ancient El Camino parked by the doors. He took a small road that led past the BP and further up the hill.

The truck stop was massive. Tricky Dick hadn't been lying about that. A dozen cars occupied the civilian pumps, their drivers shivering as they refilled their tanks in clouds of their own icy breath. A line of semis filled up on the commercial side. Other rigs were parked in a lot that wound around back of the building. He parked the truck and went inside.

He was surprised at how many people milled around through the snack food and audiobook aisles. He double checked his watch to be sure, but it was indeed almost two AM. This was the only decent exit for quite a while, he reminded himself. Still, it wasn't a holiday weekend and the amount of bodies wandering around half-dead was odd to say the least.

The coffee station was busy, most of its eight machines in use, and that was less of a surprise. Pouring himself a small cup, he fished in his pocket for a crumpled bill and stood in line at the register. A teenage girl worked the machine, blonde hair pulled into a ponytail, pasty skin and a hanging chin already marking her as one of the Night People. When you were on the road as much as Randy, you became intimately familiar with the Night People. Graveyard shift workers mostly, though there were a few insomniacs peppered into the mix who congregated at those select places open in the dead of night. The Night People were far from the picture of health. Even the most robust of them, the ones who ate well and exercised regularly, bore the marks of abusing the body's natural cycles.

When it was his turn in line, he tossed the bill onto the counter and asked about Lucille.

The girl blinked. "Lucille?"

"Yeah," he said, all grins. "Have you seen her?"

She blinked again.

"I heard she was here."

The girl scanned the room and tucked a stray piece of hair behind her ear. She turned back and looked him up and down.

"There's a Ms. Pac-Man game in the little arcade back over there by the showers. Some folks like to pull a chair up to that all backwards like and sit in it while they play."

He nodded, grabbed his coffee, and headed into the arcade. It wasn't a large room. The walls were dark colored and the lights dim and, even with no door on the room and the lights in the white hallway outside of it so bright, it only added to the almost instant sense of claustrophobia. Electronic chimes and beeps sounded from several poker machines along with the occasional plinky string of music. Aside from him, the place was empty.

There were two video games that were not gambling related: one a "Walking Dead" shooter with a plastic shotgun attached and the other a thirty-year-old Ms. Pac-Man with the decals peeling from the side. He pulled what looked like a wrought iron dining room chair over to it, spun it around backwards, and straddled the seat. Plopping a quarter into the slot, he pressed the "Single Player" button and waited for the game to start.

It had been fifteen years since he had played a video game. Not since Debbie left in the middle of the night with the kids, leaving nothing but a note. They had taken their Nintendo with them and he never played a video game again, not even those cheap ones that you could get on your cell phone.

He wondered how his two boys were doing. Sam would be... twenty-one now? Was that right?

That would make Bobby twenty-four. Jesus.

Their absence hit him hard and sudden and he wasn't sure why. Maybe it was the stress or the lack of sleep, he didn't know. Whatever it was, he wished desperately that he knew where they were right now.

Debbie had not left a forwarding address, but it wouldn't have been impossible to find her even in those days before Google and Facebook. Why he hadn't even tried was also something he didn't entirely know. He suspected, sure. Suspected that she had been right and that the drugs and the drink had gotten to be too much, suspected that she had been right to never forgive him for losing control and popping Bobby across the mouth hard enough to bust the boy's lip. The question for him had never been "Why did she leave?" but was instead "Why did it take her so long?"

He missed *her* some nights, too, if he were being honest.

Quitting was something he should have done right when they left, but hadn't. He had lost whatever fire he had somewhere along the way. Even before Debbie and the kids left. Whatever spark had been inside of him that made him buck trends, that made him carve his way, that made him give the finger to the arrogant sons-of-bitches that he worked with as he walked out the door to find a better job, whatever spark had fueled those parts of him had been snuffed out. The drink and the drugs made him feel like he had that spark again, but it had just been a pale imitation. Smoke without a fire. It took years and years to realize that he was burning himself to death from the inside out. And even then, that realization didn't fully hit him until the girl.

That poor girl.

"Heard you're looking for Lucille."

He turned from the game that he had only half been paying attention to. A tall, thin man stood in the doorway, the light from the hall making him little more than a skeletal silhouette.

"Yeah," Randy said and stood. "Heard she might be here."

They stood and stared at one another in silence for a long and uncomfortable moment.

"Alright," the man finally said. "Follow me out back."

The light in the hallway allowed Randy a better look at the man. He was thin but wiry, dry knots of muscle running down the length of his forearms. He wore a black T-shirt and jeans and Randy wondered how he could stand the cold without a jacket or sweater. They passed through a back door and across the parking lot, the freezing rain pelting them both. The man paid the rain no mind. Shoving his hands in his own jacket packets, Randy thought the man should have at least had the decency to shiver a little.

They weaved through a few trucks until they were at the very back of the parking lot. Massive rigs on either side of them blocked out most of the light and the man was once again little more than shadow.

"Here's good," he said.

Before Randy could reply, footsteps sounded behind him. He spun in time to see a board swing toward his face, the movement cutting a *woosh* sound into the winter air.

There were stars and pain and blood. The concrete beneath him was rough and damp and smelled of motor oil. Had he fallen? He must have. His head rocked, his thoughts sloshing around and refusing to steady.

Hands dug through his pockets. Two voices went back and forth in rapid-fire gibberish, nothing either said making sense to Randy.

Footsteps pounded away from him. All he was left with was the sound of the wind and rain and the distant rumbling of an engine.

Pressing himself to his feet, he almost vomited. The world pitched hard one way and then the other. He steadied himself with one weak hand on the wet metal of a trailer. His other hand wiped the blood from his face. Gingerly, he felt around for the wound. The gash itself was small, but there was no way to tell what it had done to his skull. He was standing, that much was good, but his head felt like it had been sawed open and packed with broken glass.

He fought his way across the parking lot and back into the truck stop. In the bathroom, he washed his hair and face with cold water, the blood streaking across the porcelain as it spiraled away. Checking his pants, he was relieved to find they had only taken his wallet and not his keys. He kept spare cash and a credit card in a safe in his truck in case of emergencies.

The cards in his wallet would need to be cancelled. He slid his phone from its holster to find the screen shattered. From the fall, he assumed.

Stumbling out into the station proper, he headed toward the counter, prepared to tell the Night Person working what had happened and to use her phone.

There was no one there.

He looked around the station. The entire place was empty.

That couldn't be right. He shook his head but doing so hurt and made him queasy. He walked over into the deserted Subway and sat, waiting for the pain and nausea to subside.

The station was quiet aside from the hum of refrigerators and a percolating pot of coffee.

Tricky Dick...

He should have known from the bastard's handle. He'd heard stories his entire career of dirty sons-of-bitches luring truckers in for a Lot Lizard or what have you and then jumping them, but in all his time on the road it had never happened to him. He had been careless. He should have never followed the guy into such an isolated place.

And for what? The chance to get high?

Lucille had always been his weakness. A little coke, a little speed, a little meth... Every time he'd seen Lucille, the concoction had been different but never any less satisfying. Most truckers didn't take anything harder than 5 Hour Energy and a Starbucks double espresso, but for the ones that did, Lucille kept them going long and hard. She'd kept him going for days on end in the past.

And then everything went to Hell.

He felt someone sitting across from him before he heard them. They shuffled into the booth, the seat emitting a faint squeak.

Looking up, he knew that whatever he had been hit with had caused him serious damage.

The girl smiled, her hands folded over one another on the table. Long brown hair fell onto her brown leather jacket. A green turtleneck reached for her chin and brought out the color of her eyes.

"Hi, Randy."

"Who...who are you?" He managed, even though he knew.

"I am Lucille."

He laughed. It hurt. "Lucille isn't real."

She was quiet.

"Did you do this to me?"

"No," she said and shook her head. "You did."

"What?"

"Who do you think I am?"

His lips quivered and he looked down. "The girl. The girl I killed that night."

"Go on."

He took a deep breath. He had never said any of this aloud and the words were hard to find, but once he started they tumbled out. "I was fucked up. Real high. Don't know what was in the mess I snorted that night but I was real jittery. All over the road. And then there you were, your car on the shoulder, hazard lights on, a flare on the road behind you. You hadn't done nothing wrong. And I..." His voice cracked and his breath hitched and he wondered if the hotness on his face was tears or more blood.

She was as still and quite as the grave.

"You come for revenge? Is that it? Make sure I pay for what I done? For getting away with it Scott free?"

"Did you get away with it?"

"Ain't no one saw me that night. No one else on the road."

"That's not what I asked."

He stared at her, unsure at first what she meant. Then he shook his aching head. "No. I've lived with it. That's for damned sure."

"And that's why I'm here. To offer you a way out."

"Out of what?"

"This," she said and motioned around her. "And this." She leaned across the table and touched a finger to his forehead.

"I don't understand."

"I know," she said. "You don't really need to, I suppose. But I'd like you to." She stood. "Join me outside? I promise you won't get attacked again."

The world tilted when he stood and he gripped the table until it righted itself. Then he followed her outside.

She led him past the empty gasoline pumps and into the massive parking lot. It was surrounded by night, the dark thick and crowding in on them as though it had been painted onto the canvas of the world. The only vehicle in the lot was his truck.

Walking over to it, she stood on the running board and extended a hand toward him. He took it and she helped him up.

Staring in the window, he saw himself impossibly slumped in the driver's seat. Small flecks of white powder dotted his shirt.

"It was strong this time," she said. "Maybe too strong. There were a few other things mixed into it as well. You have to be careful what you cut it with."

The blow to his head had knocked him unconscious, he thought. He was still lying on the pavement and all of this was a horrid hallucination.

"No," she said. "The hallucination was everything after Chattanooga. You in that truck? That's real. You scored tonight and your heart couldn't take it. You're on the verge of slipping into the abyss, just tumbling over into angry oblivion, and yet you refuse to give in."

"But the attack..."

"You thought that up on your own. I can't say why." She glanced into the cab at his body. "Maybe it was what you wished had happened instead of this?" She turned away from his body and looked at him. "Or maybe what you thought you deserved. Who knows this time?"

Staring at his own body made him shiver. Inside the cab, his head was turned at an awkward angle and a silver strand of drool dripped from his chin. He wondered if he was as fat as he looked now as well, sprawled across the seat like he had collapsed there.

Maybe he had collapsed there, he reminded himself.

He wanted to deny what she was telling him, but he knew it was true. He could feel it.

Working up the courage to speak, he asked, "So, are you Death then?"

She laughed. "No. I told you. I'm Lucille."

"What do you mean by that?"

She stepped down from the running board. He took one last look at his wheezing, corpulent body and followed.

"It doesn't matter what I mean. You wouldn't understand it anyway." She placed a hand on his cheek. "Just...give in. Let go and give in."

Her eyes were such a deep and vibrant green that he had a difficult time looking away.

"All the pain... The loneliness... Debbie... The kids... The girl you killed... All of it. Gone. Just like that."

"Where...where do I go?"

"Nowhere," she said. "That's the beauty of it. Everything ends here. No more memories. No more shame. Just...*nothing*."

They were sitting inside the truck stop again. He didn't remember walking back in but, damn, was his head killing him. He was surprised that he was awake.

You're not, he thought, and then shook it off.

"Well?" she asked.

Staring at her across the table, he thought her smile looked a little too perfect. Too straight. Too white.

"I ain't ready," he said.

She grunted and slapped the table. "Goddamit. What do you have to live for? Huh? You tell me?"

He opened his mouth to say something and then stopped. What did he have to live for? Taco Bell's Crunchwrap Supreme and reruns of *CSI: Miami*? Driving back and forth across the country for the next ten years until he had a heart attack? He didn't have anything to live for. And whose fault was that? Just his. As much as he wished he could blame Debbie or the kids (or that girl, that goddamned girl who did everything she was supposed to do and yet he still plowed right into her), the fault could only lie at his feet.

She smiled and leaned back into her chair, calming some as the despair washed over him.

But just because he had ruined it all up until now did not mean it had to stay that way.

Her eyebrow rose as he had the thought.

He *could* track down the kids. They may hate him, may not want to talk to him, but he could at least try. He felt he owed them that before checking out.

She stood and placed both palms onto the table. "They don't hate you. No, no. For that, they'd have to think about you at all. But they don't. Debbie remarried. They have a father. At best, you're a sperm donor."

He knew that she was telling him the truth.

"Why do you do this?" he asked.

She cocked her head to the side, her face twisting in confusion. "What?"

"Why? Why do you do this?"

Staring at him with a strange expression on her face, she lowered herself into her seat. "No one's ever asked me that before." She thought for a moment. "No. They've asked 'Why me?' or 'Why now?' but not..." She shook her head.

"Why?" he asked again.

"It's just what I do," she said, her voice sounding small and weak. "There is a hole in some people. In a lot of people, truth be told. And they fill it with booze and pills and sex. For a while. But eventually they realize that the hole is too deep, too wide, and that nothing will ever fill it. That's when they turn to me and I help them slip away. It's a service I offer, one that I'm good at." Her voice regained its former strength. "I've had famous actors and comedians, musicians and writers. I've had politicians and soldiers. And I sure as hell have had truck drivers. When living gets too much to bear, I am waiting there to take it all away. For some, it's a needle. For others a noose. It doesn't matter. I am always here and I always win."

He didn't like how confident she was.

How arrogant.

Something rumbled deep within him. It was small and hot and had the potential to blossom into flame. He hadn't felt it in a long time and, damn, how he had missed it.

"To hell with this," he said, nurturing the spark inside of him and wondering why he'd ever let its warmth die. He stood and slipped from the booth.

She was instantly beside him, walking along as he headed toward his truck again. "Why? You have nothing. Not a goddamned thing to live for. And don't say your kids because you know they don't want you to call."

"Spite," he said as they walked through the double doors at the front of the gas station.

"What?"

"I hate arrogant sons-of-bitches more than anything and I figure you're one of the most arrogant I ever met. So lady, I tell ya, even though I should be dead, I'm sticking around just to piss you off."

She stopped, her mouth hanging open at the sheer audacity of it.

He continued to his truck. As he climbed onto the sideboard, she sprinted over to him.

"Randy," she said. "I don't lose. You realize that, right?"

"I know," he said as he opened the door.

"I am always waiting here. And you will come to me one day."

He knew she was right. That was the worst part about it. One day he would just say "fuck it" and come looking for her.

"But not today," he said as he climbed into his truck and back into himself.

He gasped and sat up so quickly he almost smashed his head into the steering wheel. The world rocked and swayed and it took him a moment of sitting absolutely still with his eyes closed for everything to calm.

His chest ached horribly and his nose and mouth were raw. He opened his eyes and at first thought that he was still alone. He flicked his wipers on, pushing the sheet of rain from his windshield, and saw that the parking lot was crowded.

"Hot damn," he said.

The throbbing in his head was horrible. He rubbed his scalp and his hand came away spotted with blood. He looked up to see a bit of blood on his doorframe.

The head injury? He wasn't sure.

He thought about firing the engine up and hitting the road again, pushing through the last hundred and twenty miles to Birmingham. But he was tired, so damned tired.

Crawling back into his sleeper, knowing that Lucille would keep him awake, he thought he'd just curl up and relax for a while even if he couldn't sleep.

Lucille.

It had not been a dream or a hallucination. He knew that in his gut. She was there waiting for him. Patient as the day is long. Knowing that he would come looking for her.

They always do, he could hear her say.

And he would. Was it depression? Addiction? Something worse? He didn't know. Maybe he'd see a doctor one of these days and find out. But, eventually, it would all get to be too much for him and he would find her again. Maybe here at Rising Fawn. Maybe elsewhere out there on the long, dark road.

"But not today," he said again as he pushed the pillow beneath his head and closed his eyes.

He was asleep in minutes.

Joseph Spencer was born in 1978 in Peoria, Illinois. After graduating summa cum laude from the College of Mass Communications at Southern Illinois University-Carbondale, *he embarked on a 10-year career as a newspaper journalist before transitioning to a career as a manager of a 9-1-1 emergency communications call center. He has utilized his writing and public safety experience to create the* Sons of Darkness *novel series featuring paranormal crime thrillers* Grim *and* Wrage *published by* Damnation Books.

NEVER LOST AGAIN

Joseph Spencer

"IT'S A SHAME HE'S DEAD."

"Who?"

"The guy singing *It's the Most Wonderful Time of the Year* on the radio—Andy Williams. Christmas ain't Christmas without Andy Williams. That's the bitch about getting old. You outlive everything you love."

"About that, listen, Mac, I heard about your wife. She was a great lady. I'll miss her coming around here with you. Dinner's on me, alright?"

Terry MacGlothan's mood turned as dark as his platter of Salisbury steak. "Nah. You don't have to do that." He set down his fork and stared at the lumps in his mashed potatoes. He'd suddenly lost his appetite. "She loved it here. You know, there's not many diners like this left nowadays. She used to say that sitting down at the counter here was like taking a time machine back to when we were kids."

"Dinner's on me, and that's all there is to it. It's the least I can do."

"Hey, Joe. Can you fill me up over here?" A bleary-eyed young punk with a Spartanesque strip of black hair running down the middle of his otherwise bald head banged hard enough on the white Formica counter with his black coffee cup that the porcelain lip cracked. He rubbed his eyes and licked his lips, making sure to show off his silver stud tongue piercing to Terry. He made clacking noises with it as he gnashed it against is teeth. It matched the piercings in his nose and eyebrows and the studs on his black leather jacket.

"I told you once already, spaz." The angry Italian hash slinger furiously wiped down the counter with his white rag. His bushy black eyebrows slanted sharply downward and his lips quivered, making his fast-reddening round cheeks shake like a steaming teapot. "The name's Lou. There's no Joe. And you're paying for that mug."

"Why the hell does the sign outside this dump say Joe's Chili Bowl if your name's Lou?" The young hooligan rolled his eyes, folded his arms, and leaned back in his chair. "And I ain't paying for that shit. It was cracked when you gave it to me."

"Dump, huh? My Grandpa Joe opened this *dump* in 1945." Lou puffed out his chest and pointed at the yellowed black and white pictures hanging on the wall. "He packed 'em in four deep just for a bowl of chili back then. Anybody over the road on Route 66 in these parts knows Joe Rodgers' Chili." Lou put his hand over his heart. "I'm carrying on a legacy here. That's why the sign says *Joe's* Chili Bowl. As long as I'm breathing, it'll stay that way."

"Bet your gramps didn't serve darkies like him at the counter back then." The punk leered smugly and shook his head at Terry. He rolled up his sleeve to reveal a tattoo of an eagle clutching a swastika in its talons on his forearm. "Whaddaya think? You think Grandpa Joe woulda let your kind sit on that stool back then?"

"Not sure about *my kind*," Terry said with enough sarcasm dripping from his voice that it matched the stream of gravy spilling off his plate. "My dad and his brothers? I'm pretty sure they were welcome in any parts those days. They went over to

Europe in the last Great War and fought boys marked up like you—*your kind.*"

The thug biker pointed to patches on his jacket. The top one featured an iron cross resting on the cheek of a skeleton wearing a winged crown. "If *my kind* fought your daddy, boy, you'd never have seen your daddy again. *My kind* never backs down."

"That's it!" Lou slammed down his rag and pointed at the door. "You break my mug. You insult me. You insult my customers. Get outta here now or I'm calling the cops."

But Lou's bully pulled open his leather jacket to reveal a silver revolver tucked into his waistband. He patted it, smirking smugly like a goon used to taking what he wanted if he couldn't get it any other way, and dared the frightened restaurateur to make a move toward the phone sitting by the cash register. "You ain't gonna call nobody, *Joe.* Got it? Cuz if you call the cops on me I'll fucking kill you and him. That'll be the last fucking bowl of chili you'll have to worry about. Got it, Joe?"

"I got it. Listen, I don't want any trouble..."

"Well, it's a little late for that, Joe." The punk spit a plug of chewing tobacco onto the tiled floor. He ran his tongue over his yellowed teeth which made his stud piercing click like the hands of a clock counting down how much time his captives had left. "Trouble's here, don't cha think?" He turned his head sideways and ogled them. If the punk's eyes truly served as windows to his soul, then he'd either drawn the curtains or no one was home. "You got a truck, don't you, boy?" The punk pulled an elaborately-marked pocket watch out of his leather coat and muttered under his breath. "It's time-to-get-the-fuck-outta-here-o'clock. Why don't you give me a ride?"

"Where did you get that?" Terry knew he should be worried, but he couldn't help himself. He'd seen a watch like that long ago. The shock of seeing it again overrode his senses. He had to know where this young punk had gotten that watch.

"The fuck did you say?" The troublemaker turned his gun sideways and stomped over to the counter. As he stood over

Terry, the gunman put the cold barrel up to Terry's temple and pressed it hard against his skin. "I'm not playing, man. Get the keys to your fucking truck and let's fucking go. Otherwise, *Joe's* going to have some smoked dark meat for his chili."

"Go ahead. Pull the trigger, chicken shit. You think I'm afraid to die?" With the barrel of the gun still pressed firmly against his head, Terry pointed at the punk's pocket. "I'm not taking you anywhere until you tell me where you got that watch."

Headlights suddenly filled the room. A car pulled into the parking space closest to the front door and the bright glare of its lights replaced the familiar gloom of the Midwestern winter skyline which had turned so gray and murky from the disappearance of the early setting sun. When the lights finally flicked off, the outline of the car became recognizable. No mere run-of-the-mill family van or grocery-getter station wagon had pulled up. This black and white Monte Carlo had lights mounted on the roof, and a golden police shield on the car door.

"I don't know who fucking called the cops, but you're fucking dead now...both of you." The degenerate pulled back the gun from Terry's head and pointed it at Lou, who whimpered and cowered from the barrel.

"No one called," Lou cried. His voice cracked like a teenage boy. He swallowed hard as he held up his palm to plead with the punk. "It's just Lumpy. He comes in every night...orders a bowl of firebrand, extra meat, no beans...like clockwork. Just play it cool. He won't know anything's going on."

The barrel of the gun danced precariously in front of Lou's face as the spiky-haired gunman's hand shook with indecision. Sweat beaded his forehead as his glance alternated nervously between Lou and the doorway.

"C'mon. Don't be stupid." Terry's outburst drew the punk's attention and the barrel of the gun. "Nobody's getting hurt, you hear me? Just go and don't come back. We won't say nothing, will we, Lou?"

"That's right." Lou sounded like a mouse squeaking.

"All right. All right." The punk feverishly buried the barrel of the gun back into his waistband. He scowled at Terry. "Don't ever tell me what to do again, man. You better hope we never meet again." He swung his leather jacket closed to hide the gun, and stared at Lou and Terry as he backed away slowly from the counter.

The punk nearly jumped a foot in the air when the bell above the doorway jingled. Chatter from a police radio filled the air as a balding cop in a blue uniform stretched tautly by the paunch gut hanging over his belt removed his hat from his head and shook off a light dusting of snow from the brim. He loomed larger than life in the doorway, as wide around as he was tall, despite being tall enough to have to duck his head under the door frame. The oaf's face scrunched as he sized up the scene. The confusion of recognizing the tension between the punk, Terry, and Lou without knowing what was going on registered on his face.

"What do we have here, Lou?" Lumpy popped a knuckle on a hand as gnarled and thick as a root of an oak tree. He eyed the sweaty punk who stood so still he didn't look like he was even breathing. "Is everything all right?"

"What we've got here is a bowl of firebrand, extra meat, no beans, just how you like it." Lou could've won an Academy Award for his business-as-usual performance. He nodded at the punk, and rolled his eyes. "He's another first timer. He tried some of your firebrand, and couldn't handle it. It's coming out of his pores. He's just going to get some air, cool down. Weren't cha, pal?"

"Yeah…that's right." The punk laughed anxiously. He fanned his sweaty forehead. "I need some air."

Lumpy laughed heartily as he patted the punk on the shoulder. "It wouldn't be the first time someone played with the firebrand and got burned." He patted the belly bulge sagging over his belt. "Not everyone has my cast-iron constitution."

The punk nodded agreeably as he backed his way to the door. He eyed Lou and Terry warily, and when they didn't rat him out he darted quickly out the door.

"Poor lad." Lumpy hiked a tree-trunk size leg over his customary stool at the counter, and eagerly accepted a bowl from Lou. "I remember my first bowl of firebrand. When I shit, it burned my ass so bad that I didn't sit or walk right for a week."

As Lumpy slurped spoonfuls, sighed his approval, and belched contentedly, Terry's thoughts turned toward the punk and that watch. He knew he should be relieved his brains weren't splattered over the walls like the chili in Lumpy's bowl, but he couldn't let it go. How could he? *It's our anniversary for Christ sakes,* he thought.

"Are you okay, Terry?" Lou asked another question entirely with a wide-eyed glance and a nod toward Lumpy.

Terry knew the right thing to do was to tell the cop about the young thug and his gun, but that would take time and that's the one thing Terry didn't have. If he had any qualms about his decision, seeing that punk with that watch erased them. It had to have been a sign he was doing the right thing.

"I'm fine. I think I'll be going now. Gotta make up some time on the road." Terry hated lying to his friend, but he couldn't very well tell Lou what he intended to do. "What do I owe ya?"

"It's on the house." Lou waved his hands as if Terry's money was no good. "You be careful out there."

Lou nodded toward Lumpy again. "Are you *sure* that you don't have time to tell us about your adventure? I heard it was a doozie."

"Nah. He's probably better off getting on the road." Lumpy ripped open the plastic on a package of saltines with his teeth. "I'm working a double shift tonight because some weirdos are coming to town to hold some paranormal convention. I guess there are some ghost stories working the freaks up around here. People swear they've seen a ghost bus or van or something like that. I'd leave, too, if I could."

Terry finished his goodbyes and headed out the door. A blast of cold air belted him like a Joe Louis uppercut as soon as he ventured out into the night. His teeth chattered, and he tugged on the collar of his wool overcoat to try to shield the nape of his neck from the chilly bite of the wind. As if angered by his impudence, the gale howled and whipped a forceful draft so bitterly cold into his face that it stole his breath from his chest.

"I won't miss this weather," Terry muttered under his breath at the cold. The only sounds he heard came from the click of the blinking lights on the neon sign above the restaurant, and the howl of the nipping wind which dispatched waves of pain throughout his achy joints. "Fucking arthritis; I won't miss you, either."

Each step on the unforgiving, frozen concrete of the parking lot sent throbbing pains through his knees. They felt so wooden and stiff he thought he might fall. The light snowfall had already melted, leaving an even more dangerous cousin, black ice. It was just as slippery as regular ice, but the slick sheet of ice remained unseen, looking like nothing more than a glossy sheen on the pavement. He'd learned from a long trucking career that the night was full of unseen terrors just waiting to turn a peaceful run into a nightmare.

Terry had parked at the truck stop which shared a large rectangular lot with Joe's. It resembled a concrete jungle, full of trucks, bright red lights, smoky exhaust fumes, and purring engines. Yet, the jungle had no signs of life. He didn't mind being alone anymore. There was a time in his life when the prospect of growing old alone scared him more than death itself, but now he preferred the isolation. He'd pushed away anyone who'd tried to help him so that he could be completely alone over the past year. Although, he'd be lying if he said he was ever completely alone. Her memory and the guilt of failing her weighed on him every waking moment as if he were doomed to pull a cart full of his failure for eternity.

Only, Terry didn't feel completely alone. He could've sworn he heard more than the howl of the wind as he shuffled to his truck. He felt eyes upon him as if he were constantly being watched. He stopped periodically to look around, but he never found the mysterious watcher whose gaze unsettled him.

Terry sighed in relief as he saw his bright red Peterbilt truck. Just as he reached for the door to climb into the cab, he heard a loud squeaking noise from somewhere nearby. He craned his neck to look at the rear of his trailer, but he didn't notice anything unusual. He slowly crouched down on his hands and knees to look underneath it. But nothing was there. He couldn't hear anything anymore either. The popping and creaking of his stiff joints as he bent awkwardly underneath the running boards were the only things breaking the tense silence which made his whole body tingle with unease.

"Jesus Christ. It's cold." He cursed his absentmindedness for forgetting his gloves as he balanced himself with his palms against the concrete to push himself up.

"My mom says never to go out in the cold without gloves."

"What the..." Terry swung around to face the girlish voice he heard coming from behind him. A girl no older than ten looked up at him. Her eyes haunted him. *They're Cathy's eyes.* He knew his mind betrayed him for as he studied this girl more closely he saw his dead wife in all of her features. "I'm sorry, little girl. Are you lost?"

"No." The girl smiled brightly.

She even smiles like Cathy.

Tears formed at the corner of Terry's eyes. He noticed his hands had started shaking and he couldn't seem to catch his breath. He never thought he'd see another look at him the same way she had. He froze, unable to talk, unable to breathe, unable to move.

"My teacher said you're the one that's lost," she continued.

"Excuse me?"

"She knows about you; what you're going to do." The little girl pointed across the lot to a large yellow school bus Terry hadn't noticed. "She said it's not your fault. She said to stay away from the railroad tracks."

Red-faced, Terry turned away from the girl to hide his shame. *How did she know? How did her teacher know?* "I don't know what you think I'm going to do, but..." Terry stopped his reply short when he turned back around to find the girl had gone. He frantically swiveled around to find any trace of where she'd vanished, but couldn't spy her anywhere. He noticed the bus he'd seen had disappeared as well.

"I must be losing my mind," he muttered to himself and climbed up into the cab. Cathy smiled down at him as he slammed the door shut. The picture of her always greeted him from its perch atop the driver's seat visor. It was his favorite. They'd picked up handfuls of the chocolate birthday cake and smeared it all over each other. The black frosting dripping from her honey-kissed brunette curls and the tip of her chin made him smile every time. He chose to remember her that way rather than the last time he'd seen her.

As he turned the ignition and eased his truck off the lot, Terry shuddered as his last glimpse of Cathy ran through his head. He remembered the coroner pulling back the white sheet to reveal her bullet-riddled body. The nightmare of the bloody craters left in her chest and forehead brought tears to his eyes.

It should've been me.

He'd failed her. He told her that she'd never be lost in his arms. He told her she'd be safe. How had he repaid her trust? He didn't protect her like he promised.

It's all my fault. At least, it'll all be over soon.

Terry's thoughts wandered as he steered the stretch of Route 66 as familiar to him as the back of his hand. He'd decided to end it all where his life began. The memory of that hot, humid summer day made the whistling winter winds, the soft, wet snowflakes pelting his windshield, and the nip of the frigid night air on his exposed skin fade away.

He remembered the school bus with smoke pouring out from underneath the hood. The frightened children along the shoulder of the highway chattered and fidgeted anxiously as they stood thirsty and sweaty in the sweltering August heat. That summer became infamously known as The Drought. Throughout Illinois, no rain fell from mid-June to late September. Everything shriveled and turned brown.

That's when he noticed his Cathy. How could he not? Unlike all other signs of life, she defiantly wouldn't wilt under the blazing sun. She stood unfazed, in a dress as serene and blue as the ocean, as she pulled apart boys who were fighting and comforted girls who were crying. From the moment she looked up at him with her pleading eyes as big and brown as caramels, he knew he had to pull over. She called him her heaven-sent highway hero. He told her she'd never be stranded alone anywhere again.

Every summer during her vacation from teaching, they made it their routine. They'd stop at Joe's for a bowl of chili, and then make the short trip to the old mission next where the bus had broken down. She confessed to him that she never worried because she felt the Hands of God that day. She said it was no coincidence the bus broke down so close to Saint Anthony's. She gathered strength from the nearby marble statue, and knew she wouldn't be lost for long. Before she kissed him, she'd always say that God delivered him to her that day.

As he pulled off to the side of the road, Terry looked up at the statue as tears welled in his eyes. "I've been lost for so long. Why haven't you helped me?" Saint Anthony, clad in his robe with a babe in his arms, looked solemnly down upon him. Only silence answered Terry's cry.

Terry had come this far. He knew he had to finish what he came to do. He pulled back on to the highway, drove a few hundred feet, hung a right, and stopped in front of the railroad tracks which intersected the side road he turned off on. "God forgive me," he cried. Tears streamed down his cheeks, and he sniffled to keep snot from running down to his lips. He put the truck back in gear and eased it on to the tracks. He waited until his cab sat firmly in the middle, and stopped.

"I'm so sorry, sweetheart. I couldn't do it without you."

Terry had a friend who worked for Burlington Northern. He knew this was one of their railroad lines. He knew the lights of a locomotive would be bearing down on him soon. He knew they'd never get it stopped in time. The 30 freight cars the locomotive lugged behind it would make sure of that.

Terry figured his final moments would be different. He thought his life would play out in his mind like a movie, but that wasn't the case at all. His mind raced back to earlier in the day. He thought only of the punk and the watch he had no business owning. He wanted that watch back.

How did he get her watch?

A series of loud taps snapped Terry out of his reverie. As he looked over to the driver's side window, a muzzle of a gun slammed against the glass. The glass shattered, and as shards fell into Terry's lap he felt the coolness of the barrel at his temple again.

It's him.

"What the fuck d'ya think you're doing, darkie?" The punk clacked his tongue piercing against his teeth and licked his lips. "If I'd a known you wanted to die so damn bad, I'd a capped your ass at the greasy spoon back there."

"Do it then."

"Maybe I will." The punk smiled as he continued clacking and licking his lips like a lizard. "I want to make you work for it first." He reached into his pocket and dangled the watch in front of Terry's face. "You've seen this before, haven't you?"

There was no mistaking it. The pocket watch bore the flaming heart of Saint Anthony and the inscription Terry had engraved on it for Cathy—*Never Lost Again.*

"Yes." Terry managed to blurt out his answer before he sobbed deeply. He fell into a coughing fit from the snot running down into the back of his throat.

"Well, asshole." The Goth goon jammed the barrel of the gun into Terry's head and smiled. "You wanted to know how I got this watch. I killed her. You must know her. You know this watch, so you musta given it to her. I killed her, boy. Me and my partner killed that whole busload a kids. You see, we knocked over a gas station. As we were leaving, they pulled up. Talk about the wrong place at the wrong time."

"But...but...but why?" Terry pointed to the watch.

"They saw us, man." The punk spit a piece of his tobacco at Terry's face. "That's the first rule a knocking over places. Ya don't leave witnesses."

"Why did you take it?" Terry cried as he grabbed for the watch.

The murderous madman rammed the butt of the gun across Terry's face, gashing him across the forehead. "Ya sit there and be a good little boy." Terry's tormentor laughed and started clacking again. He sounded like a hissing snake readying to strike. "Why? Why?" He mocked Terry, yelling in his ears. "Because I could. I take what I want. The rest a this whole fucking world can burn."

Grief-stricken and outraged, Terry moaned and reached for the watch again. His captor cut another jagged gash in his forehead with the butt of the gun.

"Be patient." He giggled as he jammed the barrel into Terry's temple again. "I'll kill you, too. But you've gotta drive some more first. I've got warrants. If I get stopped, I'll get pinched for sure. I need you to drive north to Iowa. That's outta range of the warrants up there. They won't drag my ass from there back to here for bullshit DUI charges."

A strange noise drew the demented delinquent's attention and the barrel away from Terry. It sounded like children's laughter coming from behind Terry's trailer.

"Who's back there?" The passenger from hell jumped off the running board to the ground and held the gun with both hands as he aimed toward where the sounds had come from. He looked up in disbelief, pointed the gun at Terry, and motioned for him to get out of the truck, too. "Stay where I can see ya. I don't know what's going on, but you're dying the first sign of anything fishy."

The laughter started again. It came from the passenger side of the trailer this time.

"I'm not fucking around, kiddos. Come out, come out, wherever you are." The gunman swiveled to face the sound of the laughter. He looked flustered as the gleeful sounds seem to surround the trailer.

"What the fuck?" The punk started shaking. Terry could see the sheer terror in his eyes. He kept pointing the gun in different directions, but found nothing or no one to shoot.

At the front of the truck, excited squeals pierced the air. Terry traded looks of disbelief with his tormentor, who had lost his cocksure attitude along with all of the color in his cheeks.

"You go on the other side of the tracks where I can see you." The pale-faced punk yelled at Terry. "Tell me where those fucking kids are."

Terry grudgingly obeyed. He gingerly put one foot in front of the other with his eyes glued to the front of the truck. As he slowly inched his way to the other side of the tracks, he stared blankly in disbelief at what was in front of his truck—nothing at all.

"What the fuck, man?"

"There's nobody there."

"The fuck d'ya mean there's nobody there? I can fucking hear 'em."

"Look for yourself." Terry shrugged. He couldn't believe his own eyes. He'd heard the children, too.

The punk walked around to the front of the truck and kicked the grill. "I'm fucking cracking up. It's probably from talking to a damn darkie all day." He sat down on the bumper, and smiled as he pointed the barrel back at Terry. "It's about time for our little chat to wrap up and hit the road. Cheer up. The sooner I get to Iowa, the sooner I can kill you."

Peals of laughter rang out from behind the trailer, and suddenly the truck lurched forward. It threw the punk off the bumper and knocked him down between the tracks. The gun went flying out of his hands and landed far out of his reach on the other side of the tracks.

"My legs!" He tried to push himself away from the truck, but his pants leg was wedged firmly underneath a tire. He couldn't move anywhere. "C'mon, man. What the fuck is going on? Who is in the truck?"

Terry turned to look at the cab, but the headlights abruptly turned on and blinded him. He turned his head away from the glare, and put his hands over his eyes. "I can't see."

The truck began rolling forward.

"Aahh!" The punk yelled as the crunching of bones could be heard over his screams. The laughter picked up again as the truck slowly made its way across the tracks. "Help me. Help me, motherfucker," the punk screamed. Terror shot out of his pained eyes as he held out his hand toward Terry, but in an instant he'd disappeared under the truck.

To Terry's disbelief, the truck and trailer gradually made its way across the tracks and came to a stop once it was safely on the other side. As soon as it stopped, the headlights turned off and the laughter died away.

For a moment, he stood awestruck, staring at his truck. There's no way it could've moved on its own. The tracks rested on an incline. If anything, the truck would've rolled backward if it moved at all. But that didn't matter, as the brakes were on. He walked around to the back of the trailer and gasped. There were handprints in the snow clinging to the rear of it, but that wasn't what took the air out of him.

There, dangling from one of the handles to open his trailer, hung Cathy's watch. The moon light glinted on the inscription on the back: *Never Lost Again.*

R. B. Payne's work can be found in anthologies such as All American Horror of the 21st Century: The First Decade, *and* Permuted Press' Times of Trouble. *Upcoming work is featured in* Expiration Date *from* Hades Publications, Unspeakable Horror 2: Abominations Of Desire *from* Dark Scribe Press, *and his post-apocalyptic story* Spark *will be published in* Dark Discoveries *magazine in mid-2015. His first novel* The Night Watchman *is nearly complete and will be published in early 2016. Updated information can always be found at* www.rbpayne.com.

BIG WATER

R. B. Payne

I AM A SIMPLE MAN.

And this is a simple story.

Well, at least it started out that way.

My name's Roy Kincaid, nice to meet you.

For starters, I drive a big rig named Janet 784 and what you need to know is I've got security clearance to the Air Force's Flight Test Centers including the mother of all locations, Detachment 3. You might not recognize the official name because everyone calls that patch of worthless Nevada sagebrush Area 51, Dreamland, or Paradise Ranch.

Area 51. Every alien conspiracy nut in the world eventually cruises the Extra Terrestrial Highway hoping to score a photo of Gort out walking the dogs, or maybe a Colonial Viper zipping by. Fat fucking chance. Most gawkers eventually get bored and end up at the Bunny Hutch getting their oil changed along with the regulars that work Highway 375 for a living. At the end of the day, all those rubberneckers ever get is a selfie with some roadside hooker's tits.

And I'm not a sexist for saying that because every geek I've ever seen standing next to the Black Mailbox with a camera and a giant lens was a dude. Which isn't to say there's not weird shit roaming this planet. The fact is: You only see what they want you to see.

And that's the simple truth, my friend.

Anyway, this whole thing started with a "cammo" guy named Big Ben. He and Charley were designated greeters. But not at Area 51, that location is strictly for tourists. Dreamland is military sleight-of-hand; a roadside attraction designed to lure the lame of mind. The real deal is *Slick Rock*, south of Moab, Utah. About twenty-eight miles from goddam nowhere and six miles east of Canyonlands National Park.

That's where I first met Mama.

But I'm getting ahead of myself.

For all intents and purposes, Big Ben and Charley are contract killers and I should have realized that up front. But they worked for the Department of Defense and that sort of made everything legal. At least I thought so back then.

Big Ben and Charley run perimeter management at Slick Rock and spend most of their day cruising the desert in a four-wheel drive keeping John Q. Public at arm's length. And even though they're technically civilians, they wear camouflage gear like they earned it. Who knows, maybe they did earn it somewhere along the line.

Anyway, when the cammos spot an unauthorized individual approaching the site, the first warning is typically a glint off the lenses of binoculars. That sends most people scurrying away like cockroaches in a bright light because the signs on the highway say *Use of Deadly Force Authorized*, *Do Not Enter* and, if that's not clear enough, there's a Skull and Crossbones.

If a second warning is needed, Big Ben pops off a couple of shells from an AA-12 Semi-Automatic Shotgun. In a harmless direction, of course. His official mission is to "observe and deter." Keep local idiots and nosy reporters out. Still, there is no third warning. Big Ben and Charley boast that they've permanently deterred over a hundred trespassers. My guess is that's bullshit talking and there's no more than a dozen bodies buried in the desert backcountry.

So on the day all this shit started, I ground the gears as Janet 784 rolled to a stop at the Slick Rock checkpoint. I flashed my ID like I always do. Two pimply soldiers checked my Bill of Lading like they always do.

Janet 784 purred. She's a Freightliner with about 400k miles. Sweet. And she's a reefer. Did I mention that? A lot of the shipments are moved cold. I never know what's in the trailer. I don't want to know, in fact, I'm paid *not* to know. All I do know is that I cruise in light, and I roll out heavy. I pick up at Slick Rock; I drop off at Dayton. I snag another load in Utah. I drop off at Okie-City.

That's how it works.

The two guards glanced to the ridge behind the guard station for authorization. Big Ben leaned against the fender of his Jeep. I can still see him in my mind's eye. The morning sun made everything clear and bright although the temperature was nearly a hundred and twenty degrees already.

Off to one side of the Jeep, Charley took a piss. Big Ben barely moved in the oppressive heat, just nodded his head once.

All clear.

I gave the two guards a mock salute. They smiled. I jammed the gears and headed to the labs. Up until that day, one week on the road was pretty much like the next.

Shit, I can see I've confused you. So let's down another couple of shots of *Tres Cuatro Y Cinco* and I'll tell you the whole story from the beginning.

∾

Big Ben grinned and slapped me on the back. He leaned closer. His breath smelled like cigarettes and hamburger with a beer chaser.

"How'd you like to score a million bucks, pal?" he whispered.

"Yeah, right," I said.

He'd never called me *pal* before.

"Seriously."

"You jerking me?"

"Nah, serious as shit. A million freaking bucks."

Well, maybe it's a legitimate offer. I figured something was up when Big Ben and Charley suggested hoisting a few beers *off campus* in the middle of the afternoon. But I don't know why he whispered; we were the only three customers in *The Celestial Kingdom*, a brewpub in Moab. In the evening, the bar would fill with mountain bikers and rock climbers. Right now, the bar was all ours.

"I'm listening," I said.

I played it cool but my heart raced. I tilted back in my chair and balanced on the aluminum legs. Took a long sip of beer. Charley gave me the eye as Big Ben made his pitch.

"No questions. We load your truck. Whatever you see, you forget. You deliver to San Pedro out in Cali. We provide a Bill of Lading. You pick the route. Me and Charley ride bitch. We don't make it there, you don't get paid."

"Is this official?"

"Fuck, does it sound official?"

"Is it legal?"

"I said no questions."

"Yeah, but I can't see me doing hard time."

Big Ben glared. Charley shifted his butt in his chair. I tried to figure if this was the real deal or some sort of security screening.

"Alright, I'll think it over," I finally said. I didn't know how to play my cards. Shit, did I even have cards?

"Tonight, Roy. It's tonight. No time for thinking."

Then I felt it. Big Ben was proud of his Heckler & Koch Mark 23 and I could feel its barrel pressing on my balls. The corners of his mouth curled in what he must consider to be a smile.

"The correct answer is *yes*," said Big Ben.

The chair legs slipped and I crashed to the floor, beer soaking my shirt. The gun disappeared but I knew it was still nearby.

Charley, grinning, gave me a hand and I struggled to my feet.

Truth is, like many Americans, I'm dead broke. It isn't that I don't work hard or that I've screwed up. But, for some reason, my truck payment is always a few months late, and Janet 784 is my meal ticket. Finance company wants it back pretty bad.

And I've had my share of misfortune, but who hasn't? I don't believe in complaining. Bottom line: I don't have a fancy retirement plan and I can't remember the last time I could afford to see a dentist. Well, that might just be laziness on my part.

But why shouldn't I look out after myself? Screw the credit card companies. They're the reason I live in my truck week-to-week; shit, the bank took my house during that so-called recession where it sure seems like a lot of people got richer.

But not me.

Maybe this opportunity is an equalizer. My lottery ticket. My chance to join the one-percenters. I smiled at Big Ben as I dabbed a napkin to dry my shirt.

"Do you think you could make that a million...and a half?"

Hell, it never hurts to press and I figured they were low-balling me anyway.

Charley clapped me on the back as Big Ben yelled to the bartender.

"Hey! Three more beers over here."

We had a deal.

ᘒ

On Underground Level 4, Corridor 13, Lab 9, a creature floated in a massive glass aquarium. Oddly, the rear glass panel was papered with an enlarged photo of a coral reef. Somebody's warped sense of humor. The glass box was no kid's toy and the thing inside was no fish. Monstrosity. Now that's a big word, and yep, I know what it means and I meant to use it.

A fucking monstrosity.

"What the hell is it?" I asked, keeping my distance. I never knew this kind of shit went down at Slick Rock.

I scanned the room. Beakers and test tubes covered a workbench. Wires ran everywhere. I didn't recognize much of the gear other than a few monitors bleeping like in a hospital.

"Beauty, eh? She's a *bio-engineered entity*. We call her Mama," said Big Ben.

Charley tapped on a panel of the aquarium's glass with the edge of his security pass. Flippers pulsated and the creature slowly rotated to face us. A single indigo eye stared from the center of a bulbous head covered in orange mushroom-like growths. Stringy. As the currents in the water moved, the 'shroomy things almost looked like hair. Blue-green scales the size of my open hand covered her body and click-clacked faintly as she moved. Like she might be breathing through her skin.

Then I noticed she had two human arms, small, but sprouting out from under her flippers. Each arm had a hand. Mama reached and touched the glass, palm flat. Yep, a human hand, for sure. The monstrosity had fingerprints.

Her lidless indigo eye darted as it studied the three of us.

"Jesus, she's a big as a Volkswagen," I said.

"Careful, Roy, she might take offense to you mentioning her weight," said Big Ben.

Charley laughed, Big Ben farted, and I wondered what the fuck I was doing here.

Oh yeah, money.

At that moment my legs went weak and I wanted to run. I felt sick, really sick. And where the hell was everyone? A top-secret government laboratory and we'd waltzed right in? Sure, the lab stood down because it was the Friday night before Labor Day and most of the science-types had taken off for Vegas, or god-forbid, Salt Lake City. Still, I expected somebody to be around. Soldiers. Security guards. Foot patrols.

"Where is everyone?" I asked.

A voice resonated in my head.

Sleeping.

I looked at Mama and her eye stared back, unblinking.

Sleeping, the murmur came again.

"Did you hear that?" I asked aloud.

"Hear what?" asked Big Ben, as Charley slammed a ladder against the side of the aquarium and climbed to the safety railing. The tank hung on a set of ceiling rails so it could be repositioned. Or moved elsewhere for experiments, I figured.

Charley unhooked the safety catch and clicked on the power. Somewhere a motor whirred, and the water in the tank shimmied. The giant aquarium lifted from the ground and swung free.

"Nothing," I said. "Just my imagination."

"Then shut up and let's get Mama on the truck," said Big Ben.

Big Ben revved the engine on a military loader. We slowly rumbled toward the service elevator with Mama sloshing in her tank. Up at the loading dock, Janet 784 waited with her lift gate down and trailer doors open.

At the end of the corridor, I peeked into the guard station. Yep, that voice in my head was right. The guard slept.

"Would have been easier when she was the size of a kitten," observed Big Ben, braking to a halt outside the access elevator. The doors slid open.

"Amen," said Charley, swiping his security pass on the elevator controls and punching the G button. "Super easy. But who woulda known which one to take?"

"You got me there," conceded Big Ben.

At the loading dock, we secured the tank onto the trailer's floor panels. Triple straps, just to be safe. We were ready to roll.

In the darkness, Big Mama emitted a pulsing blue-green aura. Her indigo eye cut through me as I slammed the trailer doors shut.

The three of us clambered into the tractor.

"Make it cold," said Big Ben, as he scribbled the destination on my clipboard. The docks at San Pedro. Pier 9. California.

"Super cold," said Charley.

I must've given them a look because Big Ben added, "It keeps Mama calm."

"Super calm," added Charley.

I cranked the reefer as cold as she'd go. We pulled away and a few minutes later we rumbled to the Main Gate. A searchlight beamed lazily into the night sky. Next to it, two soldiers sprawled in the dirt, rifles askew. Asleep.

A voice drifted into my head.

Dead.

All dead now.

෮

For hours, we rolled down 191 toward Arizona and soon Utah disappeared in the moonless dark. I kept my focus on the road, one eye peeled on the rear view. Any minute I expected to see the flash of Johnny Law on my tail or maybe a military bear in the air. Nothing. Meanwhile, Big Ben smoked an entire pack of AS Menthols.

Back in the sleeper, Charley sawed a few logs.

At five AM a ribbon of orange on the eastern horizon meant dawn approached. Fuel gauge said we were dry; luckily Tuba City loomed not far ahead.

Dimly lit billboards gave way to the electric glow of a truck stop. I rumbled off the highway and fueled Janet 784. She was one thirsty girl. After paying, I pulled into the back row of semis where the truckers slept. Maybe we could catch a little shut-eye.

Under a flickering lamppost, three lot lizards were looking for the last John of the night. I knew one of them, Tiffany. I wouldn't say I was a regular, but there'd been a time or two I'd needed a friend.

Tiffany, in hot pants and a mesh top that read *Lakers*, approached the cab. The other two women, seeing that Tiffany had a natural, wandered off.

"I'll get rid of her," I said.

"Nah," said Big Ben. "Let her in the cab."

Charley woke.

"I'm not interested in a party with you guys," I objected, but by now, Tiffany had hooked her arm on the side mirror and peered in the driver's window. I rolled it down.

"Hey, Roy. You're looking good."

"You too, Tiffany."

A lie. She looked worse than ever. The meth does that to you. Thin, and when she smiled, toothless. Of course, in her line of work, that might be a plus.

Tiffany grinned wider.

"I see you brought some friends, baby. Maybe I can give you my three for two special."

Before I could answer, Big Ben said, "Sure, sweetheart, climb on in." He reached across me and unlocked the door. Tiffany scrambled into the cab. She slid onto my lap and wiggled her bony ass.

"What have you naughty boys got in mind?"

Big Ben smacked her head with the butt of his Heckler & Koch Mark 23 and her skull made a hollow pop. She collapsed onto the center console.

"Let's move," said Big Ben, pointing the gun at my chest.

We rolled back onto the highway, heading west. Tiffany groaned but she didn't come to.

"What the hell did you do that for?" I asked.

"Mama's hungry," said Big Ben.

Charley laughed.

"Super hungry."

And that's when I knew I'd gotten myself into some serious shit.

☙

Once upon a time, there was a dog.

Now this isn't your typical boy and a dog story because I didn't have that dog long. Certainly not long enough to fall in love. Not even a whole day. But, for the sake of argument, let's just say I felt something for that mutt.

I first saw her limping on the roadside about halfway between Sloan Lake and Highway 25 heading to Casper. About five years ago, maybe six. Anyway, Wyoming's no place for a loose dog, and certainly not in the heat of August.

After I passed her, I pulsed the air brakes and about fifty yards down the highway I coasted to a stop. The dog approached. Her ribs heaved as she panted. But her eyes weren't wild, they were sad. Starving. Dehydrated. Looking for someone to save her.

I had a half-eaten Mickey-D's and a bag of Fritos. I gave them to her along with a bowl of water. She scarfed the food. Might have saved her life for a day, but no more. She didn't have long to live unless she accepted help. I stepped away from the cab door.

"You wanna go for a ride?"

She whimpered and edged closer to the coolness that flowed from the air-conditioned cab. She thought it over. Clearly, she belonged to somebody; a leather band encircled her neck.

"Okay if I take a look at your collar, girl?"

She didn't back away as I kneeled. I ran my fingers through the fur on her head as I read the tag. *Randi*. An address in Casper about forty miles ahead. But no phone.

"You're a long way from home, Randi," I said. Her ears perked and her eyes sparkled at the sound of her name. I offered her my opened arms. She didn't think twice, and I lifted her into the cab. Before I could even buckle myself in, Randi fell asleep in the passenger seat.

A trucker's always got time for a good deed, so I headed for Kirkwood Avenue in Casper. Tonight, Randi would be home with her family.

Technically, I'm not supposed to cruise on side streets in neighborhoods, but the trailer rolled empty and I figured I could sweet-talk any law enforcement Johnnie I came across. Cops have a soft spot for lost animals; just don't ever ask them to admit it.

I cruised down Kirkwood Avenue. A nice neighborhood full of houses built before Sputnik. Big grassy lawns. Shingle roofs. Brick foundations. Nothing ritzy. Just good ol' American homes.

Randi whimpered awake when I rolled to a stop. In a yard enclosed by a picket fence, a middle-aged dad played baseball with two young boys.

"You're home, girl," I said, but Randi didn't move. She turned her back to me and snuggled into the leather of the seat.

I hopped from the cab, and the man came to the fence. I expected friendly. But his walk looked mean and the way he held the baseball bat didn't make me comfortable at all.

I smiled. "Hey. I've got your dog in the cab. I found her about forty miles down Highway 25."

"We don't have a dog, Mister."

The man spat a wad of phlegm at my feet.

"You haven't even looked at her. She's got your address on her collar."

The two boys ran to the fence.

"Did you find Randi?" the older boy said.

A woman, carrying a toddler, stepped onto the porch. Even from the front yard, I could see one eye ringed in a dark shadow. Behind me, Randi jumped from the cab and ran weakly through a gate to the young boys who both wrapped their arms around the dog's neck.

"You kids get in the house."

Without a word of protest, the two boys abandoned the dog and scurried across the grass, up the brick stairs, and past their mother. She followed the kids inside. The screen door slapped shut behind her.

Randi collapsed onto the grass.

"You better get her to a vet," I said.

"I told you. We don't have a dog."

The asshole raised the baseball bat and smashed Randi's hindquarters. I heard her hips break. Then he popped her rib cage. I heard the snap of bones splintering. I expected Randi to fight or squeal or growl or bite, but mercifully, she just slipped into unconsciousness.

The man raised the bat at me. I barely knew what to do.

"Look, I'll give you a grand for the dog," I said.

The man nodded at Janet 784.

"Get moving. And mind your own fucking business."

I looked at Randi lying in the grass. She hadn't been trying to find her way home; she'd been trying to escape. And I'd brought her back.

"I'm sorry, Randi," I said, but that dog couldn't hear a word I said. But the man did. He raised the bat to strike Randi again but changed his mind and threatened me instead.

"Don't make me hurt you, Mister. You don't know what trouble that dog caused and now you've gone and fucked everything up."

Now I know it's illegal but truck-jacking is more common than you think. Underneath my driver's seat, I keep a Smith and Wesson .357 Magnum. Not a weapon like Big Ben's Heckler & Koch Mark 23, but big enough to scare off amateurs.

I stepped slowly to the cab like I was making to leave and reached in. I flashed the gun at the man. He backed away. Every fiber in my body wanted to put a bullet in his head.

Instead, I put a bullet in Randi's head. Mercy, that's what I call it. She died without a whimper.

I raised the gun at the man again and I didn't care how many of his neighbors saw it. I figured they already knew what a dickwad he was and didn't mind if someone called him to task.

"My trucker friends and I are going to keep an eye on you, asshole. Every time you see a big rig I want you to wonder if it's me or my pals. If I ever hear about you hurting your wife or kids again, the same thing will happen to you. A bullet in the head. Now get the fuck out of here."

The man hurried to his house and slammed the porch door behind him. I lifted Randi's body to the rig. Nothing left of her but skin and bones and now a bullet hole. I buried her in the mountains outside of Casper and not a day goes by that I don't think about that dog and how pretty she could have been if someone had just loved her.

But right now, I thought hard about that gun stashed under my seat, Tiffany, Big Ben, and Mama. Maybe I could salvage this situation. Maybe I could make everything right.

"Find a side road and pull off," said Big Ben.

Tiffany groaned.

"It's feedin' time," said Charley.

My stomach curled.

ℰℛ

Rumbling into a forest, I parked Janet 784 on a Forest Service road some fifty miles west of Flagstaff. Moments later, two black helicopters roared overhead. From the forest's edge, I watched as they thundered past, headed to the far horizon, then arced back our direction.

I heard Big Ben calling me.

A moment later, three of us stood at the rear of the trailer, Tiffany lay unconscious on the ground because Big Ben had popped her in the head again.

The helicopters thumped toward us.

"Shit," said Big Ben, running to the cab. Throwing open the passenger door, he yanked out a duffel bag. A split second later, he shouldered something like a bazooka, but smaller.

Charley hurried to his side. His voice carried in the stillness of the forest.

"You think it'll come to that?"

"It will if they've seen us," said Big Ben. "You disabled the rig's GPS, right?"

"We're running super dark. Promise."

"Then keep calm. Let's feed Mama."

By now, the military birds were nearly on top of us. We were a quarter-mile off the highway, and I doubted the 'copters knew we were hidden beneath the tall pines. Still, we'd left a few tracks in the dirt road.

I slipped to the driver's side of the cab and retrieved my Smith & Wesson. The CB radio squawked unexpectedly and I nearly squeezed off a shot. I hid the gun under my tee.

"Janet 784, you got a copy? This is Rebel 33," the speaker's voice reverberated with military precision. "You got your flappers on? We know you're out there."

"Bluffing," Big Ben's voice carried as I hustled to the rear of the trailer. "If they knew where we were, they be on us like shit on a dog's ass."

"Let's get this horror show on the road," Charley said to me. "Open the fucking doors."

Out over the highway, the helicopters swung west, and disappeared. Big Ben was right. They were flying blind.

I popped the refrigeration locks and slid the cams open. A wave of fog poured into the dry desert air as the doors swung wide. A layer of ice coated the interior of the trailer; all of the humidity coming off the tank had frozen on the walls.

Mama stared, awake. But the refrigeration unit had cooled her tank until it thickened with ice shards. She flippered to rotate, cutting a path in the thick water to face us. I swear her indigo eye stared at me, and only me. Her human arms stretched out to all of us, fingers twitching, hands grasping.

Hungry.

Eat.

Big Ben hoisted Tiffany's limp body onto the floorboards of the trailer and climbed up after her.

Eat humans.

"She eats people?" I asked aloud. I couldn't help myself.

"DNA," said Big Ben. "She thrives on DNA. I figured we could make it to San Pedro but then this hooker came along, Too good to pass up, man. Charley and I don't know how to make the soup they feed her. I sure hope this works."

"You hope this fucking works?"

"Shut your cake hole."

"You never mentioned killing anyone."

"We're not killing anybody. She absorbs them. Look at the arms. She didn't have those the first time I saw her. They fed her a cadaver. A day later she sprouted those. As far as I can tell we're offering what's-her-name eternal life."

"You really think it's wise to give her a meth addict?"

"You got a better idea?"

I kept my trap shut. I didn't have a better idea unless I killed them all. I rested my palm on my Smith & Wesson. A freaking dilemma. Maybe Mama needed saving. Maybe she needed killing. I didn't have a fucking clue.

So I hesitated.

A plexi lid covered Mama's aquarium and Big Ben unfastened it and slid it aside. Jumping to the floor, his hand clasped Tiffany by the neck, and in a single lift, he thrust her scraggy body into the tank.

Mama didn't move; and Tiffany's body neither sank nor floated.

"Dammit," said Big Ben. "There's a sheet of fucking ice."

"I'll take care of it," said Charley, scrambling atop the aquarium to look. Straddling the ice, Tiffany made a cooing noise in her throat. She stirred, waking. Must have been the coldness of the ice.

"What's going on?" slurred Tiffany.

"You got a crowbar, Roy?" asked Charley. "I gotta break this up. It's super frozen."

An explosion of ice clattered against the trailer walls. Mama rotated in the tank and her human arms shot to the surface, smashing the ice and yanking Tiffany into the tank. For some reason, I expected a blinding flash of light, but nothing much happened except that somehow Mama consumed Tiffany. Mama had no mouth so maybe absorbed described it better. Regardless, a moment later, only a floating Lakers top, hot pants, and a sinking pair of platform stilettos remained of Tiffany.

"Wow. Son of a super bitch," said Charley, and those were the last words he ever spoke. Mama's hands flashed again and a split-second later, Charley's cammo clothing floated free in the icy water.

Big Ben leapt from the trailer, and together we slammed and bolted the doors.

"Shouldn't we put the lid back on?" I asked.

"Hell no. They can deal with this in San Pedro," Big Ben yelled as he climbed into the cab. For the first time, there appeared a crack in his armor and fear in his eyes. I jammed the gears and rolled back onto Highway 40, heading west. I slipped the Smith & Wesson back under the seat.

Big Ben didn't seem so big anymore.

౿

Later, Big Ben lit another cigarette and exhaled a cloud of blue smoke. Over the last few hours, he'd smoked nearly a pack. But he hadn't said much.

I squinted into the oncoming headlights. Neither of us had slept for two days. Just past midnight, traffic was scarce across the California desert heading to Barstow,

"Just what the hell is Mama?" I asked, for the umpteenth time.

Big Ben puffed his cigarette for a few more miles. Clearly, he thought about what story to spin. Finally, he spoke.

"You ever heard of Roswell?"

"You think I'm an idiot?"

"Well, it's like that, but for real."

"What? Are you trying to tell me Mama is...alien?"

"No. Yes. Well, sort of. A saucer crash happened, but not in New Mexico, and not in '47. Walla Walla, Washington, that's the place. November 24, '63. Two days after Kennedy. The saucer exploded in the atmosphere and crashed in a snowy field in the middle of freaking nowhere. A saucer team out of Slick Rock recovered a truckload of metal and some critter tissue the size of your pinky. That's it."

Big Ben lit a new cigarette from the butt of his old one. The ashtray overflowed, so he opened the window and flicked the butt out.

"So?"

"So, the military spent the last fifty years trying to clone the tissue. Or grow it. Or replicate it. Or fuck whatever, I'm not a scientist. All I know is that Mama is the only one of thousands of experiments that survived past a few weeks. Of course, she's not pure. She's a random mix of a thousand gene sequences. Frog. Cat. Gator. Whale. Gorilla. Alien. I've got no idea what's in her. All I know is that she's worth fifty million if we can deliver her to that ship in San Pedro."

"Fifty million bucks? Are you kidding me?"

"Nope. Mama's pregnant. Self-replication, they called it. And somebody wants her bad."

"You're selling out?"

"I'm cashing out of a shit system," said Big Ben. "You, of all people, ought to know that."

A blinding light suddenly flooded the windshield. I couldn't see a damn thing. Janet 784 shuttered to a stop as I hit the brakes. All of a sudden it struck me that I hadn't seen any traffic on the highway for the last half an hour.

A helicopter thumped overhead. Through the bright light I could see some sort of a barricade on the highway. An amplified voice spoke.

"Get out of the truck and lay face down on the ground."

I might have laughed at the cliché if I hadn't been scared shitless. Not for me. Not for Mama.

I feared for the soldiers.

☙

Roy.

Spread-eagled on my stomach, my face pressed into the gravel on the shoulder of the highway. My cheek hurt like fucking hell. Some jerk eighteen-year-old E5 pressed his boot harder on my shoulders.

The voice drifted into my mind. *Help.*

Now I'd swear, until the day I die, the voice I heard was Tiffany. I twisted my neck to see what the hell the soldiers were up to. Floodlights splattered the sides of Janet 784 with bright light.

On the highway, in the distance, two helicopters rested on the asphalt. A couple dozen men in Hazmat suits disembarked from convoy trucks. More than a few of them hoisted flamethrowers.

Not a rescue party.

Nearby, Big Ben spun a tale to an officer about how he and Charley had been forced at gunpoint to help in the kidnapping of Mama. He gestured at me and flashed his ID card again and again as he spoke.

Bastard.

Still, I remained calm. I knew what had happened at Slick Rock. I knew what Mama could do. Was the military that stupid? Maybe no one had told them what really had happened.

On the flip side, Mama had anxiety. Based on what I'd seen at Slick Rock, she could easily take care of a squad of soldiers. Why, then, ask me to help? Seriously, what could I do, that she couldn't?

I heard the shatter of glass and a wall of water slosh onto the highway. I couldn't see what was going on.

I decided to warn them.

"Jesus Christ," someone said through a breather. "Keep your distance, men."

The E5 kicked me in the ribs.

"Get up," he said.

Men with flamethrowers ran to the rear of the trailer.

I rose to my feet.

"Who's in charge?" I said. "I need to speak to him. Now."

"Shut your face," said the E5.

"I need to warn you about her."

"We're not scared of the bitch," he said. "We know what she can do and we know how to stop her. Now, turn around, I have to cuff you."

Then he fell to the ground.

As did they all.

So much for knowing what to do.

Big Ben looked at me as he collapsed, a grimace on his face. He looked in pain and I hoped it killed him.

So, there I was, the last man standing.

Roy.

I carried the bazooka to the rear of the trailer. Mama sat free in the open air. Scales clacking. Blue-green aura. Her indigo eye stared. Like the blob she was, she was helpless out of the tank.

Now, I'd never fired a bazooka but Big Ben had left it loaded. I clicked what appeared to be the safety.

Roy, the voice echoed in my head.

Help.

Raising the bazooka to my shoulder, I focused the crosshairs of the sight onto her bulbous body. I put my finger on the trigger. I started to squeeze. Surely, the right thing to do.

Mama quivered, I swear she did.

And then I thought of Randi.

Maybe Mama was a stray I could save.

The voice pleaded.

Big water.

Please.

Then I got it. That had been her plan all along. There hadn't been fifty million bucks. No ship in San Pedro. The whole stupid idea had been planted in Big Ben and Charley's minds. I dropped the bazooka; it clattered on the highway. I slammed the trailer doors shut and headed to the cab.

I rammed through the barricade of military vehicles.

Mama could do many things.

But she couldn't drive a big rig.

❧

Once I hit I-15 in Rancho Cucamonga, I knew the military would never catch me. There's twenty-one thousand miles of road in Los Angeles filled with cars, trucks, and taco wagons. The soldiers had no idea of my destination.

I gradually worked my way through the morning traffic. When the commute finally cleared, I put the pedal to the metal and went balls to the wall. I shot past downtown Los Angeles and headed straight for Manhattan Beach.

That's where we'd find big water.

Near the Chevron refinery, there's a parking lot with access to the Pacific. Now the Angelinos are an odd lot, and right on the beach, next to the refinery, ran a path filled with joggers, bicyclists, and skateboarders. I blew the air horn and backed onto the sand. But my wheels spun freely and I couldn't finish that last fifty feet to the ocean.

I set the brake and ran to the back of the trailer, throwing the doors open. I had no idea how to get her to the water as the blast of refrigerated air hit my face.

Mama saw the ocean; her sides clacked excitedly and she edged forward, anxious. Son of a bitch. On her underside, four human legs had appeared. Charley and Tiffany, no doubt.

Mama lumbered forward, unsure.

I hit the switch and lowered the gate to the sand. Mama stumbled onto the ground.

Big water.

Super cool, baby.

The day had blossomed bright and sunny with a trace of high clouds framing the horizon. On the beach, a couple of twenty-something girls were setting up a net for a volleyball match.

A family cruised by on the bike path, pink streamers from their toddler's bike sparkling in the sunlight. A group of middle-aged men jogged by, breathing hard, but the words *stock market* and *good investment* floated on the sea breeze.

Mama ambled toward the surf on those four human legs. She twisted to look at me with her indigo eye.

Join?

Join?

I thought it over.

No thanks, I responded.

Mama turned to face the ocean.

"What the hell is that?" somebody yelled from down the beach. I heard screaming from the bike path. People running.

A large wave washed around Mama and she screeched "Big water, big water, big water, big water, big water."

Of course, only I could hear her.

Mama hurried to the waves. Hurried might be an exaggeration. She moved as fast as she could on her new legs. A moment later she disappeared leaving only an odd track of footprints in the wet sand.

Then I heard a police siren. No doubt some soccer mom had dialed 911.

In my heart, I knew this might be the end of the world. Maybe I should have stopped Mama in Barstow. I don't know if I could have. But it didn't matter.

Things that are alive deserve to live.

But now I needed to save Janet 784.

Behind the tractor, I hurriedly uncoupled the air lines and yanked the pigtail. Then I pulled the 5th wheel jaws open and ran for the cab, where I jammed the truck into gear. The trailer slammed down onto its jacks as Janet 784 and I struggled free. Without looking back, I headed for the interstate. A minute later, two Highway Patrol cars shot by apparently heading to the ruckus at the beach.

Merging with freeway traffic on the 405, Janet 784 and I set course for Baja Mexico. I punched on the cruise control.

෴

A few months ago, I found myself in a bar in San Felipe. It's a nice town where people don't ask too many questions. Even though a year has passed, I figure it still isn't safe to show my face north of the border.

On a flickering television above the rows of multicolored liquor behind the bar, the local news team reported more surfers missing off Inspiration Point near Santa Barbara. Biologists and surfer dudes alike attributed the attacks to a Great White Shark.

But you and I, my friend, we know better. So what do you say, the moon is out and the grunion are running. Shall we go to beach and take a look? Have another shot of tequila. Too drunk? Come on. I've heard the grunion have sprouted legs. It's worth a look.

And if you're lucky, I'll introduce you to Mama's children.

At the age of eight Daniel P. Coughlin was sent to a psychiatrist by his loving parents because of the dark content of his stories. Since then, he barely graduated from high school, served as a machine gunner in the last of the Marine Corps Amphibious Raider Units, graduated (with good grades this time) from California State University Long Beach *with a Bachelor of Arts degree in Film/Screenwriting where he interned for Wes Craven as a script analyst, authored five published novels (*Ted's Score, The Last Customer, Craven's Red, The Heartland *and* Sunny California*), has had four original screenplays produced into feature films (*Lake Dead, Farmhouse, Ditch Day Massacre *and* Diary of a Psychopath*), got married to the love of his life Kelli-Rae, with whom he is expecting their first baby boy, has become an active member of the Los Angeles chapter of the* Horror Writers Association *where he met and befriended some of the greatest people on earth (and in hell), and resides in beautiful Southern California.*

DOWNSHIFT

Daniel P. Coughlin

THIS PART OF THE DESERT WHISTLES at night and it's warm. One of those nights when the moon is set high and full and yellow and that luminescent energy cascades your being and captivates your thoughts and the feeling you get is almost like a drug. Well, I don't notice any of that as I speed past her. She's walking, drifting really, along the highway and I know it's her. My wife. Mrs. Ron Burkard. The wife that was taken from me. Her life cut short and placed deeply into an infinite sleep. And now I miss her. Enough so that I see her sometimes while I'm hauling cargo in the middle of the night. She's usually dressed in that simple white nightgown, the one I'd bought her at Walmart in Kentucky, but the way she wore that knee length slip you'd think I'd bought it at some fancy store in Times Square, New York City. The kind of store where you're served champagne while shopping. God, she's beautiful, flawed, everything. I'd always savored each of her flaws and hoped one day we'd have a child that would possess her traits. But that would never happen because of the vile man. And tonight I've seen my love more than fits comfortable. It's bad enough, the dagger of despair still sticking outwardly from my chest like a coat hook for death's jacket.

Downshift.

The next time I see her that gorgeous nightgown is crimson and slick in the moonlight, each pore of its purity wet and shiny. I don't often see her like this, mostly on the nights when I haven't slept in two or three days. The bird dog squelches, but I know there are no bears around this part of the desert looking for speeders and drunks to arrest. And I swear there's a woman's voice drowning in the static, a sad radio squelch begging for a strong hand to lift her outward and return her to the land of the living. These sounds and sights are simply sleep deprivation tugging at my senses and sanity. It plays tricks on you, sleep deprivation. There's a coop up ahead, but I know I won't be able to call it a night.

Downshift.

There are two rigs lined up just inside the closed chicken coop even though it's all locked up. Everything is set. The boys have come through. I shake my head, look out the window. Can I do this? *Hell yes I can.* The bird dog and CB start squawking again. This time it's high pitched. Not the usual static. This is the sound a computer would make if it were human, being murdered and dying. Then the distinct sound of my girl screaming explodes from the speakers. In the throes of death while that vile fuck does her in with garden sheers. She'll never rest. I don't care about myself. I'll dance haunted until the end of my days and then burn in hell for eternity if it means she'll finally rest.

Downshift.

She's full on screaming. I turn to the passenger seat and see her. Her presence has never been so near. The swollen, ripped edges of her flesh where her wounds pulsate blood onto her nightgown makes my stomach sick. The endurance of her pain drives me into madness. I smile and tell my woman, "You'll sleep the sleep of a queen before sun up. He'll never steal another restless night."

And then time stands still. The air becomes stale and even the scent of night and undertones of fast food and air freshener cease. My rig halts but not abruptly, bluntly, or jarringly. It seems the Earth has hit the brakes. The fresh blood lathering my beautiful bride evaporates and retracts inside of her wounds, the wounds that now mend themselves. This black magic will work. I can feel it. Sense it. The unseen plane of existence living beneath simple thought and sight is bleeding into our worldly plane of existence. And that's why breathing no longer matters. And when the gore completely evaporates from my love I think for a moment that my heart will stop. She's so beautiful. Effortless. Stunning. I don't want to leave this moment. I've not known a moment like this since before he'd taken her from me. This beautiful woman sitting beside me has captivated me to the point that time has stopped.

And her smile allows me the confidence to shake the jitters dancing, kicking, and marching through my veins like fire ants. I can move forward with this plan. The sign reading *SCALES CLOSED* only means that I won't be bothered while I do to this man what he's done to my bride.

Downshift.

Billy the "Big Rigger" appears from behind a gaggle of poplar trees and directs me into the back lot where the bears like to park and keep the peace. But not on this night. The guys from base camp made sure of that. No officers will cross this route until sunup. Good old Teddy Buckskin served in the Marines with the Highway Patrol big wig in charge of this stretch of highway. For the night, this stretch of highway is law free. And it'll remain safe. Nobody will miss a piece of shit like... I can't even say his name, not to this day. But the maniac that took my beloved. Can't say her name either. It's like a mental block. Every time I try and push the sweet sound of her name or the bitter scratch of his out of my mouth, my throat kind of heats up and cinches off. Anyway, that old piece of shit has been cargo inside of a refrigerator in Billy's rig for the last seven hours. It's only my good luck he hasn't passed in transit. No way in hell I'm not gonna take care of this vile man by myself. My doubts are many, but I'd do anything for my love and if ending this shitbag in a vile manner will allow my love to rest then that's what his demise will entail.

She whispers, "I want to sleep in your arms for eternity." I park my rig, jump down from the cab, and wander over to my fellow rig nuts gathered near the forest edge. I smell cigarette smoke. Smoking lamp is on and a couple of cherries glow bright red in the distance. I could use a smoke about now, but I'll not have one. Maybe when I'm finished. Definitely when I'm finished. I've never killed. Sure, a few doe and a couple bucks when I was a boy, but never the most dangerous, if you know what I mean.

My nerves run rampant when I hear the sound of the vile man huffing and puffing in the very near distance. My head starts to spin and my stomach clenches up. Hustling to the nearest tree I dry heave into the cool grass. Feel better. Shaking, I raise my hand and suddenly I can feel her hand wrap around mine and I know it's her. I mean I know it's her because her slender fingers intertwine with mine and then she's squeezing tight and I'm squeezing tight and then I feel and smell the distinct humidity of her breath when she whispers, "I no longer wish to be tired." And I understand her request clearly.

By the time I reach him he's figured out who I am and he's smiling, welcoming death.

"I'll only do worse to her on the other side," he says, smiling. It's not the comedic, senseless babble of a maniac, but the cool

sadism of the devil and I realize that without a doubt this demonic fuck is serious and the thought of my wife, tortured, restless on the other side causes me to hesitate, which is something
I cannot afford right now. The guys look to me with detached
humiliation. They know the silliness with which I debate and
they don't approve. These men have sacrificed a great deal in
order for me to put my love to rest.

"Is he handcuffed?" I ask Billy.

"Cop cuffs. This dipshit ain't getting' loose." Billy responds.

I thank the fellas for their part in my plan and then excuse
them. They argue and debate for a while. Jethro and Ken even
beat the maniac into unconsciousness and knock out a few of
his teeth before I'm able to convince them that I can manage
from this point. What finally gets them to back off is when I
explain that I want to take him to the place where he took my
dearest and slayed our future in the dark. They understand and
now I'm back on the road headed into the most desolate part of
the desert. There are areas of this country where very few men
have gone. Rare Native American tribes are the only lifeforms
out here and the pure spirituality of what is about to take place
keeps them at bay.

Downshift.

He's still antagonizing me. Spouting off horrid words of
what he's done to my love. And the only time silence steals his
vile tongue is when my love appears in the desert. Far at first
but gliding toward us. I'm captivated by her beauty and he's
mortified. Knowing that something more than his demise is at
hand. *Death* he could deal with, but not the confrontation of his
undead victim. This affects him deeply. Grabbing at his chest
I watch as he sucks at the night hoping to expand the lungs
suffocating beneath his rib cage. Then the most beautiful form
is standing amongst us in her white nightgown. She smiles at
me and a warmth finds my chin when she touches me there,
leans in, and kisses my lips. The sheer ecstasy of this touch and
kiss sends me into a lucid state. Many, many years ago drugs

had taken hold of my life, but nothing I'd ever ingested could touch the high sensation of this kiss from my deceased lover. I'm sent into a comatose state and I'm barely able to witness my love when she leans in close to the vile man that took her life so many years ago and begins to scream. Her scream is soft at first, a normal scream, but then it grows as does the vile man's terror and by the time the volume of her agony is at full capacity his ears are bleeding and then he's sobbing tears of crimson blood and that's before his skin begins to rip and he's now just a screaming skull with raw, taut cheek muscles and chattering gums. When my love finishes releasing the anger and rage that she's harbored for so long she turns to me and smiles. Joy has found my love and to express this she laughs while embracing me and I'm uncertain, but the sputtering engine of my rig kicks into gear and somehow my love has shifted and it's not down-shifting now but the wheels spin and what looks like pink sugar spits up into the early morning light of this beautiful desert. When I'm done loving my wife, which is true heaven on earth, I see that the vile man has been sprayed into a mist and frosts the delicate desert sand, except for a torso and chattering skull, but my love and I wish to turn away and now I know that I never have to worry because my love and I speed down the empty highway experiencing the wonders and beauties of the open road and we are together and this is my heaven. We'll never be apart. We are together for eternity. And death is perfect.

Upshift.

Sometimes the road least taken is the road best followed. Regardless, no road is best taken alone.

Eric Miller (who prefers C.W. McCall's Wolf Creek Pass *to Convoy) has worked in Movie and TV Transportation for over 20 years, using his CDL on films such as* The Joyriders *with "Rubber Duck" Kris Kristofferson,* The Last Producer, *which was directed by and starred "The Bandit" himself, Burt Reynolds, and the* Taken *series with Liam Neeson. When not working as a Teamster, Miller is a screenwriter with credits including* Mask Maker, Swamp Shark, *and* Ice Spiders. *He also edited this book. The idea for this story came to him one night while driving a truck through the seemingly endless highways of west Texas, where something was singing to him from the darkness. It was the tires, of course. Yeah, right...*

SIREN

Eric Miller

"I DON'T KNOW HOW you can listen to that crazy stuff every night," Gary said, looking across the cab at his middle-aged co-driver Phil, who was behind the wheel. Phil had just turned the truck's radio to the AM dial, like he did every night at this time to catch his favorite radio show, *Coast to Coast AM.*

"*Coast to Coast* is not crazy," Phil replied. "If you'd take off your headphones every once in a while and actually *listen*, you'd find out some pretty interesting stuff. "

"Like where the aliens really landed in New Mexico? I mean, who the hell would fly all the way across the galaxy just to visit Roswell? You've been there, right?"

"Sure. It's not that bad. But they *crashed*, that's why they wound up there instead of Vegas or something. The real story is how they secretly took over the White House in '52 and tried to start a war with Russia, which was really being run by a renegade gang of telepathic Yeti from Siberia."

"What are you—" Gary looked over and saw his partner grinning wide.

"Gotcha."

Gary shook his head and smiled. "Never knew you had a sense of humor, Phil."

"Lots of things you don't know about me, kid. Lots of things."

"I'm sure there is," Gary nodded. Phil was obviously fishing, trying to get Gary to ask about his life. But Gary shied away from most small talk. The company had put him with a never-ending stream of co-drivers since he signed on with them three years ago, most of them good guys and good drivers, but a few were obnoxious enough that he quickly lost his desire to learn more about the next person. Sometimes he regretted that; Phil was obviously a nice guy with a very fatherly personality, but the last thing Gary needed was a new friend. He had lost enough of them in his three deployments overseas, and wasn't really ready to make more. And besides, the company would shuffle him off to a new rig and partner in a few months anyway, and he might never see Phil again. So he did what he always did; he retreated into his own world, putting in his earbuds and cranking up the music that for a little while every day took him away from the world.

"Suit yourself. You can listen to your rock and roll all you want. I'll let Mr. Noory and a few special guests get me through the night."

"It's Waylon tonight."

"Excuse me?"

"Waylon Jennings. And a little of his kid Shooter mixed in for fun. I'm not really a rock and roll guy."

"Lots I don't know about you, too I guess."

Gary smiled. Phil really was a likeable guy. "Maybe tomorrow we can talk about when you got kidnapped by those Russian Yetis."

Phil smiled back and turned up the radio as the ads finished and the bumper music to *Coast to Coast* came out of the speakers. "You got it."

Gary nestled back in the passenger seat and turned his music player up. The earbuds cut out a lot of the sounds from the rig's cab, and the music covered up the rest. Even though he was off shift and could be in the sleeper, Gary always felt more comfortable up front in the seat, where he could see the road through the big windshield. He slept more soundly knowing he was close to the outside, to escape, rather than being closed up in the sleeper. He never told the VA shrinks about that, and why should he? They'd just tell him what he already knew; he was afraid of being caught inside another vehicle, like the troop carrier he'd been riding in on the road to Kandahar when the roadside bomb exploded. For a second, the screams of his squadmates echoed in his head, and he could see the fire and blood and smoke all over again as he tried to free himself from the twisted wreckage and help them, but then he turned up the music and it all faded away. There was nothing there but the dark, lonely West Texas highway unrolling through the windshield outside. He was alive, and that was all that mattered for tonight.

Gary settled back into the seat, closed his eyes, and drifted away.

He wasn't sure what woke him up—the eerie, piercing, hypnotic sound of the tires singing that was just barely audible over the music, or the sudden change in the truck's ride as it left the highway and rumbled over the rough shoulder. Maybe it was both at the same time, but whatever it was, Gary snapped awake in an instant and looked around.

It was still dark outside, and the Freightliner was still doing at least 70 down the road. Or more accurately, off the road, he saw in a horrified instant. They had drifted out of their lane and were onto the shoulder. Gary's eyes whipped to the other side of the cab to see Phil fast asleep in the driver's seat.

He started to yell and jump to grab the wheel, but then he froze when he looked past his partner's sleeping form and out the driver's side window of the truck. A woman floated there, outside in the night air and somehow pacing the speeding rig, black hair floating gently around her achingly gorgeous face in defiance of the rushing wind. Her mouth was open and Gary knew in an instant that the strange sound was coming from her.

She was the one singing.

Not the tires.

Gary willed himself to move, to try and reach across the cab and grab the wheel, and as he did so the woman saw him. Shock flooded her face, and then anger, and Gary could somehow read her enraged thoughts.

You should be asleep!

But he wasn't. As he lunged for the wheel the cord to his headphones pulled out of the player. The music stopped, and the full force of her terrible song hit him like a sonic sledgehammer. Gary could feel his consciousness slipping away, the song pulling him to sleep like it had obviously done to Phil. But he was already in motion, and a fierce desire to right the truck—*to save his friend*—coursed through his veins and he shook off the sleepiness.

The woman screeched as the song lost its grip on him, her pretty face turning hideous and evil in an instant. Then she flew straight up out of sight, her dirty white dress fluttering as she disappeared from the window frame.

Gary grabbed the wheel a moment later, tearing his gaze from the side window and back to the windshield. The whole encounter had taken only a second, but it was enough for the speeding truck to go further off the road. He pulled the wheel as hard as he could, fighting Phil's sleeping grip and the soft dirt of the shoulder, and the truck started to come around. He got the driver's side wheel back on the pavement and the trailer was just starting to follow, but just as it did the road fell away into a culvert. It was the kind of water channel drivers passed over a thousand times on the road and barely even noticed. But tonight was a different story.

The passenger tires slammed into the ditch at the same instant the guardrail ripped into the nose of the truck like a huge machete. The tractor bounced in the air as it hit the far side of the culvert, and the trailer followed, both tilting dangerously as the whole rig started to roll over. Gary lost his grip on the steering wheel. Phil stayed put, still asleep and firmly belted to his seat. Then the truck came back to earth with a grinding crash. Gary's head cracked into the windshield and he blacked out.

℘

The first thing Gary felt was the cold ground under his body, then pounding pain ripped into his head. He groaned and forced his eyes to stay shut while he willed the world to stop spinning. A few moments later it did and he risked a look around.

He saw the stars first, the gleaming ribbon of the Milky Way stretched out above him in the sky.

The sky? He thought. *How did I get outside?*

He twisted around and saw that he was lying on the pavement. He had been thrown clear of the truck. His left arm was twisted under him, numb and possibly broken. Blood smeared his face from a cut on his forehead. The earbuds were still in his ears, as forgotten as the cord that dangled from them.

We wrecked. Oh God, we wrecked. Phil...?

He tried to look around for his co-driver, but couldn't see him from where he lay. Doing his best to avoid his left arm, he rolled over and struggled to his feet. The world spun again, and he almost vomited, but he fought for control of himself and the dizziness subsided. By the light of the moon and an inexplicably still-shining headlight he could see the wreckage of the rig scattered across the road. It was a spectacular mix of shattered truck, leaking fluids, underbrush, and the hundreds of boxes of auto parts that had spilled out of the ruptured trailer. There was no sign of Phil, so Gary limped closer to find him.

As he got closer he saw one of Phil's rattlesnake-skinned boots sticking out from behind a battered box. Gary moved as fast as he could around the box and saw his partner lying on the pavement, bruised and bloody.

Phil wasn't alone.

The woman was there too, squatting above Phil's unconscious body. As Gary watched in stunned silence, she leaned over and stuck out an impossibly long tongue and licked a rivulet of blood off of Phil's cheek. She shuddered in ecstasy as she swallowed the fluid. Then she opened her mouth wide, revealing rows of jagged razor fangs, and leaned in to bite Phil on the neck.

"HEY!" Gary screamed. It was all he could think to do.

The woman's eyes snapped up to see him standing there, and she snarled at him. She stood up, seeming to flow to her feet rather than stand, and rushed toward Gary.

He stumbled backwards, mind reeling. "Leave him alone. Leave us both alone."

She answered him by singing. The eerie song she had been singing before the crash lilted through the night air, and Gary instantly felt drowsy. He kept backing away from her, and she followed like a stalking panther.

Tired, he thought. *So tired. I should just go to sleep like Phil did. Everything will be all right if I can just get a nap...*

His eyes stayed closed longer each time he shut them, and the woman was closer each time he opened them back up. Still walking backwards, he tripped over a box and fell on his back. Pain shot through his injured arm, and the sleepiness disappeared. He opened his eyes and saw the woman looming over him, claw-tipped hands reaching for his face.

He scrambled for a weapon as she closed in, and his good right hand closed on a tire iron laying on the road. Strength flowed into him from somewhere, through the elemental metal and rushing up his arm and into his brain.

"Shut up, bitch!" he snarled, and swung the tire iron as hard as he could.

It smashed her across the mouth with a meaty *thunk*. She rolled away, the song once more turning into an angry screech. Gary forced himself to his feet and limped after her. As he walked, his hand fumbled at his belt.

He cornered her against the trailer. She opened her bloody mouth to sing again, and again the strange warbling pierced the night. But Gary just smiled at her this time instead of going to sleep. She gave him a confused look, and he pointed to his waist. The woman craned her head, trying to understand what she was seeing. Gary tapped the iPod on his belt, now plugged back in. Loud music blasted his ears from the earbuds and drowned out the Siren's song just as it had in the truck.

"Sorry. I can't hear you. Got my Waylon cranked a little too loud. Dude can sing circles around that crap you're putting out."

Her song turned into another screech as she understood. Then she hissed at Gary and bared her fangs. She launched herself at him and in an instant was on him. Fangs gnashing, claws scrapping, Gary was driven back by the furious assault. But he struck back with the tire iron, beating the woman again and again. They fell to the ground in a snarling embrace, rolling across the pavement and battering each other relentlessly. As he rolled on top, Gary stabbed at the woman, putting all his weight on the iron bar and driving it into her stomach. It punched through, and her scream drowned everything else out.

She threw him off in a violent convulsion and stood up. Black gore oozed down the front of her dress. She pulled the tire iron out and it clattered to the pavement. She staggered, almost falling. Then she gave Gary one last hateful glare and whooshed up into the air and disappeared.

Gary tensed up for a moment, expecting another attack, but nothing happened. He cautiously turned down the volume and took his ear buds out. The soft sound of crickets chirping floated through the night air. Convinced she was gone, he hurried over to Phil.

He saw that Phil was breathing, and apart from minor cuts and bruises seemed to be all right. Gary shook him gently.

"Phil. Wake up, man. Wake up."

Phil's eyelids fluttered then opened. "What...? What happened...?" he mumbled.

"We wrecked. Went off the side of the road."

"Oh no," Phil groaned. "I was just about to a million miles."

"Sorry, partner, but you're gonna have to start your safe-driving counter all over again."

Phil pulled himself to a sitting position. He saw Gary clearly for the first time, the hobbled arm, the scratches and bloody clothes. "Are you all right?"

"I'll live, I guess."

"I'm sorry, Gary. I really am. I fell asleep at the wheel and could have killed us both."

Gary gave Phil a curious look. "Asleep? You don't remember the woman?"

"What woman?"

The image of the screeching Siren flashed into Gary's mind for an instant, and he wondered how much he should tell. Or how much Phil would believe. And for that matter, how much he himself even believed. He did bump his head on the windshield pretty hard; maybe the whole thing was a hallucination? Finally he shook his head. "You didn't fall asleep, Phil. Some crazy woman ran out into the road and you swerved to miss her. Saved her life."

"I did...?"

"You did."

A dim memory came to Phil. "I kinda remember her. Black hair, white dress?"

"That's her. She was gone when I woke up. Maybe the cops will find her out in the desert somewhere."

Phil nodded. "Gonna be a helluva accident report on this one. I'll be lucky if I don't get fired."

"Relax, Phil. That's what they pay a billion dollars a year in insurance for. They'll have us in a new rig in no time."

"Us...?"

Gary smiled. "Yeah, us. While I might find your taste in radio programs questionable, at least you don't listen to rock and roll. The next co-driver they put me with might. So I think I'll ask the office if they can make our arrangement permanent."

"I'd be fine with that," Phil smiled back. "And I agree with you, by the way. The stuff that passes for music these days is pretty unbelievable."

Gary looked up into the night sky, where the woman had disappeared. "Yeah," he said. "They sure don't sing them like they used to."

Half man. Half machine. All Bigfoot. Shane Bitterling was raised around truckers and race drivers, but learned nothing about either. Driven by his hatred of basketball and humidity, he was forced to move from Indiana to Los Angeles and become a screenwriter. With seventeen—and counting—produced movies under his belt, including Beneath Loch Ness, Desperate Escape *and the very successful* Reel Evil, *he still cries oil for the ones that didn't get made. His not-so-short story* They Go in Threes *appeared in the* Bram Stoker Award-*nominated horror anthology* Hell Comes To Hollywood. *His screenplays for* Kill Everything, Red Rain, *and* Black Sunrise *are currently in development. A true hillbilly at heart, he dedicates this story to Uncle Jay Moondoggie and the Star City Streak, both of whom have left a legacy of rubber around this great land.*

WHISTLIN' BY

Shane Bitterling

AS THE GRAVEYARD RACED PAST the passenger window of the truck, Hayward Lawson's forehead tapped the steering wheel. He was as close to blacking out as he had ever been. His glassy eyes stared blankly at the Ding-Dong wrappers that whirled around his work boots. Pulsating veins popped out on his forehead and neck like Indian burial mounds ready to cut loose with avenging war cries. His final breath escaped his pursed lips in a slow sputter as his semi truck drifted into the opposing lane. A growing strand of spittle pattered to the beat of the wheels hitting the highway's median caution strip. Pah-dup-Pah-dup-Pahdupahdupahdup. But he wouldn't give in and take a breath. Not here. Not this trucker. No oncoming cars in sight, so odds on a lonely death were high.

The pungent odor from the open bottle of smelling salts duct taped to the center of the wheel wormed its way into Hayward's nostrils. The stinging vapor made his dead fish eyes flutter to life. He jolted upright with a snort, sucked the spittle rope back into his mouth, and punctuated his rebirth with a meaningful but understated, "Dang."

Hayward jerked the wheel and the eighteen wheeler eased back into the correct lane. He snapped his eyes open and shut to get the ocular juices flowing and knock out the dryness. Then worked his nose back and forth as he sniffled out the smelling salts and running snot. He looked into the passenger side rearview where the last of the tombstones receded into the distance. Hayward sucked in the stale air of the cab, clicked his fingers, and pulled the cord that operated the air horn twice in victory.

"Dang right," he said as the purple color left his face and settled on his normal hue of pasty. "Y'know?"

He glanced around the cab, nodded his head, and smirked to nobody. Lord only knew if his gestures came from the fact that he'd cheated death again and was proud of it or if he refused ownership of a colossal act of stupidity. But Hayward wasn't stupid. Hayward was superstitious.

He had been that way since he was riding on training wheels. It was his mother who hammered wives' tales and "gonna getcha's" into him from the moment he greeted planet earth. Mother wasn't always on the money, but she had been right enough to warrant that he pay attention and keep the cautious flag waving. Most people leave their strange beliefs behind when they cut the apron strings, maybe holding onto one or two for nostalgia sake or the odd peccadillo. But not Hayward. He held onto all of them as Gospel, gathering more as the years rolled on. Don't walk under a ladder. That's just good sense. He kept an acorn in the windowsill to keep the lightning out. It works. Bite the heel of your shoes and they won't give you a blister. Never put a hat on a bed. A cricket in the house is a sign of good luck, much to his sleepless wife's dismay. Hairy women make great lovers, which is why he asked that sleepless wife out on a first date. There wasn't much practical use for most of them, but he kept them in his mental file for when they might be needed.

But there was one that Hayward faced on a daily basis. And it was a whopper that kept him constantly on edge. Cemeteries were some of the biggest obstacles on his road trips. There was one or more every few miles on the Midwestern backroads and two-lane highways. Most of those little burgs barely had a working stop light, but they always had a graveyard on one end of town or the other. If you blinked, you would miss many, populated only by a single family or three. But as you neared a bigger town, or what passed as a city in these parts, the cemeteries sometimes sprawled for miles. Hayward often thought that more people were underground in these rural areas than above it. And some bastards were on the wrong side of the dirt entirely.

Big or small, they posed a danger. Hayward was of the firm belief that if you breathed in while passing one, an evil spirit might get sucked up your nose or worse, swallowed into your gullet where it could cause serious digestive embarrassment on a good day. Full on soul displacement and hellish torment on a bad one. Now, a hat on the bed was bad luck, but nothing a series of walking backwards and eating a banana from the bottom up couldn't cure. But demonic possession was an entirely different animal and Hayward didn't have the remedies or personal contacts with any particular parish that could help with such a thing. He'd checked.

So Hayward passed every cemetery with respect and the same risk avoidance measures. He would stiffen in his seat, his eyes would go wide, and a small sweat would bead. He would exhale all of the air from his lungs, then suck it all back in at the exact moment his front bumper would cross the cemetery border. He'd hold the air deep down in the bottom of his lungs until the rear of his trailer passed the other boundary. Some areas had so many cemeteries, Hayward would gasp and blow so hard and quick, he'd hyperventilate and have to pull over and breathe in a paper bag. He practiced holding his breath in preparation for the bigger ones, but a life of cheap beer, fast food, and sitting for hours on end only allowed so much lung capacity. The most exercise he got was from bouncing over potholes. He didn't know what his breath gobbling record was, but he began to feel the burn in his lungs at just over a minute. He'd heard of people holding their breath for over five minutes, but that couldn't be right. Nobody trained harder than he did. When he began to feel the burn, his temples would pound until his eyes began to bug. Air would escape from his lips in farting sputters. He figured about a minute and half was when he would start coughing and wheezing. That was more than enough to get him by. And if his drills failed him on any given day, his right foot had a mind of its own and would jab the pedal down. Better to get a speeding ticket than a trip to an exorcist.

Although he tried to avoid certain areas entirely, sometimes he just couldn't. Mainly, the places with the flesh-eating ghouls people didn't like to talk about, but he was obsessed with. He knew how to fix their wagon. Meat. And lots of it.

Hayward's list was long and tedious for others to attend to. Nobody could do anything without him raising an eyebrow or a ruckus. They were such a part of his existence, they created a lifestyle of fear. Some whispered that ol' Hayward was scared of his own shadow. He wasn't. But he was terrified that somebody might step on his and cause him all kinds of problems and suffering.

The idiosyncrasies were a mainstay at home, a living Bible, really. Hayward's Commandments, they were called, and Moses would need far more than two tablets to carve them on. Two mountains, perhaps, would suffice. But they also followed him on the road, where he'd spent at least five days a week or more for the last twenty-two years. His rig, and the employ of Amicus Freight Lines, took him all around the Midwest and beyond, delivering facial creams, sticky hair goop, and various sundries to dime stores, truck stops, and whatever hole in the wall the waybill sent him to. He loved being at home with his cricket sleepless wife and listless boy, but his true calling was life on the road. The majority of his hauling time was spent by himself, marveling at the glorious countryside provided by the U.S. of A. by way of the Almighty, collecting his thoughts on everything from motor oil to puppy breath and listening to apocalyptic wasteland audio books. He didn't like to pay the price for the actual items he found in the truck stop shops, but his oldest friend, Red Alpert, did a real good job of reading yard sale paperbacks into a cassette recorder for him. He had all the voices down pat, made a pretty decent explosion sound with his lips pursed to a tin can, and even made a little beep when the tape needed to be turned over. More than his onboard entertainment, Hayward enjoyed the peacefulness of the road, away from others. He'd rather be stuck in O'Hare International traffic in the safety of his cab, for hours on end, than have to deal with somebody who would break one of his multitude of rules, thus putting his life in danger, or merely putting a severe crimp in his day.

A few miles separated him from that last tombstone back on the road. Hayward was breathing easy now, and his passing out wasn't a big deal to him. It barely registered as an occupational hazard at this point. He screwed the lid back onto the bottle of smelling salts and would leave it be until he neared the next major cemetery. His GPS displayed them, with a little skull and crossbones icon, as places of personal interest, just as he had other settings for designations such as truck stops, derelict roadside attractions, and that restaurant that sold the pecan log rolls. But Hayward had driven these roads so many times, he could cruise the routes with his eyes closed. And he sometimes did whether he meant to or not. He didn't need the GPS, but he liked to see the icons scroll by.

Hayward had already delivered his haul hours ago, and didn't have anything coming up for a couple days. The terminal dispatcher told him to enjoy a nice, extended weekend with the family. And he would. He wished he could spend more time with the boy. He was growing up, and mostly out, these days. Hayward checked in several times a day, and noticed the boy's cracking voice only since yesterday. He knew that pubes were already popping and girls were on the horizon. Brought a tear to his eye.

Last year, Hayward had asked what the boy wanted to do on his spring break from school. They didn't have much money, so he feared that he would want to go ride the coasters in Ohio. But they would have found a way. He got good grades and didn't fight much with the other kids. He deserved a little something now and then. Hayward asked again on the last day before the break. His heart melted when the boy told him the only thing he wanted to do was ride with his daddy on one of his hauls. He had it all worked out, in case Hayward was against it. He promised to be mostly quiet, do everything he was told, wouldn't tease the lot lizards, and would hold his farts until they got out of the cab. All things Hayward lived for.

That was the first and the last time the boy got to go with him. They laughed and had manly conversations about engines and wrestling all over the countryside. That two-day trip created a bond most fathers and sons dreamed of. Hayward had never been so proud to be called daddy. Until the drive home. The boy had adhered to all the rules and observed all procedures. He was so good at holding his breath, Hayward thought that one day he could be one of those five-minute dudes. But all started to go south when they showered up at a truck stop. The boy was becoming a man, and with that, manly smells start to seep out of the body. The constant farting was nothing a rolled down window wouldn't settle. But the sourness emanating from the kid's armpits was something else entirely. It just sort of hung around. Got trapped in the nose and wouldn't shake loose. He bought the boy some Irish Spring soap from the gift shop. He was embarrassed for a spell, probably because he noticed it himself. But Hayward told him that's what men use and ladies like. The boy's face beamed proud. He lathered up and couldn't stop smelling his fresh self. And that's where it went wrong. The boy wouldn't stop whistling that jingle from the commercial.

Over and over. Sometimes you hear some ditty somewhere, and it gets stuck in your head. Won't cut loose no matter what you try to do. The boy just couldn't stop whistling that jingle.

They were coming up on a cemetery. The boy's head was bobbing listlessly from highway hypnosis. Hayward nudged him.

"Suit up," he said.

The boy nodded through his grogginess. They'd been through this a dozen or more times that morning, so Hayward didn't see it coming. On the count of three, they both sucked in and held their breath. But the boy was just going through the motions then. They'd almost cleared the cemetery when the boy shook himself truly awake. He looked right at Hayward and smiled. Then whistled that damn soap jingle. And not just the one time. He had started a reprise until Hayward shot him the stink eye and cursed through gritted teeth. The boy was about to wail, but Hayward cupped his hand over his mouth and put the hammer down.

They say that whistling past the graveyard was a sign of showing perseverance in the face of adversity. But Hayward took it as showboating to the dead.

Nobody rode in the cab after that. Nor did they want to.

സ

Hayward dreaded driving the route from the terminal to his home. The same one as the damned whistling incident. About an hour and a half was all it would take, but treacherous beyond belief. A gauntlet of final resting places and other snafus. He'd already passed most of the little boneyards that he'd encounter, but just this side of the homestretch was the double punch of Mount Hope Cemetery and Devil's Dip. One right after the other.

Mount Hope was the largest cemetery in the region. It seemed to stretch as far as the eye could see. Even if he weren't a superstitious sort, he'd hold his breath passing by. The local soy bean plant smelled so bad, people thought the odor was coming from the graves.

This is where all of Hayward's training would come into play. It was his Olympics. Go time, and the main reason for the smelling salts strapped to his steering wheel. Hayward wanted nothing more than to run and gun his way past the place, but it was a reduced speed zone and well-known hangout for Kojak with a Kodak. Cops with radar guns. There was heavy enforcement here because just beyond Mount Hope was the most frightening area of all. Hayward's bowels rumbled just thinking about it.

The patch of snaking road was called Shiloh on any map you'd find. But everybody from the region called it Devil's Dip. The turns were fast and sharp. It wouldn't take much for speed demons to lose control and go over any embankment along the stretch. Most turns didn't have rails and it was a steep drop into a wooded area. Sadly, so many did just that over the years, the name stuck. Roadside memorials with flowers, white wooden crosses, teddy bears, bottles of booze, and whatever the deceased were into were placed on every turn on both sides of the road. Some had been there for years, replenished, polished, or fixed by loved ones. New ones cropped up every month or so. Devil's Dip was bad business. And it got worse.

The area was known to be haunted by those who fell prey to the curves. Their bodies were laid to rest in Mount Hope just a few hundred yards away, but somehow here they were. Being where they weren't supposed to be. Lost souls with unfinished business, the pissed off kind, looking to add to their army of roaming damned with a bloodlust that would make Dracula blush. The legend went that if the dead weren't appeased with a sacrifice, they'd pull you down with them. Hayward heard it that slow moving drivers, the Sunday morning type, or those in rigs, would saunter through The Dip slow enough that one of the flesh-eaters could hop a ride home with you. And then hitchhike onto your neck with their teeth. Hayward never picked up a hitcher, alive or dead, no matter how nice the rack.

Hayward pulled his rig to a stop on the berm, grabbed his cooler, and ran into the Stop 'N Go Market, a do-all place with an attached squat and gobble diner with a sign that read, "Eat here and get Gas" above the neon marquee outside. They had fine food and cheap gasoline that kept the locals coming. But Hayward had never eaten there in all his years, and they didn't pump diesel. What they did offer for him was the freshest choice cuts of meat a caveman could ask for this side of the Heartland. Locally grown beef, pork, poultry, and the occasional bucket of frog legs. They had it all and they'd prepare it any way the larger stores refused to do anymore. Hayward passed the snack cakes and chip aisles, something he only did here, and made a beeline to the meat counter. He didn't know the butcher's name, but they'd traded business so many times over the years, they were beyond that type of thing now. They greeted each other with a smile then Hayward put his game face on.

"What can I do you for today?"

Hayward looked at the beautiful rows of meat lined up and displayed behind the glass counter.

"Two pounds of each. Same as always," he said. "Forget the tripe. They won't like it."

"Most don't because they ain't had it."

The butcher worked his way down the line. Scooping all kinds of chuck, sirloins, chops, butt, and on through the animal kingdom onto Styrofoam plates. He placed each on the scale until he hit the mark then placed it in a clear plastic bag.

"No need to waste those bags on me. Just put 'er in the cooler. All of it."

The butcher gave him a curious look as he placed the last bit of meat into the cooler with a slap.

"Buddy, you need to invite me to one of your barbecues one of these days. You sure do know your meat. I may even bring some extra for the grill."

"If I ever have one, I'll let you know. You think you can pour some of that blood in there?"

"How's that?"

Hayward was superstitious to the extreme. But he didn't want to broadcast it to the world. "Keeps it fresh for the ride."

"Anything you want," the butcher said as he scooped up some of the excess blood from the trays and dumped it into the cooler. Hayward paid the man in cash and lugged the cooler to the rig with a groan.

❧

The sun got ahead of schedule and was already setting over the horizon. Hayward turned on his lights and was feeling antsy. The demons of Devil's Dip didn't slack off during the daylight, but he figured they really liked to cause problems at night. Scary stories rarely occur at high noon. And he'd already called home and supper was getting cold on the table.

He barreled down the road and saw the green road marker that told travelers of upcoming gas, lodging, and food. There was another sign posted just underneath like an addendum. Mount Hope Cemetery was just a mile ahead.

Hayward puffed a couple breaths of air in and out of his lungs as a warm-up. Cleared his throat and got straight in his seat. He unscrewed the bottle of smelling salts on his steering wheel. The vapor slowly permeated the cab. He took solace in the odor. This wasn't the cheap crap you can get anywhere. This was souped-up Chinese menthol with a tiger on the label that he had found online.

His headlights caught the outer boundaries of Mount Hope. Stone masonry stacked six feet high and painted white. Black metal fencing on top of that. The cemetery kind. The creepy type with the sharp points on top that made you wonder why they needed anything at all. Nobody was getting out and any-body who wanted in was a damn fool.

Hayward blew all the air from his lungs and heaved it back in with a wheeze. His finger tapped the wheel as he slid his eyes from the road to the cemetery and back. Immediately over the gates, the newer gravestones shone in the moonlight. Beyond them, the older ones creeped in the darkness. Floating above the others. He was starting to feel heaviness in his chest already. A bit too soon. He goosed the engine a bit, but eased off immediately when he saw the bubblegum rollers peeking over a hedge. He glanced at the police car as he drove by and saw the cop aiming with his radar. Hayward was just under the limit, so he was fine on speed. But speed was what he needed right now. He had other things to worry about.

Maybe it was the chili dogs and onion rings he had for lunch talking, but Hayward wasn't feeling up to his usual snuff. He still had a distance until he cleared the cemetery perimeter, but his lungs were already burning something fierce. His eyes started to bug more than usual and he could feel that black pressure veil of consciousness squeezing in on his head. He checked the side mirrors and the policeman was still in view. He pushed the accelerator just enough to give him a little boost. His tapping finger started to drum like a conga line and he bounced a bit in his seat.

His throat clenched on him and he knew what was next. The air from his lungs worked its way up into his mouth. His cheeks ballooned and spittle bubbled from his pursed lips. He panicked as smelly breath erupted from his mouth. He worked his lips back and forth, trying to grab it back in. He fought hard to keep what little air he had left in him captive. A blood vessel burst in his eye and the last thing he saw before passing out was the bordering wall of the cemetery. He'd passed his first hurdle of the gauntlet.

A weak smile crossed his lips as his bobbing head hit the steering wheel. His front tooth shattered on impact with the bottle of smelling salts. A low whistle escaped through the vacant spot.

He awoke with a "Dang it."

Hayward gasped for air and shook the cobwebs out of his head. He was already barreling into the first turn of Devil's Dip when he realized his foot was crushing the accelerator harder than King Kong stomped villagers. He was going fast. Too fast for the curves. He saw a white wooden cross nailed to a tree whiz by his window. A makeshift memorial of somebody he felt bad for. But didn't want to meet anytime soon. He jerked the wheel going into the turn and over-corrected. The wheels howled as the semi fought to stay on the road. He wrestled the wheel like he was fighting an enemy and got his rig on a steady course around the second bend.

He could feel tingling heat in his cheeks and his mind was still foggy. He caught a glimpse of something white and shimmering pass by the window out of the corner of his unfocused eye. Whether it was a ghoul or the escaping cotton batting from a child's stuffed Easter rabbit, he wasn't sure, but realization smacked him across the face. Hayward rolled down his window and stabbed his other hand to the passenger seat. He flung the lid off of the cooler and snatched the first piece of meat he could.

"Here's a chop," he said as he threw it out the window, careful not to get any of the dripping blood on the side of the cab. He repeated the process as fast as he could, calling out the names of the cuts as he raced through the turns. He hoped that naming the meat would satisfy the unseen ghouls, in case one would give him a stay of life in wait for their favorite dinner.

Hayward was running low on meat, but only had a few more turns until he reached the ass end of The Dip. He blindly dug around the bottom of the cooler and pulled out a nice bone-in ribeye as he navigated a hairpin. Blood sloshed all over his lap and the inside of his door panel, running into the window sash.

"Shitdamn." He rubbed his shirt sleeve back and forth over it, sopping up the spillage. The rig drifted onto the road's shoulder. The cooler slid to the far side of the seat, banged against the door and toppled to the floor. Blood and the last remaining cuts of meat tumbled out and created a hell of a mess.

Hayward winced as he reached for the fallen cooler. It was just beyond his fingertips. He repositioned himself on his seat and tried again, peering just over the dashboard so he could navigate the turns. It was no use. Slowing down was not an option.

"One, two, three!" he said as his head darted below the dash and was able to clutch the cooler between his middle finger and thumb and hoist it onto the seat. He felt the vibration and heard the sound of tires leaving the paved road and turning on the loose gravel of the shoulder. He puffed between his newly gapped teeth and righted himself. His eyes went wide and the puff became a girlish scream when he saw the colony of makeshift memorials bearing down on him. This was the most dangerous turn of them all and it had taken the most lives over the years. White, wooden crosses with loved ones' pictures taped onto them, wilted flowers and fake ones, teddy bears, and packs of smokes. All seconds from coming through his windshield.

Hayward yanked at the wheel and tried to right the rig. A cross busted his headlight and bounced over the cab. A stuffed octopus slid around the hood and wedged itself under a windshield wiper. Tentacles flapped in the wind as if waving at him.

The damage to the front of his truck didn't concern him. He would assess it in the morning when he was safe. Money could fix dings and dents, but it wouldn't cure an eternity of torment.

The cab lurched and his fists tightened on the wheel. He tried to turn it but it would only respond with a shaking sound. The thought crossed his mind that if he just drove with caution, rather than littering the road with slabs of beef, he wouldn't be in the mess he was in. He didn't know why such silly things entered his head. He heard a loud skid that was swathed in one of the worst sounds a trucker could imagine. Metal on metal. He looked in his side mirror and saw it. The tail end of his trailer had already swung into the other lane and was gaining on him. This was Hayward's first visit to Jack Knife City.

Then everything spun out of control.

☙

Hayward stood from the wreckage with a groan and stumbled away. In a daze, he tripped around the debris, trying to get his bearings. The truck was in a heap and he knew it would be a total loss. This wasn't a company rig. He worked for years so that he could own it. With only a few months left until it was paid off, this one hurt him to the core.

He slowly put it all together and took in his surroundings. The dark woods. The steep hill in front of him. The graveled edges of the road above. The moaning gossamer woman with bleeding eyes shuffling toward him with her arms outstretched.

Hayward yelped and turned away. He was surrounded on all sides by them. Twenty or more by his count. Men, women, children, and even what looked like a wiener dog. All translucent and milky white, save for patches of crimson that shone bright in the moonlight. Some were missing body parts. Others were contorted and had car parts sticking out of here and there. And they all glided over the wooded floor toward him, moaning blood.

Hayward screamed as he tried to scale the hill leading to the road. He couldn't get his footing and only understood why when he looked down. His ankle was fully twisted around so his boot pointed behind him. He gulped as the blood-dribbling ghouls glided toward him.

Above, he heard a low, constant thumping sound approaching. Then he saw the lights cutting through the darkness overhead. Somebody was coming. Normally, he hated those kids who played their music with the bass thumping so loud it shook the neighborhood into incontinence, but he had never heard anything as welcome as this. He clawed at the ground, digging his fingers into the dirt. He slowly worked his way up the hill.

Hayward crested the top and managed himself to his feet along the side of the road. He saw the lights skimming through the trees and knew that the oncoming music fan was just around the nearest turn.

He turned his eye-popping gaze down the hill. Some of the ghouls waited below, their dead eyes boring into him. Others floated listlessly toward him. The wiener dog spun in a circle.

The pounding beat was getting louder. He looked back to the road and started waving his hands above his head. He saw the car coming straight at him. They couldn't miss him.

"Hey! Help me! Hey there!"

The driver of the car, a young kid with a funny haircut, looked right at him.

"Right 'chere! Help me!"

The kid's mouth opened wide and red brake lights illuminated the road behind him. The passenger, a pretty girl with wild hair, was also looking straight at Hayward with disbelief. She leaned into the back seat.

Hayward limped toward the car. "We gotta get outta here. Scary shit's on the way."

The boy's mouth was agape. He stared at Hayward with saucer eyes. The girl nudged him and hollered. He threw something hard and fast out the window and the car peeled away.

Hayward heard the screams as he watched the flung object coming straight at him. He raised his forearm to block it, but it went straight through it, creating a puff of smoke as it exited and went through his entire body.

He heard the slap as the thing hit the road behind him. He turned to it and recognized it immediately as a tenderloin steak and licked his lips.

He looked to the edge of the road. The damned were upon him, circling him, but they weren't after his blood or soul. They were welcoming him into eternity.

"Dang."

After attending the private Christian college John Brown University *with thoughts of entering the ministry, Del Howison dropped out and backslid all the way to starting, with his wife Sue, the most famous horror store in America,* Dark Delicacies. *He edited the acclaimed horror anthology series* Dark Delicacies *as well as* Midian Unmade, Tales of Clive Barker's Nightbreed. *His story* The Last Great Monster *appeared in the horror anthology* Hell Comes To Hollywood II. *Del has been awarded the* Bram Stoker award *from the* Horror Writers Association *and the* Il Posto Nero Award *from Italy.*

LUCKY

Del Howison

"...wind moaned beyond my room as if a million pipes played the air."

—Patricia Cornwell

IT WAS TO BE A SHORT but annoying trip in shitty weather. It always was short and mostly annoying when you're running empty in one direction. The shitty weather was only an added bonus. This was a drop and hook run with the deadhead she was hauling for free in exchange for a supposedly preloaded double-tiered livestock trailer moving hogs south out of Indiana to a Tennessee packing plant.

She'd read something once that said if you lined up semi trucks with the amount of grain it takes to feed Indiana's pigs in a year they would stretch from Indianapolis to Disney World. She believed it. There were a lot of hogs in Indiana.

Ray didn't much care for moving livestock. She'd done it a few times before. The shifting of the animals, the noise, the smell, plus it made her feel a little strange. She was a meat eater but loved animals. She had a hard enough time joining those two ideas in her mind without taking them to slaughter. Hauling them in weather like this was even worse than putting up with the summer smells. The freezing cold would rush through the metal grid work of the trailer with a nasty wind chill. Every time she'd arrived at the processing plant in the winter there would be a few animals frozen alive to the metal walls. The workers would come out with tools and pry the pigs loose while they squealed and squirmed to get away. On several occasions they would rip themselves out of their skins in the process.

She never would have taken this run except for the fact that she had not had a run in a couple of weeks, rent was coming due, and the cupboards were feeling a little bare. She was lucky to have gotten the job no matter how shitty it was. She had been lucky her whole life. Not big lucky but lucky enough. Always getting by when things seemed at their darkest, like this crap run when she was desperate for money. If Cullen would get off his fat ass and find a job things wouldn't be so tight.

When money was absent the fighting at home grew worse than it normally was. Maybe the break of being on the road would calm things down. Cullen had called her every fifteen minutes since she'd left, probably to bitch. She never picked up. The idea was to get away for a couple of days and let things calm down. She'd let her voice mail pick it up. With the battery running down from the constant ringing Rachel plugged her phone in and turned the ringer to vibrate. She took the last swig of cab-in-temperature coffee and set the empty cup back in the holder.

The wind was spinning the snow around so hard that it appeared to be falling horizontally. The trailer bounced and swerved behind her, yanking the rig from side to side. Without any weight in the trailer she had to keep her speed down just to stay on the interstate. She was only about 50 miles out from her pick-up dock but at this rate she would never make it before they closed the gates. She grabbed the radio mike and double keyed it before speaking.

"Hey boys, any of you still in dispatch?"

She was met with the same kind of snow on the radio as she was looking at outside. She keyed it again.

"Hey, Pacer Trucking. Anybody there? This is Ray coming at you from the blizzard in Indiana. I'm northbound on the 69 just south of the Marion exit. Todd? Hello?"

Nothing. The storm seemed to be screwing everything up. She'd try again later but in front of her she could see the bubble-gum lights of a police car flashing. She hung the mike back on the radio and downshifted. Even picking up that small amount of drag made the trailer swim and flutter as she slowed it all down to a crawl. Rachel could see the running lights of a couple of other rigs in front of her along with another couple of cop cars. There was an officer walking through the snow toward her with both hands up, palms flat, telling her to slow it down and stop.

She pulled up to him and brought the truck to a standstill. Ray rolled down the window and the officer stepped up on her running board. He wiped snow from his eyes and started to say something, then turned and stepped back down onto the snow. He started waving somebody through when an ambulance, lights and sirens cutting through the snow, drove past him and on down the road in the direction Ray was headed. The cop stepped back up to her window.

"Yes sir?"

"You can see what these conditions are like. You've got a layer of ice under a layer of snow. We've closed the highway at the next interchange. Too dangerous. You're going to have to wait there until morning. Then we'll see where we stand. How are you on fuel?"

Rachel glanced down at the dashboard.

"I'm good for the night," she said.

"It's zero out right now and expected to drop another ten degrees during the night. With this wind the chill it should be about thirty below. You'll need the heat blasting all night."

He glanced in the cab.

"Hope you've got something to eat. The truck stop at the interchange won't be open until about 5:00 in the morning and that's if the crew can get in to work."

He started to turn away when he thought of something and turned back to the window.

"Do us all a favor and stay away from the pumps when you pull into Squire's. There will be plenty of drivers needing to fuel up first thing in the morning. There is plenty of flat lot space down the sides and around the back of the restaurant. Pick anywhere there you want to camp on."

"No problem officer."

Rachel smiled at him.

"I'll just snuggle down in the cab with the heater and catch some sleep."

He looked her over one last time.

"You do that," he said and jumped down from the truck, waving her on.

As she rolled up the window she could see him slowing down the next truck. *I wouldn't want that job*, she thought with a shudder. Even with the heater blasting, having the window open just that short time gave her the chills. She started driving toward the interchange. The wheels slipped and then grabbed on the ice-covered highway but she gradually picked up a little momentum. She wanted to make the off-ramp incline without any problems. Hopefully there wouldn't be any stopping at the top of the ramp as she didn't have chains on. The road was becoming slipperier by the moment. Loose snow that was drifting across the roadway wasn't helping things either. Her empty trailer bounced about, sitting on top of the snow.

The cell phone buzzed. She didn't even bother looking at the screen. She knew who was calling. This was a good night to just cool off and try to get beyond the fighting. Ray reached over to where the phone sat and pulled it out. She tapped the button and the screen shut down. She laid it back on her passenger seat.

"Tomorrow," she said. "Tomorrow."

Through the snow and steamed windshield she could see the red and yellow running lights of the trucks that had already managed to find their way to Squire's Truck Stop off to her left. Ray would have to climb the off-ramp and then make a turn at the top cresting the bridge all without stopping. If she had to stop for any reason she may not be able to get the rig rolling again unless she backed all the way back down the ramp and had another running start. Not a good idea. She glanced at her side mirror to see how far behind her the next truck was. The headlights didn't seem to be moving. It was probably still stopped, talking to the cop.

Ray pressed down on the accelerator, allowing her some more speed. Too much of a punch and her trailer would swing around and pull her off the road. Then she'd be fucked. The back end bounced and bucked but held the road. The snow came out of the darkening sky in big handfuls of white like badly made snowballs. The wipers merely piled the snow in long thickening strips on each side of her blurry windshield. Despite the defrosters working full blast the steaming and icing of the glass threatened to take away all of her vision. She kept wiping at the inside of it with her gloved hand.

She gambled and pushed the accelerator a little more, swearing and fighting to control the truck. A white arrow on a sign with a green background almost obscured by the snow stuck to it suddenly loomed to her right. She had almost overshot the ramp. There were only seconds. Ray swerved, trying not to jerk the wheel.

"Easy, Goddamit!"

The ramp rose to her right and she had to get over even further. The vibrations from her tires changed up and she knew she had slipped off the asphalt and was thumping over the gravel and frozen grass. She needed to get over as the truck attempted to climb the ramp. The trailer was dragging her left toward the snow-choked embankment. She would certainly be stuck.

She might even roll over. It was now or never. She yanked the wheel to the right and as soon as she hit what she felt was the ramp swung it back to the left. The trailer bounced and tried to pull her nearer the slope. She was gone and she knew it. At the last moment the side of the rig's rubber hit the reflector rail. The force bounced the empty trailer straight behind her as she headed up the ramp. It all happened in a blurred frenzy of slow motion.

"Fuuuuuck."

Ray made the top of the ramp and swung the cab to the left. The trailer stayed with her and together they crested the bridge. On the other side of the highway she pulled into the truck stop and swung around past all the sitting dinosaurs to the back corner of the lot, pulled the brake and stopped dead. She dropped her head on the steering wheel and took a deep breath. She had always been lucky.

"Well, that was a Kansas City shuffle."

Rachel grabbed a cigarette out of the pack and lit it up. A couple of deep drags slowed down her pounding heart and she stared out the windshield at the driving snow wondering why she was here instead of at the bottom of the embankment in a bunch of twisted steel. Luck.

It was a white sheet in front of her headlights covering a mattress of ice. She blew out a long cloud of smoke. The trailer tire would have to be checked to make sure she hadn't busted the bead. Even though she wasn't a fan of sub-zero temperatures it was better to check it now than in the morning. The same temperature always felt colder in the morning when she was just getting up. Awakening to a flat tire would suck.

Trying to find a reason to stall opening the cab door Ray picked the cell up off the floor where it had bounced and turned it back on. It was still working. As it lit up it bleeped three missed calls. Cullen was tenacious if nothing else. Ray plugged the charger adaptor cord that had pulled loose back into the phone. She had a feeling that whenever it was that she decided to call Cullen it was going to be a long conversation. She'd better be fully charged up and ready for it.

Gloves on, head tucked in under her hood and coat buttoned tight, she was as ready as she was going get. She took the flashlight from the toolbox on the floor, checked the beam and put her shoulder to the door. It shoved open into the breath-snatching blizzard. The snow pushed past her into the cab as the vacuum that opening the door created sucked out all of the heat. Ray's feet hit the ground, shot out from under her and she landed hard on the icy turf. Getting back up was difficult what with the bumpy, glacial ground and the icy wind which threatened to take her back down at any instant. She stood back up, grabbing at the truck for balance. Then hand-over-hand she leaned against the trailer and made her way down to the rear wheels. When she arrived Ray bent down at the trailer tire. She was shaking with pain but able to pull off her glove. Her flashlight shone on the wheel and she ran her fingers along the edge where the rubber and metal met to make sure she hadn't popped a tire. It seemed smooth, tight. The rubber tire must have slammed against the guard rail and bounced the truck back onto the exit ramp. She could feel the indentation in the rim but it hadn't popped the tire. Damn lucky break. She lowered the light and looked how the tire sat on the snow. It appeared fully inflated.

Slipping her fingers back into the glove she pulled it down tight over her hand with her teeth. Then, mimicking her previous trip down the trailer, Ray made her way back up to the cab. It took several tries against the wind but the cab door finally pulled opened and she flung herself inside. Reaching back she slammed the door.

Ray grimaced as she tried to find a comfortable way to sit in the driver's seat. It had been a damn good whop on her tailbone but she didn't think anything was broken. There would be one hell of a bruise come morning.

Great, she thought. *Bruised, stiff, and cold at the loading dock in the morning. I can hardly wait.*

As the trooper had mentioned, Squire's Truck Stop was closed so there was no getting something warm from them. She had her cooler, some energy bars and a pillow. Ray decided to hunker down and make the best of it. She only wished that she could pee out of her cab while sitting sideways in the seat with the door open like the male truckers. She could make it until early morning when the Stop opened. There was no way she was going to crouch in that weather. The wind would probably blow it back over her anyway.

Stripping off her gloves she held her fingers in front of the blowing heater to warm them and noticed she had missed another call while she'd been out checking the tires. Ray took two aspirins in hopes of waylaying the pain in her backside by morning. She knew it was probably a futile gesture. After fiddling around with the knob and not surprisingly discovering there wasn't much to pick up on her radio she decided to just click it off and settle in for some sleep. The truck was rocking her to sleep as the blasts continued their relentless buffeting. Like a baby, she drifted off to dreams of Cullen asking for forgiveness for arguing with her.

જી

The lot was still shrouded in darkness when she jerked awake. The mellifluent outcry of the wind gusting against her empty trailer rose and lowered in volume as it pummeled the truck. The rig seemed to shudder and then settle back to brace itself against the next onslaught. Ray touched her phone and the digital display told her she had a half hour before the truck stop was due to open. She smoked another cigarette. From where she sat she couldn't see the front of the building. Ray had to pee. She needed to pull around toward the front so she could tell when the morning crew arrived. She unplugged the cell phone and slipped it in the front pocket of her coat, then sat up straight and prepared to drive up around the side of the building.

Ray dropped the transmission in gear and stepped on the accelerator. The motor wound up but she wasn't moving. Bumping it out of gear she dropped it back in and tried again. A lot of motor, no movement.

"Shit."

She knew what it was. Snow and ice around the brakes had frozen overnight, effectively seizing them up. She would have to crawl underneath with a hammer and smack the ice off. Then wind rocked the truck again.

"It's going to be colder than a polar bear's toenails."

The toolbox under the front seat had the hammer and she pulled it out. She rechecked her empty coffee cup from last night with desperate hope that the coffee elves had visited while she was sleeping but it was still empty. Ray threw it on the floor and grabbed her flashlight. Taking a deep breath she shoved open the driver's door and slid her feet out onto the snow.

"Fuck me," she muttered as her bruised back reminded her of last night's fall.

Ray slammed the door behind her. At least she would have a warm cab to crawl into when she finished. Stooping down at the side of her cab she aimed the light across the width of the truck at the backside of the front wheel on the passenger side. The snow was drifting up on one side of the tire and the inside of the wheel looked fairly packed. She pulled her stocking cap down against the gale wind and then tightened and tied her hood as well as she could.

Dropping flat on the ground, Ray scooted under the cab and up on her side facing the inside of the driver's front tire. Even though her gloves were too light for this weather they would have to do. She could feel the cold in her fingers already. They were what she had and she didn't have any extra money to buy a heavier pair. This was unusually cold weather so she would never use a better pair often enough for her to spend on them. She dug out any packed snow with her fingers. She could feel the wet and cold through to her skin. Ray grabbed the hammer and began to tap at the brake pads, chipping away at the layer of ice. When she was satisfied that she had knocked it all away she rolled up onto her other side facing the passenger side. In that direction the snow blasted her square in the face. She used one hand to shield her eyes and belly-crawled under the truck to the opposite wheel. Once she was at the tire it hid her face from a direct onslaught of the windblast.

It was now that she realized she'd left her flashlight at the other side. But the day was graying up and she could see well enough to tap these brakes and get back inside. She didn't want to stay outside any longer than needed. Her hands were stiffening up. Ray just wanted to get this ordeal over with. She was lying on her left arm so she dug out the snow one-handed. Then she picked up the hammer and tapped the brake pads with the hammer when a strong gust slammed the truck. The truck creaked and began to shift on the icy ground. Before Ray could comprehend what was happening it slid about an inch and then sank down through the snow enough to pin her between the axle and the ground.

Despite how she struggled to free herself Ray was stuck on top of the icy ground on her left side with one arm pinned beneath her. Her free hand, cold and wet from the snow, was quickly becoming useless. She'd lost all the feeling in her left arm as it fell asleep with her body weight crushing down on it.

"Help! Help me!" she yelled.

Most of the trucks had their engines running to keep the heaters on and probably radios or phones. The wind sang and howled around the vehicles as if screaming a taunt to Ray to escape its icy clutches. There was no way anybody was going to hear her. Then her phone vibrated. Cullen! He was up and had started his barrage of calling her. The phone hummed in her pocket but she could only move her top arm from the elbow out from under the axle. It wasn't enough to get to her pocket. She tried to twist and squirm but to no avail. Then the vibrations stopped.

"Help me! Somebody help!"

The wind snatched the words from her lips and spun them to the artic ground. Her squirming became tighter. It was as if the ground had reached up and grabbed her coat. But the thirty below wind chill gale had caused the sweat she had worked up to freeze her damp coat to the ground. Ray was packed against the truck axle on her one side and frozen to the earth on the other side. The one hand she could slightly move had become a club. It felt like a hunk of ice.

Then the phone buzzed again. Cullen was trying to reach her. He knew. She knew he knew. It was like a second sense or something. He must have felt she was in trouble and Ray shouted out to him.

"Cullen! Help me!"

If she could just figure it out she might be able to get the voice activation function to work. If she could bump it just right while it hummed in her pocket maybe... Then the vibrations stopped again. It had gone into her voice mail. He'd call back. She knew he would. If nothing else she knew he was a persistent son-of-a-bitch. He had to call. He would. As Ray attempted to wriggle around she realized she was freezing to the ground over a greater area of her body. Her movement was nearly stifled.

The wind whipped around the tire, changing directions and blasting snow in a hodgepodge of directions taking her breath completely away at times. By this time she had shouted herself hoarse. Although she had lost all track of time she knew she had been lying there for hours by now. Cullen's calls had come and gone. The phone had buzzed and shaken in her pocket but she had been helpless to reach it.

Ray was in complete agony as her body began to shut down in different areas. Her clothes were frozen to her body encasing her in a numbing cocoon. She blinked at the snow and only one eye opened back up. The wind had frozen her other eye shut with her own moisture. Blinded in one eye her line of sight had become extremely limited. The phone vibrated again and slowly moved in her pocket. It had moved a little bit each time Cullen called. It would have moved further if she hadn't had her voice mail picking up the call.

Then she heard a snatch of conversation, human voices, and close. Cocking her head ever so slightly and looking out the corner of her good eye she could see the legs of two people standing beside her cab. Snow swirled and danced about them. They were facing each other engaged in conversation.

"Help."

Ray shouted out but her voice was weak and couldn't travel past the sound of her own truck's motor. She wasn't even sure she had said anything as she could no longer hear it herself. The wind laughed at her. It chattered her teeth and numbed her mind. She wanted to kick her legs against the truck to get their attention but she couldn't move her legs. She couldn't reach down and pick up the fallen hammer to slam it against the metal above her. All of her struggles were internal now. Her mind, which had worked frantically for the first few hours, was slowing, stumbling. Her body was stilled. A cigarette butt bounced on the ground, snatched up by the air and carried past her. The two men walked on past the back of her trailer toward the warm interior of the truck stop. Rachel cried and it froze to her face, making a zigzag track down her cheeks. She was afraid her other eye would soon be blinded shut. She was getting tired. So tired.

☙

She slowly woke. She'd been dreaming of the potbellied stove in the shed behind her trailer. All her tools had been laid out and a warm fire glowed through the grate on the stove's door. She was home and she was warm. It terrified her to awaken to what should have been the dream from what should have been reality. The phone hummed again. That was what had awakened her. Cullen. He hadn't been in her dream. It hummed again and shifted in her pocket.

Had she passed out so long that it was night again? Everything was black. Her brain took a moment to realize her other eye had frozen shut. It was okay. There was no feeling to it. Time was meaningless now. She was so sleepy. Surprisingly she was warming up also. It was just the way she had felt in front of that stove. That was lucky. It must be having the tire block some of the wind. Maybe it was her frozen clothes blocking the air.

Rachel had always been lucky. Her father said she had inherited that from her mother along with independence. Cullen called it something else. Wherever she had gotten it from it was working now. She was tired and warm enough to fall asleep. Her mind shut down and Ray slipped back into her warm dream.

The cell phone in her pocket hummed again. It vibrated itself out of her coat pocket and fell out on the ice. Her voice mail picked up the call.

Along the way to way to becoming a successful writer, John Palisano used to work for his uncle's towing company and loved that time in his life. He's also related to the Klipsch family of Saint Louis, who run a large trucking company. A ride along in a big rig as a kid inspired a lot of what happens in Happy Joe's Rest Stop. *Take from that what you will. John's fiction and non-fiction has been published extensively, including the horror novels* Nerves *and* Dust of the Dead. *He has been nominated for a* Bram Stoker Award *multiple times. Check out more at* www.johnpalisano.com.

HAPPY JOE'S REST STOP

John Palisano

"AFTER YOU." The man in the white cowboy hat stepped aside and smiled with his mouth closed. The smell of cooking hot dogs came through the doorway. Greg was hungry, and one of those Big'Uns sounded perfect. He'd get right to it, probably round it up with a big sweet tea and some chips. His Papa would be right behind him, once he finished filling up. His dad was going to have to park the rig just outside the stop on account of all the truck parking spaces having already been filled.

Greg was more worried about getting a drink and a snack than his dad's long walk inside. "Thank you," he said. The man smelled funny, kind of like a wet dog that'd recently been flea dipped.

He hurried past and found himself right in the middle of the frenzy unique to a Happy Joe's. The shop was not set up all in a line, like most stores. Instead, there were several stations all around where people could do a variety of things, including checking out. You didn't have to wait for someone to take your money. Some people happily filled their own sodas. Others topped hot dogs. Some shopped for magazines. Greg stopped for a moment at the magazine rack and pretended he was checking out the monster truck magazines, but his eyes really lingered on the fashion magazines with the pretty, half-naked girls on them.

"Mister Fisher, your stall is ready." That was the PA, and the voice of a lady with a Southern Accent. Greg thought it was slightly strange to hear one, because they were in Nevada. It felt right, though, because there were Happy Joe's all through the southern United States. Greg just figured she'd probably been transferred from another location.

He made a beeline for the hot dog station. Dad would be along soon enough, he knew. Of course he would. Where else would he go? Greg looked around the shop and made his way first to the drink stations where, unbeknownst to him, his father had been only minutes before. His father always told him to get the drinks first and then grab any food or snacks he wanted. "That way," he'd said, "if you get to the bottom of your drink while you're grabbing other stuff, you can go back for a refill."

Once he found a medium cup, Greg went to the middle of the machine. There was a big guy with a long grey beard filling one of those monstrous jugs the size of a two-liter. "Be out of your way in a sec," the fellow said.

"No problem," Greg said. "Of course. I'm probably going to get some root beer, anyway. I don't like diet stuff."

The guy gruffed, finished, and stuck a lid on his drink. Then he was off. Greg noticed he was wearing a T-shirt with an eagle cartoon on the front. He always liked how the guys and gals on his dad's routes always seemed to love the country. It made Greg feel like they were all together, and working for the same goals.

He found his root beer and filled his cup.

That's when the lights went.

Not only the lights—the whole place seemed to just turn off. The people turned off, too. Everyone froze for a moment. Greg thought maybe he was having some kind of episode, that maybe it was him. A moment later, he saw people moving. *I bet they all just froze from the shock of losing all their light,* he thought.

One fellow in a cap that read "This Flag Don't Run" looked around and made eye contact with Greg. He nodded slightly. They were both thinking it was only a temporary thing and the power would go back on any second, and they'd be back to the Big'Uns and the 64-ouncers, and then be on their way.

"Welcome." The voice was soft, but because it was so quiet, everyone could hear it. Greg turned and saw the man in the white cowboy hat from the door, only he wasn't standing; his feet were a good two feet off the floor.

Greg looked toward the front door hoping he'd see his dad, but all he saw were plumes of black smoke completely covering the glass.

Something exploded outside. Everything shook. There was little he could do other than stand his ground.

There was a brief moment of silence before everything returned to normal. Turning around, Greg saw everyone looking every which way, trying to figure out what had happened. The man in white was out of sight. The music still played. He heard fizzing; a man at the soda station had kept his cup under the nozzle too long. Soda ran over the cup and fizzed into the main drain.

What was the bang? What had happened? Maybe a rig had hit the side of the building? Maybe it was an earthquake. He wasn't sure, but Greg knew he'd have to find his dad as soon as possible. This was way not cool. Not cool at all.

A second larger boom rocked the rest stop.

Greg crashed into a display of audiobooks and barely kept himself upright. Others weren't so lucky. He spotted the guy with the eagle shirt and grey beard lying flat on his belly, his giant drink spreading across the floor in front of him.

What in hell was happening? Earthquakes? What else could happen so fast?

Terrorists. That had to be it. They were under attack. They'd hit the heartland. Why Happy Joe's? They were in the middle of the desert with no one famous or notable—no one powerful enough to justify such an event. Could one of the truckers have been transporting something or someone no one knew about? He supposed it was possible.

"Dad?" he said, making his way through Happy Joe's. There were people lying all over the place. Most were trying to sit up and recover. Greg didn't see his dad amongst them, though. He wasn't even sure if his dad had made it inside. He made to step toward the window, but there was a boom so loud he instinctively covered his ears with his hands.

"Dad!"

Nothing.

The rest stop jolted, and Greg swore it went up instead of back and forth, as if a whale had head-butted it from below.

Where the hell is Dad? Why am I in here all by myself?

None of the other adults even looked his way. He was surprised. Didn't they notice a kid standing there alone? Well, he reasoned, he was big for his age. He was almost thirteen, but most people thought he was almost eighteen. He'd gotten what his mama'd called his father's "football figure," and by that she meant he was big boned, strong, and hearty. He didn't look soft one bit. Still didn't mean he wasn't worried about his dad. Or himself. Why wouldn't he be? It sounded like the world was falling apart just outside Happy Joe's.

He spotted that fellow—the one he swore had hovered—the Man in White. He stood near the front of the store, still sporting that big grin across his face. Greg knew there was something wrong with the guy. Who'd be smiling during what was going on all around them? What the heck? None of it made any sense.

Greg made his way to the front of the store, toward the man in white. When he neared the front, the Man in White said, "Where do you think you're going?"

"I think my dad's out there." Greg pointed to the window.

"Son?" said the Man in White. "I don't think anything's out there right now."

The Man in White was right: The area outside the rest stop

seemed to have vanished, replaced by pure inky black.

"What the...?" Greg said. "Where's...?"

The Man in White shrugged. "Beats me," he said. "It was here a few minutes ago." He hadn't lost his smile the entire time.

"You don't seem...concerned," Greg said.

The Man in White said, "Should I be?" He laughed and gestured toward the darkness outside. "This is what I wanted."

"What is it?" Greg asked.

"Nothing and everything," the Man in White said.

Glowing orbs the size of baseballs hovered near the window. On each, wing-like things fanned from four of their sides, matching their phosphorescent bodies. Their tips looked sharp. One came toward the glass and dragged its razor tip downward, making a scraping sound.

Greg stood back. "My father's out there," he said.

The Man in White said, "He's probably gone now. Left under a parade of the Isogul."

"Iso-what? What did you call them? Is that what those things are outside?" Greg said. "Where'd they come from?"

The Man in White said, "It's all magic, my boy."

"My dad," Greg said. "He's out there with those things." He thought, *who talks like that? My boy? Is he from England or something?*

"Do you want to go out there with them?" he said.

Greg said, "No."

"That's good," said the Man in White. "Because they're coming inside."

Without further prompting, one of the Isogul put its colorful wings against the glass and moved it in an S-shaped pattern. Other Isoguls followed suit.

"What the hell are those things?" a man next to Greg said. "What's going on? Where'd the world go?"

"We better move," Greg said. "If the glass breaks, they'll be in here. On us."

People stared at him.

"Come on," he said. "We need to find places to hide."

"Where is there to hide?" the Man in White said. "They can get through anything."

"Guess we'll just find out," Greg said. "Won't we?" He turned and hurried toward the back of Happy Joe's.

✌

Two Isoguls broke inside the rest stop. One flew right into some poor guy's head, splitting open his face right down the middle. The guy, a big bear of a fellow, cried out just before his face broke apart, revealing the workings inside. Greg saw white and yellow shapes that quickly turned red. Blood streamed out. The fellow's hands were up and at the Isogul, but it was useless. The thing had nailed him. He dropped to his knees and the Isogul made its way inside his head. He fell facedown. The Isogul burrowed its way out from the back of his head and flew into the air, coated in a slick layer of blood and bile. A small proboscis slithered out from a slit that Greg thought might have been a mouth. It licked some of the gore before slipping back inside the top part of the Isogul.

The second Isogul headed right for Greg. He ducked, but the damn thing found him. His heart raced a million miles a second. This is it. I'm done. I'm a goner, he thought.

Greg gulped; the Isogul hovered right in front of his nose. He tried to get a good look at the thing, but it spun around on itself so quickly he couldn't really pin down any single feature, other than it was as dark as night. The Isogul lunged. Greg ducked, half expecting the thing to catch him in the face, just like it had for the big guy.

It did not.

Instead, it hovered in front of him for a few moments before it flew past.

He turned, looked, and saw the Man in White, his arms outstretched in either direction, his palms up, an Isogul hovering over each. He'd been controlling them—Greg knew it was the Man in White who'd been the catalyst.

Greg didn't know what to say or do. He just wanted his dad.

The Man in White turned his gaze on Greg. His smile faded. His chin lowered. Then he turned dark. It was as if his skin had grown see-through, only not with light, but with dark. Greg's heart sank, in the same way it had just before he went over the first hill on a roller coaster, or when he stumbled upon a dead dog, or when he knew he'd done something wrong and was waiting for his dad to come home. Dread. That was what he was feeling.

The Man in White turned, his eyes like two spinning dark holes. His mouth opened, revealing an endless chasm as far and deep as Greg could imagine.

If he gets closer, he's going to swallow me up and I'll never be seen again.

Get out.

Of here.

Now.

Or else.

Dad.

Got to see Dad.

Got to find him.

Get us out of here.

The Man in White went even darker. He was nothing. He was everything. The Isoguls gathered round. Happy Joe's Rest Stop faded in places. People were on the ground, spread out. The very earth beneath their feet rocked to and fro. Greg felt like he was on a boat, if a boat could somehow be anchored in the middle of the desert. Pieces of the floor fell out. In them, there was the same endless darkness as in the man in white's empty face.

A woman wearing a baseball cap with a piece of Wisconsin cheese embroidered on it slipped near one of the holes. A man reached out, grabbed her forearm. "Babe!" he yelled. "I gotcha."

But he only did for a few more moments. Two Isoguls flew in, hovered, and then dipped down. In a blink, the man's forearm slipped apart from the rest of his body. They'd cut him so clean and quick, reminding Greg of when he cut a piece of ice cream cake for his cousin's birthday using a knife they'd dipped in hot water. He saw a circular shape in the middle of the arm, right before it and the lady wearing the Wisconsin Cheese hat slipped into the black hole. She didn't scream. She didn't seem to react at all. One of the Isoguls followed her inside. The fellow who'd tried to save her yelled—he made a sound like he'd been kicked in the gut. Greg saw him staring at the stump of his arm left behind, right before the Man in White appeared behind him. With one fast kick, the Man in White sent the man with the severed arm over and into the black hole. An Isogul chased him, too.

"What the hell is happening?" Greg didn't know where the voice had come from, but the Man in White with the missing face turned in his direction. A hole appeared where his mouth would have been and opened like the unhinged jaw of a snake about to swallow its prey. Black tendrils rolled outward, like fifteen-foot snakes, and slithered around the parts of Happy Joe's that hadn't turned into black holes.

A guy with a big Steelers shirt jumped up behind the Man in White. He had something in his hands: a huge hammer, the horns pointed toward the Man in White.

The hammer hit the Man in White square in the back of the head.

Dark light, for lack of a better description, exploded out the back. The hammer-wielder ducked a bit, shielded his face with his arm, but the damage had been done. The black light burned hundreds of little holes wherever it'd touched. Greg thought it looked like he'd gotten nailed with buckshot...buckshot from hell. The poor guy screamed. Half his face was littered with little holes. They bled, but only for a few moments.

Grey smoke drifted out from the holes. The man shook. He

cried out, but then then was silent as his head slowly caved in. First his eyes went blank, and then he collapsed, as if the darkness that had shot inside him ate him from the inside out like an evil batch of otherworldly termites. Then the rest of him flattened, caved, and dropped, his remains a pile of steaming flesh and burned clothes. He was gone in maybe thirty seconds.

Greg froze. What the hell am I supposed to do now? He didn't know, but he felt he had to do something or else it was only a matter of time until the Man in White turned his gaze on him once more. Then what? He'd have to find a way out. But he knew the Man in White could see and sense him. It didn't stop him in any way, shape, or form. It's like he's toying with me, Greg thought. He wants me to see all of this.

The Isoguls flew through Happy Joe's. They found people hiding behind chip stands, they broke through doors to get into the bathrooms and the showers, and in each place, people begged, people screamed, but people always went quiet. This kept up until there were no more people anywhere Greg could see. He crawled toward the end of the aisle, where there were piles of smashed sunglasses, bags of Doritos, large remnants of a mirrored display, and tons of blood. The only thing untouched was the Happy Joe's theme song, still playing over the house speakers.

Where you gonna go when you've got to go... Get refilled. (Killed.)
Happy Joe's. Happy Joe's.
Fill up your tank (skank)
Get a drank (drink)
At Happy Joe's. Happy Joe's.

Greg kept to his place through most of the carnage, unsure of what to do. He thought if he moved the Isoguls would be drawn to him. The entire time he hoped against hope his dad hadn't been in the bathroom, or hidden inside a closet, when the Isoguls searched and slaughtered, sliced and diced.

Where are you, Dad?

The dark black holes spread, swallowing several pools of red gore. The folks were all gone, though, sucked into the endless nowhere the Man in White Without a Face had brought. Greg crawled on the floor, but he didn't get far. The Man in White stood at the end of the aisle, all the Isoguls spinning around him.

He had no face, but he spoke, and the Man in White used Greg's father's voice to do so.

"I'll eat your fear. Saved the best for last, kid. Made you the most scared. Sweetens the meat."

Greg looked around. He didn't see any way out. The Man in White Without a Face stepped toward him. The ground under his feet faded and turned dark, revealing the great nothingness beneath. Even his feet faded; several green tendrils slid out where his feet had been, their tips like razor-sharp knives.

Crawling back, Greg nearly lost his breath.

"Come on, Kiddo. One last walk. You won't feel a thing."

Don't look up. Don't listen. It's not Dad. It's a trap. Just get the hell out of here. Somehow.

"Kiddo. You won't hurt anymore."

I'm not hurting now. What the heck?

"One last walk."

Greg felt burning on his skin, as though someone were shining a flashlight filled with pain at him. He grimaced, but did his best to avert his eyes and ears.

The Man in White's voice changed. It still used his dad's, but whatever his native voice was, that blended in, too.

"C-come on, K-Kiddo. O. O. O."

It sounded like his dad, but it didn't sound like his dad, too.

"K. Kid. Do. Doh."

There were weird noises mixed in, too: sounds unlike anything Greg had ever heard.

His arm hurt so badly. His forehead did, too.

Need something to protect myself with. Something to hide behind.

He pictured his dad then, and hoped against hope he was all right. If he was here, what the heck would he be able to do against these things, anyway? Then, he knew. Dad's smart. He always has a way to fix things and make things okay, no matter what.

No matter what.

He turned away, twisting around. Saw the pieces of broken mirror in the debris. Reached for a bigger piece. Spun around with it, still keeping his head down. Did his best to aim it back at the Man in White Without a Face.

Like when we used to aim the rearview mirror back at jerks that'd tailgate us with their high beams.

Give it back to them.

Give it back to him.

Greg held up the mirror, catching the Man in White Without a Face in its reflection. Everything the Man in White Without a Face had given—all his dark energy—every bit of it—shot right back at him. It happened before he knew it, and before he could turn away.

The Man in White Without a Face made the loudest, worst noises Greg ever heard. Even worse than when his cousin played him that grind core metal stuff he'd found on YouTube. That was funny. The Man in White Without a Face was anything but.

He's trying to burn me out like he did the others. Trying to take me.

He held the mirror higher.

Then he peeked, just a little.

Greg looked into darkness so vast and hopeless—so empty and bleak—he wanted to give in. *Fall inside. There's nothing here worth living for. Everything is hopeless. Everything is for nothing. Just dust floating in a cosmos that's collapsing into nothing. There is no meaning. There is no being. No consciousness. Be one with the universe. End your suffering. End the pointlessness.*

No. I don't believe it.

"There's that 'I' again. Always this meaningless self-preservation. Always this arrogance and belief that you matter."

We do. I do.

"Tell me why? There is only this."

Greg's face hurt like he'd been stung by a million bees. Same with his arm. *This is what a tattoo feels like. Just a tattoo. You'll look cool. You'll be grown up. The riders are going to think you're okay now. A man.*

Greg knew what he had to do. He raised the mirror shard upward and tilted it until it caught the Man in White Without a Face. Then the Man in White Without a Face stepped back, clutching at the amorphous black that stood in for his head.

There were spots of darkness...sub-darkness...growing on him. His own projections had reflected back and erased parts.

He stumbled back.

A tendril reached out, flapped around, and went for Greg. He slammed the edge of the mirror down on it, severing the tip. The Man in White Without a Face let loose a horrendous screeching noise. He stepped back again. His head expanded and contracted in several places; its shape and movement were otherworldly and complex, as though made from a dense, stringy cloud. Quickly, his entire body turned into the same. The scream turned into several voices, then more, countless more, until there sounded a hellish choir of trapped souls. The voices slid through several chords, notes changing, somehow drawing a sick feeling deep inside Greg's gut.

In a flash, the dark remnant of the Man in White Without a Face rose and then rolled itself out and away, going through one of the black holes it'd opened inside Happy Joe's.

It was gone. Greg stood. The piece of tendril it'd left behind had shriveled and darkened. When Greg kicked it, intending to send it into the abyss, it crumpled into black dust. That, too, blew away until there wasn't a trace.

There was a path to the front door, to the outside. He hurried over, past the simmering dark holes, piles of debris, and moist human remains.

At the door he saw the pumps. Saw the cars at the pumps. Saw the rigs. When he made it outside, he saw something else: his dad.

Greg rushed out the front doors.

His dad smiled. Spread his arms. Greg couldn't believe it.

"Hey, kiddo," he said. "Long time."

"Dad," Greg said. "So glad you're safe."

He ran toward his dad, but thought: *Weird. Dad never hugs me like that. Hasn't called me "kiddo" in years. What the heck?*

Greg glanced down. He did, as he ran forth, and saw his father's feet weren't quite there. They were cloudy—ghostly—and something moved where they should have been. Something unnatural. When Greg looked up, his father's eyes were empty, replaced with the same endless chasm he'd seen in the Man in White's face.

It wasn't his dad. Not the one he knew.

"C'mere, Kiddo. Gimme a great big hug."

He tried to run past, but something caught him—phony dad's arm. Handless, the fleshy tip ended in what Greg thought might be a snake's tail. It wrapped around him in a millisecond, squeezing him like an anaconda.

"Great big hug."

The Dad Imposter glitched. The outside melted in places, revealing the same dark cloud he'd seen take over the Man in White.

It'd crawled into one hole and came out another, mimicking his dad.

As Greg remembered his dad, so, too, did it. He pictured his dad in his jeans, a black T-shirt, and his favorite red Peterbilt baseball cap. The thing mirrored the picture in Greg's head. He switched it up, trying to recall his dad swimming with him on their trip to Lake Eerie. He'd worn those new, long hip-hop-inspired trunks, and Greg had been shocked at what good shape his dad had been in. While he did, the thing did its best to pull together, appearing just as Greg had remembered his dad. It squeezed tighter.

"Just a hug."

There was no way Greg would get out of its grasp.

He had an idea.

An image.

His dad, leaning over him. Immeasurably sad. Greg lost his breath and faded. His dad looked on as he passed. Sadness filled him tip to toe. He cradled his son's body. Greg's vision went. He slipped away. It was the only way.

Dad. Worse off than any person could possibly be. Dad. Standing over me. Lifts his hands to his head. Lets me go. He has something in his hand. Raises it to his face. Looks at it. I can't see too clearly. Everything's going black. Then there is a loud boom. A white flash. And I am falling...drifting away from his grasp.

Its grasp.

Only a moment.

Get up and run. Don't wait until your eyes work again. Go for it.

Greg ran.

He never looked back.

The thing screamed. He knew it was rushing after him. Felt it opening black holes. Knew it was coming.

He didn't look back. Wouldn't. If their eyes met...

A sound like the earth cracking.

Don't look. Ignore it. Run.

He made it just past the pumps, and to the small fence at the end of the parking lot. There was their big old red Peterbilt cab. It was fuzzy. He ran as fast as he could. When he made it past the fences, everything cleared.

He made it to the cab, and looked around. "Dad?" he said several times.

At one point, he looked behind, back at Happy Joe's Rest Stop, and saw nothing. A big pit of darkness had swallowed the whole thing, or so it appeared. There seemed to be some kind of vapor surrounding the area. He couldn't place what it was. He heard screams. Some sounded human. Some sounded formerly human. Some sounded like they were from hell.

"Hey?"

Someone touched his shoulder.

He turned.

His dad. It was really him.

"Dad?"

"Uh-huh," he said. "Ain't you a sight for sore eyes?"

"Where'd you go?" Greg studied him, not entirely convinced he was real.

"Came out to the rig real quick. Got a message we have to get to Memphis three hours earlier," he said. "But when I went back to get you...I couldn't get in."

"What's happening, Dad?" Greg asked. He couldn't believe his dad had just been standing there. It seemed too easy. He always was pretty matter-of-fact and reserved, so Greg wasn't expecting him to be doing a dance or anything more than he had. And that was another reason he knew it was really him, and not an imposter.

"I don't know," his dad said. "But let's get the hell out of here. I'm glad you're okay."

"Not sure I even saw what I saw," Greg said. He ran through the events in his head. None of it seemed real now that he was with his dad. It felt like it had to be a bad dream, or a movie.

"You're right about this not seeming real. Can't say how glad I am you're safe. Climb in. You can tell me what happened on the road," his dad said. "Just promise me one thing?"

"Shoot."

"Don't tell your mom. I don't know what to make of this. I can't believe it's even real. But I do know that we've got a load to deliver. There are people that are counting on us. You good with that?"

Greg smiled. "How far is Memphis?"

"About six hours," his dad said, clamping a hand on his son's shoulder.

"Great," Greg said. "So long as we don't have to make any more pit stops, we should make it."

"Nope," his dad said. "No more damn pit stops."

"Those places are hell."

They spoke like everything was normal, but Greg knew, just underneath, they were both still rattled. His dad, as always, was a rock.

As they drove away, Greg looked at the dark chasm that'd once been Happy Joe's, and wondered what others would make of it if they found it. Would it make the news? Would it be swept under the rug? Would someone figure it out?

"That they are," his dad said, and they pulled up the on-ramp and headed south on the highway, toward Memphis. There were tons of trucks and cars, with long, dark shadows, and strips of orange light stretching in every direction—a more comforting sight than either of them could imagine.

Hal Bodner is the author of the Bram Stoker Award-*nominated short story* Hot Tub, *as well as the best-selling gay vampire novel* Bite Club *and the lupine sequel* The Trouble With Hairy. *Hal has also written a few erotic paranormal romances— which he refers to as "supernatural smut," most notably* In Flesh and Stone *and* For Love of the Dead. *While his salacious imagination is unbounded, he much prefers his comedic roots and is currently pecking away at a series of bitterly humorous gay superhero novels. Those readers who enjoy his work can send him adoring fan mail at* Hal@wehovampire.com.

PURSUIT

Hal Bodner

CLEVER, VERY CLEVER. Whoever they were, they were exceedingly clever. But I am cleverer still. Less than half an hour out of town, I spotted them. A gray car, maybe dark blue. Twilight made it hard to tell and as the evening deepened, it became more difficult.

I carefully wove in and out of traffic so as not to alert them that they had been "made" as the detective novels phrase it. A white SUV moved to within kissing distance of my rear bumper and, for a moment, I thought they had managed to switch vehicles without my observing and were closing in on me. But it turned out to be some harried soccer mom with a carload of kids. I'm not saying that it was beyond the realm of possibility that one of the children was involved. But I've found that the people following me do not generally advertise their presence by hanging out of car windows and throwing chewed pieces of gum at my windshield.

Enlisting the aid of children was not, however, inconceivable. How many times had I gotten the distinct impression that someone had been rooting through my garbage, looking for evidence against me? Oftentimes, as I was about to toss in a plastic bag filled with chicken bones or carrot parings from the previous night's dinner, I noticed that the contents of the cans had been rearranged. The children playing in the vacant lot next door to my building were the only possible culprits, taunting me to challenge them with their nasty jeers and their pointed fingers. But it was better, far better, to let them believe I was unaware of their surveillance.

Misdirection has always served me far better than confrontation. Those who would entrap me are many and, though I am adept at outwitting them, I am only one person.

I stayed on the freeway for as long as I could emotionally handle it. For safety's sake, I needed to get to the desert as quickly as possible. As much as I hated driving at night, I couldn't very well have hitched a ride with a friend or asked a neighbor to drive me. This had nothing to do with any shyness on my part, or reluctance to impose, but rather because I have few friends and I don't know any of my neighbors, nor do I care to. Familiarity leads to nosiness and thence to curiosity and, ultimately, disaster. I've learned to cherish my privacy.

My anxiety kept building toward a point where I knew I would not be able to stand it any longer. The knowledge that I was being pursued, the feeling of them closing in on me, the thought of what might happen if I were to be caught: All of it was becoming too much for me to bear. My thoughts revolved in endless spirals of disaster. Cyclic thinking is the term the mental health professionals use and, though I tried, I could not seem to break the pattern.

That feeling of impending dread grew more immediate. I imagined that all of the air was being siphoned out of the car, leaving only a vacuum behind. Though I knew the notion was ridiculous, I started gasping for breath and soon found myself in danger of hyperventilating. It was an iron test of will to force myself to take slow, deep breaths and relax. Otherwise, I knew I might pass out at the wheel and at this stage of the game, after all the precautions I'd taken, getting caught because of something as mundane and stupid as a traffic accident would be one of the universe's more perverse jokes.

Even after I calmed down, the unease was ever-present. I dimly recalled a baby-faced psychiatrist asking me, in a smarmy superior-than-thou voice, if I had considered the possibility of mild paranoia. Was he real, or only a dream? Was all the effort I took to avoid getting caught naught but needless self-torture? Whether the man was truly flesh and blood or merely a phantom of my mind, did it even matter? In both cases, he was still an idiot.

I was far too clever for the doctors, far more intelligent than the police, far more canny than the nameless and faceless people who persisted in following me, who continually observed my every move and hoped I would slip up, who persecuted me for no other reason than for their own amusement. They were inexorable but, so long as I kept up the facade and continued to evade them when they drew too near, I would be fine.

With that more positive thought in mind, I forcibly drew my focus back to the immediate tasks at hand.

To further calm my nerves, I took a lesson from what little I knew about alcoholics. Instead of living one day at a time as the adage dictates, I tried measuring my life in individual moments, at least for the duration of this trip. Surprisingly, it worked. Even better, the physics of my journey helped; so long as I remained traveling at the speed limit, I could count on every minute of travel bringing me roughly a mile closer to my destination. It was strangely comforting, the consistent decrease in the amount of time remaining before I would arrive, and I took solace in it. But I had to be careful not to grow too complacent in predictability; it would be dangerous to allow myself to be lulled into any kind of self-hypnosis.

I fought the urge to go faster. Being pulled over for speeding would be catastrophic. I had spent far too long keeping my head down and studiously refraining from drawing attention to myself, hoping it would be sufficient camouflage. My one and only slip up was due to a rash, impulsive moment that never would have happened had I not been under such tremendous stress. Though I still think it was perfectly reasonable for me to assume that the man who lived down the street was installing cameras so that law enforcement could spy on me, I should have realized that it was approaching Christmas and taken into consideration that he might simply be hanging holiday lights.

Fortunately, he suffered no injuries other than a few scrapes and a twisted ankle, and agreed to a suspended sentence so long as I agreed to get "help." I made a fine show of sincerely regretting my misguided actions and, when the court mandated that I undergo therapy, I meekly agreed. I even managed to create the impression that I was enthusiastic about people probing my mind, if not downright grateful for it. It was altogether a brilliant job of fakery as the only thing I truly regretted was making a mistake that not only got me caught, but which put me "on the radar" of the authorities, so to speak.

Resolving to make the proverbial lemonade from lemons, I decided to use the analysis to my benefit if at all possible. After all, I had never before considered that enlisting the aid of a professional might help me better deal with my fears. Not that I agreed for one minute with any of the doctor's suggestions, rendered with a patently false sympathy, that perhaps I had a tendency to overreact. The duplicitous quack pretended to be my friend, but I could see the truth in his eyes. He never believed for one instant that I was, indeed, a target of those who would harm me.

Am I mentally disturbed? Perhaps. The fact that I cannot recall if all of the doctors I have supposedly seen were completely real or just figments of my imagination seems to suggest that I cannot always rely on my own faculties. Yet, I take solace in the fact that few people could withstand the kind of persecution I've been subjected to these past few years without a small screw or two coming loose.

It never helped that I was never able to describe who was after me with any specificity. Obviously, they are minions of law enforcement. They are constantly there, usually hidden just out of sight, watching me. They enjoy inflicting their petty torments, creating that stifling sense that they are about to pounce, relishing my fear at the knowledge that should they ever decide to move in for the proverbial kill and manage to catch me at an awkward moment, I am doomed.

Two more vehicles joined the grey-or-blue car. A brown sedan cleverly slid into the chase from an onramp while a van masquerading as a plumber's truck crept up from somewhere in our wake. The sedan pulled up close behind me and started honking its horn. To any observers, it would have looked like the driver was merely impatient to pass. I knew better. The three cars were trying to hem me in, to herd me like a stray sheep being driven to the slaughtering pen.

But I am no sheep.

When I could endure the tension no longer, and without any warning, I yanked the wheel to the right and cut across the van's path, taking some small satisfaction at the squeal of brakes behind me. My wheels jolted over the shoulder and the entire car shuddered as it raced across the grassy embankment before my tires made contact with the macadam of the ramp. I had cleverly waited until my little cadre of oppressors and I had almost completely passed the off ramp before making my move. The ruse was successful. Unable to back up on the freeway, they drove on, no doubt cursing the ingenuity with which they had been foiled.

For the moment, at least, I was free from pursuit. But I had a nagging suspicion that my liberty would not last very long. I needed to seek shelter of a kind and to hide my car, at least for enough time to allow my trail to grow cold.

Conveniently located at the base of the ramp was one of those intentionally rustic restaurants, designed in accordance with some misguided person's idea of what buildings must have looked like in the Wild West. Railroad ties lined the parking lot. Two huge wagon wheels framed the path leading to the front door and added to the sense of preciousness. A wraparound porch, complete with a line of rocking chairs which seemed woven from heavy reeds, was testament to the architect's apparent fixation with the O.K. Corral.

I made certain to park in the narrow space between two 18-wheelers. If anyone happened to be driving along the freeway trying to find me, the bulky trucks would make it almost impossible for them to catch a glimpse of my car. Once I was sufficiently hidden, I switched off the ignition and sat for a few moments trying to catch my breath and regain my composure. When my head no longer felt like it was going to explode, I got out of the car and made my way up the wooden steps to the faux-saloon doors leading into the little coffee shop. As kitschy as the place was, it was as good a spot as any for me to wait things out and hope that my pursuers would overshoot their mark.

Less than thirty seconds after I was inside the building, I was overcome by an attack of the shakes. I don't know why. Maybe it was a reaction to being in a state of relative safety, after having spent the past few hours exposed on the open highway. No matter how illusory my haven might be, at least it had four stout walls, even if they were designed to look like Lincoln Logs, and it helped lessen that horrible sense of agoraphobia that sometimes plagued me. In retrospect, I guess that I had been poised on the edge of multiple adrenalin rushes for so long that the sudden absence of immediate danger just took the stuffing out of me, as one of my aunts used to say. In any case, I started to tremble and my bladder clamored that it was about to burst. Fearful that I was going to wet myself, I bolted past the counter and down the aisle between the booths toward the back of the restaurant where the bathrooms can usually be found.

I barely got my trousers down in time. Not only did I have to pee worse than I could ever remember, my bowels let loose as well. I sat on the toilet, still shaking, while my insides emptied out. After I finished my business and was washing up, my guts knotted for no discernable reason and I rushed back into the stall, retching and evacuating from the other end. When I was reasonably certain that there could not possibly be anything left inside me, I washed my hands and face thoroughly and rinsed the taste of bile from my mouth. I was covered in cold sweat and considered dunking my head under the faucet as well. But there were no paper towels in the restroom, only one of those cloth roll-towel machines on the wall. Walking back through the restaurant with a sopping wet head of hair was a surefire way to draw exactly the kind of attention I wanted to avoid, so I contented myself with blotting up the excess perspiration by jamming a wad of toilet paper under each of my armpits.

The waitress looked at me queerly when I took a stool at the counter. I don't know why as my order was unremarkable, just a cup of tea and some whole wheat toast. Though I certainly did not need the caffeine, I always feel a trifle guilty walking into a business only to use the bathroom without making a purchase. People sometimes remember when that happens, whereas if you order something, however small, you become just another customer. Besides, my insides were still churning and I hoped the toast would help settle my stomach.

Nevertheless, something prompted her to give me that dubious look and it certainly wasn't anything I'd done. For a moment, I felt the surge of panic again but I was able to repress it with the rationale that, perhaps, she was just the naturally suspicious type. After all, it was far too much of a coincidence even for my leaps of logic to think that she was an undercover cop who happened to recognize me. On the other hand, stranger things have happened and I resolved to stay on the alert.

Luckily, there was a large mirror behind the counter which extended the entire length of the wall. It would allow me a fairly good view of what was going on behind me as I ate. By leaning forward only slightly, I had a good line of sight to the front entrance as well. Without intending to do so, I had picked an excellent vantage point. If there was anything about my position to criticize at all, it was that any diners sitting the booths at each of the far ends would have their backs to me and I would not be able to see their faces. I could live with that handicap.

While I waited for my order, I had time to think, time to resent the dice that Life had thrown for me. What had I ever done to deserve this kind of persecution? I ask myself that question a dozen times every day. I've always sought to do the right thing, the things that must be done and sometimes even the things that other people hadn't the courage or conviction to do. I take terrible burdens upon myself, burdens I could easily refuse to shoulder if I were just an ordinary person like most of the ordinary and boring people in the world. But I'm different. I'm one of those rare people with a sense of responsibility. I know why I've been placed on this Earth and, for that, I risk being branded a criminal.

My order arrived accompanied by another odd look from the waitress. I began to suspect that she might not be as pedestrian as she seemed. It strained credulity that my pursuers could possess precognitive powers that told them the exact moment that I would decide to take evasive measures on the freeway; there was virtually no way they could have anticipated that I would end up in this particular diner. Their network of operations would have to be far larger than I had ever suspected for them to have installed one of their agents in every eating establishment and rest stop along this stretch of the road. No, if I allowed small events like getting the fish-eye from a random waitress to propel me into a realm where I began to believe that the people who were following me possessed bizarre supernatural abilities, I would be the architect of my own insanity.

Meticulously, I buttered my toast, taking solace from the mundane activity, enjoying the sense of accomplishment when I successfully managed to spread both pats of butter so that each of them fully covered a slice on its own without any nasty dry areas left over. I had just taken my first bite when a reflection in the mirror caught my attention.

My mouth froze in mid-chew. I must have looked ridiculous with my jaw hanging slackly to display half-eaten, saliva-moistened toast for all the world to see. Frankly, I wouldn't have blamed the waitress for giving me funny looks had she happened to glance my way at that very moment! But she was occupied at the far end of the counter. A long moment later, I mustered the self-composure to finish chewing and swallow. I dropped the remains of my toast onto the plate uneaten. Any appetite that I might have had was gone.

Naturally, it was the boy who first caught my attention. No, not a boy. A youth. In his late teens or very early twenties. An adult, but not by much. Hopeful and innocent, easily misled. With the pure heart and empty head of youth, according to an expression I'd once heard one of my grade school teachers use. It was a very dangerous state to be in, especially when there was a predator nearby. They were attracted to naiveté like jackals to a corpse.

Possibly as a result of some innate gift, I've always been attuned to these sorts of things and so I recognized the situation instantly. Odd how just moments before I had been feeling almost resentful of my calling. A mere look at this youth reminded me of how important my duties were, how vital it was that I banish all doubts that what I do is *right*, no matter how many forces might be allied against me.

One look at the young man's face was enough for me to realize that he was terrified even though he was doing his best not to show it. He fiddled with the silverware, studiously avoiding looking at the face of his dining companion. Instead his eyes flicked toward the exit, back and forth, measuring. It was clear that he despaired of ever reaching it should he attempt to try. My heart broke at his imagined plight and I ached to reassure him that help was on the way. But the time was nowhere near ripe.

For the moment, I could only sit and observe, silently willing my sympathy might reach him over the empty space between us even though I knew that such communication was possible only in fantasy stories. The emotions of his plight were contagious to someone like me. I had no way of fending off the waves of bleakness and hopelessness that invaded my soul. I had only my experience at such things to enable me to cope with them, to avoid being crushed by the feelings he was projecting.

My heart reached out for him, an athletic lad with biceps and shoulders straining the dingy white T-shirt he wore. His hair was longish, the mottled yellow of roses just on the verge of turning brown. Fear-induced sweat caused strands of it to mold to the back of his neck and plastered a small lock to his forehead. I could not quite see the color of his eyes but I imagined they might be green, gold-speckled verdigris.

He was handsome and strong in his youth, a prime target. A natural-looking boy, I could not imagine him walking down the streets of any city or, if he did, he would do so blissfully unaware of the dangers that surrounded him. There was a freshness about him, an aura of innocence, a boyishness at odds with the more mature physique that caused the T-shirt to cling to his torso and outline the muscled frame underneath.

He was exactly the kind of prey ripe for a certain kind of predator. And unless my eyes deceived me, his dining companion was typical of the type.

A burly bear of man who appeared to be in his forties, one look at him and I could tell that he probably stank of old sweat and unwashed flesh. Barrel chested with overly developed arms, he had a body builder's belly which was destined to shortly run to fat if it had not already begun to do so. Unattractive tufts of wiry hair emerged from the open collar of his shirt and peeped disgustingly from his underarms where the sleeves had been crudely hacked off.

His several days' growth of stubble was in marked contrast to the boy's clean, smooth face, and the harshly square line of his jaw and the bushiness of his eyebrows suggested a bestial nature. His expression was severe, his brows furrowed, the scowl on his lips seemed a permanent fixture. Instead of lifting his sandwich to his mouth, I almost expected him to put his face into the plate and ravage his meal, grunting and spitting while he devoured it.

The boy shifted in his seat. Several times, I thought he was about to try and rise, perhaps to attempt an escape. But it took only a glare from the older man, a twist of his lips that bordered on a snarl, to freeze his unfortunate victim in place. When they had finished their meal and paid, they rose to leave.

To the waitresses and cashier—to anyone who lacked my powers of observation and my extensive experience—it must have looked like the man was guiding his young companion to the door with an avuncular hand on his shoulder. But I saw the way the tattoos on the man's arms shifted when he flexed muscle to tighten his grip on the boy's shoulder. I watched the tacky cartoon devils and realistic cobras and impossibly large-breasted women seem to move of their own volition. I witnessed his raggedly clipped fingernails digging painfully into the youngster's flesh, probably deeply enough to leave marks on otherwise unblemished skin. I was testament to the twitching of the youth's shoulders, as if he was stretching away a kink, when it was obvious to me that he was really trying to shrug free of the older man's relentless grip.

To the uninitiated, it all passed for something mundane and innocent. I knew better; I could sense the sinister purpose underneath. I shuddered when familiar feelings stirred within me. Flashes of memory streaked across my mind, almost as if I was re-watching selected scenes from a movie I had seen fifty times. There was a sharp pang in the pit of my stomach, not from nerves this time. For an instant, the welling emotions were so powerful that I had to forcibly choke back a sob. But there was no time for that now.

I could not wait for my check or they might evade me and the young man's fate would be sealed. I hastily threw a few dollars onto the counter and followed them into the parking lot. Casual. I kept my movements deliberately casual. Not only did I have my own followers to worry about, I now had the additional burden of not wanting the old pervert to notice me either.

They walked directly to a well-worn 18-wheeler. I could see the way the animal's paw cruelly kneaded the muscle underneath the young man's shirt. I saw the expression on his face when the lad climbed into the cab of the truck, and the way his gaze lingered for long seconds after the door was shut and the youth was trapped inside. It both sickened me and filled me with dread.

I don't know how I came by the knowledge other than by way of my long and sad association with other innocents who had been corrupted by lust, but at that moment, I saw in my mind's eye exactly what horrors he had in store for his young victim. It was as if my brain had become a movie screen and the brutish man's depraved lusts were projected upon it, in full color and sparing me no grotesque or sickening detail. I knew I had to prevent that horrible excuse for a human being from doing it.

It's both ironic and sad, isn't it, when you realize that it was for this, this lifelong obligation that had been thrust upon me, that I was so horribly persecuted?

My personal plight faded in importance and I banished thoughts of my own pursuers from my mind. There was a far more immediate need to rescue the blond youth from the danger he was in. How he'd gotten himself into this predicament didn't matter. My suspicion was that he was a hitchhiker who had unknowingly chosen to accept the wrong offer of a ride. I could have been wrong, of course, but that was the scenario I was most familiar with. He looked far too wholesome to be one of those hustlers who sometimes plied their trade along the highways, kneeling in the tangled brush of the berm to offer blow jobs for twenty bucks a pop.

I got into my car, started the engine, and waited anxiously for the predator to pull out of the lot, confident that the beast of a driver was unaware that he himself was being stalked. The two large trucks I'd parked between blocked me from his view but simultaneously prevented me from having a clear sight line as well. Fortunately, he had to drive past the end of the row, virtually right in front of me, in order to reach the freeway on-ramp. As soon as I saw him accelerating to merge, I hurried to catch up.

I followed for a good half an hour, wondering how I was going to effectuate the boy's rescue. Fortunately, both our vehicles seemed to be headed in the same direction and traffic was fairly light. Once we reached the desert, there would likely be even fewer people on the road. Every so often, just to fool the driver in case he happened to see me in his rearview mirror, I sped up and passed them briefly. But I was always careful to do so only on open stretches of highway where I knew there were no off ramps; I did not want to overshoot an exit and have to backtrack. It would be the height of irony if I were thwarted by the same technique I had used to elude my own pursuers earlier in the evening.

On and on we drove until the greenery along the highway gave way to tattered scrub and, in turn, to the occasional desiccated tree. Dry, twisted limbs punctuated an ever increasing expanse of rocky sand dotted with cactus and withered palms struggling to survive. It was after midnight now, and the 18-wheeler showed no signs of stopping. Luckily, I had filled my gas tank before leaving the city, so I had no worries about finding myself stranded. Even so, the traffic was reaching that point in the middle of the night when it was at its thinnest and I knew I had only a certain amount of time to make my move before it would start to become congested once again.

We had been driving a good ten minutes with nary another car in sight, and my original destination was fast approaching. I repeatedly checked my rearview mirror, well aware of how easily my intense concentration on the young captive in the vehicle ahead of me could distract me from remaining wary of the possibility that someone had once again picked up my trail. Even now, they could be following just out of sight with their headlights extinguished. Though I had managed to evade them for years, it was always more difficult to stay alert when I was involved with what I sardonically thought of as one of my Good Samaritan missions. And they were tricky little devils, apt to take advantage of a momentary lapse in my judgment to swoop down upon me.

Neither I nor the poor lad in the truck could afford that eventuality.

Instinctively, I knew when the time was right. We were driving in the middle of a long stretch of nowhere. This far out, at this hour, we were unlikely to be interrupted.

As I've confessed, I know very little about the large 18-wheelers but I understand that they do not stop as easily as smaller vehicles in emergencies. Many times, I've seen them forced to slam on their brakes or lay onto their horns when a smaller car whose driver undoubtedly has a death wish has cut them off to reach an exit or is stupid enough to risk Paradise simply so that he can change lanes.

I pulled alongside the cab of the truck and steeled myself against what I was about to do. This close, the size of the rig was intimidating. Any misjudgment on my part would seal not only the young man's fate, but my own as well. I jerked the wheel to the right and then back again, as if I was thinking about cutting across his lane but was not quite sure if I could make it. Brakes squealed in response, accompanied by an angry blast of his horn. Emboldened, I did it again, this time making sure to clip his front bumper before retreating back into my own lane. I flinched at the grinding of metal against metal and made sure to clutch the steering wheel with a death grip so as to maintain absolute control of my car during the brief period of contact.

The truck slowed even more, the brakes working overtime. But slowing wasn't enough; I needed him to stop. I laid onto my own horn and merged directly into his lane, fully cutting him off. I could only imagine the colorfulness of the language that must have been echoing in the truck's cabin just about then!

Precision was crucial. Given that with only the slightest acceleration on his part, the 18-wheeler could have flattened my car like the proverbial pancake. I had to slow down enough to cause an actual impact while avoiding my car being dragged under his front wheels. The stunt was within the purview of a far more consummate driver than I was. That I was able to pull it off at all was far more due to luck than to any skill on my part.

I ended up stopping in a spot that could not have been more perfect than if Nature had designed it with my particular needs in mind. The embankment where I was parked wasn't very wide. Just a few yards from the edge of the asphalt, it began a steep slope down to a dry wash. It was a unique feature of the terrain that was about to come in very handy.

Of course it was possible that the truck would not stop even though I'd hit it. I'd driven away from a number of fender benders myself, mostly because my tormentors were getting too close and I lacked the time to tarry. On rarer occasions, I fled the scene because it was obvious I had been set up. Thus, while it was possible he'd keep going, it was highly unlikely.

I pride myself on being an astute judge of human nature. I've been gifted with an innate ability to deduce what certain personality types are most likely to do in a given situation, a modest talent but a useful one. I doubted the man I'd seen in the diner would be the type to shrug off even a minor scratch to his vehicle. I'd gotten the distinct impression from the way he sat in the booth, both glowering and gloating over his victim, that he possessed the kind of primitive psyche that was quick to anger and which relished any opportunity that provided him the slightest justification to indulge his more brutal nature. He'd been cut off, not once, but three times; he must be furious. Once he saw me parked, I strongly believed that he would be incapable of resisting the opportunity to pull over himself and give me a piece of his mind. Very likely, he would be eager to add a punishing physical element to the chastisement as well.

When the rig continued past my car, I had a brief moment of concern that my instincts had failed me and he was going to simply drive on by. I was just about to start my engine and dive back into the chase when his brake lights flashed, vindicating my initial instincts. His passing me was explained by the way he angled the truck in front of my car when he parked; he had deliberately hemmed me in. Doubtless, he sought to block me from easily pulling around him and back onto the highway should I decide at the last minute to try and escape his wrath.

Chuckling to myself at his presumption, I reached into the space behind the passenger seat to grab what I might need to defend myself and got out.

The driver's side door sprang open. Only a fool could have missed the torrents of anger spewing from the man; his fury was palpable even without the stream of incessant cursing. He approached me with a lumbering and aggressive gait, belligerent from the very start. I'd been right about the brute's propensity for violence; his hands were already spasmodically flexed and clenched into fists. His chest was thrust forward over his burgeoning belly. I'm sure he was proud of the imposing picture he thought he presented.

This close, I could tell that he was a few years younger than I'd first assumed from my brief glimpses of him in the diner, perhaps in his mid-thirties. His slovenly demeanor and the brooding scowl were partly responsible for my error. Then again, I'd been concentrating on the plight of his younger companion and hadn't paid as close attention as I normally would have.

He stopped an arm's length from me. Given the picture of myself that I intentionally present to the world, I doubted he'd throw a punch right away. At first glance, I appear to be the quintessential victim, unassuming and unthreatening, even frail. Bullies of his type can rarely resist basking in the opportunity to threaten someone they perceive as weaker than themselves. They get off on using intimidation to reduce their targets to begging and tears and they enjoy the humiliation almost as much as they enjoy wading in with their fists. The reality where I am concerned, as my pursuers and a select few already knew, and as this barbarian was about to find out, is quite something else altogether.

As I'd surmised, instead of attacking me physically at the start, he vented his spleen for a while using the foulest language imaginable. I stood quite still, concentrating on maintaining the illusion that I was helpless, assuming the most innocent and apologetic demeanor that I could. Eventually, he ran out of steam and I thought I might finally be able to get a word in edgewise.

"I know about you," I said. I kept my voice quiet and casual. It has been my experience that angry people will stop shouting if you speak softly, for no reason other than it is impossible for them to hear you if they don't.

My words brought him up short. He stood, blinking for a moment, and his brow furrowed uncertainly.

"About you and that young man." I clucked my tongue as if to say, "Shame on you."

"Leave my brother out of this," he spat.

"Ah! Your *brother*. I see." By both my expression and my tone, I let him know I was not going to fall for the lie. I may even have smirked a bit. "It's always a brother, or a son or a nephew, isn't it?"

My meaning penetrated and his cheeks took on high color.

"You sick fuck," he spat.

"Me?" I put my hand in the center of my chest, in a questioning gesture I knew he would interpret as prissy and overly effeminate and would enrage him even further. "I know what *you're* planning to do."

His face, already flushed, took on new depths of color. I've taunted others of his ilk in the same way before. They usually contrive a righteous indignation, unable to comprehend that their dirty little secret has been exposed. But it never lasts for long. Eventually, they are forced to realize that the jig is up.

Some of them prove themselves not to be completely irredeemable, having the good graces to show at least a little shame for what they've done, or had been about to do.

This beast, however, was not one of the nobler breed of perverts. Though it was clear to me that my accusations had struck home, he displayed not a shred of remorse. His response was typical. Like so many others, he first tried to explain away his actions. It always starts the same way, with the cretin snarling, "Not that it's any of your business but..." In this case, he had some cockamamie story about driving the boy back to college cross country. I do not know whence comes this compulsion to justify themselves but, in my experience, a majority of them try to get away with it. They cast themselves as the heroes, these monsters do, always claiming some altruistic motives, foolishly determined to prove that I have misinterpreted what I've seen.

It never works of course. And their failure to convince me makes them even angrier. Typically, the trucker was working himself into a frenzy again and I was guessing that I had perhaps another minute before he'd begin swinging his fists. I never understood the notion of trying to prove by violence that the truth was a falsehood. Nor was I able to reconcile his bizarre logic that, instead of exposing his depravity, I'd contrived to insult him. In any case, I was already weary of his protestations and of his tawdry display of temper.

The crowbar made a hefty dent above his left ear.

I'd taken the precaution of turning off my headlights when I stopped, leaving only the parking lights to illuminate our little tableau. In their yellowish glow, I could not tell if the chunk that flew into the air was an actual bit of skull or merely a nice-sized swathe of hairy scalp.

He teetered as if about to fall over and he felt at his wound with a comically wide-eyed expression of surprise that never fails to amuse me. I don't know why people sometimes do that. Perhaps they want to make sure that no cranial fluid leaks out. Like most scum, they are concerned only for themselves, obsessed with their own hurts. At times like this, I suspect they give little thought to the feelings of their victims. One thing is for certain though, few of these deviants ever stop to consider that, in nature, even the most skillful predators may find themselves victims of something more vicious still.

His mouth opened. But whether it was to speak, to cry out, to beg, or perhaps even to vomit, I had no interest in finding out.

I hit him again.

Harder.

The crack of the iron against his skull made my arm muscles shudder such that I almost lost my grip on the crowbar. With the third swing, I both heard and felt the satisfying crunch of bone giving way. I knew there was no need for a fourth swing; he was already dead. I didn't need to stand there gawking like a tourist and watch him collapse onto to the ground to confirm it.

I set the crowbar aside and started toward the van. Before I had taken more than a few steps, the passenger side door swung open and the young man clambered out.

"Karl?" he asked. "What happened? Are you okay?"

His voice was deep and resonated in his chest. I found myself wondering what his screams would be like, whether they would remain in that attractive lower register or if they would slowly climb in pitch until they came close to hurting my ears. In either case, if I could work quickly to subdue him and cover my tracks against the incessant pursuit, I would have plenty of time to find out.

Taser guns are truly inspired creations and rendering the blond unconscious was ridiculously easy. Even better, they do the job leaving nary a mark. Absent the two small punctures from the Taser, which could be easily overlooked, the youth's body would be like a fresh canvas for me to create upon. Obviously, you can't do what I do without causing some damage. Nevertheless, I like to begin each session cleanly. Accidental bruises and such are an indication of carelessness. While my ministrations are unavoidably messy, I try to pay attention to details and I abhor blatant sloppiness.

I'm strangely fussy, I suppose, and I want my subjects to be physically pristine at the start; it lends an ambiance of purity to the occasion. I take a certain satisfaction in knowing that every slice is deliberate and that nothing is ever mutilated or cut away by accident. If something is crushed rather than removed, or burned rather than cut, it is done for a precise purpose or to provoke a particular reaction. Technique is what counts, technique and patience. With proper technique, one can happily spend several days enjoying oneself. For the moment however, as tempting as it was to begin on the spot, I simply secured his wrists and ankles for travel with zip ties and left him where he'd fallen. I had more than enough time to gag him before stowing him in my trunk; for now, he was out cold anyway.

As for disposing of the older man, his body had tumbled over the lip at the edge of the asphalt and now lay in a hollow of earth slightly below the surface of the road. It was as good a place as any and, with the addition of some dry brush, the corpse was concealed from any but the most observant of freeway travelers who might happen to be looking at the precise spot at the exact right moment. I was just happy that it saved me the time and effort of a burial. If I were at all lucky, it might be as much as a day or two before he was found. That was more than enough time for my purposes as my trail would grow cold in a matter of moments and the young man and I would be safely at our destination within the hour.

My pursuers might deduce who was responsible, if not specifically by name, at least by way of style. They might even step up their efforts, following me more closely, more intently seeking an opportunity to "collar" me, as they say on the television crime shows. But as my years of avoiding them had proven, their having knowledge of who did it was a vastly different thing than their having the ability to stop me.

Moving the truck was problematic. Once I got behind the wheel I realized that I had no idea how to even start the thing. I originally had some notion of driving it into the desert and perhaps concealing it on the far side of one of the dunes. It didn't need to be very far, just out of immediate sight of the highway. But the stick shift was intimidating, much larger than I'd expected, and all those buttons and levers baffled me. In the end, I simply left it by the side of the road with the doors unlocked and the keys in the ignition, hoping that some enterprising criminal might steal it before anyone realized it was abandoned.

Hoisting bound young men onto my shoulders is never an easy feat. They seem to weigh far less when they're fully conscious. Then again, when they're awake and have an inkling of what's going to happen to them, they tend to flail about, making them difficult to keep hold of. Everything else being equal, in spite of the increased difficulty, unconscious is better. I carried him back to my car, opened the trunk...and stopped, confronted by my own stupidity.

Every incident has its own wrinkles and unexpected complications. Fortunately, they are usually minor ones and can be easily overcome. This time, I'd been so caught up in the excitement of the pursuit that I had completely forgotten about the other boy!

It was a terribly foolish oversight on my part, especially since the only reason I'd been headed out to the desert in the first place was to dispose of the body. Praying that the corpse was not still in a state of rigor, I breathed a sigh of relief when he folded quite nicely, leaving just enough room for me to tuck my new acquisition in beside him. It looked like a tight squeeze and the blond was apt to be a tad uncomfortable, but things would have been much more unpleasant for him if I'd had to "hack and stack" by the side of the road.

By this time, the young man had regained consciousness and he began to struggle. There was fear in his eyes, as well as an understandable anger and frustration at his helplessness. But he seemed determined to hide his fright and he did it well. It was only when he realized that his traveling companion was already dead that his terror surged and he began desperately writhing and straining against his bindings.

I placed my hand on his chest to reassure him, admiring the way the muscles flexed beneath my fingers as he fought to free himself. He was strong. Good. He would last.

"Shhh," I crooned. "Just relax and everything will be fine."

My eyes darted up the road and I squinted. For an instant, I thought I'd seen a flash of something bright, as if light was reflecting from the metal grill of an approaching car. I waited for several long moments before concluding that it must have been my imagination. As eager as I was to bury the one youth and get to work on the other, I resolved to take my time and proceed with my usual caution. The people who I feared were adept at sniffing out vulnerability. Should they descend upon me while the two young men were bundled in the trunk, I would indeed find myself vulnerable!

I turned back to my captive. Naively, he was still testing his bonds, hoping even while hope faded that he could summon the strength to break free. Oh, he was a feisty one indeed!

"I've got everything under control."

I hoped my even, relaxed tone would calm him down a little. If he continued thrashing so strenuously, I was concerned that he'd hurt himself.

"You needn't worry. I'm always very careful."

I bent over the open trunk. Our faces were so close that we would have been breathing each other's exhalations had he not been gagged. I always find the smell of helpless terror intoxicating. A single trickle of sweat ran down the strong column of his neck and pooled in the hollow of his throat. I was captivated by the sight of it.

There is an unavoidable intimacy to what I do. A rare few of my young men come to understand that and, when they do, it makes the time we spend together far more meaningful. Something told me this youth might be one of the special ones. As if stimulated by that thought, my tongue darted out with a mind of its own and, before I quite realized what was happening, I licked up the droplet of moisture. The salty tang of it sent delicious shivers of anticipation coursing through my entire body. Yes, I knew this boy was going to be special.

"There's nothing to worry about."

Though my voice was a soft whisper, it was laden with the promise of what was to come.

"After all, they haven't caught me yet."

Meghan Arcuri writes fiction and poetry. Her short stories can be found in various anthologies, including Chiral Mad *from publisher* Written Backwards, *and* Insidious Assassins *from* Smart Rhino Publications. *She lives with her family in New York's Hudson Valley. You can visit her at* meghanarcuri.com *or* facebook.com/meg.arcuri.

BEYOND THE BEST SEASONING

Meghan Arcuri

"SO WHAT DO YOU THINK'S IN IT?"

Dex sighed. They'd barely pulled out of the loading dock, and Kyle was already talking about the damn thing.

"Don't know." Dex hoped brevity would end the conversation.

"Food?"

Dex sighed. Guess not.

"Guns? Drugs?" Kyle laughed that dopey laugh of his. "Porn?"

"Jesus, Kyle." Dex took a hit off the joint he'd just lit. According to the GPS, the ride was supposed to take four hours. Four damn hours. On the back roads of upstate New York. With this stupid idiot. No way he could do it without altering his state of mind.

"Hey, man," Kyle said, shoving his hand in Dex's face. "Gimme a hit."

Dex hesitated. This was the shit from his brother. The good shit. He didn't want to share.

"Please," Kyle said, whining like a four-year-old. He probably wouldn't stop.

Dex passed him the joint.

"Thanks, man." Kyle took a hit. Made a big production out of it.

Tool.

"So what do you think's in it?" Kyle said.

"Mr. Fitch told us not to ask any questions."

Fitch owned the trucking company Dex and Kyle worked for. *Fitch's Delivery: Service with a smile.*

Original, Bob Fitch was not. But he ran a tight ship. And, known for being discrete, he made all kinds of deliveries. He trusted Dex with his most delicate customers. Kyle, not so much. He was a big dope, and even Fitch knew it. But Kyle was his new girlfriend's son, and he needed a job. And at 6'3", 250, he had the right stuff for loading the heavy deliveries.

Not that this one was heavy.

"I guess. I wouldn't wanna ask that dude questions, anyway," Kyle said.

"Fitch?"

"No, man. That dude we got the package from. Fucking freak, if you ask me."

"Did he scare you?" Dex liked messing with Kyle sometimes.

Kyle sat up straighter in his seat. "No way. Used to beat the fuck out of skinny fucks like that in high school."

I'm sure you did. Probably afraid of them, too.

"Nah," Kyle said. "That dude was just straight up weird. Slicked back hair, sunglasses at night. And did you see those fingers?"

"They were pretty spindly."

"Huh?"

"Like a spider's legs."

"Exactly." Kyle waved his fingers in front of Dex's face and made a high-pitched noise. "They're gonna get you!"

Dex slapped at his hand. "Knock it off."

More of that stupid laugh.

"He kept saying weird things about it, too," Kyle said. "'It's delicate,' 'needs to join with the other six,' 'it would be a sin if it didn't make it.' Then laughed like he'd made a joke."

"Yeah..." Dex thought he was odd, too. "I think he's just a strange guy with some strange things. Fitch deals with a lot of guys like him."

"Well, I hope I don't have to deal with them too often."

"It's a job, Kyle. You do the work and get paid. And don't ask too many questions."

Kyle took another huge hit off the joint.

"Gimme that," Dex said. "Shit, Kyle."

He'd left Dex with hardly anything. Dex finished off what little was left.

Kyle huffed a laugh.

ᴄ⁄ᴈ

They had driven for a while in silence when Kyle said, "Seriously, though, man. We can ask each other questions, right?"

"Of course." But Dex didn't really want to. As much as he didn't want to admit it, Kyle was right. Weird just scratched the surface with that guy. Sure, he looked a little different, but other things set off Dex's Freak-O-Meter. The guy was quiet. Too quiet. And his voice, when he did speak, reminded Dex of some creepy B-movie vampire.

Not to mention the upside down cross he wore. Dex'd thought that meant atheism, but at one point, the guy looked to the sky and said, "Unworthy, my Lord." Who knew what that was all about?

Plus, the strange package.

"So?" Kyle said.

"So what?"

"What do you think's in it?"

"I have no idea." And usually Dex didn't care. When he had a job to do, he did it. Pick up the package, transport the package, drop off the package. Get paid.

But something about this package intrigued him, too.

"I mean, it was so damn big but light as a fucking feather," Kyle said.

That and its unusual shape.

Dex had never seen anything like it.

Kyle's stomach rumbled.

"Didn't eat dinner, huh?" Dex said.

"I figured we could stop somewhere."

Dex laughed. "It's the middle of the night. And there aren't any stops on this route. It's all back roads, small town shit."

"Damn." Kyle downed the last of the coffee they'd bought before they'd left. His stomach rumbled again.

"Check the glove box. Sometimes Ron or Cheeks leaves stuff in there."

Kyle opened it. "Nothing but some stupid wet wipes and ketchup packets. Should've known. Those fat fucks eat everything. I'm surprised this stuff is still here. But..." He snapped his fingers. "Sometimes there's a cooler in the back."

"I don't remember seeing one."

"Are you sure?"

"Pretty sure."

"100% sure?"

"What is this, middle school? No, I'm not 100% sure."

"Then let's stop and check."

The cab jerked as the truck hit a pothole. A drop of Dex's coffee splashed into the cup holder. He finished the drink.

"Where do you suggest I pull over? No shoulder on these roads."

"Who cares? It's the middle of the night. So what if our tail's hanging out on the road a little? Not like we've seen another car in a while."

He had a point. Miraculously. And if pulling over would get him to quit whining about his hunger, then Dex would do it.

"Fine." Dex stopped the truck.

They went to the back and opened the door.

The box hadn't moved much, due to the expert loading job Dex had done. The box itself was almost as wide as the bed of the truck, but not as long. A few straps and a couple of blankets took care of that. Kyle had stood by and watched as Dex had packed it. If the shape and size of the box hadn't been so large and unwieldy, Dex would've been able to do this job himself. Would've kept all the tip money, too.

Mr. Daddy Long Fingers may have been a freak, but he tipped well. Best tip Dex'd ever gotten, even with splitting it. And he'd promised more at the destination, if the package arrived safe and sound.

That thing must be pretty important to the guy.

Kyle hopped into the back of the cargo compartment.

"Careful," Dex said.

"I'm fine," Kyle said. "Thing looks like a giant, weird-shaped pizza box."

"You're just hungry." Although he pretty much nailed the description. The large box was brown and plain and about a foot thick. It looked to be sealed with one piece of packing tape.

"What the hell shape is that? A pentagon?" Kyle said.

"Heptagon," Dex said.

"I always sucked at math."

Apparently.

"Pentagon's got five sides. That thing has seven."

"Well excuse me, Alfred Einstein."

Oh god.

"Albert."

"Huh?"

"It's Albert Einstein. Not Alfred."

"Whatever." Kyle stood on his tiptoes and looked around the back of the truck. "Dammit."

"What?"

"No cooler."

"Told you."

"Now we know for sure." Kyle didn't move, his eyes seeming to linger on the package.

"Let's go, man. We've got three more hours ahead of us," Dex said. "I just want to get this trip over with."

"It'd be easy enough." Kyle didn't look at Dex, his normally booming voice now almost a whisper.

"What the hell are you talking about?"

"Opening it."

"The box?"

"Yeah."

"You're crazy, man. We're supposed to deliver the packages, not open them."

Kyle looked at Dex. "You really think we'd be the first guys to open one?"

Dex had heard all sorts of stories in his five years at Fitch's company. "No. But it's not something I do."

"Well, aren't you a big, fucking Boy Scout?"

"No, but it's just not right."

"Whatever, man." Kyle pulled out his pocketknife and, before Dex could blink, sliced the sole piece of tape.

"What the hell, Kyle?"

Dex wanted to rip the knife from his hands, shove him from the box, and get back into the cab. But Kyle was huge, and Dex had never been one for confrontation.

"Relax, man. We've got plenty of tape. We'll just peek in, see what's so special, then tape it right up. Like nothing happened." Kyle pocketed the knife and lifted the top of the box. Hinged at one side of the heptagon, it opened like a pizza box, too.

Sweat formed on Dex's upper lip. His heart raced. This was wrong. He wanted to hide in the cab. But pride kept his feet rooted.

And, if he were honest with himself, so did curiosity.

"We really shouldn't be doing this." One last, feeble protest.

"Too late, bro," Kyle said. "And don't you smell that? I think there's food in here."

Dex wanted to protest, tell Kyle his hunger was getting the best of him. But damn if he didn't smell food, too. Something savory and delicious.

Kyle dug through a sea of packing peanuts. "Go get a flashlight."

Dex complied, grabbing the big Maglite from under the driver's seat.

It's gone this far. Might as well see what it is.

He jumped into the back and held it over the package.

"So weird," Kyle said. "All that packing shit...for this?"

Kyle had moved the peanuts to reveal a small, pine chest. About two feet by one, it had two bronze hinges and a simple, bronze latch. No lock.

Kyle undid the latch and lifted the top.

"Hallelujah," Kyle said. "It's like my prayers have been answered."

The flashlight shone on dozens of piping hot bacon cheeseburgers.

Dex's favorite.

Now his stomach rumbled.

The chest seemed too small for such a large amount of food, but before Dex could voice the thought, Kyle had reached in and grabbed one.

"Kyle, don't." Dex grabbed his arm.

Kyle looked at Dex's hand. Dex let go. "There's a ton of food in there. They're not gonna miss one. And I'm fucking starving."

Kyle bit the burger, devouring half of it at once. Cheese dripped onto his finger. He licked it off.

God, it looked good.

What the hell? There are so many in the damn chest. They won't miss two.

Dex grabbed a burger and bit into it.

Amazing.

"Best burger I've had in a while."

Kyle swallowed. "What the hell are you talking about?"

"Cheddar cheese. Bacon. Medium rare. Doesn't get much better than that."

"Can't handle your weed, huh? It's not a fucking burger. It's fried chicken strips."

Sure they'd had some weed. And the good shit, at that. But Dex felt fine. Kyle had hit the stuff harder than he had.

"You must be high. It's a bacon cheeseburger."

"Look in that thing, Dex. It's a pile of the hottest, crispiest fried chicken strips I've ever seen. Best dinner in the world." Kyle took another bite.

Dex checked the chest again.

No chicken. Just burgers. Steaming hot. Crispy bacon. Awesome.

But how did they get so hot?

Who the hell cares? Keep eating.

He took another bite.

"You're telling me you see a bunch of fried chicken strips?"

"Yes." Kyle wiped his mouth with his hand.

"Well, I see bacon cheeseburgers."

"You're high."

"I'm fine."

"Then you're an idiot."

Something was off.

Dex dropped the burger and jumped out of the truck. He needed to be away from the smell. Needed to clear his head.

"Aren't you gonna finish?" Kyle said.

Dex wanted to. He really did. But the burger/chicken thing seemed off.

That's an understatement.

"No. And I think you should stop, too."

"Why?"

"'Cause I see burgers where you see chicken. Doesn't that seem weird to you?"

"Yeah, but who cares? I'm hungry." Kyle grabbed another burger. Or chicken strip. Or whatever.

This is definitely messed up.

"You've gotta stop, Kyle. Even if we didn't see different things, this is not our food. We've got a job to do."

Kyle inhaled the food in two bites. Wiped his hand on his pants. "Fine, man. Done. I should be good for the rest of the trip."

He closed the pine chest and found an extra roll of packing tape. After sealing the large box, he grabbed Dex's half-eaten burger.

"You sure you don't want this?"

"I'm sure."

"Suit yourself." He shoved it in his mouth as he jumped down and closed the door.

He patted Dex on the back with two heavy thumps. "Ready?"

They got in the cab and continued on their way.

"You're not even a little freaked out?" Dex said.

"I'll tell you what I am." Kyle let out a low rumble of a burp. "I'm fucking satisfied. That's what I am."

"Fine."

"I mean, sure, it's weird. But I was hungry. There was food. I ate it. Now I'm not hungry."

Airtight logic, if there ever was any.

"All right."

"Don't get your panties all bunched up, Dex. There was so much food in there, they won't even notice."

"But you saw chicken and I saw burgers."

"What can I say, man? You really need to lay off the weed."

"Shut up, Kyle."

That damn laugh.

⌘

They drove in silence for another hour, the winding, tree-laced roads keeping Dex alert, but also giving him time to ponder the pine chest. None of it made sense. The weird guy. His huge tip. Cheeseburgers. Chicken. Who knew? Maybe his brother had put something extra in that marijuana.

Kyle's stomach rumbled, louder than the last time.

"What the hell, man?"

"Don't know," Kyle said. "Guess I need some more chicken."

"No way."

Kyle laughed. "Just fucking with you, man. I can make it."

But in the next few minutes, Kyle's stomach wouldn't shut up. Then he doubled over.

"You okay?" Dex said. His stomach started making some noise, too.

Kyle moaned. "Don't know. Never been this hungry in my life."

"Seriously?"

"Uh-huh. It hurts. Please, man," he said. "You gotta pull over again."

"We can't."

"Just one piece, I swear." Kyle groaned.

Dex shook his head. "Fine." He pulled the truck over.

Kyle scrambled out of the door, as Dex grabbed the Maglite. By the time Dex got to the back, Kyle had opened the door and sliced the packing tape of the big box. He shoved the peanuts aside and opened the pine chest.

"What the hell?" Dex said.

The light revealed a bunch of doughnuts.

Kyle's hand, already in the chest, grabbed a glazed one.

"Kyle. Don't."

"But I love chocolate chip cookies. They're warm, too."

"You see cookies?"

"You don't?"

"I see doughnuts," Dex said. "This is crazy. You can't eat that."

"I'm so fucking hungry."

Pain hit Dex's stomach. An intense hunger cramp like he'd never felt.

Holy hell.

"It was chicken and burgers before. Now it's cookies and doughnuts. Something is seriously wrong with this chest."

"I don't really give a—" Kyle dropped to his knees. Grabbing at his stomach, he groaned and grunted. He doubled over, swearing.

Then he shoved the food in his mouth. Chewed a little. He leaned on the wall of the truck, eyes closed. He swallowed. Sighed. Opened his eyes. "Much better."

Dex massaged his stomach, the cramping becoming more like shredding.

"You should eat something, too," Kyle said.

The chest was freaking Dex out, but his stomach: the growling, the wrenching, the twisting. Like something clawing at his insides. Primal urges outweighed logic. He ate a doughnut.

And the pain disappeared.

"Shit." Kyle closed the chest, re-taped the heptagonal box, and closed the door. "I think we're done here."

"Hell, yeah." Dex fished the keys from his pocket, and they hustled to the cab. "What was that all about?"

"I don't know, man. I've never been that hungry before in my life."

"Me, either." Dex started the engine. "Where did all those sweets come from? I thought we were delivering burgers—or chicken."

"Who knows? But I'm thinking we need to get the hell away from that box. How much longer we got?"

Dex pulled onto the road. "Less than two hours. Hopefully that snack'll tide us over until we get there."

"Where is 'there,' anyway?"

"You weren't paying attention, were you?"

"That guy was a freak. I just wanted to get out of there. And based on what's going on with that box, I think I was right, wasn't I?"

"Can't argue with that." Dex swerved around a dead raccoon. "Potsdam."

"Is it as middle-of-fucking-nowhere as this?" Kyle gestured out the window.

"It's pretty far out there, but we should be able to find a diner and a hotel, if you feel like crashing for a bit."

"After this crazy night? I think I just wanna go home."

Dex didn't disagree.

※

Under an hour from Potsdam, Dex's stomach growled again.

"No way, man." Kyle stared at him. "You can't possibly be hungry."

Another growl.

"Shit!" Dex slammed the steering wheel. "What the hell is going on?"

Kyle grabbed his stomach. "Mine's doing it again, too. There's gotta be someplace to eat around here. Someplace not involving that box." He took out his phone.

"I've done this route a bunch for Fitch. There's nothing until Potsdam."

"Dammit." Kyle tapped on the screen of his phone for another minute or two. "Nothing."

"That's what I just said." Fear and panic mixed with the anger in Dex's voice. More sweat formed on his upper lip. His pulse pounded again. If his body followed the same pattern as last time, that stomach pain would set in at any minute. And it would be bad. Real bad. Dex didn't know if he could deal with it one more time.

"All right, man. All right. Calm down." Kyle didn't speak for a minute. Then he said, "Okay. Here's the deal. We go back to the box one more time."

"Are you crazy?"

"Just hear me out. The hunger waves seem to come every hour or so, right?"

"Yeah."

"And we've got a little less than an hour until we get there, right?"

Dex looked at the clock on the dash. "Yeah."

"So we go to the box and grab a snack. That'll keep us full until we get there. We deliver the package. Good fucking rid-dance. And that's about the time we'll be hungry again. We find that diner and, boom, we're done. We can order a bunch of stuff to go for the ride back."

Usually calm in a crisis, Dex had trouble focusing, his hunger becoming his only concern. But damned if Kyle's reasoning didn't make sense.

"Okay."

"Yeah?" Kyle said.

"Yeah. Let's do it. Before that pain comes back."

Dex pulled the truck over and grabbed the flashlight, the noises in his stomach threatening to turn into cramps.

Kyle climbed into the trailer and opened the big box. His hand flew up to cover his mouth and nose.

"What's that smell?"

The scent of rot filled Dex's nose. Still standing on the ground, he waved the Maglite around to see if they'd hit anything. Or if anything had already been hit.

Nothing.

"I don't think it's coming from out here." He hopped up next to Kyle, who opened the pine chest.

"Oh my god," Kyle said. "It's dog shit. A fucking pile of dog shit!" He jumped out of the truck.

Dex didn't see dog shit. The box held what seemed to be an old turkey carcass, moldy and quivering. But it wasn't really quivering. A bunch of maggots moved en masse around the carcass.

Dex dry heaved. Which seemed to be at odds with his growling stomach. He slammed the lid of the chest shut, fumbled with the packing tape, and sealed the big box.

He jumped out of the truck and closed the door. Kyle lay on the ground, writhing and twisting, coughing and hacking.

Hunger's vice grip seized Dex's stomach. The sensation of tearing, shredding. All started again. He dropped the Maglite and fell to the ground next to Kyle.

The pain soon subsided enough for them to sit.

"What the hell are we going to do now?" Dex said.

Kyle looked at him without speaking.

Is he eyeballing my leg?

"I got it," Kyle said.

"What?"

"The glove box."

"What about it?"

"It's got ketchup packets." Kyle stood and rubbed his stomach.

"That's not gonna do anything."

"Better'n nothing." He disappeared. Doors opened and closed. He returned and threw three packets in Dex's lap.

"That's all?"

"Yup. Six altogether." Kyle held up three other packets. "Three for you, three for me. Dig in."

But the ketchup brought back the pain. As Dex went fetal, Kyle walked toward him, a weird look in his eyes.

"Get the hell away from me," Dex said through groans.

"It's all right, man." Kyle knelt next to him. "We'll get through this." He put his hand on Dex's arm and squeezed. A tight squeeze.

Dex felt for the Maglite. As soon as he found it, he swung.

After it hit Kyle's head, Dex blacked out, the pain overwhelming him.

જ

Dex woke to a headache and sore hand.

But no stomach pain. In fact, he was more sated than he'd been the whole night.

He sat up and looked around, but the sun still hadn't risen yet.

"Kyle?" Dex's sticky lips tasted strange. Unfamiliar.

He got up and walked to the driver's side door. As he turned the corner, the Maglite lay on the ground, still lit. It shone on a body.

He hustled over to see Kyle, facedown in a pool of blood.

"Kyle!" Dex turned him over.

His bloody, swollen face reminded Dex what he'd done before blacking out. But the guilt didn't come.

Son of a bitch was gonna eat me. Self fucking defense.

He scanned the rest of Kyle's body. A dark patch on Kyle's inner thigh gave him pause. He grabbed the Maglite.

"Holy shit!"

Blood had begun to dry over a shredded, messy hole.

Dex licked his lips. Sweet. Metallic.

"Oh my god!"

He jumped over the body and scrambled into the cab. Adjusting the mirror, he shone the light on his face. Blood covered his mouth. Dry bits of...something stuck to his cheeks.

Memories from after the blackout started to come: swinging the Maglite again, straddling Kyle's chest, throwing more punches. Kyle's still body. Chest barely moving. His summer clothes revealing bare arms and legs, thick and meaty.

Dex waited for the gorge to rise in this throat, but it didn't. A strange calm settled over him. He took the wipes from the glove box, tearing open each one and cleaning his face as best he could.

The dashboard clock read 5:00 AM. Almost two hours since he'd last eaten. No pain yet. He felt good. Strong. But a whisper of a stomach rumble told him he would need to eat again. Soon.

As he climbed out of the cab and stepped over Kyle's body, a faint odor of smoke hit his nose.

Maglite in hand, he passed the back of the truck, the door still raised.

The big box was open, but the chest was gone.

What the fuck?

Another memory, faint and foggy, came to him: dark sunglasses and spindly hands, clutching pine. And a whispered voice saying, "No humility...definitely not worthy."

More rumbling. The beginnings of cramping.

"Fuck it."

He followed his nose through the woods. After about a half mile, he found a clearing. Two cars. A fire pit. Two tents.

No one was by the still-smoking fire.

Must be sleeping.

Dex's stomach started to ache as he approached the site. Two coolers sat by the pit. But he didn't open them.

He needed something a little more substantial.

He unzipped a tent.

Janet Joyce Holden was born in the North of England, and is a writer of dark, supernatural fiction. She is the author of the novels Carousel, The Only Red Is Blood, *and* The Origins of Blood *vampire series, as well as a number of "on the dark side" short stories. She lives in Southern California, where the true trucking horror is the speed limit...*

TAKE THE NIGHT

Janet Joyce Holden

"You think you've seen it all? Heard it all?
I did not simply stare into the abyss.
I embraced it, and let it whisper in my ear.
And tonight, I will tell you what I heard,
I will show you what I saw.
I will give you everything."

DANNY'S HANDS WERE SHAKING. It was the first thing Rob noticed when his friend climbed into the limousine. He also looked thin; even the legendary potbelly had gone.

"I'll be fine once we start playing."

"Have you seen a doctor?" Rob had already taken a guess—long-term nerve damage, Parkinson's maybe, but after another rebuttal he decided to keep a lid on it. Instead, they swapped tales of wives and kids and indulged in the usual industry gossip, all the way up the Interstate until the conversation, as usual, spiraled into one of Danny's legendary rants.

"Well, did you read it?"

Rob nodded. Yes, he'd read it—the latest online screed from their charismatic frontman, Ed Visalli.

"He's an asshole."

"He's just playing to the crowd."

"And what kind of crowd do you think will show up, after this?"

As if it mattered. Rob figured Ed was simply pulling out all the stops for the last hurrah. They'd had their official, final reunion gig weeks ago, and this was billed as a special encore for their diehard fans. One final moneymaker before they closed the lid on three decades of rock mayhem.

He settled back and assumed his role as caretaker, while Danny hurled bitter invectives and let off steam. Until finally they pulled in at the venue, and Danny's barriers were down.

"I have a doctor's appointment next week. But don't tell the others."

"Danny—"

"Shush. Not a word. Not on the final gig. Especially to Ed and Alan."

Rob held up his hands. "Swear to God."

"Okay, then."

They left the vehicle and were approached by two young women bearing clipboards and exuding efficiency. One of them pressed a lanyard into Rob's hand.

"To be worn at all times."

And just like that, he was sidelined, relegated to a hanger-on.

Dutifully, he looped the all-access credential around his neck. If nothing else it would serve as a souvenir. His daughter collected them; she had a hundred of them strung on the back of her bedroom door.

They were backstage and he couldn't see much, but they'd played here before and he remembered the venue well enough—a natural, open-air auditorium, nestled in the foothills at the eastern edge of the Los Angeles Basin, surrounded by hills of dry brush that did nothing to dampen the acoustics.

He caught up with the others, climbed the steps, and walked out onto the stage. From here, he could see the entire front of the house and the view made his heart quicken. He waved at the guy on the soundboard, perched on an island in the middle of the arena, and when he turned, he saw Danny grinning from ear to ear. Yeah, he felt it, too. Just a moment between them before Danny was swallowed by a gaggle of technicians about to embark on the final sound check.

No sign of Ed, or Alan, their aloof guitarist. However, their bass player, Tyler, was already plugged in. Rob's eyes veered toward the row of amplifiers, and instinctively he patted his empty shirt pocket. Memories were washing in like the tide, and already he was dying for a cigarette. He was their roadie, back in the day, and had been responsible for the entire backline— setting it up, breaking it down. Not to mention driving them from gig to gig in a succession of vehicles, including their first big truck after the second album hit and the record company decided to pay attention. But those days were gone, and now his primary function was managing their mercurial drummer's legendary temper.

Satisfied Danny was fully occupied, he retraced his steps and headed backstage, and at the top of the stairwell he had a good view of what it took to put on a show these days. No turning up in a shitty old van with a few battered amps, hoping and praying the venue's ancient PA system worked. Now it was multi-consoles, computer controlled lights, giant screens, pyrotechnics...

He looked down at the row of jet-black big rigs, meticulously lined up, trailers painted with the "Take The Night" logo, each one capable of a thirty-ton payload. But instead of the usual four dedicated vehicles, he counted six.

He took inventory once more. Six trucks.

The lift gates were down on four of the trailers and he decided to investigate. He could hear Danny on stage, already laying down a backbeat, and his feet instinctively matched the tempo as he descended the stairs. He approached two guys who were wearing standard issue tour shirts. "Something special for tonight?" He gestured along the line. When they offered him nothing but shrugs and wary glances, he left them behind and headed toward the extra vehicles.

Their livery was identical. No sign of the drivers. He walked the length of the final trailer, and for no particular reason, ran his fingers along the paintwork. Just for an instant, before his hand recoiled.

Feeling foolish, he stopped and reconnected, this time pressing his palm flat against the trailer wall. He gritted his teeth, while an odd sensation washed over him, as if he'd been trapped like a mouse. No more recoil. Instead, something inside had the measure of him, and it didn't want to let go.

He broke free, and considered he'd imagined it. He felt the beginnings of a headache. Common sense told him he'd endured a long journey with Danny bellowing in his ear; he was hungry, thirsty, and probably suffering from the late afternoon heat.

Abandoning the vehicle line, Rob headed toward the shade offered by the enormous stage scaffold. The catering crew had already set up, and he gathered two cans of 7UP and a turkey sandwich. Minutes later, after ingesting the contents of one of the cans and the sandwich, he felt a whole lot better.

Another limousine crept through the gate. It stopped near-by, and he saw the driver get out and scurry to the rear passenger door. Soon after, Ed, Alan, and a guy who appeared to be Ed's latest "spiritual guru" stepped out of the vehicle.

Rob raised his hand and waved. None of them reciprocated. Instead, they turned and headed toward a big, luxury coach parked near the gate, Alan's posture was like that of a gangly stick insect, while Ed followed, hands in his pockets, his gamine profile overshadowed by his strange companion, who bore a ghastly pallor reminiscent of a vampire.

Rob frowned. Usually, Ed waved back. Which meant something was up. Under normal circumstances he would have followed them, hung out, and indulged in a little small talk. Instead, on this occasion, he figured he'd wait it out. All these years, and he could read his bandmates like a book: Alan pretending that Rob didn't exist, Ed behaving as if he had one foot in another world, Tyler bearing a shield of perpetual stoicism, and Danny displaying his usual belligerence, especially if he was on the wrong side of a bottle of whiskey. There were nights when Rob wondered how they managed to pull it all together and play. But play they did, and their fans adored them.

The sun was beginning to fall behind the hills and more people were arriving backstage, despite Ed's decree of keeping everything to a minimum—no families, no friends. Rob saw a cameraman wielding a digital Red, and a group of girls talking to their social media guy. He heard the beginnings of a powerful riff coming from the stage platform, courtesy of Alan's guitar tech, and he watched the girls' faces light up. Others had stopped what they were doing; everyone was listening. The night was already taking shape and it reverberated through his bones.

He spotted Ed's nosferatu companion, over by the line of trucks. The guy was wearing a black duster jacket that hadn't been cool since the eighties. Rob stared, and there was a moment of eye contact before his hand began to ache, the one he'd earlier placed against the trailer. He wriggled his tingling fingers, while common sense whispered platitudes. *A mild discharge of static.* He shrugged it off.

The music stopped. They were done with the sound check, and soon enough he saw Danny striding across the compound toward the motorhome, his hair plastered to his scalp, his T-shirt already dark with sweat. Rob downed his second can of soda and followed, and he almost made it before the fireworks started.

"All that *embracing the dark* shit. What the fuck was Ed thinking?"

No sign of their frontman inside the vehicle, but Alan had his feet stretched across the aisle and was trying hard to look bored under the weight of Danny's verbal assault. "Superstitious, Danny?"

"Sure. Where is he?" The drummer made an attempt to push by and get to the rear of the coach. But the guitarist had other ideas and sprang to his feet.

"He's resting. Leave him be." He was taller by a good six inches, and normally it wouldn't have mattered, but as Rob sprang on board to stop the altercation, he couldn't help notice how frail his friend had become.

"Hey Danny, let's go grab something to eat." Two seconds of silence, maybe three; the heartbeats counted it out, hard and relentless. "C'mon, let's go."

"Sure. Why not." Danny's shoulders slumped, and Alan's lips twitched in triumph.

Rob breathed a sigh of relief when they were back outside, until Danny hesitated. "I'm not hungry. I think I'll go take a nap in Tyler's Winnebago."

"Look, about Ed. You know how protective Alan is—"

"Hey, I wasn't going to kick his ass. I'm tired of all the devil crap, and those two shutting themselves off, is all."

"Okay, I'll walk you over, and keep your screaming fans at bay."

On another occasion, Danny would have laughed.

ℰℛ

An hour later, Rob wandered the compound, feeling restless. They were starting to let the crowd in. He could hear the excited murmur from beyond the stage and it added to the tension. Everyone was here to see the band. No additional acts for this particular show—it was stripped down, lean and mean, despite a logistics crew hauling the equivalent of a small town into the foothills.

Over by the row of eighteen-wheelers, he thought he saw Ed's strange companion skulking around again, and he realized he'd never popped the question to Danny. *Why the extra trucks?* Probably because it hadn't seemed important, and yet...

"Rob."

He turned, and saw Ed standing behind him; still wearing his street clothes—black jeans and the ubiquitous black T-shirt— still looking like a rock star, despite his middle age. The guy bled cool, and always had. Even at the start of their career, when the press had discovered Ed's real name carried an aristocratic title and their street cred had plummeted. Those same journalists had subsequently unearthed an ancestor who'd dabbled in the Occult, and all of a sudden Ed, and the band, were back in business.

The Occult, or devilry, as Danny called it, had proved an irresistible lure, one that Ed and Alan had subsequently woven into their lyrics. And while Tyler hadn't cared one way or another, Danny had expressed his opinion right from the start. "One day, it'll bite us in the ass, just you watch." And there had lain a bone of contention for the next thirty years.

"How is he?" Ed continued.

Rob closed the distance between them, and seconds later he'd subconsciously matched the other man's posture. Hands in pockets, eyes on the dark hulk of the stage rising into the night. No need to ask about the subject of discussion. "You noticed."

"He looks ill."

"He'll be fine. He's just a little pissed about what you said—"

"He thinks I'm courting demons." He placed a hand on Rob's shoulder. Narrow fingers dug into the flesh beneath his shirt. "All these years, and I've never had to worry about what *you* believed."

"You mean the devil worship? Come on. The fans love it, but—"

"I want you to promise me something."

"Sure."

"Whatever happens, take care of Danny and Tyler. Will you do that?"

"Why? What's going on?"

Ed winked, broke away, and set off toward the motorhome. "Too late to explain. Not long now, before the show begins."

Unease rippled in Rob's gut. "What's inside the trucks, Ed?"

He received no reply.

※

Time.

He hung out, stage left, and wallowed in the excitement borne by the crowd. It was like sitting on a roller coaster as it headed slowly, relentlessly upward, toward the first big drop. As always, they'd kept the platform dark and Tyler was opening up with his signature bass riff. In seconds, he had the entire auditorium clapping along with him, and when Danny joined in with a rapid, staccato beat, the crowd howled its approval.

He saw Alan waiting to go on stage, a slender ghost, his hair completely white. Alongside him, Ed had changed into a tighter pair of jeans and now sported a ragged bandana and a tangle of fetish necklaces. Their stage manager counted them down, and Rob watched them disappear into the gloom. He couldn't see the crowd, but he could feel them, lying in wait, bleeding anticipation. And when Ed's dark, eerie chant erupted through the mike, they fell completely silent, until three, two, one—Alan's guitar kicked in, and the lights ignited with a blast of pyrotechnics. The crowd began to scream, and goose bumps ripped across Rob's flesh. It happened on every single gig and it never got old.

He stood and watched, with a wild grin on his face, while his right foot tapped out the beat. No need to worry about Danny. He and Tyler were in the pocket, right from the get go, and after two numbers, Rob began to lose count. He was caught up in the magic, the same as everyone else.

Until eventually, the earlier headache began to reassert itself.

The sound faded momentarily, and he had to catch himself before he stumbled and fell. Confused, and unused to feeling faint, his heart began to hammer. He saw Danny, surrounded by a blistering array of percussion instruments, still true to his word, no sign of his earlier tremors, so Rob took a step back, followed by another, while he tested his balance. Maybe he needed a breath of fresh air; God forbid he was getting too old for this.

"You okay?" A young woman pushed a bottle of water into his hand. Her attention was back on stage before he could answer.

He took the water bottle; it felt inordinately cold in his hand as he headed for the stairs. And as he took a seat on the top step, he heard the pounding rhythm and soaring guitar cease, and Ed's sotto voce lyrics take over—

"—and when the light is gone,
when your heart's undone.
Give into the fight, and—"

Rob began to hear the chant, this time coming from the crowd—

"—take
the
night—"

It gathered momentum and made him feel dizzy all over again.

He downed half the contents of the water bottle and rubbed his eyes. Back stage, the lights were dim, but he could see the regimented line of eighteen-wheelers, an odd, ambient haze surrounding the furthest. He blinked, and figured he was imagining it. But instead of disappearing, the strange light clung to both truck and trailer like a halo. There was movement, too, over by the vehicle's liftgate.

An inner alarm began to ring. He forgot all about his lightheadedness, and began to descend the steps. When he reached the bottom he reckoned he could make out two, maybe three people standing alongside the truck. No sign of anyone else. Barring security at the gate, he figured most folks would be watching the show.

Under normal circumstances he would have walked over there. He had every right. But on this occasion it felt prudent to be cautious and not announce himself, despite feeling an utter fool as he crept toward the nearest vehicle. Damned if he knew what was going on, but some primordial sense of self-preservation was telling him to be careful. Better still, to turn around and stay away altogether.

Instead, he crept from the shelter offered by the first truck and approached the second. His headache wasn't getting any better, but at least the dizziness had gone. Logic put up a good fight, and reasoned they were hiding some kind of special effect to mark the end of the tour. And sure, Ed or one of the others could have told him about it, but whatever. The sooner he got this little mystery squared away, the better.

He approached the radiator grille of the third truck and his stomach did a loop-the-loop. He doubled over, clamped a hand over his mouth, and barely managed to silence the accompanying grunt of pain. He dropped to one knee, and from there he could see beneath the cab where the odd glow appeared larger and was spreading across the compound, intent on reaching the rear of the stage where he'd only just left.

He heard the whine of the liftgate motor. He wanted to stand, in order to get a better look, but his gut had other ideas and kept him crouched low like a frightened cat. The band was still playing but he barely heard them. He was caught up in an inexplicable net of terror, and inside, he railed at his own cowardice.

Voices.

They spurred a reaction from his joints and he scrambled to the fourth truck, still staying at the front of the line, away from the action taking place at the rear. He stopped, and risked a quick glance along the gap in between the trailers. He saw the nosferatu guy, bathed in a sickly, lavender light. Rob immediately ducked out of view, heart hammering in his ears, lungs bellowing short and fast. There was something inordinately bad about this, but what?

You're being an idiot, common sense told him. *Imagine what Danny would say, if he could see you now. Why don't you just stand up, walk over, and ask—*

His headache grew exponentially until something popped inside his skull. His upper lip grew wet; he tasted blood. He dropped to the ground and crawled beneath the fourth tractor. In the foreground lay a forest of axles and tires, and beyond—

The light was undulating, fluttering around a vague, domed object. *It's a prop; something for the show, you fool.* And perhaps it was, but why did its proximity fill him with such belly-clenching horror? Flat on the ground, he pushed himself along. His nose still bled, pebbles of gravel tore at his shirt, but he felt so much safer with a roof over his head.

A jellyfish, he thought, as he scrambled for a better view. It looks like a stupid, giant jellyfish. Directly below it was the tall, pale guy. A ridiculous notion, but Rob expected him to sprout fangs at any moment.

He struggled, and attempted to claw back some modicum of reality. Here he was, hiding like a trapped rat beneath one of the trucks, while some of the crew unloaded props for the show. Meanwhile, another jellyfish floated into view, presumably from the sixth vehicle. The light they exuded increased, and Rob became temporarily blind. When his sight returned, he could see the objects gliding up the steps toward the stage.

Come on, they're balloons. It's like a Floyd gig.

Rob's gut told common sense to shut the fuck up. Right now, his hands were trembling as hard as Danny's. But instinctively, they stopped when he saw movement to his right: one of the drivers, climbing into the fifth vehicle. He heard the gates closing, and the engines kicking in. The sixth big rig began to pull out of its parking space.

Rob retreated; he crawled from his hiding place and crept back along the line. His heart beat loud and hard, and he didn't realize the music had stopped until he was part way across the compound and he'd remembered to breathe.

Way above him, the light show on stage had shifted, had become an easy, hypnotic pulse of purple and blue. No sign of Ed's voice and Alan's haunting guitar, or Tyler and Danny's pounding rhythm. Behind him, the two trucks were now on the move, the first already pulling beyond the security gate.

He headed toward the steps. The stage was the last place he wanted to go, but all he could remember were Ed's last words, about taking care of Danny and Tyler. He began to climb. Dread took a firm hold on his spine. Common sense had pulled an about turn, and was now expounding the virtues of retreat. But it wouldn't take long, he assured himself. A short, steep climb, go grab the guys, and get the hell out.

His manner of ascent was markedly different than the last. This time he stayed low, he used his hands and crawled up there like a lizard. Almost there, he risked a peek. He could see back-stage—the manager, the girl, a few of the others—backlit into silhouette. They were silent, immobile, like a row of cardboard cutouts.

He rose onto the platform. Another few steps and he could see their faces, blank, staring beyond the stage, into the arena where the two glowing objects hovered like a pair of giant Por-tuguese men-of-war, their tendrils hanging low, brushing the heads of an enraptured, silent audience. He saw a sea of hands, holding smartphones aloft, allowing thousands of electronic eyes to bear witness, while their owners were hypnotized by the gargantuan, fluttering creatures above their heads.

"Christ," he heard someone mutter. It was one of the techs, coming out of his stupor.

Rob ran onto the stage. Alan was staring out into the arena, a beatific smile on his face, while Ed was on his knees.

"What the fuck did you do?" He grabbed Ed's shoulder and spun him around.

The vocalist rose to his feet, slow and deliberate, and Rob didn't like the look on his face. "I bought us a few years of fame and fortune, my friend, and now it's time to pay the price."

The objects were now floating toward the gates, and the au-dience was beginning to follow. He saw Tyler slowly, reverently, placing his bass guitar on its stand. He looked about ready to join the crowd.

Ed punched him hard in the chest and got his attention. "Do as I told you. Take the others, and run!"

"You crazy bastard." Rob turned and reached Tyler before he jumped off the platform and broke his ankles. "Don't look!" It was the only advice he had to offer, and he began to haul the bassist toward the rear of the stage. Out in the arena, he heard someone scream. Not everyone was enraptured.

Danny was hunched forward, surrounded by snares and high hats; he had his eyes screwed shut. Rob had to kick some of his instruments away in order to get at him.

"Move! Now!" He grabbed none too gently at Danny's stringy arm, and with some effort, began to push and pull his two bandmates toward the exit. Memory threw him a left hook, and reminded him of similar acts back in the day, when fights had broken out and Danny and Tyler had been too drunk to move. Some things never changed.

He risked a glance toward the front of the stage. There was no sign of Alan. Had the cowardly bastard abandoned them and made a run for it? Or had he jumped, as hypnotized as the rest? Beyond the platform, light still danced and the crowd seethed; it had become a unified, living thing. Rob stared in horror as he recognized Ed, now aloft, in the grip of one of the luminous tendrils. He hung high above the arena floor—limbs spread, head reclined—the consummate sacrificial lamb. The sight was breathtaking, part of a spectacular show, until the creature tightened its grip, and a thick, wet rope fell toward the crowd.

Ed let out a blood-curdling scream.

Immediately, the mood shifted. Panic raised its head, and a single crack of gunshot rang out, closely followed by another. But it wasn't enough, and despite a number of people dashing for the emergency exits, most continued to follow the glowing creatures in an orderly fashion, out of the auditorium.

Rob kept on pushing and hauling, and by the time they had descended the backstage stairs, Tyler appeared to have regained his wits.

"The Winnebago," he yelled. "It's our only chance."

Danny was also coming around, and all three began to run across the compound. The lights were back on, and others were wandering about, looking dazed, as if they'd recently awakened from a very bad dream. One of the security guys was standing alongside the wide-open gate, bewildered and scratching his head.

They reached Tyler's R.V. and climbed aboard.

"What about the others?"

"Fuck the others." Danny was leaning over one of the banquettes, staring out of the window. "This is all their fault." He glanced toward Rob. "And what the fuck happened to your face?"

"Hang on," Tyler said. He was in the driver's seat, already gunning the engine.

Rob wiped his bloody nose, sat down, and did as he was told, while their bassist pulled an adroit reverse in the cumbersome vehicle. He shifted gears, and drove at speed through the gate. A gravel track took them to the right of the arena, where they were able to look down on a sea of vehicles. And in their midst—

The two missing big rigs were parked with their trailers facing the turnstiles, their doors open, their tailgates down, allowing the crowd to climb aboard, while the two giant glowing creatures hovered above. They had shifted shape, had become elongated, almost squid-like. Their fronds now floated horizontally, and ethereal limbs were reaching out, beckoning everyone forth. Directly below, men and women were scrambling over parked cars, trucks, and SUVs. They had one single purpose, and that was to climb aboard the trailers. A trick of the eye, perhaps, but it appeared dark within, terrifyingly dark, as if those who'd already climbed inside had been swallowed, and had taken any available light with them.

"It's like the fucking Pied Piper." Danny's face was pressed close to the window, looking out. Rob wasn't about to argue with the metaphor. The music had brought these people here, after all.

He narrowly avoided head-butting the window as Tyler took a sharp right to avoid another vehicle. Not everyone was caught in the net. Others were trying to escape, too, their tires kicking up dust until it was difficult to see much of anything.

A few more turns, then Tyler pulled off the road and drew to a halt. Danny was now in the front passenger seat, and while Rob's attention had been captured by the chaos, the drummer and bassist had decided on a detour, and instead of becoming log-jammed with everyone else, along the only road that led to the highway, they'd doubled back and climbed higher.

"What the hell?" Rob regarded them as if they'd both lost their minds.

"I'll tell you what the hell." Danny stabbed a finger in his direction. "And don't tell *me* you didn't know this was coming."

Tyler had risen, and was pulling the latch on a nearby cupboard. A door swung open, revealing the contents, and Rob could only stare, dumbfounded.

"You hear the gunfire? The screams?" Danny continued. "It's our fans, fighting for their lives. They came here to listen to our music; they came here for us. And Ed Visalli—the fucker—sold them out. We're going to rescue them, and put an end to it."

Still in shock from what he'd already witnessed, and grappling with what Danny was suggesting, Rob helped unload. He knew Tyler and Danny sometimes went shooting together. He'd poked enough fun at them over the years, so he guessed he should have been prepared for the blistering array of weaponry now being spread across the table, hitherto tucked discretely within the confines of the R.V. Three pistols, a revolver, two assault rifles, a sawed-off shotgun, and enough ammunition to hold off an army.

Tyler handed him two heavy 9mm pistols, and gestured toward three spare magazines.

"But how do we know this will work? You saw those things. If we get close—"

"We're guessing you're immune," Tyler said. "So you can watch out for the two of us."

"He's fucking tone deaf. That's why he's immune." Danny was grinning like a maniac, while cradling a short-barreled Heckler and Koch as if it were a baby and he the proud father. His hands were steady as a rock.

They got out of the vehicle. Ahead, at the base of an easy incline, lay the parking lot, and in front of the auditorium gates, the trailers were gaping wide, all the better to swallow the world, while their mesmerizing heralds floated above, still intent on gathering their flock. Rob wondered what would happen once they'd gotten their fill. Perhaps the doors would close and the tractors would come to life, and they'd drive off toward Hell, or somewhere worse...

Danny jabbed him hard in the ribs. "Let's do this, and if I see Ed, or Alan, I'm taking out both those bastards." With a determined stride, he began to descend the slope.

Tyler was carrying a mean, long-barreled rifle in a manner that suggested he knew how to use it. "Dibs on Ed's guru." He winked at Rob. "Come on, man, let's take the night." He set off after the drummer.

No need to worry about Ed. Rob hung back for a moment and watched his bandmates as they reentered the fray. He had a pistol in one hand, another wedged in the small of his back. The night was young, they hadn't even completed their set, and here they were, with brand new instruments, about to finish the gig and perform an encore. Fear crawled through his vertebrae and whispered of his mortality, but he shrugged it off like an old skin. All those wasted years on the sidelines, all the bullshit and the excess. He was now back in the band, a full member, and about to do something good and right.

He caught up with his companions. And as they advanced toward the insidious play of darkness and light, Danny was already letting loose with his weapon, his posture energized, his rat-a-tat gunfire synonymous with the rhythm of his drums.

And the band played on.

Charles Austin Muir came straight off the Pork Chop Express to tell you a story about blood, guns, and golems. He's known a King Shit *or two, excepting his gracious editors, who previously published him in small-press magazines and anthologies such as* Cthulhu Sex Magazine *and the* Stoker-*nominated anthologies,* Dark Visions: Volume One *and* Hell Comes To Hollywood. *He says* King Shits *is about a war he lost inside his head. "It's for anyone fighting a phantom enemy. And for my dogs."*

KING SHITS

Charles Austin Muir

FOR CLAY HALLER, pain was another delivery. Like anything else he transported across thousands of miles of open road. It was a job, like driving 11 hours or calling his dispatcher or backing his 53-foot trailer into a tight dock. But unlike his other deliveries, pain was a secret load, a shadow operation within the one he got paid for.

His war against King Shits.

According to the Internet, a King Shit was someone who overestimated his importance. The seven men across the street were real big shots, if muscle defined importance. The blazing sun painted their torsos pink and copper, ridges and bands of armor forged with gym machines and steroids. To passersby they made a startling sight, quaffing from plastic cups and 40-ounce bottles in front of a bungalow. Not even old ladies and minors escaped their drunken taunts.

On the sidewalk, a hulking bald man from whom the others took their cue intercepted a black teenager. "What up, *nee*-gro?" His mock jive-ass falsetto shrilled across the street. Whatever the kid replied, Chrome Dome spat beer in his face.

Clay munched on a gummy bear, watching from inside his truck cab. He had been waiting on the light at the head of the street when he decided to investigate these Mr. Universe wannabes. They made quite a spectacle. Since parking on the side street catty-corner to the bungalow, he had seen them harass a woman in Daisy Dukes, menace an old Vietnamese lady, and yank the American flag off a drooling man's mobility scooter. But what he saw at the traffic light prompted his surveillance.

A scrawny, Jesus-bearded dude stumbled down the driveway, coughing blood. One of Chrome Dome's buddies—a Filipino who looked like Rufio from the Peter Pan movie, but with twenty-inch arms—tossed Jesus Beard in the bed of a pickup truck parked on the street. Three rounds of rock-paper-scissors ensued between him and a mop-headed kid wearing a lifting belt. Rufio beat Mop-head, paper over rock.

As Mop-head drove off in the pickup, someone shouted a line from the movie *Road House*:

"PAIN DON'T HURT!"

And Clay recalled another line about pain as he circled the block to his present position, a motivational saying, *pain is something*. He was still trying to remember it when the black kid stalked away, passing a dude wearing a scarf in the ninety-degree heat. Scarf Ace stopped before the Great Wall of Chrome Dome.

Clay zoomed in with binoculars. Chrome Dome gesticulated like a hard-sell personal trainer. Scarf Ace, ashen, shook his head, then pinched up a smile. He followed the others up the driveway through a tall wooden gate. His view cut off, Clay nibbled on gummy bears and waited.

Grabbing the binoculars again, he saw Scarf Ace stagger through the opened gate, sans neckpiece and bleeding from the forehead. Right behind him, Chrome Dome swept him up in a bear hug and dropped him into the pickup bed where Jesus Beard had been. Once again, Mop-head lost to Rufio's paper. Minutes later he returned—wherever he dumped Chrome Dome's victims, it was nearby.

Pain is weakness leaving the body. That was the saying. Marine Corps ad or something. Since King Shits were made of weakness, what would happen if he tested the axiom on Chrome Dome and Co.'s magnificent bodies?

Clay got out and crossed the street. A breeze stirred his hair as he walked past the neighboring houses. Eyes straight ahead, he felt the group push without touching him, a psychic bum rush of liquid courage and testosterone. They allowed him to pass, belching and carrying on, waiting for their leader to command respect. Finally a tank of thinly veiled muscle stepped in Clay's face.

"Hey man, wanna stick fight?"

Chrome Dome stiffened like a point man sensing danger, despite his hundred pounds over the thin, middle-aged nobody reflected in his gold Elvis sunglasses. To feed the man's beast of self-satisfaction, Clay shrank back a step.

"I, uh, well, I'm afraid I'm not really into blood sport."

Along with his buddies, Chrome Dome snorted. "'S'not like that. Gentlemen's rules. No head shots, no groin shots, no hitting when a man's down. Just for fun."

Fun.

As in, *pain don't hurt.*

"I'll even give you a free beer. Come on, Jim Carrey." Chrome Dome felt his alpha maleness now. Though people often mentioned Clay's resemblance to the actor, they didn't also chuck him in the arm with a gap-toothed grin.

"I do like beer..."

"Good man."

Clay followed Chrome Dome through the wooden gate onto a covered patio. He pretended not to notice the scarf folded in a corner, the abstract floor art made from Jesus Beard's sputum and Scarf Ace's head wound. Grabbing beers from a cooler, Chrome Dome launched into a prolegomenon on the art of stick fighting. "Have you ever watched the opening scene from *Rambo III...*?" Clay imagined his predecessors withering inside while Mop-head and another bodybuilder slapped each other with rattan sticks. The sight of the seven bare-chested, sweat-oiled beefcakes brought to mind a 'roided reenactment of the beach volleyball scene from *Top Gun*.

"No blood, no foul," Chrome Dome said. "But don't try anything funny. We go for arms and legs only. And if you spill any of these I get a free shot and vice versa." He swept his arm at the drinking containers bordering the patio. Clay gathered the "free shot" wasn't for refreshment.

"Not having second thoughts, are you?"

"Well—"

"Get us those sticks," Chrome Dome shouted. Taking his pair, Clay weighed them in each hand as if awestruck by their virility, dildos of impossibly manly proportion.

Chrome Dome flashed gap teeth again. "Ding-ding." Backing into a corner, he stared Clay down while a crony removed his Elvis sunglasses. Clay glanced at the eager-eyed behemoths crowding around the patio. He wondered how many men waylaid by Chrome Dome had had second thoughts and still wound up in Mop-head's pickup truck.

The kid threw down a fist and lost a third time to Rufio's paper. Mop-head cursed and stepped between the two fighters. He removed his lifting belt and raised it like a start flag. "Begin."

Twice, circling the ring, Clay flinched in anticipation. But he redeemed himself sidestepping a wild swing and tapped Chrome Dome's log-like upper arm. The big man retaliated with a backhanded strike that should have caved in Clay's skull. But Clay dodged the stick and smashed his against Chrome Dome's nose, spraying both men with blood.

"Carrey's a ringer," someone said.

Gurgling a war cry, Chrome Dome raised his stick, but the smaller man hooked around behind him.

Knifing his stick between Chrome Dome's legs, Clay ended the fight.

Chrome Dome fell on his face, convulsing around his sudden vasectomy. A hollowed-out, miniature watermelon filled with red liquid skidded onto the grass as his size-11 Adidas kicked out.

A phantom, a flicker of temperature behind Clay as someone charged in. He took Rufio out with a liver shot, then wheeled amongst the onrushing bodybuilders. Sticks arcing in the sunlight, Clay taught Chrome Dome's crew that pain hurt immensely. Mop-head fell last, beaten by wood instead of paper. When he was done, Clay drank in the sight of weakness leaving bodies, the suits of living armor now scattered and broken around the yard.

As the groaning men fell silent, other sounds arose. Birds chirping, dogs barking, children laughing down the street. Clay was always amazed at how tender the world could be in the aftermath of violence. He despised men like Chrome Dome who profaned life's sanctity, forced their will down the world's throat like some orally obsessed rapist. For their viciousness surpassing all other animals, he felt *they* should be raped. Yet Clay couldn't perform that function—his sex organs weren't wired into his will to break King Shits.

Instead, he found other methods of punishment.

Clay dropped one of his sticks and rolled Chrome Dome on his back. Then he took the hollowed-out miniature watermelon from the grass and cupped it to the injured man's drooling, gap-toothed orifice. Red margarita dregs spluttered from under the cup and mixed with crimsoned vomit. Holding the cup in place, Clay drove the other stick through the rind, impaling Chrome Dome's soft palate with blood-soaked rattan. He stopped when he had punched through the first cervical vertebra.

"My free shot," he said, and departed.

∾

A mile or so from Chrome Dome's bungalow, Clay stopped at a restaurant. He entered through the bar side and ducked into the restroom. He cleansed his face and hands. Then he waited. Moments later his bowels seized and he slammed the toilet seat back. Brownish, chunky liquid shot from his mouth and filled the bowl. He flushed and returned to the sink. He was lucky. Once he had pulled off the highway and barely clambered over the passenger seat to splatter the roadside. The last shadow jobs, he puked afterward even though he didn't eat much. It was as if conscience struck through his digestion, rejected his vigilantism through his gorge.

What puzzled him was that it tasted earthy, like mud. Clay washed up again and frowned in the mirror. He sat at a booth in the restaurant.

Since his Rebirth, he needed little food. But he still enjoyed the ritual, sitting down to a meal and "playing" at eating. Ensconced among objects dedicated to a single task. The plastic menu stand, votive candle, and salt and pepper shakers on his table were like the knobs, gauges, and caution stickers inside his truck—a microcosm where chaos didn't reach. As a young man he became a trucker to escape the world's noise, tumult, and disorder.

While he nibbled burnt toast and watched pigeons out the window, Clay forgot his gut problems and his war against King Shits. Then voices rose behind him.

"Yo cunt, I'm talkin' to you."

"Shhh, T, she'll hear you."

He had barely noticed them when he came in. The restaurant's only other patrons, two booths behind him. Talking about the waitress, the Kim Kardashian look-alike arranging silverware by the bar. The man was black and the blonde white woman wore short-shorts. A second woman at the table muttered something inaudible.

Then: WHAAAP cracked a fist on the tabletop. "I said, hey, BITCH, I'm TALKIN' to you."

The first woman said: "For God's sake, T, I'll get us some napkins. Just leave her alone, will you?"

"Fuck off, Iris. 'Sitcher ass down 'fore I smack you into next week."

Iris sighed.

Clay laid his butter knife next to the toast. He pitied Iris and the other woman. And he pitied the waitress. No wage was worth dealing with venomous shitheels like T. She deserved Employee of the Month for the way she was enduring his goading. Clay admired her swelling backside as she bent over utensils, moving so minutely she looked like her celebrity twin's wax double. Maybe she'd found the best way to handle men like T was to freeze like a squirrel before a large dog.

"The ho hears me," T said. "Right, ho? You hear me. Been hearin' me for the last five minutes and actin' like you Helen Mirren."

"I think you mean Helen Keller," Iris said.

"Whatever. Bitch better serve us."

"I think I've got some toilet paper in my purse," the second woman said.

"The hell for? Jesus, Betsy. Aiight. If that bitch don't come in ten seconds I'm goin' over dere and give her some a' big T."

Betsy said, "Actually, I've got tissues too."

"Ten—"

"T," Iris said.

"Nine—"

"Who wants some tissues?"

"Eight—"

"I promise they're not used."

"Seven—"

"T, please..."

"That was a joke. Come on, T, just take my—"

WHAAAP! cracked the fist again, this time on bone.

"Damn it, T!" Iris.

"Not a peep from you tricks. You wanted to use them tissues, girl, use 'em."

Betsy sobbed.

"Oh, NOW I got your attention," T shouted at the waitress. "Don't look at me like that, you deaf-actin' bitch. You stay right where you are. You just keep playin' with that silverware while I tear dat fat ass *up*."

Clay got up and marched toward the table. T, on his feet, wiped his knuckles on his jeans leg and scowled. "The *fuck* you want, you Jim Carrey-looking motherfucker?"

He was Clay's height, but beefier. Wearing a sleeveless T-shirt. A lifetime of urban desolation and rage exuded through his pores. Clay had read about pimps: Confused, desperate young girls fell for their promises of protection and prosperity and wound up drug-addicted, sexually battered, and often pregnant from their coercions.

Iris, the blonde, turned in her seat and gaped up at Clay as if he'd punched in the code for a nuclear missile launch.

T was out of the booth and swinging when Clay stepped inside and drove his fist into T's sternum. T's legs meant to wheel him back ten feet but the wall absorbed the impact and he slid to a sitting position on the floor. Iris yelped when Clay pushed her gently back to her seat. "But he can't breathe," she said. Guppy-eyed, T sucked at air as if fellating an under-endowed John.

The waitress said, "Holy shit," as Clay bent T over the table. He twisted the pimp's arm back and nodded at the puffy-eyed Latina between Iris and the wall. "Cover your eyes." From the plate of chicken fried steak under T's belly, he extracted a steak knife slathered in sausage gravy. He drove it into the base of T's neck, paralyzing him.

Iris shrieked. The waitress shrieked. Betsy shrieked, peeking through her fingers at T's blood leaking onto her French fries. Without use of his legs, the pimp was like a 200-pound dead fish.

"Napkins," Clay snapped. The waitress quieted down and did as told. Clay tore a hole in the napkins pushing them down the knife in T's neck.

"Here's your damn napkins. Have a nice day."

Iris gaped. Betsy shrieked again.

Clay left a hefty tip.

∾

The town was called Wanting. Population 94, a gas station, a general store. Nearest post office was twenty miles north, in Dayton. The Hallers and family dog lived in the old Wanting fire station. Mr. Haller, fresh from the military, worked in Dayton and dropped Clay at Dayton Elementary each morning.

This was Clay's first year there. Seventh grade. One day at recess, Chris Kezzlewick, an eighth-grader and the biggest kid in school, challenged Clay to a fight. When he refused, Chris made to tackle him and slipped. The nimble new kid dodged him all around the playground until a teacher stepped in. How he finally caught Clay came a week later, after school.

It happened on the forest road that led to the bus stop. Backed by buddies David and Quinton, Chris jumped Clay and dragged him into the forest. David and Quinton braced him against a tree in crucifix position while Chris pummeled him. A low blow dropped Clay to his knees. The sight of him kneeling, wet with tears, inspired the bully to relieve himself. Clay gagged on blood and Chris's copious piss, still in his captors' clutches, in Christ pose.

Dusk in those woods, pencil beams of sunlight stabbing through the murk of old growth. Next they turned Clay toward the tree and laid him face down. Dirt and pine needles sandpapered his cheek. "I said hold him!" Chris barked, behind him. Quinton's hand clamped down on Clay's wrist. The other boy, David, grabbed the other. "Don't move, Clay," he whispered, and it sounded like advice, like how Clay's father advised him where to place his thumb when he drove a hammer. "Hic," Quinton said, Quinton who always had hiccups because he ate like a famished dog, "hic."

Clay heard Chris unbuckle his overall suspenders. He was like some fat snake crawling over Clay now, breathing hotly. His hands found Clay's fly, pulled his pants down, underwear next, cold earth kissing his shriveled penis and indrawn testicles. Time stretched Clay on a rack of pain and humiliation. Then finally the nerve ends in his broken boyhood granted him mercy and he passed out.

He didn't tell his parents what had been done to him. Only that three classmates had beat him. His torment snowballed over the next few weeks when Chris Kezzlewick spread a rumor in school that Clay was a "homo." Even teachers looked at Clay like some sort of pervert.

How hatefully some of the boys called him names, Clay wondered if they, too, had been taken to those woods.

He grew so despondent that finally his parents moved from Wanting, population 94, to Los Angeles, population two-million-something. The Hallers took an apartment in a neighborhood where white, undersized, timid boys were singled out on the street. After so many Band-Aids and ice packs, Clay's dad enrolled him in a Kung Fu school in the building where he worked.

The instructor warned Clay that the training was monotonous and repetitive. Children want action, he said, big movement. Clay followed instructions and, a year later, not even three of his enemies together could beat him. He stopped coming home bruised and bloodied.

From then on, Clay avoided conflict. He made it a practice to treat others with kindness, compassion, and restraint. As his skills developed, so did his ability to find peaceable solutions. Trucking seemed a natural entry into the real world, a life of solitude and purpose. Sealed in the bubble of his semi, he reduced his chance of running into Chris Kezzlewicks and street toughs. Of course, he could never completely avoid bullies.

He was between shifts at a bar in Butte, Montana. Rowdy place. Friday night. A big man, like Chrome Dome but more fat than muscle, bumped Clay in passing. He turned on Clay and shoved him off his barstool. Clay reseated himself. Felt Big Man watch him. Didn't see Big Man's friend come up from behind and crack a glass stein on his noggin. Next thing he knew, two Big Men had him on the floor, working him over with steel-toed boots.

Visions of Chris Kezzlewick and his buddies flashed through his nerves. Chris pushing inside him, becoming part of him. Hic. Hic. Something in the brutal touch of his attackers awakened memories buried in his cells. Flipped a switch. Pain sloughed off Clay like old skin, and the kicks to his skull and rib cage, the commotion around him, passed through him like light through water.

Training took over. He rolled to his feet. Jabbed his fingers in each man's throat. Slipped outside them, gave one a liver shot and the other a knee breaker. Dragged them by the wrists out the front door. Training turned into something other than self-defense. Clay pierced eyeballs. Broke fingers. Stomped scrotums. As the men screamed, he no longer saw pain as an end to conflict but as the beginning of a conversation. A lesson in how much can be broken if he plowed the body deeply enough.

Brutalizing those men, Clay felt nothing. No rage or hate. He followed a script in his muscles, the way a predator takes down its prey. Witnesses gaped when, with an air of punctuality, he urinated on his victims. Even then he felt no pleasure, no satisfaction beyond a job well done, like delivering a load to his next receiver. Pain and humiliation, right on time.

He drove his rig the hell out of Butte, Montana. Next night, walking another town's streets, he followed his shadow. And he realized he felt no rage or hate because he *was* those things, a negative incarnation of the principles he had lived by. Clay Haller died under a rain of steel-toed boots. His body now was like the shadow at his feet. A resurrection, a Rebirth of opposites. Like the men he had beaten, shadows of power driven by fear and weakness. The world, nothing but shadows.

Time to stop running from them.

Realizing that, Clay shed biological imperatives like food and sleep. One night he watched a TV show about a golem. A magical entity formed from clay, like his name, unstoppably pursuing the mission it was made for. He'd never heard of such a thing, but here he was, like that golem, a monster created from pain and humiliation to give the self-crowned kings of the earth—King Shits—a taste of their own medicine.

But how would he find them?

How could he reach so many?

Then he realized the answer was parked right outside his motel room.

స్చ

Surfing the Internet on his laptop, Clay came across an item on cop killer Clint "Herc" Walker. Herc was well over six feet and resembled his granite-jawed, movie-actor namesake, at least in the mug shot. He was a hard drinker with a vicious temper. One night a deputy called on him, responding to a disturbance call. Heated by drink and bad poker hands, Herc bludgeoned the lawman with a bronze sculpture.

Paroled after 25 years in prison, Herc was back in his hometown, the article said. Grimsbo, population 1,100, on the way to Clay's next pickup.

A temper like that, Herc might need talking to.

The temperature was in the nineties when Clay rolled into Grimsbo the next day. He checked into a motel. After weeks of napping in his truck, a private bed called to him. Curtains closed, A/C whirring, crisp sheets beneath him. Normally he didn't need but an hour of rest, but the bodybuilders and T had drained him. Drifting off, last thing he saw was Chrome Dome's gold Elvis sunglasses and gap teeth. *Come on, Jim Carrey.*

Next thing he knew he was sitting up straight throwing punches in the dark. He kept on going till he realized he was hitting air. Shadow boxing.

"Clay!" The voice so close, like Chris Kezzlewick at his neck, while he ran the shower. Dripping wet, Clay shot into the bedroom, found no one.

He peered through a gap in the curtain: Dusk out. He got dressed. Stared at himself in the bathroom's cracked mirror. He threw back the toilet seat, puked mud and conscience.

"Clay!" Calling him from the door of the town watering hole.

Where he thought he might find Herc, or get a lead on him. The sort of place where peanut shells littered the floor and deer heads lined the walls. Business was good. Clay sat near some old-timers and scanned the bar's patrons. Was someone stalking him, or was he getting twitchy after so long at war?

"Smashed a bottle on a guy's throat, Herc did," an old-timer said, wiping beer froth off his mustache.

Minutes later the legend himself walked in. He reminded Clay of rock stars who hadn't seen the limelight in decades, a jarring contrast to yesterday's portrait. Herc looked old, stooped, and milk-pale, with wispy white hair and pinkish eyes. "Kidney cancer," a Stetsoned old-timer said. Only his height and granite jaw identified him as the hard-drinking juggernaut who beat a peace officer to death twenty-five years ago.

Grimsbo's drinkers, they patted him on the back and made way for him. Herc smiled through the welcome reception, eyes downcast, edging through the crowd. He nodded at Clay, the small-town courtesy, as he brushed past and joined a frumpy redhead sitting in back. A waitress served him ice water.

While this went on the old-timers talked about how Herc had become an ordained minister in prison. Clay was about to leave when Herc's spitting image—from the mug shot—lumbered through the door.

"Even worse than his old man, back when," the mustached old-timer said.

Herc Jr., it seemed. Slightly shorter, but beefier. A few more steroid injections and he could be with Chrome Dome's crew. He looked to be in his mid-twenties, wearing a baseball cap turned backward and a skintight T-shirt that said "Dick Diesel." Grimsbo's drinkers, they greeted him and his entourage with a scant nod.

"Them dogfights up at Sin Mountain," the Stetsoned old-timer said.

"What up, Meat!" The shouter had fewer pounds on him than the gold chains he wore over his Yankees baseball jersey. Meat gave Pencil-Neck a fist bump and led his entourage to the bar.

Clay guessed none of them could fight. Not Meat, who measured toughness in biceps' peaks. Not the tousle-haired Frankenstein's monster showing Pencil-Neck some karate block. Not the mutton-chopped beach ball rolling his head around like a boxer and shrugging to a twenty-year-old rap song he picked on the jukebox.

A row of shots was set before them which they raised toward Herc. "Welcome home, dad!" Meat downed the shot and slammed the glass on the bar top. His father, at the rear of the bar, nodded gloomily.

The buxom waitress drifted over to Clay, smelling of gum and perfume. "Sorry to keep you waiting, hon. Can I get you anything?"

"You can get *me* something, Maria," Meat shouted before Clay could speak. "Name of that fake casting agent who creampied up your slit. Nice video on Jizzhub!"

Maria made a face like she was counting to ten, then stormed off, crunching peanut shells underfoot.

Clay had seen enough. He nodded to the old-timers and went back to his truck. He parked in a lot across the street facing the bar. An hour later Meat and his boys climbed into a black Escalade. Clay tailed them through side streets and turned off when they entered a cul-de-sac. He cruised the area a few minutes, then parked on the street facing the cul-de-sac. The turnaround was packed with SUVs, pickup trucks, vans, motorcycles, and hoopties.

Rap music boomed from the biggest house on the dead-end street.

Somewhere behind the house, dogs were crying.

❧

The party raged into the early dawn. All night people went in and out of the house, drinking and smoking. No one seemed to notice the black 18-wheeler parked down the street. Clay saw nothing of interest until just before noon, when a van cruised past his truck and stopped on the lawn.

Meat came out to greet it. Through his binoculars Clay watched the van's side door open and a Mr. Universe wobble out with two leashed pit bulls. The driver, a gorilla in a cutoff army jacket, went to the back of the van, grabbed a bucket of 5/8-inch steel chain and followed Meat and the dog walker into the house.

Clay wiped his binocular eyecups on his shirt and mopped his brow. Hot as hell out.

Hotter in his chest, where an old memory caught fire.

Old Man Gardner. He was why Jimmy, Clay's dog, his twenty-pound Boston terrier, never made it to Los Angeles. Clay wanted to blame his father for not mending the fence where Jimmy escaped, but in the end it was Old Man Gardner who pulled the trigger, who blew the back out of Jimmy for crapping in his yard. Jimmy and his butter-soft coat, how he leaned on Clay's chest and rolled his eyes up for attention. Old Man Gardner left the dead dog on the road outside his gate. This he declared on the Hallers' front steps, reeking of cheap whiskey and self-satisfaction—Chrome Dome's granddaddy with a shotgun.

Clay sweated in the cab, thinking about Jimmy.

About the pit bulls.

What the old-timer had said: "Them dog fights up at Sin Mountain."

He'd read about dog fighting. How so-called "dog men" beat and starved the dogs to make them more aggressive. Set them loose on "bait" animals, like cats or smaller dogs, to sharpen their taste for blood. Chained them in cages or steel drums.

Drowned, strangled, shot, or beat against the ground the dogs who lost or were severely injured. He'd seen pictures of dead dogs in trash bags, blood-spattered walls. One image, the combatants locked like Kama Sutra lovers, bleeding all over each other, the bottom dog staring at the camera, infinitely rueful.

The pit bulls from the van, they looked like they'd survived such a contest—barely. Faces like meat tossed under a lawn mower.

Clay's dad didn't let him see the body when he picked it up, but that didn't help. For weeks he kept picturing Jimmy raped by Old Man Gardner's shotgun. Post-traumatic stress disorder, he didn't know the term back then, he only knew that what happened to him in the forest transformed how he would see life forever. Every show of strength, every flaunting of power, extended the rapist's will, thrust a knife through the core of him.

These trailer-trash King Shits, these gangster-wannabe King Shits, these muscle-bound King Shits with their chains and cages and fight rings. They were rapists of the animal kingdom, Old Man Gardner with a god complex.

Thinking about Jimmy, Clay realized his war was only his boyhood self still searching for redemption. A mask he hid behind, like the truck he spent so much time inside, a mask he couldn't take off.

He should have driven away, he should never have followed those men from the bar. What he had seen today, written on those pit bulls' faces, was the end of every King Shit in Grimsbo, population about to drop. Even Meat's three-story headquarters looked like a King Shit house.

Blue sky, a day promising to top a hundred, a day for glaring sun and bug splats on the windshield while he tore up the interstate, and Clay sat in his truck picturing the .50-caliber Desert Eagles he kept in a briefcase. Nasty way to send a man to the underworld.

Little by little, like dawn breaking over years, Clay had made peace with death. He knew that for every man he hunted, he

brought death closer. Chasing down foes in his 18-wheel King
Shit chariot, Clay the ultimate King Shit, a King Shit killer of
King Shits. That, he'd learned in his forty-one years, was how
the universe worked. When shadows peeled back the world and
all you saw were your sins, reflections of reflections, mirrored
to infinity. Whether he died in the next few minutes or lived to
fight another day, a King Shit killer was coming for him.

So bright the sunbaked asphalt, so sour-sweet the gummy
bears he chewed while he stared at the opened side of the van
where the pit bulls had been. Thinking about them, about Jimmy, voices from the past chattering in back of his mind—and
then:

"Don't move, Clay," David, still thirteen years old, making
Clay wait after all those years. Some wisp of foreknowledge
sampling from his worst memory, guiding him into another
dark forest.

Minutes later, Meat pushed out the front door.

"We're heading out," he said to someone inside.

So that was why Clay's subconscious urged him to wait. Meat
would lead him to Sin Mountain.

Clay watched over twenty people stream out of the house
and disperse into vehicles. Beach Ball and Frankenstein's Monster and Pencil-Neck. Van Driver and Dog Walker, minus the
dogs. All dudes except for a skinny blonde in a Jeep convertible,
turning out of the cul-de-sac onto the lane intersecting with the
dead-end street. Clay started the truck and followed the proces-
sion to a freeway on-ramp. A mile out of town Meat's Escalade
turned right onto a rural road and led the convoy up a steep,
golden hill. Clay followed, hanging back so he'd have plenty of
room to pull over when they reached their destination. This
turned out to be the gravel drive of a big white farmhouse.

The only house within miles, atop a blaze of arid land known
as Sin Mountain.

Through his binoculars he scanned the trees and fence ob-
scuring the property. Place like that, they didn't want you crapping in their backyard.

"Well, Jimmy," Clay said, "looks like we're finally gonna pay back Old Man Gardner."

⟨⟩

Over the top didn't begin to describe them—the hand cannons under his armpits. Bought from a guy on the Internet at a reasonable price, if your tastes included signed Picassos and rare Scotch. Over four pounds each, ten-inch barrels, titanium gold finish, custom gold-plated grips featuring a black dog with glowing red eyes. Hellhounds. The seller gave them funky names from Welsh myth, but Clay just called them Jimmy One and Jimmy Two.

So far, the Jimmies had only shot pumpkins. The exit holes so big Clay could put his fist through them.

Truly a King Shit weapon, how a shotgun blast must have felt to a twenty-pound dog taking a crap. Clay's "Rebirth-day" gift to himself came with the custom double-gun shoulder holster and leather briefcase. The seller had a flair for the cinematic.

Long shot of Clay driving across open field, his big rig black as dreamless sleep, a shadow growing under the eye of the sun.

No plan, just jump down, point, shoot. Dumb as Chrome Dome's stick fight technique, but it was now or never, he should've been on the road by now.

The Jimmies hungered for more than pumpkin seeds and pulp.

Anyway, probably the whole town knew what Meat's gang was up to and all they worried about were law agencies spread too thin for some Podunk animal abusers. Last thing they'd expect was a battle with a long-haul truck driver.

Sin Mountain: Dead land ready to catch fire and a King Shit party at the far end. It could have been some farmer's family picnic, people drinking beer and standing around or sitting in lawn chairs. But then there was that pavilion-type thing back by the trees, like a wooden carport built around a large, empty sandbox. Cars parked around it, except where a wooded trail sheltered some dozen dogs chained to overturned barrels, some lumped on their sides, not moving.

Now Meat kicked something in the sandbox—the fight ring—something too small to see over the low wall. He went after it and kicked it again, while a buffed shirtless dude in a doo-rag jerked the chain on a pit bull in one corner.

Those Hellhounds, they were the most decadent purchase Clay ever made, but he knew someday he'd need them.

His last delivery: Pain and humiliation, right on time.

He rolled in slowly, honking thunder as if the crowd were kids pulling on an air horn. By now everyone was watching him. The skinny blonde grabbed something from her Jeep, and Meat vaulted from the ring, striking his best college bouncer pose in a gap between parked cars.

Clay killed the engine. Jumped down from the cab. Heat and parched grass smells hit him.

Meat's sleeveless T-shirt said, "Do you even lift, bro?"

"Jesus," Meat said, "it's Jim Carrey—"

BAWWWWMMM!

That was Jimmy One, and the blonde on Clay's right fell behind the Jeep, shotgun pointed skyward.

BAWWWWMMM!

Jimmy Two barked left at a redheaded guy reaching down the back of his jean shorts. Blood and entrails showered the tree behind him. He collapsed next to a dog lump.

Someone screamed. People ran for cover. Jimmy One followed Pencil-Neck around back of the ring, turned his face into a menstrual explosion. Guy in a feathered pimp hat had made it to the trail when Jimmy Two turned his chest into a porthole, flashing a gap in the trees ahead.

Hellhounds.

Silly, Clay knew, giving his guns personalities like he was a hit man in the movies. But then, they were his muscle, weren't they, like Chris Kezzlewick had David and Quinton? And this was *his* rape stage, *his* forest.

These metaphors of male potency, extensions of the rapist's will, forcing themselves on people where holes weren't supposed to be.

Clay heard screaming inside the ring. Doo-Rag had let the pit bull loose, and instead of charging Clay it seized in its teeth the thing Meat had been kicking. The small, fawn-colored dog thrashed in the pit bull's jaws. Flopped behind the low wall and swung up again, its cries so shrill Clay felt his blood turn to crushed glass. Jimmy Two put down both animals with a bullet through the pit bull's muzzle.

To the right: *Chakk-chakk... BOOOMMM!*

Beach Ball with Blonde Girl's shotgun, nicking a corner post of the ring.

Jimmy One and Jimmy Two tore into him, his third-trimester gut.

The spent cartridges whipped past Clay's face.

Hellhounds.

"Anyone else?" Clay pointed them, side by side, at the crowd. "What about the house?" to Meat. "Anyone in there?"

"No, man."

BAWWWWMMM!

Jimmy One saw Cell Phone Guy before Clay, scalped him with his sunglasses sitting on his head. He crumpled out of sight between a Corvette and a Buick.

Where he fell came a ring tone: *Wocka-wocka-wocka-wocka-wocka-wocka.*

Pac-Man, eating.

Meat hit a biceps shot, palming his forehead.

"Everyone put their hands up," Clay said. "No one uses cell phones. Sure there's no one in the house?"

"No, man. I mean yes. Fucking yes." Then, "What is this? You were parked back at the house, right? What the hell do you want?"

"I want your people to get in back of my truck."

"What for?"

Jimmy Two pointed at Meat's chest. The part that said, "bro." "Everyone but you."

Meat scowled. "You got six rounds left."

"That's right."

Not including the magazines in his cargo pants pockets.

"Anyone want a piece of my Jimmies?" Clay shouted.

Wocka-wocka-wocka-wocka-wocka-wocka

Meat said, "You're something, man."

"Someone should answer that phone."

"But you said no—"

BAWWWWMMM!

"Five rounds left," Clay said, Doo-Rag, still in the ring, pulling his hand back from his right boot.

"You want something to do, big man, open the trailer door on my truck. Let's go, people, form a line."

Doo-Rag went to the back of the truck. Meat next, everyone else filing after him, hands raised, the Jimmies tracking them. "Used to drive long haul myself." Doo-Rag, arms akimbo, stared up at the empty trailer. "It's going to be hot as hell in there."

"Like those dogs you got chained."

Doo-Rag turned to Clay. "Man, those are dogs, four-legged things, this is what they do." Nodding toward the ring. "You, you're killin' *people*."

"People, huh?"

"Heat stroke, starvation, whatever you got planned—it's *monstrous*."

Doo-Rag was a monster himself. Chiseled, in olive-drab fatigues and black boots—Clay hadn't forgotten the piece hidden in the right—tattoos on front and back like giant monk script, illegible against the dark canvas of muscle. Knife scar where the right pectoral tied in with the front deltoid. Bad dude, but he had a point. Clay with his Hellhounds and trailer-cum-death-chamber, like some King Shit Nazi...he hadn't thought what to do when the shooting ended.

"Two-legged things," he said finally. "Okay, here's what we do. First, everyone else gets in the trailer. Then you shut the door and go to the ring. You, too, *bro*," Jimmy Two pointing at Meat, "and you three, Frankenstein." Jimmy One waving at the sleepy-eyed brute near the back of the line. "Let's go, people, this isn't a spectator event."

Dog Walker, last inside the furnace, glared down at Clay. "You're gonna get your ass whupped."

Doo-Rag shut the trailer door.

Meat, Doo-Rag, and Frankenstein's Monster went to the ring. Clay approached from the trail side, the chained dogs eying him, ears forward, brows furrowed. He kenneled his Hellhounds, removed the shoulder holster and laid it at his feet. Stepping over the low wall, he took a spot behind the dead dogs, conjoined at fang and face. The warning he'd fired at Doo-Rag through the low wall had ripped a hole in the pit bull's underbelly, pooling guts and sticky stuff on the killing floor.

Lined behind the dog mess the three men exchanged glances.

"Two-legged things," Clay said. "This is what we do."

The ring was infernally hot, a miasma of old contests and fresh kill. Adrenaline gripped the men in place, unsure how to triple-team their opponent.

Two-legged things, doing what four-legged things do.

Outside the ring, two-legged and four-legged things dead or dying under the eye of the sun.

Hop-stepping around the dogs, Clay threw a shield up—elbows and front knee covering groin and midsection—and blocked Frankenstein's Monster's roundhouse kick. He chopped the man's windpipe, then bent his arm back so that Doo-Rag, knife flashing from the right boot, bayoneted a corpse. Doo-Rag threw a hook around the human obstacle in his face. Clay straight-arm blocked it, released Frankenstein's Monster, and stabbed his fingers in Doo-Rag's eyes.

For an instant he felt a phantom, a flicker of temperature behind him as he finished Doo-Rag with an elbow to the temple. For an instant he became a child again, back in the nightmare forest. Chris Kezzlewick snaking over him, breathing on him. "Don't move Clay." David's ghost, freezing him.

For an instant. Then he felt a death grip on his shoulders, and teeth tear into his earlobe. Clay twisted with elbow out, knocking Meat off balance.

Stepping around the dog mess again—now a heap of four- and two-legged things—he thrust his fingers into Meat's mastoid process.

Clay didn't fight people, he dissected them.

But now training turned into something other than self-defense.

Like his Hellhounds, he hungered.

A four-legged thing descended on Meat's sprawled body. A digestive tract in the guise of a man, boiling with pain and blood lust. There was a script to it, the feeding. Clamp hands around prey's neck. Smell its fear. Bite off piece of prey's upper lip, like tearing open a bag with your teeth. Create an entry point.

Clay spat out the chunk of lip—Meat wouldn't be able to pronounce "lip" after that—and bit off pieces around the mouth. Speech, what two-legged things do. Then he bit off part of the tongue—Meat wouldn't be able to pronounce "tongue" after that—chewing, rending, working through the eyeballs, ears, nose cartilage. Meat kicked and flailed under the onslaught, shrieking like the little fawn dog. He tried to whip Clay with the chain around the pit bull's neck. Clay slammed Meat's arm down, then dug his fingers in the nose holes of the face beneath Meat's face.

Monstrous.

It was a red skull Clay left when he walked back to the truck. "An eye for an eye," an ear for a face—a face for every animal that had perished where Meat now lay screaming.

Meat, he hadn't even bitten all the way through Clay's earlobe. Mistake like that would have cost him if he'd been one of his own fight dogs.

Clay started the truck.

He hit the accelerator, Meat crawling toward him, at the front of the ring. One arm over the low wall, teeth gritted in that anatomy-chart face—at the last instant he jerked up and seemed to blink his lidless, eyeless eyes. Then the semi plowed through him and the low wall and clove the roof down the middle, slamming to a halt on the jumble of dead men and dead dogs in a cloud of dust and falling wood debris.

Clay dropped down from the cab, sunlight pouring in where holes weren't supposed to be, yelling and pounding and bumping inside the trailer where people weren't supposed to be, and the floor around the tractor unit streaked with gore. Meat's body laid out in a smeary contortion of limbs and spine and what looked like a raw ham hock with hair and, "lift, bro?" more identifiable than the rest of him sticking out under the fuel tank. It reeked of slaughter.

End of the line.

Clay staggered out of the ring where he'd entered, strapped on his shoulder holster. Doleful eyes watched him. He was always amazed at how tender the world could be in the aftermath of violence. Odor of gunpowder, corpses, and spent cartridges strewn around the field and the chained dogs gazing at him like sad mothers. Sun blazing down on the rape he'd made of man and earth.

Sin Mountain, Clay's masterpiece.

I'm everything I hate, he thought.

He wandered through the carnage.

I've turned my truck, my sanctuary, into a weapon. I've turned Jimmy into a weapon. I've turned my body into a weapon. I've disgraced my teacher, my art. And I've walked on four legs, I've tasted the flesh of my enemy.

For the second time that day, Clay dropped to all fours.

His bowels seized, and conscience shot from him like it would never stop. It erupted with the force of weeping held back for years, racking gut-sobs of inestimable loss. His body wept for itself, every monstrous thing he'd made it do and remember. A river of death, sludgy and putrid, flooded from his mouth, bounteous and indifferent to his torment. He clawed the earth, hands soaked in mud and the pain of men, until only drool came and he fell on his back. Blue throbbed in his vision, death sky-written where no birds soared.

Then he slipped into dreamless sleep, black as the prison where Meat's people cried out.

એજ

Wocka-wocka-wocka-wocka-wocka-wocka
The Pac-Man ring tone jerked Clay awake.
Wocka-wocka-wocka-wocka-wocka-wocka
He got to his feet and drew Jimmy One.

Something caught his eye near the trail. A figure fleeing toward the woods. He had the impression it wasn't clothed, and didn't know how to run. Arms flailing, feet slapping down like clown shoes. Body of a lanky, undersize youth, how Clay was when he was twelve, swallowed by another forest. Only this stranger seemed eager, even desperate, to plunge into the woods.

No visible musculature, no butt crack, no hair even. The dogs saw it, too, watched it dash past, this live mannequin. They looked at Clay then. Their eyes said, *What are you going to do?*

He holstered the gun. Whoever it was could have attacked him and opted for escape. His gut—what he hadn't puked, what was left of it—told him he had a mess to clean up.

Morbid curiosity made him check the mountain he'd heaved, only to find the ground was clean. Not a scrap of Clay's moral bulimia remained in the puke-yellow grass. Like the first time Jimmy barfed and when Clay brought paper towels it was all gone, Jimmy licking his paws.

The chained pits, still staring.
What are you going to do?
The sun was still high in the sky. He hadn't been out for long.

He had five rounds in the Jimmies and four magazines in his pants' pockets. Thirty-three rounds left, and seventeen people he'd counted climbing into the trailer. Some pounding the wall now. They would be his last kills. Then his war was finished. The massacre here, it would expose him and he deserved to die as he lived, by his own vengeance. Jimmy One would get the privilege, nasty way to send a man to the underworld.

Sin Mountain, Clay's self-portrait.

His swan song.

He fed the Hellhounds fresh magazines and went to the back of the truck.

Then he heard tires and saw a car coming toward him. He stepped out to meet it, Jimmy One drawn. The pounding in the trailer doubled. People shouted. Through the cracked, dusty windshield, Herc met his eye.

Clint "Herc" Walker, the cop killer, the minister. "I'm unarmed," he said, ducking out of the Trans-Am. Eaten by disease, he looked like a dweller in darkness, not meant to stand in the sun. Eyes even pinker and more rat-like, skin like the transparent membrane of an onion.

"You'll want to raise your hands," Clay said.

Herc did.

"You shouldn't have come here, Herc."

"I recognize you. You were at the bar last night."

He'd gone to the house to talk to Junior again, he explained. Son thought he was just another born-again, a Bible thumper. Which he supposed he was. Finding the place empty, he drove out here, a place he swore he'd never visit.

"I've heard what my son does." Herc glanced at the chained pit bulls. "What I saw at the house was bad enough. Is he in there?" He nodded at the trailer.

Clay shook his head.

Herc peered past him, into the ring. Swallowed.

He wanted to try one last time with his son before he called police, he said. Kept calling Scott, Junior's childhood friend. Scott usually answered.

"I don't suppose he's in there, either," Herc said.

"Try him again."

Herc dialed a number.

Wocka-wocka-wocka-wocka-wocka-wocka

He sighed.

"I was hoping I could save him. My son. But he didn't want to be saved. Him, Scott, the whole gang, they were headed for a reckoning. And you gave it to them. What you've done here, it's..."

"Monstrous," Clay mimicked Doo-Rag.

"...something I might have done, if I hadn't spent my youth busting heads in bars." Herc smiled with one side of his face, the way some men smile after crying.

"I used to be a vindictive SOB. You may have heard I killed a man. A deputy. I was drunk that night, but I'd been fixing to kill him anyway. He stole the woman I loved."

Every brawl, Herc said, was practice for when he would finally kill that man. Then all that rage, all that vengefulness, caught up with him. God forgave him for what he did, but his body wouldn't. That was God's price, he said, giving us vessels that can't sustain our darkest impulses.

"God will forgive you for what you've done," Herc said. "Even I can forgive you. It's not too late for you, if you stop now. Let those people go. Kill me instead. I'm dead anyway. Take my car. Disappear. With your health, the sky's the limit. Save yourself. Be born again. All that rage and vengefulness, it doesn't have to kill you."

"Maybe, not yet," Clay said, approaching Herc. "Still, you've given me an idea."

He pressed Jimmy One to Herc's forehead. Kidney cancer, nasty way to send a man to the underworld.

"Maybe not even the sky's the limit," Clay said.

And pistol-whipped him unconscious.

Herc, the born-again, saving people.

Offering them redemption.

Clay got in the Trans-Am. Keys were in the ignition. Rosary draped over the rearview mirror, Christ on a chain of death and rebirth. And Clay's face in the glass—a mask of puke and gore, a mask he couldn't take off.

Monstrous.

ༀ

Flight 1580 to Athens landed right on time.

Dressed in the airline's new blue uniform, Shem Steward rolled his luggage through the jet bridge into the airport terminal. He bought coffee and gummy bears and took a table in the nearest food court.

Not that he needed caffeine, but he still enjoyed the ritual, sitting down with a cup of Joe and "playing" at drinking.

In his down time, sightseeing, Shem had learned something about Greek myth.

This ancient king of Thebes, Laius, gets rid of his baby because an oracle told him he's going to sire a son who will kill him. Years later he's traveling to Delphi in his chariot when he encounters a young man walking toward him at the crossroads. Young man won't give way, so Laius tries to run him off the path. Young man gets so enraged he kills Laius. Young man turns out to be Laius's grown-up son.

Moral of the story: Don't be a King Shit like Laius.

The young man, he's got troubles, too.

When he gets to the crossroads, he's already upset. The oracle tells him he's going to kill his father and marry his mother. And because he's a King Shit like his dad, because he won't share the road even with a sovereign, he fulfills the prophecy and doesn't realize it till way after.

Moral of the story: Don't be a King Shit like Oedipus.

For some of you, life's a Greek tragedy: You can't accept how things are, but if you think you're the one to fix them, you're begging for a beat down.

You're a King Shit.

You're doomed.

And doom followed Shem from city to city. Guts, Shem called him, born of horror and disgust, the shadow of the shadow of a man named Clay Haller. Shem sort of looked like Haller, only bald and mustached, his co-worker was sure he resembled someone famous but couldn't place it. Guts knew, though, Guts who stalked Shem across oceans, who needed no food or rest. Guts, like that golem Haller became long ago.

That day on Sin Mountain, pointing a gun at a dead man's head, Haller saw he would take his war to the skies, where no birds soared.

Since then the puking stopped and Shem Steward felt strong as ever. Like Guts, biding his time, studying his adversary, a creature of rage like his creator, waiting to give the King Shit a taste of his own medicine.

Till that day of reckoning, Shem had work to do.

That job in a bubble thirty-thousand feet in the air, a microcosm where chaos didn't reach. Annoyances yes, but only the occasional Laius type. Like the guy in 26C, wouldn't stop texting while they readied for takeoff. Ignored Shem's request three times, finally said he'd stop when he finished his message and not a moment before.

His skintight T-shirt said, "Contents of this shirt may cause choking." Woman next to him, staring at something across the aisle, had a dime-sized bruise on her throat.

Sitting at the table, Shem popped a gummy bear in his mouth and watched people go by. His coworker waved and rolled her luggage over.

Her name was Absolut, like the vodka, like Shem's attitude toward guys like 26C. Cocoa-skinned, big dark almond eyes, men rubbernecking when she sashayed down the aisle. His partner in coach sashayed toward him now, back from the deli with a mountain of curly fries she placed between them.

"That's right, you don't eat," she said, "except for those things." The gummy bears. "How do you do it?"

"I put one in my mouth. Then I chew it."

"Haha. I mean, how is it you never get tired or hungry?"

"I'm just made funny."

While Absolut dug into her fries, Shem noticed someone watching them across the food court. Guy his size, wearing black jeans and a matching hoodie. He slunk off behind the magazine rack, and Shem knew from experience he was gone, like a shadow into a shadow, the shadow of Athens, the shadow of a chariot waiting at the crossroads.

26C walked past, pausing mid-text to give Shem the stink eye. The woman next to him on the plane trailed after him, hauling their carry-ons.

Shem watched 26C go into the men's room.

"That jerk," Absolut said. "The whole flight he kept looking at me like I was naked. Where are you going?"

"Restroom," Shem said, standing. "I have a delivery to make."

"Eww, Shem. Too much. You've just put an awful picture in my head."

Shem smiled with one side of his face, the way some men smile after crying.

"Tell me about it."

To writer Tim Chizmar, the life of a long haul trucker always looked zen, as if truckers don't choose to drive, it chooses them. He sees it as a life that only a select few will understand. Since graduating from Edinboro University with his BA, Tim has written and sold many short stories and screenplays. When he is not writing, Tim is a film director, comedian, and producer living in Hollywood, CA or at least that's where he is until the road calls to him...

CARGO

Tim Chizmar

MY NAME IS LARRY AND what I'm going to say doesn't make much sense. I'm currently quite fucked. I know that. I'm just hoping that maybe you can help me—see I don't belong here, *nobody* does. This is insane. But the money was too good for me to ask any questions. I never should have looked in the back. He *told* me not to look—what I saw—wasn't right—it wasn't right. But I'm getting ahead of myself here. As I said name is Larry and I hope you can help me.

I've been a truck driver for as long as I can remember. Since I got Lucy Jane Parnell pregnant in the 11th grade with what would be our first son. In my years as a king of the open road I've dealt with all the standard bullshit from lot lizards and bend-over Billys at truck stops to white line fever, raging slabs, and more. I felt there was nothing I couldn't deal with. That's why when I took the meeting with my new employer I accepted the job without hesitation or any questions. There'd never been a problem I couldn't deal with. My own will always being stronger than that of an asshole I'd run into or a surprise I'd run into on the road. I'm sure some of you men get what I'm saying here, swig of beer for the working man! Am I right? You're goddamn right I am, Sure, there were red flags and, maybe, if I'd had more schooling I'd have seen it coming. But I'm a tad bit hardheaded and that's just how I've always been wired. Besides, it's hard to pay bills with hugs, kisses, and good intentions. Sometimes you just need a risk to get your blood pumping.

For me that risk came from this fat little Hawaiian shirt-wearing S.O.B. that said he had a job for me to run some cargo out to Erie, Pennsylvania. Truth told, I was just pleased to see that a response to that ad I put up at the Laundromat lead to some real cash. What he wanted to do was for me to transport a "black load" or "dark load" or as he put it to my face a "don't touch/ don't look and we won't have to have problems" load. His beady little eyes stared holes into me and he stressed how important this was to my future. Before that meeting I'd only ever heard of this Hawaiian shirt fella before in passing whispers from other drivers at trucks stops, tough men telling tales of his mystery jobs and solid pay, and long ago I'd decided that having never met him suited me just fine. Still, sitting across from him in the doughy flesh with his eyes twinkling at me, my mind wondered what this was really about.

The whole thing had a mafia/mob feel about it and it's not something I wanted to be associated with long term. Hard to raise your family behind bars, besides I've seen too many guys end up in the slammer for something even more innocent than this. Who knows what I was being asked to run, guns, drugs, dead bodies?! Still there was that thrill of risk that anything could happen once I was on my way. The more we talked the more I felt a stirring, a strong feeling that I wanted my own personal story to share at biker bars when the boss man in the colorful shirt's name came up in conversation. Dammit, at that moment in my thinking I knew that he had me sold on the idea.

The boss man said his name was Tim Chizmar. He wanted this mystery load done—yesterday. Ten hours to drive and a deadline by a man who doesn't like to be kept waiting. I tried to tell myself this was a one-time thing and to look on the bright side. Hell, there was no snow or ice and for October I couldn't ask for better conditions. So there was that. He had said I'd be driving a Western Star, I remember how he had eyed me up and added that it had an automated manual with 12 speeds and 4 reverse. He had asked if I could handle that. I was used to all this and told him so.

He made a few more things very clear to me at that meeting, in between sloppy bites of his barbeque wings and talking with his mouth full, shooting bits of meat in all directions—fucking fat slob; even now, after everything that I've experienced, I still remember his words, "You don't look in the back of your truck. You don't question the cargo. You just deliver the goods and when you get there you don't look at who unloads it."

He continued, "Half money up front, the other half when you return, you *do not* look at what is in the back, *ever*. We understand each other?"

"We understand each other." I had lied. Truth was I just wanted to get it over with anyway. The gross little Hawaiian-shirt Man eyed me up and dabbed his mouth with a napkin before continuing with all the details of my drive. I looked at the purchase order, the guy who bought this drive from Chizmar was Eric Miller.

Who the fuck is Eric Miller? I remember thinking.

ew

In a few days' time I kissed the wife and kids goodbye, left her some advance money from the job, picked up the truck from where the Hawaiian-shirt Man said to meet him, and I hit the road.

You're still with me right? Good because I'm not fucking around when I say I need you. There'll come a point where you see how my future depends on you. I'm desperate and scared and... and...I'll calm down. You need to understand. I'll explain.

ℰↄ

So I'm driving this truck and it's okay at first, my Dwight Yoakam tunes are playing and I'm living the dream. Cars drive by with kids, fists raised, pumping their arms for me to toot my horn, I do it and they are happy. Cars on the road make room to let me pass and flash their high beams to let me see for merging better. I was just thinking this would be a breeze when I noticed the shadows on the floor of the cab thickening. They collected like a living thing. They pooled and splashed around my feet, thick like oil. It crawled up my legs like millions of wriggling worms.

I tore my gaze away from the eerie darkness that wasn't darkness and blinked into the blinding light of the setting sun. All was normal outside my cab, but inside the darkness crawled ever higher. I felt slimy, as if I had been dipped in sewer muck. Funny how my kids enjoyed things like seeing Ninja Turtles skateboarding through sewer drains in cartoons, I'd seen that shit on their TVs and warned them that it isn't all fun; it's turds, piss, and garbage down there fuckin' hell it's not a place to eat pizza those stupid heroes in a half shell, my ass. My rant made my kids smile, they'd laugh missing the solid points I was making but anyway, I digress. My body was all of a sudden very gross and tainted by something not good, something wrong.

First it showed up under the steering area by my feet squishing and splashing about and it was thick like oil. I knew it wasn't a leak just like I knew this whole thing was madness. The stuff smelled like an old bookshop full of very old pages. I remember how the smell brought back my childhood memories. How as a child I would wait for my grandma, she would continually scour the stacks of moldy old papers. Her forever searching, I forever bored. It was so weird. But the truck ran fine and I had a load to deliver so I shrugged it all off and kept driving.

Maybe this was a symptom of something, of what I didn't know. Maybe a weaker American would stop but I thought I was stronger than that. I'd told myself that I'd see a doctor about this whole thing once the load was delivered and I could afford to see a doctor.

It wasn't much long after I decided to ignore the oil thing that I first heard the knocking coming from the back. It had to be loud and powerful for me to hear that all the way in the cabin.

KNOCK KNOCK KNOCK KNOCK KNOCK.

You have no idea how pissed off I was. I turned the radio up but it was as though the damn pounding turned up too. I was one fucking second away from pulling that truck off the road and into a tree just to stop it. Between the creepy crawly slimy feeling all over my body, the old book smell, and now this knocking...

KNOCK KNOCK KNOCK.

I was going out of my mind. That's no bullshit readers—this is a straight shot from me to you. Swatting my legs to stop the blackness I began to panic. I'm not too strong to say that—shit what would you do? The smell, the books all around me, ink and pages, I couldn't take it. I just didn't have time for any hocus pocus bullshit. I pulled over to the side of a very busy highway. I got out and staggered a few steps. The pounding still rang out. I had no time for this, not on my job, not in my life.

KNOCK KNOCK KNOCK.

A car sped past lighting up the night for a moment as it blew past. I watched them drive by as if in another world.

KNOCK KNOCK KNOCK.

I don't know how I got back to the hatch. It was like waking after sleepwalking. My hands were on the handle. That's when the pounding inside stopped. There would be no more secrets. It knew where I was. I would break the rule, the one rule I was given. Chizmar would be pissed but I was eating the apple from the Tree of Knowledge. I needed to know. I lifted it. As the gate rose, I heard typewriter keys clicking. The WORDS. They washed over everything.

Such brightness all around.

The papers, the cuts.

Where's my arms, my legs, my face?

Where's my dick?

Where am I?

Now I'm just here. HERE. Not that I'd believe any of it anyway.

I'm another missing fuckhead, why should you believe me?

☙

Here's why, there's life and there's death. I know things in here. I miss my family. I miss life. I'm not a creation. I was there and now there's *THIS*. Whatever *this* is, I can *see* you. No not like some author's creative fucking angle bullshit. I see you. I really do. I goddamn see you right now. You are holding me in your hands. I can see who you are and what you want. I see you. Stop reading *right now*. Go on, I *dare* you.

I thought so. See. I'm really talking to you right now. Please don't leave me in here. Don't leave me in this book. I'm scared! It's lonely in here...

You don't believe me. I can prove it to you. GODDAMN IT! Look at the facts. Tim Chizmar and Eric Miller! I bet that bastard Chizmar took credit for this story huh? Says he wrote it? Nah he absorbed it. He knew I'd look in the trailer, he knew it! Miller edited it too huh? Look at the cover. Miller was the guy I was taking the load to!

I was the load, I was the cargo. They knew all along...

They used me. This book is full of crushed souls and broken dreams... I will prove it to you... I have to... Don't leave me in here, it's so cold...

Edward M. Erdelac is the author of eight novels including Andersonville, Coyote's Trail, *and the* Merkabah Rider *series. Various summer vacations spent gallivanting up and down the United States with his parents as a kid instilled in him a fascination with the open road and the people who traverse it, and he still prefers the trip and every odd stop along the way to the getting there. To this day he appreciates the various men and women who cut loose on the air horn in response to his frantic pull string gestures out the back window, and encourages his offspring to do the same. Born in Indiana, educated in Chicago, he lives in the Los Angeles area with his wife and a bona fide slew of kids and cats. His other works can be found at* http://emerdelac.wordpress.com.

CROCODILE

Edward M. Erdelac

GWENDOLYN COULD NOT ENTIRELY SUPPRESS the girlish shudder that began in the pit of her stomach and somehow spread through her torso to the tips of each extremity as Brendan took her hand in his and led her toward the forest.

Brendan.

Her dark angel.

Her Peter Pan.

His hand was cold, as if scoured by a winter wind, though it was a sultry August evening after a rain, the remains of it rising as steam off the moonlit pavement and hanging in the air. Yet despite his coldness, wherever he touched her, warmth spread as if kissed by a noontime sunbeam.

She followed him. She would follow him anywhere. Particularly tonight.

She was reminded of the first time he had taken her hand and led her like this into the wild night.

❦

Like any night, she was working the counter at the Pizza Hut in the Happy Joe's Rest Stop on the edge of town, that sprawling neon and flickering fluorescent complex situated alongside the I-10 like an island of light in a dark delta, always busy with the roar of the big trucks, always stinking of diesel. Haley, the cashier, interrupted the looping Merle Haggard music to announce the vacancy of another shower.

So many big-bellied men leered at her from behind their whiskers across the counter she had ceased telling them apart. Though they came from every corner of the country, they were almost all one. One hairy, endless flannel and mesh back cap parade of Skoal chewing, pig-knuckled fathers, so like her own; inappropriate, unmannered, too loud, and overpoweringly male.

Noodler, as she mentally called the man who had approached her in the parking lot at the end of her shift while she sleepily rode her tired feet to her Honda may well have *been* her father for all either of them knew. Daddy had climbed up into the beaded seat of his Peterbilt when Gwendolyn was four, sent his rig groaning down the driveway, turned the corner, and never looked back.

The only impressions she still had of Noodler were the same sort of dull, musky, beer sweat feelings she'd let pass over her like inclement weather every six hour shift for the past two years.

Ron, her assistant manager, had warned her time and time again never to clock out and head to her car without having him come along, but Ron looked at her the same way so many of the customers did. Never mind his non-threatening clean-shaven face and pitiable acne scars. When he walked her to her car she felt just as uncomfortable. What was the difference between Ron hanging back in the name of chivalry to watch her ass and some forty-year-old pervert directing a tobacco-stained grin squarely at her tits while he ordered a greasy personal pan and a suicide?

The employees parked their cars at the edge of the lot behind the pumps. Happy Joe's required that so there was always ample parking for the endless array of customers stopping by on their way to somewhere else.

Those were the people that interested Gwendolyn. Not just the hot young guys (pickups and sports cars) and the young couples (U-Hauls), or the contented, slow moving retirees (Winnebagos or blinding, silver Streamlines) but even the families, the beleaguered fathers trying to hold down the spasmodic little kids, exploding with energy after having been confined to the minivan for untold hours, while the haggard looking mothers ordered from the menu and didn't look at her once. She extrapolated their lives by the music she heard drifting from their cars, the Kenny Chesneys, the Rihannas, the Wiggles.

Categorized as they might be, these were people with lives. Commitments, responsibilities, they might have, but they were free. They moved on and never returned.

Not like her.

Not like the truckers.

Happy Joe's Rest Stop was their home. Gwendolyn's even more so. The truckers lived out of their vehicles, but at least their scenery changed. She spent most of her life right here at this counter, wishing for something, anything to happen.

Beyond the ringing pumps were the line of employee cars, and beyond that, the rows of glittering rigs, maybe a small light in a sleeper now and then, maybe on occasion a burst of wheezy laughter or a four letter word, but otherwise nothing but the incessant rattle and roar of trucks arriving or departing, the hiss of brakes.

That was the overnight parking, where the drivers slept and woke at all hours, dreaming maybe of their destinations, always leaving, always returning.

There were women who moved among the trucks. Lot lizards. Hopping from rig to rig, tucking wrinkled dollars into their animal print bras or their garish bags, stinking as if they rode between the exhaust stacks, women who smelled of diesel machines and were little more than that, really.

There was no way Noodler could've mistaken Gwendolyn for one of those. She still had her Pizza Hut shirt on, her stained black apron over her shoulder, her tennis visor.

But he put himself between her and the handle of her car door, jutted his narrow hip out and blocked the key hole.

He wasn't fat like most of them, but he had one of those foam and mesh hats, so dirty she couldn't read the phone number for the garage it advertised, the frowning brim frayed in bursts of green thread. He had on a black Jack Daniel's T-shirt, the white writing like an old time epitaph, and tight black jeans fastened to his waist by a huge yellow enamel belt buckle, an unfurling Gadsden flag with the coiling rattlesnake. Don't Tread On Me. Boots. Not cowboy boots, heavy, treaded workmen's types with steel toes, like tanks on his big feet.

She couldn't remember what Noodler said to her. She could only see his teeth and big round eyes in the dark. She tried to push past him, but all of a sudden he was all over her, hissing in her ear, hard, rough hands on her arms, body bulging against her, pushing her against the car.

His face was prickly and scraped her neck. He smelled of liquor.

Her favorite story growing up had always been Peter Pan. Her mother had told her her name Gwendolyn was like name of the girl from the story, Wendy.

She could not help but equate the trucker to a pirate. He sneered, and he was dark, and rough and strong and drunk, just like one of Hook's crew.

That was when he had appeared.

Brendan.

Her dark angel.

Her Peter Pan.

Noodler was off of her suddenly, jerked away as if someone had hooked his belt to the back of one of the departing Freightliners. He slammed against Ron's Nissan and fell to the oily pavement.

Noodler came up with something shiny in his fist, sharp, like a lion's tooth made out of steel. She heard it click as it opened.

He jumped up to his feet, lunging. Her savior was just a boy her own age. Slight and short-haired, the back of his neck very white and clean. She saw the trucker's knife disappear into his stomach, heard the sound it made punching through his skin, tearing his shirt.

She screamed, but it was muffled, her own hands flying up to her mouth to stifle it.

The boy didn't fall. He swiped his hand down as if to brush the offending weapon away, and she heard another sound, a crackling. This time it was the trucker who screamed. The knife clattered on the ground, the hand twisted horribly, hanging loose at a severe right angle from his broken wrist, like Noodler, the pirate from Peter Pan with the backward hands.

The boy's other hand shot out and caught Noodler by the throat, the fingers pushing together hard enough to pinch out the scream.

He lifted the bigger man up with one spindly arm and brought him down hard on the hood of Ron's Nissan Sentra, hard enough to crack the windshield and dent in the metal. Then he sprang up and straddled him. He put his other hand to Noodler's throat and leaned in as if whispering a secret.

The only sound Noodler made was when his heels battered and scraped at the hood of the car. His arms swung at the boy, dealing hard blows to the side of his head with his good hand (the other flopping grotesquely at the end of the snapped wrist) to his neck and ribs. The boy didn't even flinch. The flailing arms weakened and fell to clawing, then surrendered all effort completely. His limbs twitched as they dangled over the edge of the Nissan, and the boy straightened, just as a car swung away from the pumps.

The headlights briefly illuminated him as he reared back.

He was as young as Gwendolyn, and more beautiful, with ivory, blemishless skin, unmarred by any body hair that she could see. His loose red shirt was partially unbuttoned, revealing a narrow, lean chest. He had an angular look, a narrow, sharp face, and dark eyes. His hair was brown and neatly trimmed, the natural waviness barely constrained.

He stared at her from beneath a downturned brow in that moment, and she saw his lips were bright red with blood, as were his abnormally long teeth. But she wasn't scared. She felt the first flutter, as he touched her with his eyes.

She knew right away what he was.

She had read all the books in the break room, in the car before and after work, in the secret place of her room. Lestat and Edward Cullen had long ago supplanted Peter Pan in her girl's heart. Just like she had prayed as a girl for Pan to float into her room and lead her past the first star on the right, now she would every night amid her pink bed sheets wish to see a pale, longing face at her window beckoning her to step into the dark.

The headlights turned their attention back to the entrance ramp and he moved. She heard the hood of the car groan and pop as his weight was lifted.

"Wait!" she called, breathless. "*Please* wait!"

A shadow moved and became the boy. The blood was gone from his lips, and his teeth, still sharp, but nowhere near as long. Had she imagined it? He was so close. Vampires moved faster than regular people she knew. His eyes were like a wolf's. His nostrils flared like those of her pet rabbit Bunnicula, taking in her scent.

"You know what I am?" he asked. His voice wasn't deep, but it wasn't a boy's either. He could be a hundred years old, she knew.

She nodded, unable to even say it.

"You're not scared?"

She shook her head. She was only scared he would leave.

She couldn't smell him. He had just fought and killed a man and there was no sweat. His hair wasn't even mussed or damp. He wasn't breathing.

She smiled, thrilled.

He smiled back. His teeth looked completely normal now.

"Your teeth..."

He drew his lips closed, as if embarrassed.

"No," she said, touching his lips with her fingertips, feeling the thrill of it deep within. "I love them. But..."

"They only come out when I'm..." he shrugged, letting the words trail of meaningfully.

She nodded, understanding.

He had the face of an angel. A dark angel.

She felt something ice cold close around her hand and looked down. The blood in her palm grew warm and shot up her arm, filled her cheeks. She trembled at his first touch.

"Come with me?"

She nodded.

They ran off through the maze of silver trucks, into a new and wild night, newer and wilder than any night in her life.

She was not afraid with him. He had killed to protect her. She would do anything for him.

But that first night, he didn't ask for anything.

He held her hand tightly, and they walked, along the road, through the fields, and down the dark streets of town, for hours and hours.

And they just...talked.

But the things they talked about!

She gushed a lot, babbled out to him her whole life story, all her daydreams, her secret surety that some of them were real, her boundless delight in vindication. When she was finished, she begged to know his story.

He told her his name was Brendan, but that he had once had another name back when he'd been mortal, "in Bible times." He told her he had come from a wealthy family of merchants. He had befriended a young Roman soldier named Messala who one day rose to the position of provincial governor. When the Romans had marched into his city, Brendan and his mother and sister had been standing on a roof and accidentally knocked a loose piece of tile down into the street. The tile had hit Messala and, for the offense, Brendan had been sentenced to slavery, chained to an oar on a warship while his family was imprisoned in a Roman dungeon. During a sea battle with Egyptians in which their ship was sunk, he had saved the life of the Roman captain and been freed, then granted Roman citizenship in gratitude.

Soon after he'd learned that his family had died of leprosy while he'd been away. He renounced his newfound citizenship and instigated a revolt, leading an army of gladiators to the palace of his former friend. He ran him down with a chariot.

As he told her this, tears spilled down Gwendolyn's face. What tribulations he had faced! His life could have been a book itself, maybe even a movie.

Heartbroken by the death of his mother and sister, Brendan had for a time found love in the arms of a slave girl he had freed from Messala's house, but the gladiator army was ambushed by the Romans and they were both taken prisoner and crucified. He said the greater suffering had been to watch her die slowly just out of his reach. Then that night as he hung on a cross, a pale traveler had come upon him. Seeing he was still alive, he had taken a ladder from his cart, set it up against his cross and climbed it. Brendan had thought the man intended to cut him down and save him out of pity, but he had been a vampire, looking for an easy meal. A passing cohort of legionnaires had surprised the stranger, and he had run off, but not before his bite had infected Brendan. Using his new supernatural strength, he had agonizingly freed himself from the cross and hid from the rising sun in a cave.

He said he had never been back to Italy since.

"And that's why to this very day...I still hate WOPs," he finished, brushing her hair from her face. "You know, you remind me of her, the slave girl who died. She was a Trojan."

"What was her name?" she asked.

"Helen."

Then, as it was near dawn, he got up to leave.

She begged to see him again, and he swore that she would, sealing the immortal promise by leaning in and kissing her softly. It was like licking an ice cube, or a patch of snow. His breath smelled metallic, like the groaning pipes beneath the sink. When they parted from that first, wonderful kiss, her breath roiled in a little white cloud in his sad smile, across his deep dark eyes, brimming with a pain and sorrow that seemed to span the ages.

She knew right away that she loved him. Who else could she ever love?

Of course the police were waiting for when she got home, both because of her hysterical mother and because Ron had found Noodler's body sprawled on his car after locking up. Everyone was so concerned. She answered all their questions, said she'd decided to walk home as it was such a nice night, and hadn't seen anything.

A policewoman told her she was lucky. Noodler had been identified as a serial rapist, and no one was going to lose much sleep over him. Gwendolyn only shrugged, and thought of Brendan.

That night she dreamed of him in green tights and a red feathered cap, circling the ceiling of her bedroom and smiling down at her.

She went right back to work because she knew he would be there at the end of her shift. She knew because of the kiss.

And he was. Every night afterwards he met her in the parking lot. Sometimes they drove, mostly they walked, and talked, and kissed. He told her all about the long life he had lived all over the world, about all the people he had known through history, Genghis Khan, Abraham Lincoln, even Sherlock Holmes.

He held her till she shivered in his cold arms (but he was always a perfect gentleman, even though sometimes she sort of wished he wasn't), and he answered every question she had about vampires.

All but one.

"When will you take me to your lair?"

"Soon," was all he said, and drew her closer, taking in her scent with a flare of his nostrils, then kissing her deeply.

She always knew the time would come.

And tonight it had.

She had somehow woken in the morning knowing this would be the night they would be together at last. She had packed an outfit in the car and changed before she clocked out. A sexy black top with lace trim and her best jeans, her Victoria's Secret panties, the red ones with the matching bra. She had worn perfume for him too, something with a name she didn't dare try to pronounce in front of him for fear he'd laugh at her.

She'd brought condoms. She wasn't sure if she could get pregnant, but it was best to be safe. Did vampires cum? She didn't honestly care if he did get her pregnant. She would gladly have his child, but she didn't know how he felt and thought it best to wait until another time to bring it up. She thought she might like to bear his child before he made her a vampire, just in case vampire women couldn't have babies.

She wondered if Brendan's baby would be a half vampire, like in Blade.

If he was, would other vampires hate him? She would teach him or her to be good, to love both halves of him or herself, to accept him or herself first.

She had never thought to ask him about other vampires. Had he met any in his travels? There would be time enough to ask later. All the time in the world.

Brendan would turn her, and they could travel the world together, all three of them, see the things she never thought she'd see.

Well, everything except Italy maybe.

သာ

He led her through the trees.

They were in a forest preserve across the highway from Happy Joe's. She had never gone into these woods, never had a reason to. She wondered what his lair was like. Was there some dilapidated mansion deep within the woods that no one remembered? Did Brendan keep a normal house, or maybe a trailer with blacked out windows like the vampires in Near Dark? Well, she hoped it wasn't that. She hated that movie. She supposed she would be happy no matter where they were of course, as long as there was someplace they could lay down together, as long as they were alone.

She had waited for this so long it seemed. Really only a week, but it felt like an eternity.

She giggled. She didn't really know anything about eternity, did she?

But her dark angel, her boy that would never grow up, would show her.

She would be like Wendy if Wendy had decided to stay in Neverland. Gwendolyn had never understood why Wendy had gone home. She had been responsible for her brothers, yes, but Gwendolyn had always thought had she been in the story, she would have brought her brothers back to her parents, told them not to worry, then dove out the window with Peter and Tinkerbelle and flown in the ship back to Neverland. Anyway, with the Lost Boys to take care of, Mr. and Mrs. Darling had plenty of kids, and wouldn't have missed just one that much.

It was such a silly thing to be thinking about now. Fairy tales.

"What's so funny?" Brendan asked, looking back over his shoulder.

"Nothing," she said, beaming at him. "Are we almost there?"

"We're here," he said, drawing her into a moonlit clearing.

There was a creek nearby, which Gwendolyn heard before she saw. The silver light cutting through the trees dappled the flowing water like icing. She didn't see a house anywhere.

He put his arm around her and pointed.

Up the creek was a stone retaining wall, and in the wall was a great black hole, a dark culvert that trickled into the creek.

"Through there?" she whispered, laying her head against his shoulder.

"Mm hm," he said. "Come on."

He started to splash across the creek, felt her stop short, and frowned back at her. Then almost immediately his brow slackened and he hoisted her up in his arms, carrying her to the culvert across the water. She laid her ear to his chest and closed her eyes. No heartbeat of course. She couldn't stop smiling. She felt like a bride being carried across the threshold.

"What's that smell?" he asked, when they had reached the yawning black gap in the wall.

"I wore it for you," she said. "Do you like it?"

When she opened her eyes and looked up into his, her smile fell a little. He was grimacing at her.

"Have you ever sprayed perfume on a cat?" he asked.

"Once," she admitted. Her grandmother's cat, Jake, had come in from the alley one night reeking of whatever garbage can he'd been into. She'd thought she was doing the animal a favor, since cats didn't like water, and spritzed him with her atomizer. Jake had gone into a terrible hissing and scratching fit, every hair on end, like a wild thing. She still had the scar on her forearm.

"It hated it didn't it?" his tone was sharp, almost scolding. "It's the smell. It's too much."

Of course! He had heightened senses, like a cat's. She pursed her lips, disappointed. Had she ruined everything? Stupid! He wouldn't even want to touch her now. She felt her eyes brim. She wanted to jump from his arms and scrub herself clean of the perfume in the cold creek.

"I'm sorry," she whimpered.

"No, it's alright," he said after a minute. "It's okay. I can deal with it."

"I'll never do it again," she promised. She meant it.

"I know," he said, finding his smile again.

He set her down and climbed up into the hole. He crouched inside and turned to stare down at her, perched and smiling. He held out his hand.

"Don't you have a flashlight or something?" she asked, craning her neck to look over his shoulder at the thick darkness from which he seemed to spring.

He shook his head slowly. "Are you scared?"

She straightened, and held back her shoulders. "Not if you're with me."

She took his hand.

He pulled her lightly up into the culvert, turned, and led her into the shadows.

It was damp and the only light was from the moon behind. Her shoes splashed as she walked, and she heard his feet too. Her breath echoed back at her off the walls of the concrete tunnel. How far did this go? Would there be some kind of side tunnel leading to a maintenance room he had claimed? Maybe something he had made himself? Furnished with antiques from around the world?

It seemed they walked for a long time, until the light of the entrance was a pinprick behind. She had never been in a tunnel so long. She couldn't see the other side either. It was just black ahead. She gripped Brendan's hand tighter. She didn't think of herself as claustrophobic, but suddenly the knowledge that they were well beneath the earth weighed on her. How old was this pipe? Was the concrete sound?

"You okay?"

"How much further?"

"We're here now," he said, stopping at last. "Home sweet home."

"Here?" she asked. "I can't see anything."

"Do you want to see?"

"Yes," she said.

She heard him moving about something in the dark. Something clanked, and after a bit a camping lantern hissed to life, casting a whitish orange light all around.

The first thing she noticed was the size of the cockroaches that scurried in erratic curly-cue patterns before retreating into the dark.

They were deep in the culvert, but there was no antechamber or hidden stair. The pipe had apparently collapsed in the middle. She could see they were at a dead end, and a wall of broken concrete segments lay before them, through which only the water could hope to pass. It trickled in rivulets from dozens of cracks.

The lantern sat on a rock, evidently brought in from the creek bed, and a dingy, filthy blue and white striped mattress was propped in the muddy corner. She could smell the rotten fabric.

There were tied garbage bags of clothes in the opposite corner.

She looked around, nervous.

"Brendan?" was all she could manage.

"This is where I sleep," said Brendan, hunkering on his heels and resting his elbows on his knees, back against the wall. He motioned to the disgusting mattress. "Have a seat."

Gwendolyn looked at the mattress dubiously, then back at him.

"I don't understand."

"Vampires have to sleep in the same earth where they were made. Didn't you know that?"

She shook her head.

"But...you were made a vampire in Italy."

"Oh," Brendan snickered. "That. Listen. Have you ever seen a movie made before nineteen-eighty-nine?"

She frowned, her eyebrows knitting together. She felt strange, and hugged herself. Why did he ask her that?

"I don't like black and white movies," she said lamely. "What are you talking about? Weren't you turned into a vampire in Bible times? In Italy?"

He reached across the pipe to her and slipped her purse off her shoulder. She was too amazed to say anything when he unclasped it and began to paw through it with one hand.

"I can't really remember when it happened. Not before I wound up in this pipe. I think there used to be a drive-in where the truck stop is. I used to watch the movies."

"What are you saying?"

"Can you remember when you were three or four years old?"

"I think so."

"What happened on the first Thursday you can ever remember?"

"I don't know."

"I can't remember ever not being a vampire. I don't remember who made me into this. I think it was a man. A fat man. I think my earliest memory is of kneeling in front of him in this place. I don't even know if that was him. It could've been anybody. That's what I do here. I come here with people from the truck stop. Usually men."

He pulled out the pack of condoms and looked at her, smirking.

She felt her face color. Her cheeks were so hot her eyes felt like they were sweating.

"What were you gonna do with these?" he asked.

"I thought...I thought tonight would be...special."

"Well you wouldn't have any use for these, honey," he said, tossing the condoms into the muddy water at their feet. "I haven't had a hard-on since I became like this."

"Why are you talking like this?" she gasped, tears blurring her vision, making him run in the lantern light like a spoiled painting.

"Vampires don't drink, we don't eat. We don't piss or shit or fuck. You humans find us so attractive though. I dunno. I guess it's like the light on one of those lantern fish. Have you ever seen those?"

She stared at him, huffing in her misery, her eye makeup spilling down her face now in oily black cascades.

"Of course you haven't," said Brendan.

He stood up slowly.

She backed away, but only a little. She still couldn't believe. Didn't want to.

"Don't you love me?"

"Oh no," Brendan said, pursing his lips.

She shook now, trying hard to keep the sobs from bursting wholly from her grimacing lips. She felt like a bullet was already spinning in her heart trying to work its way slowly out of her chest.

"There it is," said Brendan, reaching out to her, his hand on her chest, cold skin to hers. She sucked in her breath sharply at his touch.

He moved very close to her now, embracing her. He ran the side of his face against hers. They rubbed noses. He kissed her and inhaled her. She trembled. She was so confused.

He moaned.

"So sweet. You're so sweet," he whispered in her ear.

He pulled her slowly down to the rotten mattress. She felt her jeans soak through from without and within. She cried and sighed at the same time. She tried to push him away, but he was iron strong. His kisses were hard and loveless. He was just tasting her, lapping at her skin, nibbling at her with his sharp teeth. They were like the bites of a cat.

His hands moved over her breasts and shoulders and back and his nostrils sucked at the skin of her neck.

"Oh baby," he groaned. "Nothing's sweeter...to me...than...a breaking heart."

She pulled him to her. She put her legs around his waist. Maybe it was a lie. Maybe he had been alone so long he didn't know how to joke around the right way anymore. Maybe...maybe they could still...

She reached for his belt and fumbled with trembling hands to undo his pants.

He laughed in her ear.

"Still trying, huh?"

She nodded.

"Uh huh," she said hotly as he kissed and licked at her neck.

Her heart was hammering. She yanked apart his jeans and slid her shaking hands behind the band of his underwear, felt down his hard stomach, fingers moving through the bristling, weedy pubic hair to the loose lump of dead flesh that nestled there, cool as a sleeping viper. She stroked and rubbed as if trying to start a fire, but he did not respond.

She worked at him furiously in her confusion and frustration. She desperately wanted him to share in her own passion, which despite all that he had said, was still waxing below her navel, fluttering like a maddened bird beating its wings against a window.

She still wanted him. She wanted him more than anything.

He said something muffled in her neck.

"What?" she whispered.

He pulled his head back. His face in her eyes, she stared in disbelief at the blood broadly painted across his face, dripping from his long teeth, spilling down his chin.

She hadn't felt the bite.

"I said 'this,'" and he flicked one of his protruding canine teeth with his finger, "is what you're looking for. On a vampire, it's *these*."

She understood. She darted her face forward and kissed him, tasting her own blood, like a mouthful of batteries. She thrust her tongue between his lips, lapping at his teeth. He nearly pulled back in shock, but she clasped her hands behind the nape of his neck and ground her heaving body against him, seeking his sharp teeth flicking at them with the tip of her tongue.

Brendan gasped and bit her.

The pain was unimaginable. She shrieked into his gulping mouth, eyes bugging in her skull.

Her tongue pierced, instantly both their mouths filled with a gush of hot blood, so copious it jetted directly to the back of Brendan's throat, warm as fresh milk. He gagged at first, but fought past it, letting her life seep down hot as whiskey to his eager, hungry belly. He sucked at her bleeding tongue, gripped the sides of her head.

Her body moved furiously against him, but he was utterly unaware of it. All his concentration was on draining her through her tongue, like a thirsty boy on a hot summer day sucking from the garden spigot.

Gwendolyn's eyes fluttered and something burst deep within her. Something that spurted fire like a Roman candle up and outwards into her whole body. Her stomach and legs locked and she fell back quivering against the grimy mattress, blood leaking from her lips, her mouth full of rust.

Tears ran down from the far corners of her eyes as she looked up at Brendan, straddling her. Blood, her blood, all down his chin.

He was heaving too, though no breath came from his lips, only flecks of her own blood dropping on her staring face. He smiled down at her with his sharp, animal teeth. The edges of her sight blurred and darkened. Maybe the lantern was going out. Maybe she was dying. Maybe it was only her mortality dying. Maybe all of this had been some rite of initiation into immortality. A lesson in letting go.

But she wouldn't let Brendan go. She strained to see him, until he became a tiny picture in a pinhole.

Her dark angel.

Her Peter Pan.

No.

No, he wasn't Peter Pan.

He wasn't Captain Hook.

He was the crocodile.

Ian Welke has never driven a truck, but has spent many hours on the interstates, having driven the length of I-5, I-15, I-40, and much of I-10 in particular. Most days he rides a desk and keyboard. His short stories have appeared in Kzine, Big Pulp, Zombie Jesus and Other True Stories, *and the* American Nightmare *anthology amongst others. His first novel,* The Whisperer in Dissonance, *was published by* Omnium Gatherum Media *in 2014. His second novel,* End Times at Ridgemont High *was released in April 2015. Follow him on* Twitter @mewelke.

SLEEPER

Ian Welke

ALONE AT NIGHT IN THE DESERT Matt feels like he's drifting in space. He knows the desert's out there. He's seen it driving during the day, but at night there's just blackness. His headlights shine over so little of the I-40 pavement, it feels like he's floating on a disk of asphalt through the void.

It's easy to get philosophical on too little sleep and after too many miles. There hasn't been much chatter on the CB. He hasn't gotten a call all day on his cell. When he pulls in for his mandatory rest, he'll have to check his email and the news on his tablet. Just the thought of the glow of that screen warms him. There's an outside world waiting for him as soon as he can log on. But the warmth turns to dread as he contemplates what follows when he has to log off and force himself to sleep. It's more than insomnia. It's worse than just missing her. Every moment alone and sleepless heaps sorrow upon sorrow and anxiety upon anxiety. Once it's just him alone with his fears, the walls of his sleeper will close in and smother him.

Twin red points, taillights of another truck, flare ahead in the distance. Matt looks for a mile marker. He'd hoped to make Flagstaff when he hit the eleven-hour limit. Time is another tricky variable when you're tired and bored. He'll have to stop short of Flagstaff. He won't be able to sleep, but the hours-of-service rules won't allow him to keep going.

The taillights zoom toward him like someone's hit the fast-forward button on reality. He checks mirrors, but there's a car that's come out of nowhere passing on his left. Matt feathers the brakes to avoid a skid. To make matters worse, the four-door Dodge on his left slows down to match speeds. At the last second, before Matt will have to commit to a full stop, the muscle car guns it and disappears into the night.

Matt releases the brake, and shifts up, pulling around the slower moving truck. As he passes, he catches the glimpse of a woman silhouetted on the opposite side of the road. A hitchhiker? It can't be. What woman would be hitching in this barren stretch of road at night? No. He imagined her, because he's tired and stressed he imagined the very image of Lucy.

Miles pass, none of them well, as he dwells on his wife's memory. When you lose someone, they say you'll keep the happy thoughts with you, keeping their memory alive in your heart. But when you lose someone to cancer, it's the memory of their suffering that sticks with you alone in the night. It's the memory of the failed treatments that haunts Matt on this dark highway. Just as the debt for the failed treatments haunts his daylight hours. He dreads the end of his eleven. The time when it will just be him in the sleeper with all his worst memories ensuring that he doesn't sleep.

A mass of lights cuts the dark ahead. A town, or at least a truck stop. His stomach growls. An hour short of his limit, he'll stop there.

❧

Matt fills the tanks before parking the rig in the back lot, next door to a diner. He's already lost the battle of willpower. Once upon a time, Matt was a vegan. In college, he was as straight-edged as they come. He didn't even drink coffee. Some of that changed after he dropped out, went to trucking school, and started driving at the port. After losing Lucy, he went off the rails. Booze. Drugs. Despair. He hasn't climbed out of the pit from that downward spiral yet, but he's been meaning to, and he keeps thinking part of that process would be eating healthier again. Temptation is a bitch though. Tonight's temptation is in the form of a bacon cheeseburger.

He licks his lips and heads into the diner.

Most restaurants off the highway don't play any music. If they do it's piped in corporate Muzak. But a jukebox plays in this diner between the waiting area and the hall leading to the restrooms. It's playing something slow and dreamy, not what he'd expect. There's an edge to it that feels out of place. It's all sweet and soothing and then there's this tinge of distortion like it's reminding you it can all go wrong at any second.

A row of four truckers sitting at the counter drinking strawberry shakes turn in unison and stare at him, before turning back and sucking on their straws again.

A waitress shows Matt to a booth in the back corner. Her name tag says "Irene." Her hair is dyed a red a shade brighter than the curtains. It all clashes with the faded-brown Naugahyde booths. "Coffee? Or a shake? We've got the best strawberry shake in the state," she says a little too fast, like she's had too many cups of coffee or is trying to save time by cutting out the spaces between words.

"Just coffee." Coffee's not the best idea at this hour, but if he's going to have heartburn anyway, he might as well go for it. While she goes off for the coffee, he looks over the menu. Might as well just top off that cheeseburger with some chili-cheese fries. That will light the fires in the gut furnace.

A car lights up the window next to him as it parks. It's that Dodge. He's considering giving the driver a piece of his mind, but he watches as five men climb out, and he decides to mind his own business when they come into the diner.

The first thing they do is spread out. One man, wearing a hat with a feather in it, stands to the left of the counter with the milkshake sipping truckers. The driver remains at the entrance. He wears a suit of some shiny material. Sharkskin maybe. His thin hair is greased back. The other three men walk into the main dining area. Two of them head to the restrooms. After eye-balling all the people at the tables and checking the restrooms they return and shrug to the man that was driving the Dodge. The driver snaps his fingers and they all file out again. The door shuts, and moments later the Hemi engine roars to life and the car drives off.

The waitress returns with a pot of coffee. "What can I get for you, hon?" She peers down at Matt through her rhinestone glasses.

"I'll have the bacon cheeseburger and a side of fries."

Irene disappears into the kitchen just as the front door opens again and a young woman walks in. For just a second, Matt's sure that she's the spitting image of his wife, but he shakes his head and rubs his tired eyes, and realizes that while she bears a passing resemblance, the length of her black hair and maybe the shape of her figure, it's just that he's exhausted and is seeing what he wants to see. He remembers reading somewhere that human eyes can't see clearly at a distance, that the brain doesn't want to admit it doesn't know something, so it fills in the blurry image with something familiar until the object or person gets closer. As the woman in the entryway walks past, the truckers ignore their milkshakes, staring at her until she's passed down the hall into the women's restroom.

The waitress drops off Matt's burger and heads back to the kitchen. The Dodge returns and its crew fan out into the restau-rant again. They search, return to the front empty handed, and shrug to the driver boss man. This time instead of snapping his fingers, the driver steps out to the jukebox area. "Excuse me," he says, loud enough to be heard over a Clash song, something off *Give Them Enough Rope*. "Did anyone just see a young woman walk in here? She's about," and he puts his hand up to show the height of the woman that's just gone into the restroom.

No one says anything.

"I see. So no one saw anything? How about you?" he turns to the row of milkshake drinkers. They look spooked. In unison, they reach forward and point to the restroom.

"So she was here. Son of a bitch." He grimaces.

The man in the hat says something in the boss man's ear.

The boss shakes his head. "No. She had time alone in that restroom. She could be anywhere. Come on."

The men follow him out the door and back to the four-door in the parking lot.

Matt leaves his meal half-finished, drops some bills on the table, and leaves the diner.

The truck looms ahead in the lot. Nights like this the sleeper is misnamed. He's in for a night of staring at the walls. And then the worry will take him and spawn its own spiral of anxiety and sleeplessness. Worrying about the worry already has his stomach upset.

When he gets to the cab, she's standing there in the shadows. "Can you help me, sir? I require transit."

For just a second, she sounds so much like Lucy he almost says yes without thinking. "Those men after you? I'd love to help, but I can't go far. I'm at my limit for the night. I drive much further and I'll need to pull over and sleep or there'll be hell to pay."

"Can you take me just as far as you can? I will wait with you while you rest." It's odd. She doesn't move her lips or even open her mouth when she speaks.

"I'm afraid... I don't do that. You see I was married, and while she's no longer with us, I kind of think it would be untrue to her memory."

"You believe I would sell myself to you?"

"Oh. I'm sorry. I didn't mean to embarrass you. You don't mean that. But wouldn't it be weird to you to just wait while I sleep?"

She reaches out and puts her palm on his forehead like a priest blessing him.

&

The next thing Matt knows he's at the wheel. He comes to with a panic attack of having just nodded off, but he's miles from the truck stop, hours past his eleven, and he has no idea how he's gotten here. He manages to keep the truck on the road at least. He knows many drivers that have crashed not because they nodded off to sleep, but because they overcorrected when they snapped back to consciousness. He keeps the wheel steady. The sky has that blue, predawn glow. He looks around the cab, but there's no sign of the girl he was talking to in the parking lot.

He's calculating how many hours he's lost, when the clock flickers and the truck loses all its power. The road goes dark as his headlights kill. He manages to steer the rig to the shoulder and in the low predawn light, rolls it to a stop on a flat, loose surface.

He's stopped for what seems like a long time before he stops shaking. First he loses time, then the truck loses all its electric power. He checks his cell phone. Dead. Same for his tablet. He's all alone out here, and he doesn't know where "here" is. He hasn't seen a sign, and his GPS is as useless as the rest of his gear.

Climbing out of the cab he grabs his emergency kit. He puts up his reflector cones. It's a miracle that he broke down where he did. There's nothing but a wall of mountain on the other side of the road. Any earlier there'd have been a cliff past the shoulder. The loose material under his feet is straw. With the light of a flare he realizes he's not in a field at all. It's a parking lot. There's a flicker of light ahead. The flicker disappears, but he can now see the outline of a building a hundred feet from him.

He walks toward it cautiously. Highways are littered with abandoned buildings and ghost towns. There might be someone

at this one who can help him. Or there might be camp of crazy homeless people. He gets about halfway to the building and
stops. The Dodge is parked at the edge of the building.

He can see a little better now, with the sun starting to climb.
The building's a boarded up roadhouse. The boards covering
the door have been removed, but are leaned against the door-
jamb to cover the opening. The light comes from a window to
the right of the door.

The inside of the abandoned roadhouse is lit by candles. The
candles form a circle on the floor surrounding a flat rectangular
object.

Five men stand around the exterior of the circle. The same
five men from the diner.

Their leader waves his hand. He's manic. Vibrating. Matt
guesses he's on a shitload of speed. "Let's get this show on the
road. Fire the damned thing up!"

One of the men reaches down to the floor. There's a series
of boxes next to him, five car batteries wired together. He pulls
a switch that's planted to the floor and sparks fly, first from the
switch, then across the row of batteries. Lightning arcs to the
ceiling, coiling around a rectangular object that Matt recognizes
as a flat-panel television. He's not sure what's holding it to the
ceiling, only that blue current flashes up on either side of it. The
television is mounted directly over the large flat object in the
circle on the floor.

The leader turns around. There's something taped to his
throat. An old-fashioned radio microphone in front of his
mouth. He raises both hands in front of him. His voice is dis-
torted, grating and metallic through the amplification of the microphone.

"Calling the hub. Listen in."

The other men say in unison, "Come in. Prepare transmission."

The leader raises his hands. "The deal is set. We await delivery through the interchange."

The other men echo this with like a call and response in a church, "Send the merchandise."

"Open the lanes. Send it through."

"We await the goods."

Glass shatters upwards from the rectangle on the floor. It flies up to the television screen on the ceiling. Behind the glass there's a spray of some viscous fluid, and chunks of wet flesh fragmented into smaller particles chased by a larger sprawling mass. A flash of light is followed by darkness.

"Lights," the boss man shouts, his voice no longer modulated.

Flashlights illuminate four circles in the room. The circles bounce and rotate around a wet mass on the floor. The mass is shaped like a boulder, but it's undulating. The top stretches, and an arm punches through the membrane. Then another arm. This is followed by the head.

Matt takes a step back from the window and realizes that he's not breathing. That head. That thing. It's not human. It is humanoid. Its eyes are elongated ovals, longer up and down than side to side. Even in the flashlight circle he can see that its eyes are partitioned. Like thousands of squares of black glass pieced together in a mosaic. Its snout stretches out like a hook squash. Four half-moon orifices ring the edge of the snout.

"All right," the leader sounds exasperated. "Help it out already."

The two youngest men pull the creature up by its arms. Its torso is the oddest part of it. Its ribcage is on the outside and the color of grey metal. Knobs are riveted to the ribs.

Matt turns to leave, trips over a rock, and lands face first in the straw and the gravel.

When he looks up, the boss man is standing over him. "What have we here? Some sort of peeper? Hey, don't I know you from somewhere, friend?"

❦

Stabbing pain expands from between Matt's eyes, filling his head with shards of hot glass. As he wakes, he becomes aware not just of the immediate agony in his head, but also of a dull ache from the rest of his body. He's covered in one great bruise. His throat is so dry the skin might crack if he breathes in. And then there's the pain from his wrists. They're bound behind his back with something tight. Electrical wire maybe.

Memories of last night come back in waves like the nausea of a hard hangover. The girl at the truck stop, the breakdown, the weirdness at the abandoned roadhouse, but nothing afterward.

He's on the floor of a motel room. He can tell by the carpet and the painting above the bed. The bathroom door is open just a crack lending the room a trickle of light.

A hot flare of pain shoots through the base of his neck. More memory comes with it. Being grabbed and thrown into the trunk of the Dodge. A needle jabbing him in the neck. With that memory, a series of visions flash past him that he can't separate from dream. An ethereal face turning to a skull in front of him. Tied to a chair in a motel room while people asked him questions in a language he's never heard before. Slumped on the floor against the wall, while the men around him discussed something and moved that painting above the bed...something about that painting. They replaced it with a new painting facing the television screen. Why?

There's a low, sad moan from the bathroom, a deep drone like a whale's song. Matt gets up to his knees, doubles over, and vomits on the floor. He pulls at the wire binding his hands, wishing he could wipe his mouth. There's another moan from the bathroom, this time more tentative, like it's calling to him.

He spits and manages to get to his feet and stagger to the bathroom door. He presses his shoulder to the door to push it the rest of the way open. There's another sound, something mechanical and repetitive, a whirring, a sucking, a gear turning, and it repeats.

The thing is there in bathtub. The thing from the roadhouse.

Thick pea-soup-colored mucous shoots out of the bottom right hole on its snout. The low moan begins again, as the machine cycles once more. The creature is hooked by its eight rivet-nipples to this thing that looks like a combination of a pachinko machine and an automatic milker. Matt can't be sure if it's milking the creature or pumping something into it or both. But he knows what it reminds him of, the chemo machines. Those horrible days when he watched as Lucy was hooked up to the machine pumping her full of poison that never worked anyway. But Matt doubts that the intent here is to cure the poor creature writhing in the bathtub.

"Would it help you if I can get you out of that?" Matt's not sure it understands him. He has no idea how to unhook it from the machine, but figures that freeing his own hands is probably a good first step. The binding is a power cable for a radio. It's tied tight, but he gets it under the sink and tries using the faucet for leverage. It cuts into his skin. He manages to get hold of the soap to the right of the sink and lathers it up over his wrists. The skin lubricated, he puts his hands back under the faucet and manages to pull the wire off.

The front plate of the machine is covered in dials and knobs. Matt hasn't any idea what will happen if he starts turning these, or if he can just start unhooking the creature. He tries to convey his confusion to it by raising his hands. The creature bellows at him, and Matt interprets that as the go ahead to proceed.

He reaches for the first of the hooks clasping the creature's rivet-like nipples. The creature's call seems to indicate that this will help. But the clasp is fastened tight, and Matt struggles to loosen it.

Matt's so busy struggling to free the creature, he doesn't notice that the men have returned. Their leader says, "That's enough of that, hero. Dope him." Sharp pain pierces his neck, and darkness swirls into nausea.

の

When Matt's eyes open, his vision is blurry and smeared like light in an impressionist painting. His chin is on the toilet seat. His hands are now bound in front of him, his arms wrapped around the base of the toilet.

The machine is still on, but now the sucking sound is more of a wheeze, as it draws nothing from the creature in the tub. There are no more moans from the beast. It lies there, still, an empty husk. The room reeks. Vomit coats the sides of the toilet. Then there's the smell coming off the dead thing in the tub. Rancid meat. Roadkill.

Matt wonders why they've left him alive. Maybe it's just less trouble? Who is he going to tell that would believe him? On the other hand, he guesses it wouldn't be much more trouble to just kill and dispose of him the same way they plan on dumping the body of this creature. He pulls, trying to free his hands, but the wire just bites harder into his wrists.

His vision flashes white. He remembers reading about stroke victims seeing bright flashes of light before they drop, and he wonders if this is it. He opens his eyes again and sees through the blurry light something that can't be. The woman from the parking lot outside the diner is climbing out of the wall mirror. The glass of the mirror ripples as she steps through and just her arm is still inside the glass. She pulls her arm through and the glass solidifies.

She looks down at the beast in the tub and blinks. As she does this Matt is suddenly filled with an overwhelming sense of sadness. The sense of loss replaces his fear for himself. For just a moment, there's no pain from his wrists, his bruises, or the two needle jabs he's taken to his neck. There is only sadness.

"Can you walk?" she says without moving her lips.

"My hands are tied." The pain returns and the sadness subsides. She kneels down and snaps the wire. He's able stand, but he hunches over and cramps up. With effort he starts to limp toward the door. "They think I know where to find you. You won't be safe with me."

"I'm not safe anywhere. But I think there's a place we can go. If you can drive me." She pulls his arm over her shoulder and helps him to the door. She places her hand over the peephole and closes her eyes. "There's no one outside. Come."

She opens the door and the daylight hits him. He can't remember the last time he's been out in the sun. Not since he left LA. The time saved by driving at night seems pointless now that he's overdue. He realizes he doesn't know how overdue he is. He doesn't even know how many days he's been inside that room. And he doesn't know what they've done with his truck.

They're on the second floor of a Motel 6. The parking lot below is empty.

As they get to the base of the stairs, a car comes off the road and turns, kicking up dust into the parking lot. The Dodge.

The woman grabs Matt's hand and pulls him around the corner of the motel. Behind the building, there's a field, and his truck. He races for the driver's door with a renewed step to his stride. They must have not even considered that he'd get away, because they've left the keys in the cab. On the other hand, they've taken his phone, his tablet, and wallet. Even the CB is torn out, leaving a spaghetti mess of wires hanging from the dash.

The truck starts. Whatever was wrong with the electrics is fixed. Matt guesses it had something to do with what they were up to in that roadhouse. *Of course the truck's fixed. Otherwise it wouldn't be here.*

There isn't all that much town to Los Lunas, but it's twenty minutes before they find the highway entrance. They join State Highway 6. Matt still hasn't come up with the right question to start. Eventually he goes with, "What's your name?"

"You can call me Mara." Before he says anything she adds, "I know that you are known as Matt."

He wants an explanation, but he's not sure what to ask first, or if he should bother. He's always wondered if this is the way things are. That if you get off the wrong exit, you'll find the world completely different than anything you'd expect. You know what things are like at home. You think you know what they'll be like at your destination, but in between there are infinitely weird possibilities.

He figures he'll wait until they reach I-25 before he asks Mara where she'd like to go. As the sun starts to set and the on-ramp gets close, his mirrors light up with headlights from the Dodge.

"Go north," she says.

"Why north, is that where you need to go?"

"No. But it is away from south. Their power comes from their base. In your town of El Paso."

Matt shifts it and takes the route north.

༄

For the first half hour the muscle car hangs back, like they're waiting to see what Matt does. When he gets close to Albuquerque and has the choice of hitting the 40, they roar even with the truck. Matt pushes the fuel pedal down. They pull even again. They play this game for a while. Matt slows down. They slow down. This pattern continues onto the I-40 headed east.

"The good news is we can outlast them until they need to gas up." Matt upshifts, the engine roars, and they gain again on their pursuers. The gauge shows the tanks are over half full. He has at least six hundred miles of range. The Dodge will have to stop well before he does.

His headlights pass over an exit sign, but the sign makes no sense. In the instant he sees it, the numbers change to characters he's never seen. They look like crosses between letters and pinwheels, then they swirl to pitchforks and sickles. He looks back, trying to make sense of what he's seen. When he looks forward again, a sign on the overpass does the same thing.

"What the...?"

"This is not good. They are altering things."

Her face conveys no sense of emotion, just as her mouth doesn't move when the words play in his head. Matt looks back at the road just in time to get the flash of headlights of an on-coming vehicle. He starts to crank the wheel to avoid the car, but Mara grabs it and "NO!" reverberates in his skull.

They pass through the lights and an ephemeral outline of an old Plymouth Valiant. The truck shudders but does not crash, and there are no signs of the car in his mirrors. Just the muscle car. Shivers shoot through Matt's wrists, up into his shoulders, and meet in a stabbing ball of pain in the center of his back.

He wipes a bucket's worth of sweat off his face, looks back at the road behind them, then back to Mara hoping for answers.

"You will not be able to trust what you see. Some will be true. Others not. It will get worse."

"How am I supposed to keep it on the road if I don't know what I'm looking at?" Matt cycles through his memories of the road ahead. Past the outskirts of Albuquerque there's nothing. Scrub brush and hills. Matt's been through here plenty, Amarillo is often one of his rest stops.

"We might be able to see what they are doing at least." Mara waves her hand over his rearview mirror. It goes to snow, like television static. When it comes back, it's the reflection from the Dodge's rearview mirror, focused on the men inside.

The boss man is driving and grinning. The man in the feathered hat sits in the passenger's seat. He's working the dial on a handheld device with an antenna. It looks like an old walkie-talkie or maybe a Geiger-counter. He pulls the dial full to the right, and the lights of a weigh station flash in front of the truck: *SCALES OPEN. TRUCKS MUST WEIGH IN.*

Matt instinctively panics and moves for the wheel before remembering that there's no weigh station here.

"So, all I have to do is ignore whatever they do?"

"No. It is not so simple. As they add power, they can make changes more than pictures. They could end the road into a cliff if they can give the machine enough power."

In the rearview, the man with the hat twists the dial full right, but nothing happens. The road ahead remains the same, straight ahead in a slow climb.

"Turn the wheel."

"Right or left?"

"Guess! Right! Now!"

He turns the wheel. The left side of the truck hits something that isn't there. Amid a shower of sparks, a guard rail shimmers into vision. The air is wavy like a heat mirage as Matt's view of the road changes from straight to slight right turn.

The Dodge pulls ahead of them.

There's no time to catch his breath, the man in the hat is moving the dial to full again. Matt does the only thing he has left. He upshifts and floors it, slamming into the muscle car. The grill and engine of the truck smash clean through into the trunk of the Dodge. Both vehicles lose control. The Dodge spins off to the left. The truck goes off the road, careening over a hill and sliding down, rumbling over underbrush before slamming into a boulder.

༄

Matt peels broken glass off his face. Through the blood clogging his sinuses, he smells something burning. Brakes and the rubber from his tires, but he also smells diesel. His next move should probably be away from his truck.

A shape on the hill must be Mara. He staggers in the loose rock to get to her. When he taps her arm, she rolls to her side. Her face contorts, breaks into separate frames, and there are two images in its place. For a second, her face is more like the thing from the motel, before the image snaps and returns her features to the way they were.

He reaches down to help her to her feet. "Come on, we've got to move." There's a light from a building uphill to their left. Remembering the roadhouse, he's wary to approach random buildings off the highway, but he hears shouts from the road behind them.

Three silhouettes are cast by the headlights of the over-turned Dodge. One of them carries a handgun, Matt can't tell if the others are armed.

The terrain gets rougher. More brush, less rock. A rusty piece of sheet metal lies flat on the ground. There are the bones of a motorcycle, but not the wheels or engine. Matt slips on something slick, an old plastic trash bag, its contents are scattered all around, crumbled and decayed.

Matt has seen these places before. These roadside dumps. Places where people have come to ditch their trash. The light's coming from the window of a trailer. Maybe the owners have a phone. Maybe they will help them. Or maybe they're with the men chasing them, and it's hopeless.

There's a toilet in the ground to Matt's right. About five feet from the trailer, there's a refrigerator turned on its side and half buried in sand. They get to the refrigerator and the trailer door swings open. A thin man in overalls with a straw hat and a grey beard steps out. He points a double-barreled shotgun downhill at him and Mara. There's a click, a sound like thunder, and a metal car door, rusted and flat on the ground is hit by the shot.

"That's what you call a warning shot. The next one doesn't miss."

Matt raises his hands. "We don't want trouble. But there's some men after us."

"They ain't after you, boy. They want that alien you got with you."

Does everybody know what's going on but me? Matt shakes his head, no time for discussion. "You'd just let them take her?"

Shouts come from the distance. The survivors from the wrecked muscle car have heard the shot.

"I got my own species to think of first, boy."

There's another crack and Matt hits the deck. The old man falls to his knees. He twists down to the ground before Matt sees that the back of his head is blown out.

Mara crawls ahead of him, over the body of the dead man, and into the trailer. Matt follows, wincing as another gunshot echoes through the night. He takes the shotgun from the hands of the dead man on the way.

The inside of the trailer looks like a long line of hoarders have lived in it. There's a stack of phonebooks that stretches from floor to ceiling. The rear of the trailer is inaccessible, the floor covered in boxes. The box on top of the pile is overflowing with hair combs. Matt throws it to the ground behind him. The next is full of cigarette lighters. Remote controls. Rubber bands. Toothbrushes.

Mara starts rummaging through the drawers stacked along the wall. "Is there a mirror in here?"

"I don't see one. Do you see shotgun shells or a phone?"

The door flies open. The man in the feathered hat steps in, gun pointed at them. Matt drops to the floor. Mara screams. Matt's head fills with pain, but somehow he can tell that he's just caught the backsplash of the blast aimed at the man in the hat. Blood comes out the man's nose. He shakes and steadies himself and aims the gun at Mara. Matt pulls the trigger on the shotgun. The remaining barrel fires and the man grimaces and goes running from the trailer in pain. The door slams shut after him. There's no blood on the wall. Matt guesses the shell was filled with rock salt.

At least the door doesn't open again.

"Hey in there." The voice of the driver.

"What do you want?"

"We don't have any beef with you, friend. We just want the girl."

Matt thinks for a second. "She's not here."

"What?" The boss sounds skeptical. Matt doesn't blame him.

"There's a wall mirror at the back of the trailer. She went straight through it."

There's a pause.

"You wouldn't mind if we came in and verified that would you?"

"How do I know you won't try and just shoot me anyway?"

"I don't know, friend. I could give you my word, but then you don't know me."

Matt looks around the trailer wondering where the old man might have kept more ammo. The only thing keeping him alive now is that the men outside don't know that he's out of shells. But there's no way out of this trailer. He wonders how long it will be until someone passes the wreck on the highway. Someone who will call the Highway Patrol. And then how long it will take the highway patrol to investigate.

The men outside apparently don't want to wait it out. A barrage of shots pierce the side of the trailer. Most of these are absorbed by the stacks of boxes and books, but one shot ricochets several times before embedding itself in the stack of phonebooks. Before the sound and dust clears the door flies open again. This time the man in the hat and one of the other men charge into the trailer, guns firing.

Mara screams, but the sound is cut off. She's hit. Matt swings the butt of the shotgun. He brings it down on the man in the hat's gun hand with a satisfying bone-snapping crack. The other man aims at Matt, but Matt's already swinging again. The wood connects with the man's jaw and sends him out cold to the trailer floor. Matt picks up his gun and gestures for the man in the hat to go out of the trailer. Using the man as a shield, Matt follows him outside.

"The girl's shot."

"It's true, boss. I think she's had it." The man in the hat's words are panicked and slurred.

"So what now?"

Matt's not sure how much longer he can hold the gun level.

"The police would never believe any of this."

"So we go our separate ways?"

The man in the sharkskin laughs. "That's the first sensible thing I've heard you say." His gun points down toward the sand.

Matt fires. This is only the second time in his lifetime he's fired a gun. The first was in the trailer, but unlike the shotgun there's no spread on the shot from the handgun and the bullet streaks off into the night.

The man in the sharkskin fires rapidly. All the shots strike the man in the hat. Except one, which passes through the hat man and hits Matt in the hip. He's sure his hip is broken. He's not bleeding, but he doesn't have time to guess how hurt he is.

Mara has crawled out of the trailer. She shrieks and it staggers the man in the sharkskin suit. Matt drops the dead man in the hat, uses both hands to steady the handgun, and fires into the leader. The boss man drops dead to the ground. Matt leaves the gun on him until he's sure.

He turns back to Mara. She no longer looks like the woman he'd seen before. She looks like the creature that was killed in the motel bathroom. Matt hears her voice in his head. "Do not worry. I am free from them. When I awaken in my home, I will be safe."

She's still. Her image flickers and warps. Her face contorts, the image wavy like a broken channel on an old television. She's Mara, then her face is Lucy's, then back to the creature in the motel. The air around her shimmers like hot air off the asphalt on a desert day, and she is gone.

Matt limps his way back to the highway, doing his best to ignore the pain throbbing from his hip with each step. The blood is all on the outside of his jeans. He checks the other side under his belt. There's a terrible bruise that stings too bad to tighten his belt again after he checks it, but it's a relief to know that the blood all belongs to the dead man back near the trailer.

When he gets back to the road, he finds his cell phone in the Dodge's glovebox, but there's no signal. As he walks down I-40, he wonders what the hell he's going to tell the cops, or worse, his insurance people. He knows he should be afraid. It should all hurt more than it does. He doesn't know if it's shock, but he's just numb. Seeing her fade makes it feel like it's all happened again. Any hopes that he'll ever sleep right again, are gone with her. There will never be enough miles in the rearview to fix him. He knows that, but he keeps limping one foot in front of the other down the highway.

Michael Paul Gonzalez lives and writes in Los Angeles. His mind was forged (warped?) at an early age by the adventures of Jack Burton and his truck, the Pork Chop Express, in the greatest B-movie ever made: Big Trouble in Little China. *Follow him at* www.MichaelPaulGonzalez.com

THE IRON BULLDOGGE

Michael Paul Gonzalez

ROOK WAS DIGGING into the worst apple pie he'd ever encountered when the kid sidled up to his table. He'd seen the type before, hitchhikers, college dropouts starting a misguided romantic journey across the states. This skinny kid couldn't have been more than a week into his trip. Clean blond hair, light stubble, didn't stink, and his cheeks weren't sucked in yet. Rook always wanted to tell them what life on the road was really like. When it's in your bones and in your blood. When you're on the road, you can't wait to get home. You get home for a few days and then you're burning to get back on the road. Instead, he just cut to the chase.

"Where ya headed?"

The kid shuffled his feet, surprised that he didn't need to go into a sales pitch.

"West?" the kid asked.

"You don't have to be so specific," Rook grumbled, kicking out the chair on the other side of the table. "Siddown and let me finish this slop, then we'll get going. What's your name?"

"Oh, you can call me—"

"Not what I can *call* you. Shit, you hippies with your damn names. Not *Moonbeam*, or *Supertramp*, what's it say on your birth certificate?"

The kid looked down at the plate of pie. "Didn't think it was that big of a deal."

"Meh, it's probably not. I'm eighteen hours into a run that was supposed to wrap up hours ago, so forgive my *brusqueness*." Rook loved throwing five dollar words at the hippies. "How far west are you going?"

"Gotta get to the ocean. I've never seen the Pacific."

"You ever see the Atlantic?"

"Yeah, that's where I start—"

"Looks the same, just reversed."

"Look, if you don't want to give me a ride, I get it. I can ask around."

"Nah," Rook laughed. "Nah, I'm just giving you a hard time. Wanted to see if you had a sense of humor. Guess we'll keep things quiet. I can get you as far as Salt Lake City, then you're on your own. Word of advice? When we get there, buy a thicker jacket. You're gonna freeze."

"I'll get by. You mind if I grab a quick bite before we head out?"

Rook shrugged. "Don't try the pie."

"You can call me Sticks," the kid said.

"Nope," Rook answered. "Your mama call you Sticks? Then I ain't gonna either."

A waitress arrived in a cloud of scent that was somewhere between knockoff perfume and nicotine addiction. "What'll it be, hon?"

"The steak special."

"Outta steak."

"Ribs with no sauce?"

"We make 'em how they ship 'em. You want ribs, you get sauce."

Sticks sighed. "Just a hamburger patty."

The waitress raised an eyebrow. "Gotta charge you the same either way. You're getting the blue plate special, do whatever you want with the stuff you don't eat." She pivoted and hustled away to the kitchen.

"Come for the atmosphere, stay for the service," Rook muttered. "You got a gluten allergy or something?"

The kid smiled. "Nah, it's just...I'm a meat-eater, you know? It's all I can eat. Don't like it when it has the tinge of other stuff on it."

"Interesting," Rook said.

"It's a long story. It's part of the journey. I'm on a dare of sorts, I guess. Took a job delivering something cross-country. Big payoff. Lotta rules."

"Well, if it's drugs or contraband, you're gonna have to find another ride."

"No, it's nothing like that," Sticks said, checking over his shoulders as he leaned in with the shiniest trust-me grin that Rook had seen this side of a used car dealership. "You ever hear of fringe archaeology?"

Rook struggled not to roll his eyes. One of *those* guys. "The study of imaginary bullshit totems and trinkets?"

"You've heard of it then? I know it's easy to scoff, but I believe, man. The world is full of objects that want to remain undiscovered. Things that people want to keep hidden by any means necessary. It's cool shit, man!"

Rook exhaled a fine spray of pie crumbs and laughter.

Sticks leaned back. "Most people feel like you, but I could show you something that would change your mind."

"You know, usually people wait until we're actually rolling down the road to start talking about looney bullshit, but I gotta say, thanks for saving me some time." Rook started to slide out of his seat, but Sticks laid a hand on the table.

"You a vet?" Sticks asked. When Rook glanced over at him, Sticks jutted his chin at the tattoo wrapping around Rook's forearm. It was his namesake, a crow wreathed in black flame, rising from his wrist and up his forearm. Floating just above the beak was a simple black chess piece, the rook, eternally just out of reach.

"Yeah, I guess you could say that. I've seen action in a lot of places. Not exactly *on the books*, if you catch my drift."

"What's it mean?"

"Guess you didn't catch my drift. Let's just say delivering freedom isn't about hopes and dreams and flowery shit. It's a dirty business." Rook scratched at the dark stubble on his chin.

"You're a soldier though. I can show you something that'll blow your mind." Sticks started to rummage through his backpack. "Anyone ever tell you that you kinda look like a younger version of Lemmy from Motorhead?"

"Nobody that wanted to keep their teeth." Rook fixed a steely glare on him.

"It was supposed to be a compliment. Rugged badass. You know? Anyway, soldier boy, this is going to slay you. Check it out." Sticks pulled a long, thin black box from his backpack and set it on the table, sliding it toward Rook.

Rook stared at the box. It was smooth and featureless, just a small seam that ran around the top edge. It had the dull sheen of fresh asphalt, and even though it looked like cardboard, Rook knew that it would be cold to the touch.

"Open it!" Sticks laughed. "It ain't gonna bite ya, don't worry."

Rook folded his arms and stared at Sticks. The young man broke, laughing and sliding the box back toward himself. "Fine. Big tough soldier guy scared of a little box." Sticks pushed a dirty thumbnail into the seam and pried the lid from the box.

A small whisper escaped the box, probably just cardboard scraping cardboard, but Rook swore it sounded like the thing hissed his birth name. Inside the box, laying in neatly piled hay, was a metal blade, about eight inches long. It was chipped and dull. Covered in rust, except for the tip which was bright polished silver. It looked like someone had been trying to restore the thing and just gave up about two inches into the job.

"And?" Rook asked.

"Guess what it is," Sticks smiled.

"You have any idea how many miles I have left to go tonight?" Rook asked.

"All right, all right," Sticks said. He leaned in closer, checking over his shoulders to make sure there were no snooping ears. "The legend is, this is the tip of a spear."

"Certainly shaped that way," Rook said, rolling his eyes. "You gonna tell me it's magical?"

Sticks danced his fingers along the edge of the box, looking at the spear, then back at Rook. "A Roman spear. Probably the most famous spear in history. That shiny part, that was used to hold a sponge once. And also used to deliver the final insulting wound to—"

"Jesus Christ," Rook muttered, sliding out of the booth and standing up. "Word of advice, kid. You want a ride cross-country, save your batshit crazy talk for whoever's waiting for you at the end of the line. Tell the next guy you see that you're taking a break from college to find yourself. Try to—"

Rook swallowed his next thought as Sticks picked up the spear tip and jammed it through his forearm. He held his arm high, the blade jutting out at an odd angle, the flesh around it puckering.

"No blood," Sticks said. "By his wounds," and he drew the blade out of his arm, "we are healed."

Rook turned on his heel and hustled out to the parking lot, yanking on his battered leather jacket. He heard a chair slide out behind him, heard Sticks' heavy steps following. Besides one disinterested waitress and two fat guys sleeping in separate booths, the truck stop was all but abandoned this evening.

Outside, the air was congealing into a cold, wet fog that had no business on a Wyoming highway. Rook jogged out to the far end of the lot where his truck, *The Iron Bulldogge,* lurked in the shadows.

"Hey!" Sticks' voice called through the fog. "Why are you running?! Come on, man, it's all just shades and shadows. Illusion! Scaredy-cat!"

Rook fumbled in his pocket for his keys. His fingers wrapped around them just as Sticks' cold hand wrapped around his bicep, spinning him around. His fingers were cold, even through Rook's jacket. The target in Rook's pocket had shifted from keys to folding knife. If he couldn't get that one out, he had a few others concealed on standby.

"You know what I am. You've known since I sat down," Sticks said.

"Who sent you?" Rook asked.

"A mutual friend. We know what you're carrying in there," Sticks tipped his chin at the truck, letting out a low whistle. "What has this thing been through, man? Where'd you drive, Hell and back?" he laughed.

Rook remained silent.

The Iron Bulldogge had definitely seen better days, and was usually scary enough on the outside to keep people from asking for a lift. The cab was scorched and burned, pocked with holes and slashes in the doors and fenders. The trailer was a short twenty-footer that looked like it had just been dredged from a swamp.

"What's your real name?" Rook asked.

Sticks stared at Rook, a brief glimmer of red flashing through his eye. "If you want to have a chance of rolling out of this parking lot, I just need to have a look inside your trailer."

"Not happening."

"You picked up a package in Shreveport, right? Little box, about a foot square. About big enough to hold a human head. Sound familiar?"

Rook shrugged.

Sticks flicked the spear tip out, holding it low and ready. "This is the key. You have the lock on the truck. We want it back. It wasn't yours to take."

"Never said it was mine. I'm just the delivery guy."

"Open the trailer."

"Whatever you say. Put your little shiv away before you bring the wrong kind of attention on us."

Rook slowly pulled his keys from his pocket. He lifted the lock on the latch of the trailer, tapping it precisely four times against the door. He slid the flat of his palm up the metal and rubbed a dusty circle on the truck before slapping the center.

"Gotta clear the hex first," he said, sliding the key into the lock and unlatching the door. "Might want to stand back."

The doors slowly creaked open, a dull purple glow emanating from inside the trailer. It was impossibly large, a museum on wheels, cavernous. The walls extended back into the darkness, the ceiling was nowhere in sight. The floor was decorated in elaborate marble tile.

"How far does it go?" Sticks asked.

"How far can you walk?" Rook asked.

Sticks shook his head. "Just give me the box."

"Go get it," Rook said. "Just tap the edge of the trailer four times—" and Rook slapped the floor hard four times, "—and hop in. Just...four...times..." Rook slapped the floor hard and kicked at the dirt, muttering "Dammit, Coogles..."

"There's no hex, is there?" Sticks said. "You're trying to trick me."

"No hex. Just a good for nothing lazy-ass Nightshade named Coogles who seems to have forgotten our secret distress call. Fiercest guardian you'll ever know, they told me. More like a flying puppy that eats everything in sight."

"Enough chit-chat. Give me the box. And no tricks."

"Tricks? Nah, I don't do tricks. Just get by on my charm and grace."

Rook hopped up into the trailer. It was no use fighting. Wouldn't be the first delivery he failed to make, probably not the last either. This one would've paid pretty damn good though. And he'd have a lot of explaining to do to the witch's sister in Portland who was expecting this package.

The box wasn't too far back. It was sitting on a low shelf near the collection of shrunken heads and Atlantean statues in the antechamber near the door. Rook tucked it under his arm and headed back to the door. He hopped down to the ground, squinting to see Sticks through the gathering gloom. The fog was thick now, tendrils of orange and blue witchfire dancing in the air around them.

"Dusted it off for you and everything." Rook started to thrust the box into Sticks' chest, then drew it back. "Who are you working for?"

"Doesn't matter."

"Matters to me. I let you have this, you do whatever you want with it, but someone's paying me for my time, trouble, and fuel."

"You don't want to go down that road."

"Mister, you don't want to know about the roads I've been down. Gimme a name."

"Or you'll do what, exactly?" Sticks reached a palm out for the box. "Give me the box before I surgically remove your charm and grace."

"I'll follow you until I figure it out."

"Horrible plan."

"I've had worse ideas," Rook scowled. He realized that he wasn't going to stare his way out of the situation and decided to hand the box over while he thought of Plan B.

No! No! A sharp voice barked from inside the trailer. *No give to bad thing! Bad, bad thing!*

A clumsy fluttering grew louder inside the trailer, a noise like a fuzzy sack of potatoes being thrown down a long hallway. A giant blur of white rocketed from inside the trailer, slamming into Sticks and knocking him back. It settled on the ground, a stout creature that was somewhere between a bat and a medium-sized dog.

"Is this your Nightshade?" Sticks groaned from the ground, pulling himself up.

"Yeah, this is him. It's all right Coogles. We're letting this one go."

No! Bad thing! Not box! Box is bad! Thing is bad! No box!

"He talks?" Sticks said.

"Something like that," Rook said, laying a hand on Coogles' head.

I love you! Coogles barked, licking Rook's hand. *Not you bad thing! Bad! Go!*

Sticks scrambled to his feet, brandishing the spear tip again. "Well, let's have the box now or I'm going to put this bad thing through his head."

"Was it Azazel? He put you up to this?"

Sticks swiped the spear at Coogles, who skittered backwards and hid behind Rook's legs, clutching at his pantleg with long fingers.

Bad!

Rook dropped the box on the ground and stepped back.

Sticks crawled forward, kneeling and slicing at the lid. "The blade is the key, the head is the lock. The secrets inside unleash the end. You had no idea what you were carrying back here..."

"I never look inside of customer's packages. Union rules."

Sticks reached a hand into the box and lifted his prize out. A desiccated human head, the lower jaw dangling slack, the skin loose and yellow. "The traitor. The interrupter. Judas the liar."

The head spun freely by the lock of hair clutched in Sticks' hand, the dull eyes looking through him.

"Inside," Rook whispered to Coogles. The Nightshade needed no further coaxing, flapping up into the truck.

"Do you know this man?" Sticks asked Rook.

"Well, you just told me his name was—"

"Do you know him?"

"Doesn't everyone?" Rook asked.

"Cursed to roam the earth forever. He tried so many times to end it. Hung himself the day that he killed the prophet, woke up the next morning and went on his way. Same thing happened to Cain. Can you imagine the eternal torment? Living forever?"

"I have a good imagination. So...you know, I never really ask people what they're doing with the stuff they give me. Point A to point B, that's good enough for me. But since this has turned into armed theft, I feel like I oughtta know what the big deal is with a dried-up skull."

"He has work to do. Many people to see, many tales to tell. So much knowledge locked in that brain. So many secrets, so much power. He's been known by so many names through history. The Great Khan. The Impaler. Rasputin. He couldn't bring death to himself so he walked through history and brought it to others. It's why they eventually cut his head off."

"And what's your job? You gonna carry a dried up head across the country and beat people to death with it?" Rook asked.

"My job is almost done. His is just about to begin again. By his wounds—" and Sticks raised the spear, driving it into the side of his own neck, "—we are healed..."

He rested the rotten skull on his shoulder as he proceeded to saw his own head off with the spear. There was no blood. No gore. Just a clean, wet slicing, like watermelon on a hot summer day. Sticks slid the head of Judas the betrayer on top of his neck just as his own head fell to the ground. He dropped the spear and stared at Rook with lifeless eyes, the color slowly returning to ancient cheeks as the wound on his neck knitted itself closed.

Judas shuffled forward and coughed twice, then drew in a sharp breath. He glanced around, taking in the thick fog that was slowly dissipating.

"I gcás ina? где я? Where?"

"America," Rook said seizing on the first English word, quickly swinging one door to his trailer closed.

"America. Long time," Judas growled. His face had grown whole, his features unassuming. He had thick dark hair and round cheeks, a chin that would be better hidden by a beard, and solid black eyes. The faint pink scar on Sticks' neck was a line of demarcation between a road tan and pale skin that hadn't seen the sun for generations. "What in carriage?"

"Don't worry about it. Food in there," Rook pointed to the truck stop, "Warmth too. Me, I have to be moving on."

"You will give me your carriage."

"There's plenty to choose from over there. Besides, you wouldn't know how to drive—"

"You have things I need. In there. Then you will take me. To ocean." Judas pointed a finger toward the trailer.

"Not going that far," Rook said, slowly walking backward toward the cab of his truck.

Judas slowly crouched down and picked up the spear. He raised it above his head and spoke three syllables, an ancient language that this continent hadn't heard since its founding. The fog in the air grew thick again, coalescing around the spear tip.

"I'm afraid I must insist. Years ago, I lost something in a river in Russia. A strange object, you'd call it. I need to destroy it. I am not strong enough to do it. Two things I need. You have them," Judas gestured toward the trailer again. "You will give them to me and deliver me to the ocean, or I will remove your head and take what I need, and leave your body here as food for the beasts."

"Museum's closed," Rook muttered. He slapped the side of the trailer twice and grabbed a strap hanging on the inside wall. "Gun it, Coogles!"

The Iron Bulldogge roared to life, rolling forward. Rook scrambled inside the trailer and rose to his feet, anxious to see Judas recede from his sight. Instead, the man walked behind the truck, keeping pace, arms outstretched as if to ask *really?*

Rook scratched behind his ear. "Coogles can drive, but sometimes he forgets what this ol' bucket can do."

Drive drive drive! Came a faint bark from the cab.

"Flip the red lever, furbag!" Rook yelled, bracing himself.

Judas took two jogging steps and leapt inside, striking hard with his palm against Rook's chest, sending him skidding further backwards into the truck.

Red lever! Red Red Red! Coogles barked.

"No no no no wait! He's inside the—" Rook shouted, but it was no use. Gears ground together and an explosive rumble bucked through the trailer. The truck accelerated from a slow walk to an all-out sprint, sending Rook sliding across the floor toward the open trailer door. As his feet flew out into the cold night air, he managed to hook a hand around Judas's ankle. The temporary brake allowed him to brace his other hand around the closed door. Pulling himself in at the moment wasn't an option because of the acceleration.

Judas had regained his balance enough to throw a kick at Rook. Rook rolled sideways, taking the impact on his shoulder but managing to stay in place. "Brakes! Brakes, Coogles!"

Race Race Race! Came the bark from the cabin.

"I really need a human sidekick," Rook grumbled. He inched further into the truck and took another kick to the head from Judas. Ears ringing, rook slid slowly backward, further into the darkness outside, the roar of the wind and engine deafening. The truck came to a curve in the road, shifting both men against the side and buffeting them back as the road straightened. They were on the interstate now.

Judas stood in front of a large rack of shelves. Rook knew that beyond that shelf, the magic that made the trailer into the cavernous space it was took hold, and the room had its own sense of gravity. Fortunately, Judas hadn't figured that out yet. The truck was holding a steady speed now, too fast for Rook to overcome. His grip was fading and he couldn't feel his fingers from the cold. One finger slipped free from the door, then another. If there was a God who received their prayers as a litany of curses, Rook was their devoted supplicant. His hand slipped, and his body slid backward, a sickening feeling in his stomach. He closed his eyes and prepared for the pain.

The only pain he felt was in his wrist. He looked up to see Judas gripping him, pulling him back up into the truck. Judas shifted back and threw Rook into the trailer as if he were a spare pillow.

"Your companion is a horrible carriage driver," Judas grumbled. "I need a reliable driver. You may continue to live. You will take me to the things I need."

Rook coughed, slowly climbing to his feet. He risked a glance over his shoulder, watching the asphalt roar by beneath the truck.

"How did you come to own this magnificent machine?" Judas asked.

"Years of hard work. Saved up my money. Union benefits. You know how it goes."

"Your cavalier attitude is wearing thin," Judas said.

"Charm and grace, like I said," Rook answered.

"Personality quirks only get you so far," Judas muttered.

Rook spun on his heel. "Quirks? Nah. Charm is a great thing." Rook pulled a necklace from behind his shirt, displaying a beaten coin encased in glass. "This one has traveled with me for longer than I care to remember. Hell, really longer than I could possibly remember. This charm was with me when Pompeii was on fire. I held it as I watched the Huns pass over the mountains and level everything in their path. I carried it at Gettysburg, had in my pocket in Dallas in '63, and it helped me crawl from the rubble in New York a few years ago. What I'm trying to say is this: If you're trying to scare me with a pig-sticker that's incapable of drawing blood, you're going to have to step up your game."

Rook stared at Judas, watching the glow in his eyes vibrate as his gaze darted from Rook's eyes to the charm, and back to the spear in his hands.

"I recognize the coin. You were there. You were there when I betrayed..." Judas's eyes welled with tears, then hardened. "You will give it to me. The spear may not draw blood, but it can remove your head from your filthy body."

Rook smiled and shook his head. He kicked at some imaginary dirt and turned slightly away from Judas. "You're not touching it. Drop the spear and get lost in the fog if you know what's good for you." Rook extended his arm, holding the coin in front of him like a ward to push Judas back. For a moment, it seemed to be working, as the demon inched closer to the opening in the truck. Rook rested his hand on the shelf near the door and raised an eyebrow.

"You expect me to retreat from a charm?" Judas growled.

"Nah," Rook shrugged. "Charm is the distraction. When the situation falls apart like this, I let Grace do the talking."

The interior of the trailer lit up with a blinding light as Rook emptied both barrels of his riot gun into Judas's head. Gore sprayed the walls as Judas frantically grabbed at the back of his skull, which was considerably more *open* than it had been a minute ago. Judas looked at Rook with his remaining eye, and what was left of his jaw was struggling to make a sentence.

Rook seized the spear from Judas's floundering hand and swiped a clean slice across his neck, liberating the head from Stick's body. The skull clattered to the floor with a wet thud. Rook reared back and drove a hard kick into the sternum of Stick's dancing headless corpse, sending it out into the night.

"Shut it down, Coogles!" Rook shouted.

Down down down down! Came the barking reply, lost in the growl of downshifting.

Rook lifted up the skull. The eyes were lifeless again, the skin dry and desiccated. His cargo had a giant hole in it and considerable damage, but all things considered, a delivery was a delivery. The recipients could try to file an insurance claim. Most likely they'd try to take it out of his hide, but when those complaints came, Rook always handled them with Grace.

He wandered through the hallways of his trailer toward the front of the truck, pausing to hang Grace back in her wall holster beneath a fading tintype photo of a young woman with steel-grey eyes and a mouth set in a firm line. Rook kissed his fingers and touched them lightly to the photo.

"Thanks, Annie." He closed his eyes, letting his mind drift back to the day she had given him the gun as she lay dying, imploring him to abide by the creed inscribed in the handle: *Deal with people in love and kindness. Deal with all else in sacred silver and lead.*

He opened the door to the cab and slid into the driver's seat, accepting a few over-excited licks and nips from Coogles in the passenger seat.

Ready for break. Break break break.

"We can't get off the road yet, buddy. Long way to go and a lot of packages to drop."

Want break! Hunt and fly! Fly fly fly.

"You can take a flight when I stop to pick up more bullets, right? Maybe we'll stop at Chef Ray's. You can have a shrimp po' boy while he blesses my ammo, huh?"

Poboypoboy!

"That's the spirit," Rook sighed. "You think we'll ever get proper thanks for saving the world so many times?"

No! No no! I love you!

"Go to sleep, Coogles."

The furry white beast curled up in the passenger footwell and muttered *sleep sleep*.

Rook started the truck up and turned on the lights, watching the remaining fog burn away into the night. He almost wished he could have kept Judas around. It would have been nice to talk to someone around his age.

Jeff Seeman is the author of two novels, Political Science *and* Guns and Butter, *and was a contributor to the* Bram Stoker Award-*nominated short story anthology* Hell Comes To Hollywood. *He's written several feature-length screenplays, one of which was adapted into the film* American Virgin. *He has written, produced, and directed a series of short comedy videos and performed stand-up comedy in Los Angeles, Boston, and San Francisco. Jeff dedicates this story to the memory of Richard Matheson.*

ROAD KILL

Jeff Seeman

1:17 AM. TWENTY-EIGHT HOURS and twelve minutes.

331 miles to Chicago.

And the blur of white lines on black asphalt shooting past in the darkness—endlessly, mercilessly. And the low, steady hum of eighteen tires on asphalt unremitting, and the high, steady whine of the engine unrelenting. And the tattoo of rain on the windshield and the squeak-swish-squeak of the wipers incessant. And the feel of the seat hard and painful against his back, the cracks in the cold brown vinyl exposing the cheap foam padding beneath, hardened and yellowed with age. And the air stale with the smell of sweat and nicotine. And the flashes of light from passing streetlamps throwing nightmare shadows inside the dark cab, then disappearing, then darting in again, like a slow, steady strobe. And the quiet symphony of static and indistinct, barely human voices drifting from the CB radio like memories from some distant, hypnotic dream. And the coffee in the extra-large Thermos had gone cold hours ago. And the supply of pills was dwindling. And he'd been driving for twenty-eight hours and twelve minutes, log book long forgotten.

And it was still 331 miles to Chicago.

And by now she might already be gone. After all, she'd left him the message over 24 hours ago. And this time she'd sounded as if she really meant it. She might have already packed up the car, taken the kids, and left.

She might have already taken all her clothes from the bedroom closet—the brightly colored summer dresses, the dark business skirts and serious blouses, the tight little black cocktail dress that she always worried made her look fat. He tried to imagine what their closet would look like half-empty. Mostly empty.

She might have already packed up all the kids' toys. The stuffed animals and the video games, the board games and the Lego sets. The doll with the fancy clothes and curly blonde hair he'd brought back with him once from San Francisco. The autographed catcher's mitt he'd gotten at Fenway. The Nintendo Wii he'd bought for Christmas, the one the kids had been so excited about, the one they'd played all day long and then never touched again. They might all be packed up in brown cardboard boxes by now and sealed tight with packing tape.

She might have already taken all her things from the bathroom. Her toothbrush from the holder on the sink. Her seemingly dozens of bottles of lotions and creams and gels that he always teased her were probably all the same thing, just marketed in different bottles. Her pink silk panties, the ones she used to hand wash and hang over the shower curtain, the ones that always used to annoy him when he wanted to take a shower but delighted him when he'd come home from a long trip and she'd sent the kids to their grandmother for the weekend and she'd greet him at the doorway wearing nothing else. And she'd run her fingernails ever so lightly over his skin as she removed his clothes, like ten tiny, precious tongues.

She might have already taken all the pictures down from the walls. The one at their youngest's first birthday party, the whole family crowded around the birthday cake, the guest of honor with his eyes wide and innocent and completely uncomprehending of the occasion. The one the waiter had taken that weekend in Puerto Vallarta, the two of them with their arms thrown around each other, laughing, wild, high on love and sex and tequila, the Pacific Ocean behind them. The wedding photograph... She wouldn't take that, would she? But leaving it would almost be too cruel. For him to come home and be greeted only by that photograph looking down from the wall on an empty apartment. No, she couldn't be that cruel. She'd take the wedding photo with her.

And for the tenth time that hour, he grabbed the cell phone from the passenger seat and hit Redial. Ringing.

Come on. Pick up. God, please pick up.

"Hi, this is Amanda. Leave a message." *Beeeeep.*

Fuck. He tossed the cell phone aside.

From the radio, Patsy Cline sang faintly, mockingly. Something about falling to pieces.

And the rain poured down. And the squeak-swish-squeak of the windshield wipers. And the low hum of eighteen tires on asphalt. And the high, steady whine of the engine. And he popped another pill and washed it down with the last dregs of cold coffee. And he checked his watch.

And it was 1:19 am. Twenty-eight hours and fourteen minutes. 329 miles to Chicago.

☙

Ttschhhhhhhhhhhhhh...

"Break one-nine."

All he'd been picking up on the CB for the past twenty minutes had been a swirl of static and a few barely audible voices. Probably due to the storm. Occasionally, he'd catch the hint of a conversation fading in and out, mostly talking about the weather or last night's baseball game. But this voice had cut through the auditory mist, more distinct than the others. A Southern drawl. A nasal twang.

"Break one-nine," it repeated.

Another distant, barely audible voice responded. "Come on, breaker."

"This here's Buzzsaw. Ah got a full grown bear takin' pictures on Old Hut—" The voice disappeared in a sea of static. *Ttschhhhhhhhhhhhhhh...*

Shit. Speed trap. He'd been trying to keep it at close to eighty since San Bernardino. He grabbed the microphone.

"Come back on that?" He waited for a response. Nothing. "Come back on that, Buzzsaw?" he repeated.

There was a crackle of static, then, "Howdy, good neighbor. What's yer twenty?"

"Old Hutchinson Road. Eastbound."

"Y'all got a bear in the bushes your side, mile marker five. Right behind the billboard for Chuck's Diner."

He peered out the windshield, through the darkness and driving rain, and his headlights illuminated what appeared to be a billboard, about three hundred feet up ahead. He eased off the fuel pedal. 75...70...65...

He passed the billboard doing sixty. Sure enough, it was a peeling, faded sign proclaiming the culinary virtues of one Chuck's Diner. He threw a glance at the passenger side view mirror as he drove by. A highway patrol car sat just behind the billboard, a cheetah waiting in the bushes to pounce on the next passing gazelle.

He shook his head. "Much obliged, Buzzsaw. You just pulled my nuts out of the fire."

Thunder boomed and a flash of lightning briefly illuminated the twisted, naked trees lining the side of the road. Buzzsaw's voice faded in and out of the ether. "Happy...help, good neighbor. Who...talking to?"

"Warthog."

"Glad...acquaintance, Warthog. Whatcha doin' out...godforsaken stretch...shit and asphalt?"

"Old Hutch? GPS sent me here. Just before the damn thing died on me. Accident back on 235. Traffic's all fucked up. Trying to find a way back to 80."

"Y'all keep headin' east. You'll hit 'er eventually. Hauling... load?"

"Nope. Deadhead from L.A. Just trying to get home."

"Folks waitin' for you?"

He hesitated. "Maybe." A swirl of emotions coursed through him. "Maybe not."

"Don't sound good. Trouble...old lady?"

Warthog couldn't resist a cynical chuckle. "Apparently on the road too much, Buzzsaw. Not home enough. On account of the whole trying-to-make-a-living-and-feed-my-family thing."

"Oh, yeah, *that* thing. Sounds...fuckin' curse...bein' a trucker, son."

He took a deep breath. "Yeah. Fuckin' curse."

"Don't see much traffic...Old Hutch," said Buzzsaw. He chuckled. "Hey, you watch out...ghost now."

"Come back?"

"Local legend. There's...hairpin turn halfway...ravine about... miles... Locals say... Dead Man's Curve...some driver...'bout twenty years ago...skidded...and... When they...found...severed...arms and...head...blood...torso...with his guts all...and his eyes... People say when...they still see his ghost...night...out on Old Hutch. What the kids say, anyhow."

Warthog shook his head. "Kids. Every town in America probably got a legend like that."

"Yup. Reckon so. Say...diner...pretty decent, you ain't eaten."

"Chuck's?"

"Yup. Only place open twenty-four hours...damn county."

"Thanks, I'll pass. Trying to make time."

"Nothin' else...for miles," said Buzzsaw. "Might want...reconsider."

"Ten-four."

Warthog jammed the microphone back into its clip and put the hammer down, pushing the semi back up to eighty. There was a flash of lightning and the thunder crashed again. The rain came down even harder, as if redoubling its efforts. He snatched up the cell phone again and hit Redial.

"Hi, this is Amanda. Leave a message." *Beeeeep.*

He cursed under his breath and threw the phone back onto the seat.

All at once, the road before him seemed to blur. He squinted and blinked several times—hard—trying to regain focus. But everything appeared as if through a haze, even the dashboard just three feet in front of him. A hot flash coursed through his body and sweat dripped down the back of his neck. His head pounded and his mouth had gone dry. He couldn't feel the pedal beneath his foot any longer. He looked down in disbelief to make sure it was still there. It was, but he'd lost all feeling in his right foot. With a start, he realized the tips of his fingers had gone numb as well. The world spun suddenly around him as if he'd had one too many whiskeys.

He gulped for air and eased off the pedal, slowing the truck to thirty-five.

The CB crackled again. "Warthog, this here's Buzzsaw. Y'all sure you don't want to check out Chuck's? Might be a surprise for you." There was a swirl of electronic feedback, then, "Ah was just there."

Warthog tried to shake the dizziness out of his head. Grasped for the mic. Missed it two times. Grabbed hold on the third.

"Ten-four," he managed weakly.

Up ahead in the distance, through blurred, bloodshot eyes and pissing rain, he caught a glimpse of neon lights, red and yellow and white. He couldn't even tell if he was on the fucking road anymore. Just aimed the truck for the lights and kept rolling.

૭৲৩

The sign proclaimed it as *CHU K'S DIN R*. Warthog pulled slowly into the parking lot, rolled to a stop, and cut the engine. He
sat hunched over the steering wheel, breathing hard, forcing air
into his lungs as the rain pounded on the windshield. His throat
was parched and his head still spun. He gripped the steering
wheel tightly and stared down at the floor of the cab, waiting
for the world to stop swimming around him. *Something to eat.
Yeah, that's all I need. I'll be fine. I'm sure I'll be fine if I just get
something to eat...*

He lifted his head slowly and peered through the windshield,
but the rain was too heavy to make out anything but the blur of
colored neon. He kicked open the door of the cab, pulled his
jacket tightly around him, and tumbled out into the downpour.

He landed hard on his feet and his legs almost gave out beneath him. Struggled to regain his balance. How many hours
had it been since his feet had touched solid ground? He steadied
himself, a weary, haggard sailor just back ashore after months
of being at sea.

The diner stood small and brightly lit against the darkness.
Warthog saw there were a couple of other trucks and even a
few cars parked in the lot. Maybe it wasn't so bad, he thought.
Seemed to be able to draw a few customers, even this late at
night. Then again, Buzzsaw had said it was the only place open
for miles. He jogged across the small parking lot toward the entrance as the rain poured down.

The tingle of a small bell announced his arrival as he stepped
through the front door. He tried in vain to shake the water from
his soaking jacket. The diner was so bright compared to the
darkness outside, the fluorescent lights fairly sparkling off the
freshly polished linoleum. A long Formica countertop with a
row of stools on his right, a series of booths on his left toward
the windows. Behind the counter, a grill where a hamburger and

several strips of bacon sizzled. Glass display cases advertised various cakes and muffins and pies. A jukebox stood against the far wall playing country music over the din of the rain. It was like every other truck stop diner he'd ever been in.

Except it was deserted.

He looked around. Two raincoats and several umbrellas hung on hooks near the front door. A wet poncho was draped over one of the bar stools. He walked slowly down the row of booths. A woman's handbag lay abandoned on one of the benches. A man's jacket. And there were definitely two semis and a handful of cars parked outside. *Where the hell was everyone?*

"Hello?"

No answer.

Warthog heard a loud sizzle from behind him and turned to see that a grease fire had broken out on the grill. He rushed behind the counter and turned off the heat, then grabbed the lid of a nearby pot and covered the piece of charred, burning meat. The smell of burnt oil hung heavy in the air.

"Hello?" he shouted again.

Nothing. Just Hank Williams and the rain.

Warthog walked slowly through a swinging door into the kitchen. It was as immaculate as the rest of the diner—countertop, gas range, sink, all sparkling stainless steel, all freshly cleaned and polished. A small connecting room contained shelves piled high with cans of sweet corn and baked beans and cling peaches, and on the far side of the room, a door to a meat locker stood slightly ajar.

Slightly ajar.

He walked slowly to the door and hesitantly pushed it open. A blast of cold air emanated from the darkness. He felt along the inside of the doorway for a light switch and found it.

The room was filled with bodies and body parts hanging from meat hooks. A young woman with long, stringy blonde hair, her right arm missing, her face twisted in horror, the hook piercing her stomach. An elderly man, still wearing his baseball cap, his left leg sawed off, suspended in the air. Various arms, legs, and other unidentifiable organs, hanging from the ceiling like so many cold cuts in a delicatessen. And in the center of the room, a naked torso—armless, legless, blood still dripping from the chest wound where the hook burst from the skin—dangling like some gruesome piñata.

From the next room, Patsy Cline sang forlornly about falling to pieces.

Warthog fell back, overwhelmed with horror and nausea. He covered his mouth as he gagged and retched, his eyes wide. Then he turned and ran, through the kitchen, through the diner, and out the door into the turbulent night.

His head spun and he lost his balance on the slippery asphalt, falling hard on his right knee. He pulled himself up and half-ran, half-staggering back to the truck. Pulled himself up into the cab and slammed the door shut. He sat breathing hard, rain hammering the windshield, sweat pouring from his brow, trying to digest what he'd just seen.

He grabbed the cell phone and dialed 911.

"9-1-1 service is not available in your area," came the automated voice. "Please hang up and call your local police department."

Warthog hit zero for the operator.

"Your call cannot be completed as dialed. Please check the number and dial again."

He tried twice more and got the same recording.

Shit. He grabbed the mic and switched the CB to channel 9, the emergency channel. "Emergency," he said, his voice shaking. "Emergency on Old Hutch."

There was a crackle, then a familiar voice. "Howdy, good neighbor. Y'all get on out to Chuck's Diner?"

"Buzzsaw, this is an emergency!"

"Emergency? Why, sounds like somebody found mah little surprise." Malicious laughter floated to him through the ethereal static. "Hope it wasn't too much of a shock for you, son. But ah figured, heck—you're used to haulin' meat, ain't ya'?"

Warthog's jaw dropped and he heard a gasp escape his own mouth. For a moment, he sat in stunned silence.

He regained his wits and rapidly switched to channel 10. "Emergency! Emergency at—"

"Howdy, good neighbor," came the voice.

Warthog squinted with confusion and checked to make sure he'd actually changed channels. He had. He switched the dial again, randomly clicking to another channel.

"Emergen—"

"Howdy, good neighbor."

He switched to channel 12.

"Howdy, good neighbor."

To channel 4.

"Howdy, good neighbor."

To channel 21.

"Howdy, good neighbor."

What the fuck? His whole body shook as he stared at the CB radio. *It wasn't possible. He couldn't be on all the channels at the same time.*

"Now at this point, son, you got two options, way ah see it," said Buzzsaw through the static haze. "You can head on back up Old Hutch. Head west to where you saw that cruiser a few miles back. Might still be there. 'Course, I ain't sayin' it is. Not sayin' it ain't, either. Not sayin' nothin' one way or the other. But it might be, and you could take that chance. You surely could. Maybe that cruiser's still there. Maybe them troopers' still alive. You could take that chance.

"'Course, that would mean drivin' back up Old Hutch, like ah said. And that there's a gamble right there. That's takin' you in the opposite direction you want to go. So that's a choice you got to make. Ah ain't makin' no choices for you, son. That's your choice.

"On the other hand, you could keep headin' east. Might be an entrance back onto I-80 in a few miles. 'Course, might not. Might be a weigh station up ahead, maybe just a mile or two.

'Course, I ain't sayin' there is. Not sayin' there ain't, neither. Not sayin' nothin' one way or the other. Just want to make sure you're thinkin' through all your options is all.

"So that's what you got to decide, son. You gonna head east or west? You gonna take a chance that—"

Warthog clicked off the CB. He sat in the darkness of the cab, listening to the rain, drenched to the bone and trying to control the violent shaking of his body.

A map. A good old-fashioned goddamn map. Before he'd gotten so dependent on his fucking useless GPS, he'd used maps. He clicked on the dingy dome light and began tearing through the contents of the glove compartment. A map of Texas. A map of Illinois. *Come on, damn it. There has to be a map of Iowa in here somewhere.*

Iowa. He pulled it from the jumble of other maps, papers, and fuel receipts. It was tattered and yellowed, thinning and tearing along the folded creases, and he unfolded it as gingerly as he could with his wet, trembling hands. In the dim glow of the dome light, he squinted at the tiny text. His eyes had clearly worsened with age; he could barely believe he'd ever been able to read these damn things. He found I-80 and traced it with his finger, east across the state. Finally found where it intersected with I-235 and traced it north, looking for where he'd turned off.

Nothing.

He retraced the route with his finger. *It had to be here somewhere.* East on I-80 to 235. North on I-235 to Old Hutch. He squinted harder in the dull yellow light as fat drops of water dripped onto the map, disintegrating the paper before his eyes.

There *was* no Old Hutchinson Highway. At least not on the map.

He peered out into the darkness. *East or west?* Back the way he'd come or forward toward God-knows-what? But Old Hutch couldn't be that long a stretch of road. If it were, it would *have* to be on the map. Wouldn't it? It certainly hadn't been constructed recently. It must have been here when the map was printed. And if the map didn't even show it, maybe it was tiny. Maybe he hadn't even been on it as long as he thought he had. Maybe his mind was playing tricks on him. Maybe I-80 was just a few clicks up ahead. Maybe...

Can't stay here. Have to find help. A weigh station. Highway patrol. Something. He started the truck and, feeling slightly reassured by the familiar roar of the engine, pulled back onto Old Hutch, heading east.

He'd been driving for only three or four minutes when he saw a light up ahead—a small, rundown gas station on the westbound side, barely illuminated by an old streetlamp. Set back behind the single gas pump was a small convenience store, and as he slowed he saw a light shining from the window and an elderly man behind a cash register. The man looked up as Warthog eased the semi into a wide left turn, cutting across the highway. As he rolled toward the station, he saw the old man emerge expectantly from the office, pulling a rain parka tightly around him.

All at once, the night was alive in a blizzard of flames. The ground shook as the gas pump ignited and a ball of fire shot skyward. Warthog slammed on the brakes, then threw the semi into reverse as flames swallowed the convenience store. Fiery debris rained down.

And then the old man emerged through the wall of fire, a living torch, his clothes and hair and skin ablaze, a blood-curdling cry emanating from his lips. He staggered forward into the beams of the truck's headlights and Warthog watched in horror as the flames melted the skin from his body and the heat boiled his eyeballs in their sockets. The man hurled one final shriek of anguish and agony into the night before collapsing into a smoldering pile of flesh and bone. He lay dead in the middle of the road like a raccoon squashed flat by an eighteen-wheeler.

Screaming and shaking with fear, Warthog threw the truck into gear and hit the accelerator.

"Howdy, good neighbor. Looks like your night's just full of surprises, don't it?"

Warthog stared at the CB radio. The cold red eye of the power indicator light stared back at him through the darkness of the cab.

But I turned it off. I turned it off. I know I did.

He clicked off the radio and turned his attention back to the road. The wind had picked up now, the rain flying straight at the windshield as he drove. He felt as if he were flying through an endless tunnel of raindrops that glittered in the headlights. The effect was like a kaleidoscope, dangerously mesmerizing. He shook his head, struggling against its hypnotic pull.

"Now that wasn't very neighborly, was it, son?" came the voice again. "You ain't gonna get rid of me that easy."

Warthog looked. Sure enough, the power light was back on.

"'Sides, ain't good to spend so much time alone. See, that's your problem, son. Too much time alone. Too much time on the road. Just like your old lady said. Spend that much time alone, your mind starts goin' places it shouldn't. That's what ah think. Ah surely do. Forget how to be a husband. Forget how to be a father. Heck, forget how to be a man. You know it's true, don'tcha, son? You've thought the same damn thing. Sure you have. Ah know you have. Only natural. That's what ah think. Damn, you forget how to be a goddamn human being's what it is. Got to re-engage with the world, son. Re-engage with people. See, that's what ah do. I *re-engage* with people." The voice broke off into laughter. "What ah call *re-engaging.*"

Warthog grabbed the microphone and took a deep breath, working up his courage. "Did you kill those people?"

"'Scuse me, son? Come back?"

"Did you kill those people?!"

"Back at the diner? Surely did, son. Surely did. Old man at the gas station, too."

A chill went through Warthog's body as the words sank in, confirming his fear. "Why?!" he stammered.

"Just bored, s'pose. Ain't you? Ain't you bored, driving for miles and miles with nothin'? Thought ah'd provide us a little entertainment's all. Oh, don't have to thank me none. Got to admit though, son, you ain't bored no more. Ain't that right?" He chuckled. "Don't you go tellin' me you're bored now, boy. 'Cause ah do not believe that. Not one bit."

Warthog took another deep breath. "Where are you?" he demanded. "I haven't seen another truck all fucking night long. Where the fuck are you?!"

"Ah, well now that's a question, son, ain't it? That's a question. Ain't easy to answer, though. Wish I could tell ya'. Ah'm here. Ah'm there. Ah'm a little bit everywhere, s'pose. Ah mean, when you're on the road, where are ya' really? You know what ah'm sayin'? 'Nother trucker asks yer twenty and you tell 'em, 'Ah'm a-headin' east on this' or 'Ah'm a-headin' west on that' or whatever. But you ain't really there. Or least yer only there for a moment. Then yer gone. Then yer somewhere else. So I mean, where are you really? You get what ah'm sayin'?"

"Are you...following me?"

"Followin' you? Well, depends how you mean, son. Not so much followin' you. Not really." Another laugh. "But ah'll put it this way. Ah'm goin' everywhere you're goin.' Anywhere you go, that's where ah'll be."

The trailer. He's in the fucking trailer. That's why I don't see his truck on the road. Son of a bitch has a CB hooked up back there and he's been talking to me from my own goddamn trailer the whole time. That must be it.

Warthog slowed the semi and pulled over to the side of the road. Pulled a flashlight from the glove compartment and fished a tire iron out from under the driver's seat.

"What you getting' up to now, son? You be careful now, hear? Don't go doin' nothing stupid. Think you may have had enough surprises for one night."

He opened the door and jumped out. The wind and rain lashed at him furiously as he walked to the back of the trailer, the beam from the flashlight slicing a narrow path through the darkness, the mud sloshing beneath his feet.

He placed the tire iron on the metal step at the back of the trailer and shoved the flashlight into his jacket pocket, beam pointing upward, in order to free his hands. Pulled himself up onto the slippery step, retrieved the tire iron and tucked it under his left arm, then pulled out the flashlight again. With the light in his left hand, he reached out with his right, his heart racing, his hand trembling. Slowly, as quietly as possible, he unlatched the trailer doors. Taking a deep breath, he pulled the right door open. A blast of cold air emanated from the refrigerated unit, turning his breath to mist in the night air. He shined the flashlight inside.

In the glare of the flashlight beam, he caught a glimpse of something shiny. Shiny and wet. He gasped.

Bodies. Like the meat locker at the diner. Like the cargo he'd unloaded back in L.A., only these were human. Suspended from meat hooks, filling the cargo trailer. The remnants of tattered clothing still clinging to their flesh. An arm. A severed leg. A half torso, split down the middle. All wet and sticky with blood.

Warthog let out a cry and slammed the door shut. He lost his footing on the slippery metal step and fell hard to the ground. The tire iron landed somewhere nearby, lost forever in the darkness. The flashlight rolled a few feet away. He crawled through the mud and snatched it up.

When had he done it? When had Buzzsaw put the bodies in the trailer? It must have been when Warthog was inside the diner. While he'd been finding the corpses in the meat locker, Buzzsaw had been loading more into the back of his truck.

He scrambled to his feet and sloshed back to the cab. Pulled himself up and slammed the door shut.

"Warned you 'bout goin' back there, boy. Didn't ah warn you?"

Warthog grabbed the microphone. "WHO THE FUCK ARE YOU???"

"Told you that, son. Didn't ah tell you? See, locals say there's a ghost haunts Old Hutch. What the kids say, anyhow. They say some nights you can see—"

"Bullshit! Fuck you!"

Buzzsaw laughed. "Okay, boy, have it your way. But in future, you best be more discriminating where you buy your automotive 'lectronics, wouldn't cha say?"

The CB radio. He'd bought it years ago, second-hand. Friend of a friend. Someone in the junk business. Recovered from a highway accident, wasn't it? Had he ever heard any details of the accident? Had anyone been injured? Killed? He strained to remember.

Warthog began frantically yanking at the electrical wire to the radio.

"Whatcha doin' there, boy?"

One more strong yank and the wire pulled free. Warthog stared at the radio. The power indicator light stayed solid red.

"Now that wasn't very friendly, was it, son? I mean really, that's what ah call downright rude."

Warthog popped open the glove compartment and began scrambling through its contents, tossing maps and papers every which way.

"That there's the problem with people these days, boy. Manners. Ain't nobody got no manners no more. Swear to God. It's a goddamn shame. Civilization going to hell in a hand basket 'cuz ain't nobody got no goddamn manners no more."

It has to be in here somewhere. Warthog reached into the bottom of the compartment and felt around. His fingertip hit something sharp. *Got it.* He pulled out a Phillips-head screwdriver.

"Whoa there, son. What'cha plannin' to do with that?"

He began furiously unscrewing the mounting bracket that secured the radio to the dashboard.

"Okay, okay. Let's calm down now, boy. No need to do anything drastic."

One screw out. He savagely attacked the second one with the screwdriver.

"Ah wouldn't do that, friend. Ah surely wouldn't. Friend? You hearin' me?"

Second screw out.

"Really, son, this is so uncalled for. Ah mean, ah ain't perfect. Ah admit that. Ah might have said some stuff. Might have done some stuff. But we can put all that behind us. We can start off on a new foot."

The Phillips-head slipped, jabbing the thumb of Warthog's left hand. He smarted for a moment, then pushed on ahead. Third screw out.

"Can't we talk about this, friend? Friend? Can't we?"

The last screw was stubborn, its threads worn. Warthog gritted his teeth and pushed hard. It finally gave.

"Aw, son..."

With a grunt, Warthog yanked the CB radio from the mounting bracket. He pushed open the door of the cab, tumbled out into the night, and strode to the front of the truck. Standing in the glare of the headlights, the rain pouring down, he lifted the radio high above his head. And then, triumphantly, threw it down. It smashed against the asphalt.

Back inside the cab, Warthog threw the tractor into gear and gunned the engine. He rolled forward just a few feet until the radio disappeared underneath the left front tire. There was a small, almost imperceptible crunch. Warthog threw the truck into reverse and backed up a few feet. The radio lay dead like an animal, its electronic guts scattered across the side of the road.

He burst into tears and crumpled in the driver's seat, his body shaking as he sat hunched over the steering wheel.

෴

It was the changing sound of the rain that finally caused him to lift his head, the steady drumbeat on the windshield having diminished to a sporadic tapping. Warthog looked up to find the rain had tapered off and the clouds had parted. Way off in the distance, a glint of sun peeked out from over the horizon. Up ahead, just a few yards away, a road sign he hadn't noticed in the darkness. He squinted to read it in the dim light of dawn.

80 EAST. 2 MILES. A wave of relief washed through his body.

He started the engine and eased out onto the highway. His head seemed clear for the first time in hours, the cobwebs suddenly blown away. He rolled down the window and a cool breeze brushed across his face. Breathed deeply and all the tension in his body eased.

And maybe... Maybe it wasn't too late. Maybe she'd changed her mind. Maybe while she was packing up her bright summer dresses and her serious blouses and her little black cocktail dress. Maybe while she was taking her things from the bathroom—the toothbrush, and the lotions and the creams and the gels, and her pink silk panties that hung over the shower rod. Maybe she'd stopped. Maybe she'd stood there, holding them in her hands for a moment. And maybe she'd had second thoughts.

Maybe when she'd taken down the wedding photo—or the one with the family crowded around the birthday cake or the one from the trip to Puerto Vallarta with their arms around each other and the ocean behind them—maybe she'd stopped for a moment and looked at them, stopped for a moment and studied the faces. Maybe she'd been moved. Maybe something had shifted.

Maybe when she was packing the kids' toys—the stuffed animals and the doll with the fancy clothes from San Francisco and the catcher's mitt from Fenway—maybe she'd stopped and held them to her breast. Maybe she'd taken a deep breath. And maybe she'd felt something. *Something.*

And maybe it wasn't too late. And maybe it would be okay. Maybe.

And it was now 5:47 am. And it was 318 miles to Chicago.

Patsy Cline again sang from the radio, this time more optimistically, reminding her lover that he belonged to her.

The cell phone rang. *Amanda Calling*, read the display.

Thank God. He breathed a sigh of relief and snatched up the phone from the passenger seat.

"Amanda? Sweetheart—"

"Howdy, good neighbor," came the familiar voice.

Every muscle in his body froze.

"Ah'm here with your lovely wife, Amanda," Buzzsaw continued. "And ah tell you, boy, she sure is a looker."

"You... You're...?"

"Cute kids, too. Seems a damn shame leavin' them alone for so long. Alone and unprotected, you know what ah'm sayin'?"

"You lay a hand on any of them—" Warthog put the hammer down, pushing the semi to 80mph.

"Amanda, she's quite the feisty one, ain't she? Don't do what she's told the first time. Got to show her who's boss. Thinkin' you might have just spoiled her some, boy."

"You son of a bitch. You goddamn—"

He pushed it to 90mph.

"Them kids could use some discipline, too. Think maybe you been too soft on 'em, boy. Got to toughen 'em up some, what it is. Toughen 'em up. That's what ah think. Ah surely do."

"Don't you dare. Don't you fucking—"

100mph.

"What ah'm wondering is, are any of them gonna call your name? When the time comes, ah mean. When the time comes, they gonna remember you? If the kids were in pain, say. If your wife...if Amanda...if she were havin' some...intense feelings of some sort. You know, the way ladies do sometimes. Ah'm wonderin' if she'll be callin' your name. I mean, I'm just wonderin' if they're even gonna remember who you are at the end. That's all ah'm sayin'..."

"You fucker! You sick twisted fuck! You fucking piece of sh—"

He was doing 110 when he hit Dead Man's Curve, a hairpin turn halfway up a ravine. Too late, he pulled his foot off the pedal and tried steering into the skid, wrenching the wheel to the right, eighteen tires screaming at the asphalt. He resisted the impulse to slam on the brakes, holding his breath and easing down as gently as he could to try to regain control. But the tires skidded on the wet pavement and the whole rig lurched sideways, the trailer pulling violently to the right. At the last possible moment, with no other option, he slammed down on the brakes as hard as he could.

The semi slipped over the edge of the ravine, the wheels spinning, the trailer hurdling down on top of the cab. And the air filled with the shattering of glass and the crunch and grind of metal on metal.

℥

Ttschhhhhhhhhhhhhh...

"Dispatch, this is 82, over."

"Go ahead, 82."

"Got a ten-fifty, half mile west of the I-80 entrance. Semi down the ravine."

"Dead Man's Curve took another one, huh?"

"Looks like. Driver's dead."

"Other fatalities?"

"Nope, truck's empty. Based on the skid marks, sumbitch must have been doing a hundred."

"Drugs?"

"Pulled a bottle of pills from the cab. Looks like speed."

"Hell, take enough of that shit, probably start thinking you can fly."

"Yup. Start seeing monkeys fly out your own asshole's what I hear."

"Okay, 82. Meat wagon's on its way."

"Roger that, dispatch."

Ttschhhhhhhhhhhhhh...

If you liked this book, please consider telling other people. Helping us spread the word is a great way for readers to find new material, and for deserving writers to find new fans.

Thank you for your support.

26686041R00171

Made in the USA
San Bernardino, CA
02 December 2015